Alexander Charles Ewald

The Tatler

Selected Essays with an Introduction and Notes

Alexander Charles Ewald

The Tatler
Selected Essays with an Introduction and Notes

ISBN/EAN: 9783337275273

Printed in Europe, USA, Canada, Australia, Japan

Cover: Foto ©Andreas Hilbeck / pixelio.de

More available books at **www.hansebooks.com**

THE "*CHANDOS CLASSICS.*"

THE TATLER.

SELECTED ESSAYS.

WITH

AN INTRODUCTION AND NOTES.

BY

ALEX. CHARLES EWALD, F.S.A.

AUTHOR OF "STORIES FROM THE STATE PAPERS," ETC.

London and New York:

FREDERICK WARNE AND CO.

1888.

LONDON:

BRADBURY, AGNEW & CO., PRINTERS, WHITEFRIARS.

PREFACE.

It seems strange in these days of "Extracts" and "Selections" that the Volumes of the "Tatler" should never have engaged the attention of an Editor to lay its gems under contribution. Though not enjoying the popularity of its more famous successor, the "Spectator," there are yet in its pages Essays which, for humour, wit, charms of style and knowledge of human nature, are as deserving of study and perusal as any in the English language. Nor as contributions to the history of the period are they less worthy of attention. Politics, fashion, literature, the tastes and prejudices of the day are all there to be met with, and shed a light upon the reign of Queen Anne not reflected elsewhere. Yet the "Tatler" is pre-eminently one of those works on the shelves of our literature which are often spoken of, occasionally quoted, and never read. This neglect no doubt arises from the mass of obsolete and uninteresting matter in which the readable Essays are so embedded as to be practically smothered. The work therefore lends itself especially to the scheme of selection. In the following pages the

Editor has been guided and controlled by the same rules and restrictions which he laid down when preparing the "Spectator" for this series. It is hoped that his selections from the "Tatler" will fill up a gap in our popular literature, and meet with as favourable a reception as their companion volume.

A. C. E.

London, *May*, 1888.

ESSAYS SELECTED FROM THE "TATLER."

THE TATLER.

INTRODUCTORY ESSAY.

THE history of the Great Revolution has been almost exclusively identified with the political character of the changes it
introduced. It is true that the reign of William the Deliverer
rang the death-knell of government by prerogative and by
ushering in government by parliament, so raised the influence
of the House of Commons as eventually to create our lower
assembly the centre and force of the State. But the Revolution
of 1688 was as much social as it was political. If it
emancipated the people from the tyranny of the Crown or the
despotism of Ministers—according to which was the dominant
authority of the hour—it no less emancipated the nation from
the evil surroundings which had so long depressed and restrained
its vitality, its energies, and its intellectual progress. With a
Court comparatively pure, with the creed of the land eliminated
from superstition and servility, with the restoration of the
currency and the consequent revival of trade, with a general
stability of affairs that inspired confidence and stimulated
activity, a healthier and more vigorous tone gradually became
apparent throughout the country.

Society which, in the days of the Restoration, had been
confined almost exclusively to the circle of a dissipated Court,
now broke down many of its barriers, and admitted within its

ranks those who formerly had been ignored. The vast fortunes made in trade—the Sir Andrew Freeports of the day—had created a powerful middle class, whose new and varied wants had to be supplied, greatly to the development of the prosperity of the nation. More leisure, more wealth, a less restricted social intercourse, a desire for the gratification of purer tastes, was now causing pleasure to flow into different and less dangerous channels. The list of the coffee-houses was swelled, and in spite of such additions, none had to close their doors for lack of patronage. The theatre, which, in the wild revelry of the Restoration, no modest woman could attend unmasked, was now, thanks to the scourging of Jeremy Collier and a less vitiated taste, a popular place of social resort, and at the accession of Queen Anne a masked female in the house was an exception—neither author nor actor giving occasion for such a veil. Perhaps the most marked feature in this transition of things, was the change in the position and treatment of woman. The fair sex was no longer the toy or drudge of man, a plaything and an inferior, but was quietly and imperceptibly being regarded as an object of rational consideration by those to whom she was henceforth to be the helpmeet and the glory. Yet one great want had still to be supplied her. Save poems, plays, stilted French romances, and heavy tomes of sermons, history and biography, there was little in the literature of the day to appeal to her leisure or capacity. Novels, newspapers, magazines, amusing essays, were all conspicuous by their absence. No wonder that the woman of the day over her _bohea_ talked and talked, for she had little encouragement to do ought else but gossip and dress.

And now it was that Richard Steele—always gallant and sympathetic when the welfare of the ladies was concerned—came prominently upon the scene. On Tuesday, April 12, 1709, there appeared, as the happy coinage of his brain, the first number of the _Tatler_. The new journal was to appeal to various sets in the community. The fashionable ladies of Soho and Covent Garden, were to read accounts of "gallantry, pleasure, and entertainment," dated from White's Chocolate House. Articles on Poetry were to appeal to the critics and men of letters who daily assembled at Will's Coffee House. The students and Templars who haunted the Grecian, were to be propitiated by articles on Learning ; whilst the warriors and men of fashion, anxious as to the conduct of a campaign or a coquette, who patronised the coffee-house of St. James's, were to peruse the latest Foreign and Domestic News. Subjects which could not be catalogued under any special heading were to be dated from the writers' Own Apartment. The name of the paper was to be the *Tatler*, " in honour," said Steele, " of the fair sex ; " and the object it had in view was " to expose the false arts of life, to pull off the disguises of cunning, vanity, and affectation, and to recommend a general simplicity in our dress, our discourse and our behaviour." The editor of the new venture concealed his identity under the *nom de guerre* of Isaac Bickerstaff—a name which Swift had a few years before made notorious by his exquisite ridicule of Partridge, the astrologer and almanac-maker.

Few men were better qualified to start and manage a paper of this nature than its founder. Without going outside his own experiences, the life led by the joyous, kindly Dicky Steele furnished him with ample material to draw upon for his " lucubrations." The son of an official under the Irish government—" a gentleman born," as he was somewhat prone to designate himself when amid the shady surroundings of Grub Street—he had known both prosperity and adversity, at one time swaggering with men of fashion in Pall Mall, at another hard pressed for a guinea to escape the sponging-house. He had been educated at Oxford, he had deserted Alma Mater without taking his degree, and had enlisted as one of " the gentlemen of the Guard " in the second troop of Life Guards ; though soon afterwards he obtained a commission in the regiment of John, Lord Cutts, by dedicating a poem on the death of Queen Mary to that impetuous and daring officer. Tired of soldiering he quitted the army shortly after obtaining his company, and led an irregular, roystering life about town, writing comedies which were not particularly successful, writing poems and articles for the money he so often needed, always a favourite and boon companion in whatever society he frequented until he was finally relieved from pressing want by his appointment, thanks to the recommendation of Arthur Mainwaring, to the post of Gazetteer, then in the gift of Harley, afterwards Earl of Oxford.

A fair but not profound scholar Steele possessed that knowledge which is not to be derived from books. He was a man of the world, and his humour, combined with his keen powers of observation, had made him a deep and accurate student of human nature. He knew the London of his day—its haunts, its vices, its virtues, the pleasures of society, the woes of want, and, to the last trick in his secret programme, the designs and wiles of the impostor. Thanks to his two marriages—especially to the temper of his " Dear Prue"—he had carefully studied that most complex machinery, the heart and aspirations of woman. More as an anatomist than an admirer, he had watched and criticised the aim and promptings of " the fair sex,"—that constant allusion to the fair sex which so aroused the ire and sneer of the mordant Swift. In the words of the French philosopher, Steele was qualified to pass judgment for he had at least " dissected one woman." He knew the excellence and the foibles of woman, her strength and her weakness, her kindness and her tyranny, her self-denial and her egotism, her indulgence and her restraint—in fact, the whole mass of contradictions which go to make up her nature. His papers, whenever he touches upon the purity or vanity of woman, her severity or laxity, are always excellent—the articles of one who knows and believes in his subject, who has weighed it in the scale and not found it much wanting. And this knowledge, always the result of experience and not of the conclusions of imagination, is apparent in all the contributions of Steele. When he attacks the vices of the day—drunkenness, duelling, gambling, profanity, the arts of a sharper—we feel that we are in the presence of one who is no closet preacher, but of one who warns and denounces because he himself has suffered and experienced. " The general purpose of the whole," he writes when the *Tatler* reached its last number, " has been to recommend truth, innocence, honour, and virtue, as the chief ornaments of life."

Nor did his intentions lack appreciation. " There is a noble difference," writes John Gay, the poet and humorous author of *Trivia*, in a letter to a friend in the country at this date," between Steele and all the rest of our polite and gallant authors. The latter have endeavoured to please the age by falling in with them, and encouraging them in their fashionable vices and false notions of things. It would have been a jest, some time since, for a man to have asserted that anything witty could be said in praise of a married state, or that devotion and virtue were any way necessary to the character of a Fine Gentleman. *Bickerstaff* ventured to tell the town that they were a parcel of fops, fools, and coquettes ; but in such a manner as even pleased them, and made them more than half inclined to believe that he spoke truth. Instead of complying with the false sentiments or vicious tastes of the age—either in morality, criticism or good-breeding—he has boldly assured them, that they were altogether in the wrong ; and commanded them, with an authority which perfectly well became him, to surrender themselves to his arguments for virtue and good sense. It is incredible to conceive the effect his writings have had upon the town ; how many thousand follies they have either quite banished or given a very great check to ! how much countenance, they have added to virtue and religion ! how many people they have rendered happy, by showing them it was their own fault if they were not so ! and, lastly, how entirely they have convinced our young fops and young fellows of the value and advantages of learning ! He has indeed rescued it out of the hands of pedants, and fools, and discovered the true method of making it amiable and lovely to all mankind. In the dress he gives it, it is a most welcome guest at tea-tables and assemblies, and is relished and caressed by the merchants on the Change. Accordingly there is not a lady at court, nor a banker in Lombard Street, who is not verily persuaded that Captain Steele is

the greatest scholar and best casuist of any man in England
Lastly, his writings have set all our wits and men of letters
on a new way of thinking, of which they had little or no notion
before : and, although we cannot say that any of them have
come up to the beauties of the original, I think we may venture
to affirm, that every one of them writes and thinks much more
justly than they did some time since."

The success of the *Tatler* from the date of its publication to
the day of its withdrawal was complete and assured. It was
as welcome to the "lady of quality" in town as it was to the
squire in his manor house or the parson in his vicarage. A
new feature in the literature of the day, it received without
stint the patronage of the powerful and the affluent. It was
all that the novel and the newspaper were to a later generation,
and appealed to a multitude of readers—readers who subse-
quently developed into so numerous a class as to cause the man
of letters to rely upon a public instead of grovelling before a
patron. It was Steele who laid the foundation of this happy
exchange. For the success of the *Tatler* no small share, as we
have elsewhere admitted,* was due to the pen of Addison.
Without disparaging the labours of Steele and the excellence of
the papers he contributed, it was the aid of his old school-fellow
and brother undergraduate who raised the tone of the journal
to the height it reached and made it the welcome guest at every
breakfast table. "The truth is," writes Macaulay, "that the fifty
or sixty numbers which we owe to Addison were not merely
the best but so decidedly the best that any five of them are
more valuable than all the two hundred numbers in which he
had no share." This praise is doubtless somewhat ex-
aggerated, but anyone who reads the paper on Tom Folio,
on Ned Softly, on the Political Upholsterer, on Frozen
Words, on the Adventures of a Shilling, and on the various
other subjects which occupied the attention of Addison, cannot but perceive at a glance how much of truth there is in the
assertion.

* See the *Spectator*, included in the series of the "Chandos Classics."

At that date Addison had crossed St. George's Channel, and was acting as Chief Secretary to the Earl of Wharton, then Lord-Lieutenant of Ireland. After the issue of several numbers of his paper, Steele wrote to his friend across the water, begging him to take an active interest in the new enterprise, and attach himself to the staff as a contributor. The application was not tendered in vain, and henceforth the genius of Addison became as conspicuous in the pages of the *Tatler*, as it became a few months later in the pages of the *Spectator*. We all know in what high terms Steele acknowledged this assistance. " I have," he writes in his preface to the fourth volume, " only one gentleman, who will be nameless, to thank for any frequent assistance to me, which indeed it would have been barbarous in him to have denied to one with whom he has lived in an intimacy from childhood, considering the great ease with which he is able to despatch the most entertaining pieces of this nature. This good office he performed with such force of genius, humour, wit and learning, that I fared like a distressed prince, who calls in a powerful neighbour to his aid ; I was undone by my auxiliary ; when I had once called him in I could not subsist without dependence on him." At a later date he again handsomely admits his obligations to the refined genius and delicate humour of his friend. " The *Tatler* was advanced indeed ! for it was raised to a greater thing than I intended it ! For the elegance, purity and correctness which appeared in the writings of Joseph Addison were not so much my purpose ; as (in any intelligible manner, as I could) to rally all those singularities of human life, through the different professions and characters in it, which obstruct anything that was truly good and great."

The two prominent contributors to the paper served as excellent foils to each other, and what one lacked the other supplied. If Steele sometimes hurried off his articles, writing them in taverns or whatever was the haunt he for the moment frequented, drawing upon his animal spirits and boisterous experiences for the matter required of him ; nothing could be more finished, more recondite in its references, more polished

in the structure of its sentences than the "copy" furnished by
Addison. Read any of his papers and never do we meet with
a grammatical mistake, a clumsy expression, a long and in-
volved period, a passage that has to be read and re-read before
it becomes intelligible ; lucidity, coherence and correctness are
conspicuous in every line of his contributions. Not without
reason did Dr. Johnson recommend those who wish to study
the English language to give their days and nights to Addison.
If Steele owing to his more vigorous nature and ruder surroundings is occasionally gross in his similes and mistakes sensuality for love and impertinence for wit ; the pen of Addison
never offends—nothing can be purer than his chivalrous devotion to woman, nothing tenderer and yet more penetrating than
his humour, never does he gloat over the criticism of unsavoury
subjects, never does he raise a laugh or inflict one of his little
stabs which strike so gently and yet go so home, but by the
aid of an art which is absolutely without reproach : in the
perusal of his pages we feel we are in the presence of a perfect
man of letters and a perfect gentleman. To us Steele appears
as a rollicking, easily led, impulsive, good hearted, literary
man ; Addison a quiet, retiring, keenly observant man of
society and man of letters. The one looked out upon life and
human nature from the windows of the barrack yard; the other
from those of his library. In the criticisms of the former we
see the man of action, in the criticisms of the latter the man of
reflection. The combination of the two gives the light and
shade necessary to their co-editorial labours.

To the social historian of this period the pages of the *Tatler*
are invaluable. In them we see life and manners in the reign
of good Queen Anne vividly and elaborately portrayed—the
dress and distractions of the "lady of quality," the gait, speech
and dandyism of the beau, the character and position of the
clergy, the favourite haunts of the day, the dissipations, recreations, employments, all held up before us as in a mirror of the
past. Let us look upon the reflection and for a moment study
the features of English life in that most picturesque of all
periods, the beginning of the eighteenth century.

And first as to her who was the object of so much homage, criticism, and confusion, the dame of fashion. The fine lady was the especial creation of the indolence, ignorance and luxury of the hour ; holding in disdain most things English and accepting without inquiry everything French. Her morning was generally spent in bed ; then after having sipped her two dishes of chocolate and yawned over a French romance, her waiting-woman proceeded to dress her head, paint her cheeks and throw over her shoulders the elegant night-rail trimmed with the rarest lace. Thus attired madam was now ready to receive her friends of both sexes and pass the time till noon in criticising her neighbour, the newest fashions, or the last play. If she happened to be free from the " vapours," her monkey, lap-dog, and grey parrot were permitted on this occasion to bask in the 'sunshine of her brightly arranged chamber if in summer, or in front of the light and portable stove in winter. At noon she rose to dress, and now the one most serious business of the day presented itself. When her cheeks had been rouged, her lips salved, her eyes brightened, and she had availed herself of all the other appliances of art to conceal the ravages of nature, her tirewoman placed upon her hair the towering headdress of the hour, so as to completely hide her fair locks ; and then were put on the fine linen, the varied petticoats, often edged with silver, the hooped petticoat so girded against by the satirists of the day, the furbelow, the open laced boddice, the green silk stockings (what does Grammont say about hose of that hue ?) the high-heeled shoes, the rich fan of India paint, the hats or coloured hoods, feathers, coats, and the rest.

Her elaborate toilet completed, the fine lady was now scented and patched to drive out shopping—the New Exchange in the Strand was her favourite place of resort—till three, when she dined, though the hour for dinner like at the present day was getting later and later, as we see from certain remarks made by Steele upon the subject. In London she seldom rode, but was carried about in a sedan chair, or drove in her coach. Steele more than once inveighs against coaches monopolising so much of the road. After dinner visits as a rule were paid, and arrangements made as to the occupation of the next day. The evening was spent in "seeing company," dancing, going to the theatre, which opened at six, or in playing cards; bedtime as a rule at twelve, though cards often ran the night into early morn. Next to flirting and dancing, the great recreation of the day for the lady of quality was card-playing. Never was the "itch for play" keener than at this date. From the *Tatler* we learn that ombre, whist, basset and crimp were the favourite games. Play was high, and frequently women of fashion were forced to break up their establishment in town on account of the heavy losses they had sustained. "Oh the damned vice!" cries Steele, "that women can imagine all household care, regard to posterity and fear of poverty must be sacrificed to a game at cards." When her ladyship, after a long course of luxury, idleness and dissipation, began to suffer physical inconvenience, she was, then as now, a great believer in change and the cure to be derived from the drinking of Spa waters. Bath or "the Bath," as it was called, was her favourite watering-place, for there the best company was to be met with its attendant attractions of music, gambling, balls and well laid-out grounds. Next to the city of King Bladud, the spas of Tunbridge, Epsom and Hampstead were the most popular. The season was from May to August, and at its height in July.

The woman of the upper middle class led a healthier and less vicious life than her more exalted sister. If her home was in the country, she was constantly in the saddle, and often rode well to hounds, she danced country dances, she interested herself in the poor of her district, she helped her mother in domestic concerns, and piqued herself upon her knowledge of preserves and the manipulation of medical prescriptions. She did not read much, for as we have said, there was little to read, but she was no mean proficient upon the harpsichord, and loved to organise little concerts in her village, she patched but did not paint and save for the building up of the lofty and ridiculous headdress, her attire was modest and attractive. If she lived in London, she was pretty constant in her attendance at morning prayers, either at St. James's or at St. Paul's, Covent Garden, (Steele complains that she looked about too much and never repeated the responses) she walked a good deal, chiefly in St. James's Park, between Story's and Rosamond Pond, she adored French dances (country dances she left to her cousin in the shires), she preferred a comedy to an opera, she had a mania for the purchase of lottery tickets, she loved sight-seeing from the newest rope dancer to the latest monstrosity, she believed in astrologers, she was fond of tea and the "thick scandal" it engendered, and of course she was passionately addicted to that great distraction of idleness—cards. Like the dame of fashion, her thoughts were much occupied with the details of dress—the choice of commodes, pinners, furbelows, quilted petticoats, silk and chintz gowns, and modish French night clothes engaging much of her attention. The laced boddice had always been somewhat careless as to the revelations it disclosed, but of late years its boldness had developed to such an extent as to cause shopkeepers to fear that one class of their wares would become extinct. Steele took the subject up and inserted in his *Tatler*, the following humorous appeal :—

" To Isaac Bickerstaff, Esquire.

" The humble Petition of the Company of Linen-drapers, residing within the liberty of Westminister,

" Sheweth,

" That there has of late prevailed among the ladies so great an affectation of nakedness, that they have not only left the bosom wholly bare, but lowered their stays some inches below the former mode.

" That in particular, Mrs. Arabella Overdo, has not the least appearance of linen ; and our best customers show but little above the small of their backs.

" That by this means your Petitioners are in danger of losing the advantage of covering a ninth part of every woman or quality in Great Britain.

" Your Petitioners humbly offer the premises to your Indulgence's consideration, and shall ever, &c."

.' The lives of the men of the upper classes, as revealed to us
in the pages of the *Tatler*, followed very much upon the same
lines. They were equally frivolous, indolent, un-cultured, and
un-domestic. To the beau and the fop, dress was as much a
matter of grave import as it was to the dame of fashion. The
buck or the maccaroni spent hours over his toilet. A long,
heavy, powdered periwig—sometimes three feet long—framed
his patched and rouged face ; around his neck was the Berdash
or the carefully disordered folds of the Steinkirk—a neckcloth
so called from the battle of that name, when the French
generals were so suddenly called upon to attack the English
as to have no time to arrange their cravats. The shirt was of
the finest linen, and its front exposed to view, the waistcoat
always being freely unbuttoned—" wearing the breast open "
was the highest form of swagger. The coat was generally
made of cloth with elaborate buttons and embroidered with
silver, at the ends it was wired causing it to stick out ; for
visits of ceremony it was of flowered silk or satin ; the
waistcoat and breeches were after the same fashion. The
hose were generally of silk in all colours, and the shoes
adorned with small buckles, the heels being often of wood
and very high. Owing to the constant habit of taking
snuff, the pocket handkerchief which was of silk and very
large, played a prominent part in the attire of the beau.
Except when dancing a carelessly hung sword, with its hilt
more or less elaborated according to the taste and wealth
of the wearer, was always carried at the side. If the beau
was a peer of the realm and decorated, he displayed on all
occasions his star and riband on his coat. When dressed for
walking, the fine gentleman surmounted his periwig with a
low crowned, broad brimmed felt hat looped up or cocked, if a
military man a feather was worn ; it was rakishly put on one
side, " one eye tucked under the hat." From the third button
on his coat hung his amber-headed cane, or, if in winter, his
muff. In the fob of his breeches was a big watch to which
was attached a broad ribbon with dangling seals. If the
weather was cold a roquelaure or cloak (do we not remember

the roquelaure of Uncle Toby ?) generally of scarlet enveloped. his manly form.

The occupations of the beau were in perfect harmony with his costume. His morning he spent in visiting. On entering the room his manner and appearance were stiff and studied but not ungraceful, the bow he made, the mincing step, the fashion after which he kissed the hands of the fair sex or gently brushed the painted cheek with his lips, for kissing the ladies on entering the room was then the vogue, his lisp, his limp, his affectation of being shortsighted or of being deaf ; his occasional dropping of the aspirate, the smile, the ogle, his way of telling a story or imparting scandal, and the rest of his arts were all acted in the most finished manner and the result of repeated rehearsals. One trick of his he was then very fond of performing, for it was the occasion of much amusement ; in the nineteenth century we call it a *sell*, in the eighteenth it was called a *bite*. "I'll teach you a way to outwit Mrs. Johnson," writes Swift to his fair correspondent at Dublin, "it is a new fashioned way of being witty and they call it *a bite*. You must ask a bantering question or tell some damned lie in a serious manner, then she will answer or speak as if you were in earnest, and then cry you 'Madam, there's a *bite!*' I would not have you undervalue this, for it is the constant amusement in Court."

As there were then no clubs in the modern sense of the word—for at the October and Kit Kat Clubs men met only to drink and talk politics—the young man of fashion, after paying his morning visits, or ogling the ladies in the Mall— the Parade, as it was then called—or flirting with the pretty shopkeepers at the New Exchange, dined at a fashionable ordinary—at Locket's at Charing Cross, or at Pontack's in Abchurch Lane, noted for its excellent claret, both of which taverns are so often mentioned in the comedies of the day. After dinner he lounged down to his coffee-house, the St. James's or the Cocoa Tree, where he talked, smoked, and, we fear, often drank (for Steele is ever girding at the drinking habits of the times), until the hour had arrived for him to occupy his favourite side-box at the theatre—at the Haymarket or Drury

Lane. After the play he returned to his coffee-house, or the particular tavern he affected, or visited that haunt of gallantry, Spring Garden, or more probably betook himself to one of the numerous gaming-houses in the town, or punted with the best of company at the gaming-house of the Groom Porter—an official specially appointed to preside over gambling, and regulate its conditions. The Groom Porter's was a favourite haunt of the cold and silent King William, where, according to the diary of Luttrell, he seems invariably to have lost.

So much for the man of fashion. To him who had to work for his livelihood the tone of life was healthier, and not unenviable. Amusements were within the price of all, living was cheap, competition had not as yet rendered work either scarce or severe, and social intercourse was abundant and enjoyable. If the middle-class man did not as now possess his palatial club he had his coffee-house where, for a modest penny, he had the run of a large room where he could hear the news, warm himself before a good fire, enjoy his dish of coffee, smoke his pipe, and there meet his friends, if necessary, for the transaction of business. If he was a young doctor, he patronised Batson's, in Cornhill; if a clergyman, Child's, in St. Paul's Churchyard; if a barrister, the Grecian, in Devereux Court, Temple; if a merchant, Garraway's, in Exchange Alley; if a stock-jobber, Jonathan's, likewise in Exchange Alley; the Jerusalem and Lloyd's were also for city men; for the man of letters there was Will's, in Bow Street; for the soldier, Old Man's, in Tilt Yard, or Slaughter's, in St. Martin's Lane; and numerous others which appealed to every class and purse in the community. The theatre was his great relaxation, and since its prices, unlike at the present day, were within the scope of all, was well patronised. Constant reference to the plays of the day, and to the favourite actors and actresses, is made in the pages of the *Tatler*. Indeed, Colley Cibber frankly acknowledges how much the stage was indebted to the dramatic criticisms of Steele, how he induced the town to come to the play-houses, and how people were attracted by the force and influence of his papers. The play began at six,

The pit was the popular seat; the upper gallery for footmen; the middle gallery for the well-to-do; and the boxes for "the quality." "The Pit," writes Misson, a French critic of English life at this date, "is an amphitheatre filled with benches without back-boards, and adorned and covered with green cloth. Men of quality, particularly the younger sort, some ladies of reputation and virtue, and abundance of damsels that hunt for prey, sit all together in this place higgledy-piggledy, chatter, toy, play, hear, and hear not." Between the acts wenches with baskets of oranges went about the pit to sell their wares. It was when acting in this capacity that Nell Gwynne attracted the attention of the Merry Monarch.

In addition to the theatre there were various other amusements. There were the fairs, at specified dates, of Bartholomew and Southwark; exhibitions of all kinds, generally held at the most noted taverns; travelling menageries, which occupied any piece of vacant ground in the town; rope-dancing; fencing bouts; boxing; bear-baiting at Hockley-in-the-hole, bull-baiting at Tothill Fields, and cock-fighting at Gray's Inn Gardens. These last entertainments excited the ire of Steele, who denounced them for their cruelty, and declared that among no other people were they looked upon as pleasures. We also hear of billiards, tennis, cricket, football, archery, and then as now the witnessing of racing was always a spectacle that afforded much delight to every class in the nation. Races for stakes of all descriptions were among the most prominent features in the pastimes of the age. Not a town of any note but had its racecourse.

To one profession the pages of the *Tatler* offer corroboration of a then melancholy truth. The position and activity of the clergy left very much to be desired. With but a few exceptions the parson both in London and the country was an idle, ignorant, servile creature, grovelling before his patron, and careless as to the welfare of his flock. According to Steele he read badly, hurried over the services entrusted to him, whilst to his laziness were to be attributed the dissensions which so

often broke out in every parish, and helped to fill the con-
venticles. Though occupying the position of a gentleman, he
was treated with scant respect, and seldom regarded by his
squire or his lady as an equal. Hospitality or attention was
rarely shown him except when he was wanted to take a hand
at cards, to fill a vacant place at the table, or to give information upon some subject of which he was supposed to possess
especial knowledge. Between him and his scanty congregation
there was little love or regard ; the one looked upon his duties
as weary and monotonous, whilst the poor knew from the means
of " Sir Crape " that their necessities could not be relieved. As
a rule the country vicar was always married, and often, if we
credit the satire of the period, to " My Lady's antiquated
waiting maid," who, perhaps, in her youth had not been cruel
to My Lord. Did not that pliant divine, the Rev. Mr. Tusher,
of Castlewood, link himself to the tirewoman of My Lady ?
Yet if the position of the rural parson was degrading, that of
the domestic chaplain was still more so. He was the butt of
the household, the object of derision to the boys of the family
he was sometimes called upon to teach, the scorn of the
servants, and, though he dined at the table of his patron, was
expected to retire when the sweets were served. If he resisted
this custom, his opposition, as we see from the *Tatler*, sometimes cost him his post. " I am chaplain," writes Addison in
the guise of one of these clerical menials, " to an honourable
family, very regular at the hours of devotion, and, I hope, of
an unblameable life ; but for not offering to rise at the second
course I found my patron and his lady very sullen and out of
humour, though at first I did not know the reason of it. At
length, when I happened to help myself to a jelly, the lady of
the house, otherwise a devout woman, told me that it did not
become a man of my cloth to delight in such frivolous food :
but as I still continued to sit out the last course I was
yesterday informed by the butler that his lordship had no
farther occasion for my service." What a flood of light is
thrown upon the position of the unhappy chaplain by these
words, " *informed by the butler !* "

When the parson took his walks abroad he was always dressed in cassock and gown and his head covered with the heavy wig of the period. Then, as now, there were dandies in the sacred profession—though only in London—who prided themselves upon their powdered periwigs, their white hands, the sheen of their gowns and polish of their shoes, the dulcet tones in which they appealed to the fair sex and the expressive sentimentality of their gaze. Steele takes these "pretty fellows in sacred orders" to task. "I therefore earnestly desire," he writes in a *Tatler*, "our young missionaries from the Universities to consider where they are, and not dress and look and move like young officers. It is no disadvantage to have a very handsome white hand, but were I to preach repentance to a gallery of ladies, I would, methinks, keep my gloves on." Nor were the arts of these "pretty fellows" wholly ineffectual. What satirist is it who said that the religion of young ladies is—curates? Thus writes in a *Tatler* Miss Penitence Gentle to one the Rev. Mr. Ralph Incense, chaplain to the dowager Countess of Brumpton. "I heard and saw you preach last Sunday. I am an ignorant young woman and understood not half you said : but ah ! your manner when you held up both your hands towards our pew ! Did you design to win me to Heaven or yourself ? " Can the nineteenth century say that the race of Penitence Gentle's and Ralph Incense's has wholly died out? As long as the mechanism of a creed has to be maintained in order to regulate and exalt its animating spirit, hero-worship of this description will never lack a shrine.

We have but alluded to the prominent features of this reign which are presented to us in the papers of the four volumes of the *Tatler*. No period is richer in the contemporary materials it offers for a complete and vivid history of its times than the reign of Queen Anne, and of these materials the essays penned by Addison and Steele are among the richest. Not a subject which interested our ancestors but is brought forward, discussed and dismissed. The style of the *Tatler* is here and there somewhat less light than that of its more popular contemporary the *Spectator*; but embedded in its pages are essays so humorous, so truthful, so suggestive, so replete with advice and instruction of the highest order, that they well deserve to be separated from their fellows and taken out of the oblivion in which they have too long been allowed to remain. This selection has now been attempted, and it is hoped not without success.

After a circulation of some twenty months the *Tatler* suddenly ceased to appear, Jan. 2, 1711. Various reasons have been given for its withdrawal at the height of its prosperity, but if we criticise the politics of the hour the one real reason is not difficult to discover. According to Steele the *Tatler* was discontinued because the world had ascertained that he himself was its editor and chief contributor. So long as he wrote anonymously and his personality was kept in the background the strength of his attacks upon gambling, duelling, and the other vices of the age was unimpaired. The sermon was excellent, provided the preacher was unknown. But what was to be said of the discourse when the pulpit orator was found to be more than liberally endowed with the frailties of our erring nature, and to practise seldom what he so eloquently enlarged upon? "I never designed in my articles," writes Steele, when announcing the withdrawal of the *Tatler*, "to give any man any secret wound by my concealment, but spoke in the character of an old man, a philosopher, a humourist, an astrologer and a censor, to allure my reader with the variety of my subjects and insinuate if I could the weight of reason with the agreeableness of wit. The general purpose of the whole has been to recommend truth, innocence, honour and virtue as the chief ornaments of life; but I considered that severity of manners was absolutely necessary to him who would censure others; and for that reason, and that only, chose to talk in a mask. I shall not carry my humility so far as to call myself a vicious man; but at the same time must confess, my life is at best but pardonable. And with no greater character than this, a man would make an indifferent progress in attacking prevailing and fashionable vices, which

Mr. Bickerstaff has done with a freedom of spirit that would have lost both its beauty and efficacy, had it been pretended to by Mr. Steele." Yet this statement is but half the truth. The stripping off the "mask" may have had some connection with the extinction of the *Tatler*, but we fancy that in Steele's dismissal from his post as Gazetteer lies the actual and dominant reason. It was from his official position as Gazetteer, that Steele was indebted for the early and trustworthy news with which he supplied his paper, and which caused the *Tatler* to triumph over all its rivals. The *London Post*, the *Postboy*, and Dyer's *News Letter*, in discussing foreign intelligence, were greatly at a disadvantage when compared with the most popular journal of the time, which drew its information direct from the fountain-head. Deprived of his office Steele saw that the days of the *Tatler* were numbered, and that it must either exist, like the rest, as a political paper, or develop its social and humorous articles. He preferred the latter course, and from the ashes of the defunct *Tatler* arose the *Spectator*.

Why was Steele compelled to resign his office as Gazetteer ? It appears that he permitted certain articles, though apparently not written by himself, reflecting upon the State, and especially upon Harley, to find their way into the columns of the *Tatler*.

As we have already related, Steele was indebted for his appointment of Gazetteer to Arthur Mainwaring, who had obtained it from Harley, then one of the two Secretaries of State, the other being Lord Sunderland, the son-in-law of the great Marlborough. Owing to the tactics of party warfare, the Whigs, divided and disheartened, were now gradually being ousted from office. At last the trial of Sacheverell completed their overthrow. Sunderland, from whose office at Whitehall so many of Steele's letters had been dated, was dismissed, and was succeeded by Lord Dartmouth, a staunch but violent Tory. A few months, however, before his resignation Sunderland had appointed Steele to a Commissionership of Stamps, a vacancy having been created by the nomination of John Molesworth as envoy to the Court of Tuscany. And now it was that there appeared in the *Tatler* three papers which were supposed to

reflect upon Harley, then scheming for supreme power.
Whether Steele penned these strictures or not he was regarded
by all parties as their author, and his periodical looked upon
with suspicion by the now dominant Tories.   In the preface
to the fourth volume of his *Tatler* Steele distinctly denies that
he wrote the articles complained of.   As editor he was
responsible for their insertion, but of the venom they contained
he was innocent.   He held the quiver, but did not manufacture
the poisoned arrows.

Denial was, however, useless.   Steele was an object of suspicion to the Tories ; he had made the now absolute Harley
his enemy, and he declined to imitate the example of the bitter
Dean of St. Patrick's and attach himself to the victorious
party.   It was considered a mischievous precedent that one
holding the post of Gazetteer should lend himself to the heat
and spite of faction.   An official, it was said, should not
" engage in parties."   Steele was accordingly dismissed from
his office, and it was also thought that his three hundred a
year, which he received as Commissioner of Stamps, would
have, after a similar fashion, to be sacrificed.   Swift, who had
been employing his efforts for the poet Congreve to retain his
official post, now performed the same service for Steele.

"I was this morning," he writes in his Diary, " with
Mr. Lewis, the Under-Secretary to Lord Dartmouth, two hours
talking politics, and contriving to keep Steele in his office of
stamped paper ; he has lost his place of Gazetteer, three
hundred pounds a year, for writing a *Tatler*, some months
ago, against Mr. Harley, who gave it him at first, and raised
the salary from sixty to three hundred pounds.   This was
devilish ungrateful, and Lewis was telling me the particulars ;
but I had a hint given me that I might save him in the other
employment, and leave was given me to clear matters with Steele."
Accordingly, Swift continues, he proceeded the same evening
" to sit with Mr. Addison and offer the matter at distance to
him as the discreeter person, but found Party had so possessed
him that he talked as if he suspected me, and would not fall
in with anything I said.   So I stopped short in my overture,

and we parted very dryly; and I shall say nothing to Steele, and let them do as they will; but if things stand as they are he will certainly lose it unless I save him, and therefore I will not speak to him that I may not report to his disadvantage. Is not this vexatious? and is there so much in the proverb of proffered service? When shall I grow wise? I endeavour to act in the most exact points of honour and conscience, and my nearest friends will not understand it so." Later—on the 15th of December—he again alludes to the subject. " Lewis told me a pure thing. I had been hankering with Mr. Harley to save Steele his other employment, and have a little mercy on him, and I had been saying the same thing to Lewis, who is Mr. Harley's chief favourite. Lewis tells Mr. Harley how kindly I should take it if he would be reconciled to Steele, &c. Mr. Harley, on my account, falls in with it, and appoints Steele a time to let him attend him, which Steele accepts with great submission, but never comes, nor sends any excuse. Whether it was blundering, sullenness, or rancour of party, I cannot tell, but I shall trouble myself no more about him. I believe Addison hindered him out of mere spite, being grated to the soul to think he should ever want my help to save his friend."

Such was Swift's story of the matter in 1710. Three years later, however, when political differences had widened the breach between Steele and himself, he published a pamphlet in which there was a less friendly account of the circumstances in dispute. Briefly it is as follows. Soon after the Sacheverell trial, Swift writes, Steele must needs corrupt his paper with politics, and libel Harley, who had made him Gazetteer. Hence, comments the Dean, when the new ministry came in, to avoid being dismissed he was forced to resign. It is also further alleged that when Steele, as a mere matter of form, tendered his thanks to Harley for his office, Harley gave the whole credit of the appointment to Arthur Mainwaring. Then Swift proceeds to say that Steele had complained to a gentleman of Harley's treatment, stating "he never had done Mr. Harley any injury, nor received any obligation from him." The gentleman (was the gentleman Swift himself?) thereupon produced the *Tatler* articles, of which Steele at once declared he was only the publisher, "for they had been sent him by other hands." This the gentleman considered "a very monstrous kind of excuse." To this remark Steele replied, "Well, I have libelled him, and he has turned me out, so we are equal." But neither would this be granted; and he was asked whether the place of Gazetteer were not an obligation? "No," said he, "not from Mr. Harley, for when I went to thank him, he forbad me, and said I must only thank Mr. Mainwaring."

"It would be unwise," writes Mr. Dobson, who has carefully considered this question in his critical and interesting monograph on Steele,* "to attach too much importance to this statement, penned in all the bitterness of party feeling, and aggravated by personal irritation. But even from this it is possible to deduce certain conclusions by no means so unfavourable to Steele as his antagonist would have us to believe. If, as Swift says, Steele did not regard himself as indebted to Harley, it is difficult to fix upon him the charge of ingratitude, especially as tradition has, rightly or wrongly, associated his real benefactor Mainwaring with the offending utterances in the *Tatler*. His error, if error it were, lay in the negligence or want of judgment, which permitted the employment of a non-political paper for political purposes. But considering how he was surrounded by the opponents of Harley—by Addison, by Henley, by Halifax, by Sunderland, to the last of whom, as we have said, he probably owed his Commissionership of Stamps, it is easy to understand what pressure would be put upon him to harass a common enemy. As regards the backwardness to fall in with Swift's schemes, which Swift in his journal professes to regard as so disheartening, it seems even more capable of solution. Steele and Addison had not gone over, as Swift had, to the Tories, nor in the turn things had taken, were they inclined, after the fashion of some of their more time-serving colleagues, to cling to him like drowning men; †

---

* *English Worthies.* Richard Steele. By Austin Dobson.
† "The Whigs were ravished to see me, and would lay hold on me as a twig while they are drowning." (*Journal to Stella,* Sept. 9th, 1710.)

and although neither of them thought it necessary to come to open rupture with Swift the friend, it is most probable that both of them resented the patronising assistance, which at this moment may fairly be supposed to have been more than usually arrogant and exultant, of Swift the politician. With respect, also, to that famous visit to Harley which Steele never paid, it would seem that if he failed upon this occasion, he had at some later time an interview with the new Lord Treasurer, which, whether Swift knew of it or not, was wholly satisfactory in its results. For this he himself is the authority. ' When I had the honour of a short conversation with you, you were pleased not only to signify to me that I should remain in this office, but to add, that if I would name to you one of more value, which would be more commodious to me, you would favour me in it.' The proof that he remained in his Commissionership is furnished by a letter of the 4th June, 1713, containing the above extract, the object of which letter is the resignation of this very post. It appears therefore that Harley, who took from him the Gazetteer's place he had given him, refrained from taking from him the Commissionership he had not given him. That he did so without some tacit understanding is improbable. But whether it was definite or indefinite, whether it amounted to an armistice, or an armed neutrality, are things we may never know. What is clear is, the *Tatler* came to an end, and came to an end so suddenly that—according to Swift—even Addison, whom he met on the very day of its decease, knew nothing of the matter—a rather incomprehensible statement, which is nevertheless confirmed by Steele himself."

The sale of the *Tatler*, according to all accounts, was very extensive, and must have been a source of great emolument to Steele. The first four numbers were given gratis, and the price was then fixed at a penny, which was afterwards doubled. The size, folio, a half-sheet printed on both sides, deserved the character which an angry correspondent gave it when it first appeared, of " tobacco-paper and scurvy letter." The *Tatlers*, however, were afterwards collected in volumes, and reprinted in royal octavo and large letter at one guinea per volume. A numerous list of subscribers, "the greatest beauties and wits in the whole island of Great Britain," engaged to take the work at that then unprecedented price. These generous subscriptions were handsomely acknowledged by Steele.

A. C. E.

INTRODUCTORY.

No. 1.   TUESDAY, April 12, 1709.   [Steele.]

Quicquid agunt homines——
nostri est farrago libelli.
Juv. Sat. i. 85, 86.*

Whate'er men do, or say, or think, or dream,
Our motley Paper seizes for its theme.

THOUGH the other papers, which are published for the use of
the good people of England, have certainly very wholesome
effects, and are laudable in their particular kinds, they do not
seem to come up to the main design of such narrations, which,
I humbly presume, should be principally intended for the use
of politic persons, who are so public-spirited as to neglect their
own affairs to look into transactions of state. Now these
gentlemen, for the most part, being persons of strong zeal, and
weak intellects, it is both a charitable and necessary work to
offer something, whereby such worthy and well-affected
members of the commonwealth may be instructed, after their
reading, what to think ; which shall be the end and purpose
of this my paper, wherein I shall, from time to time, report
and consider all matters of what kind soever that shall occur
to me, and publish such my advices and reflections every
Tuesday, Thursday, and Saturday in the week, for the convenience of the post. I resolve to have something which may
be of entertainment to the fair sex, in honour of whom I have

* This motto heads most of the earlier numbers of the *Tatler.*

invented the title of this paper. I therefore earnestly desire all persons, without distinction, to take it in for the present *gratis*, and hereafter at the price of one penny, forbidding all hawkers to take more for it at their peril. And I desire all persons to consider, that I am at a very great charge for proper materials for this work, as well as that, before I resolved upon it, I had settled a correspondence in all parts of the known and knowing world. And forasmuch as this globe is not trodden upon by mere drudges of business only, but that men of spirit and genius are justly to be esteemed as considerable agents in it, we shall not, upon a dearth of news, present you with musty foreign edicts, and dull proclamations, but shall divide our relation of the passages which occur in action or discourse throughout this town, as well as elsewhere, under such dates of places as may prepare you for the matter you are to expect in the following manner.

All accounts of gallantry, pleasure, and entertainment, shall be under the article of White's Chocolate-house ; * poetry under that of Will's Coffee-house ; † Learning, under the title of Grecian ; ‡ foreign and domestic news, you will have from St. James's Coffee-house ; and what else I have to offer on any other subject shall be dated from my own Apartment.

I once more desire my reader to consider, that as I cannot keep an ingenious man to go daily to Will's under two-pence each day, merely for his charges ; to White's under six-pence ; nor to the Grecian, without allowing him some plain Spanish, to be as able as others at the learned table ; and that a good observer cannot speak with even Kidney § at St. James's without clean linen ; I say, these considerations will, I hope, make all persons willing to comply with my humble request.

* White's Chocolate-house was in St. James's-street.
† Will's Coffee-house was on the north-side of Russell-street in Covent Garden, where the wits of that time used to assemble, and where Dryden had, when he lived, been accustomed to preside.
‡ The Grecian was in Devereux-court in the Strand ; probably the most ancient coffee-house in London. In 1652 an English Turkey merchant brought home with him a Greek servant, who first opened a house for making and selling coffee.
§ Kidney was one of the waiters at St. James's Coffee-house.

(when my *gratis* stock is exhausted) of a penny apiece; especially since they are sure of some proper amusement, and that it is impossible for me to want means to entertain them, having, besides the force of my own parts, the power of divination, and that I can, by casting a figure, tell you all that will happen before it comes to pass.

But this last faculty I shall use very sparingly, and speak but of few things until they are passed, for fear of divulging matters which may offend our superiors.

TWO BEAUTIES.

No. 4. TUESDAY, April 19, 1709. [Steele.]

ALL hearts at present pant for two ladies only, who have for some time engrossed the dominion of the town. They are indeed both exceeding charming, but differ very much in their excellences. The beauty of Clarissa is soft, that of Chloe piercing. When you look at Clarissa, you see the most exact harmony of feature, complexion, and shape; you find in Chloe nothing extraordinary in any one of those particulars, but the whole woman irresistible : Clarissa looks languishing ; Chloe killing : Clarissa never fails of gaining admiration ; Chloe of moving desire. The gazers at Clarissa are at first unconcerned, as if they were observing a fine picture. They who behold Chloe, at the first glance discover transport, as if they met their dearest friend. These different perfections are suitably represented by the last great painter Italy has sent us, Mr. Jervas.† Clarissa is by that skilful hand placed in a

---

* The Author here celebrates two beauties of those times, whose real names the Editor has not been able to discover. Perhaps Steele only remarks on two pictures of Jervas [the instructor and intimate friend of Pope], whom he certainly meant to recommend as an excellent painter.

manner that looks artless, and innocent of the torments she gives ; Chloe is drawn with a liveliness that shows she is conscious of, but not affected with, her perfections. Clarissa is a shepherdess, Chloe a country girl. I must own, the design of Chloe's picture shows, to me, great mastery in the painter ; for nothing could be better imagined than the dress he has given her of a straw-hat and a ribbon, to represent that sort of beauty which enters the heart with a certain familiarity, and cheats it into a belief that it has received a lover as well as an object of love. The force of their different beauties is seen also in the effects it makes on their lovers. The admirers of Chloe are eternally gay and well-pleased : those of Clarissa melancholy and thoughtful. And as this passion always changes the natural man into a quite different creature from what he was before, the love of Chloe makes coxcombs ; that of Clarissa, madmen. There were of each kind just now in this room. Here was one that whistles, laughs, sings, and cuts capers, for love of Chloe. Another has just now writ three lines to Clarissa, then taken a turn in the garden, then came back again, then tore his fragment, then called for some chocolate, then went away without it.

Chloe has so many admirers in the house at present, that there is too much noise to proceed in my narration ; so that the progress of the loves of Clarissa and Chloe, together with the bottles that are drunk each night for the one, and the many sighs which are uttered, and songs written on the other, must be our subject on future occasions.

THE STAFFS.

No. 11. THURSDAY, May 5, 1709. [Steele.]

OF all the vanities under the sun, I confess that of being proud of one's birth is the greatest. At the same time, since in this unreasonable age, by the force of prevailing custom, things in which men have no hand are imputed to them ; and that I am used by some people, as if Isaac Bickerstaff, though I write myself Esquire, was nobody : to set the world right in that particular, I shall give you my genealogy, as a kinsman of ours has sent it me from the Heralds office. It is certain, and observed by the wisest writers, that there are women who are not nicely chaste, and men not severely honest, in all families ; therefore let those who may be apt to raise aspersions upon ours, please to give us as impartial an account of their own, and we shall be satisfied. The business of heralds is a matter of so great nicety, that, to avoid mistakes, I shall give you my cousin's letter *verbatim*, without altering a syllable.

" DEAR COUSIN,

"Since you have been pleased to make yourself so famous of late, by your ingenious writings, and some time ago by your learned predictions : since Partridge of immortal memory is dead and gone, who, poetical as he was, could not understand his own poetry ; and philomatical as he was, could not read his own destiny : since the Pope, the King of France, and great part of his court, are either literally or metaphorically defunct : since, I say, these things (not foretold by any one but yourself) have come to pass after so surprising a manner ; it is with no small concern I see the original of the Staffian race so little known in the world as it is at this time ; for which reason, as you have employed your studies in astronomy, and the occult sciences, so I, my mother being a Welsh woman, dedicated mine to genealogy, particularly that of our own family, which, for its antiquity and number, may challenge any in Great Britain. The Staffs are originally of Staffordshire, which took its name from them : the first that I find of the Staffs was one Jacobstaff, a famous and renowned astronomer, who by Dorothy his wife had issue seven sons, *viz.*, Bickerstaff, Longstaff, Wagstaff, Quarterstaff, Whitestaff, Falstaff, and Tipstaff. He also had a younger brother, who was twice married, and had five sons, *viz.*, Distaff, Pikestaff, Mopstaff, Broomstaff, and Raggedstaff. As for the branch from whence you spring, I shall say very little of it, only that it is the chief of the Staffs, and called Bickerstaff, *quasi* Biggerstaff; as much as to say, the Great Staff, or Staff of Staffs; and that it has applied itself to astronomy with great success, after the example of our aforesaid forefather. The descendants from Longstaff, the second son, were a rakish disorderly set of people, and rambled from one place to another, until, in the time of Harry the Second, they settled in Kent, and were called long-tails, from the long-tails which were sent them as a punishment for the murder of Thomas-à-Becket, as the legends say. They have always been sought after by the ladies; but whether it be to show their aversion to popery, or their love to miracles, I cannot say. The Wagstaffs are a merry thoughtless sort of people, who have always been opinionated of their own wit; they have turned themselves mostly to poetry. This is the most numerous branch of our family, and the poorest. The Quarterstaffs are most of them prize-fighters or deer-stealers: there have been so many of them hanged lately, that there are very few of that branch of our family left. The Whitestaffs * are all courtiers, and have had very considerable places. There have been some of them of that strength and dexterity, that five hundred † of the ablest men in the kingdom have often tugged in vain to pull a staff out of their hands. The Falstaffs are strangely given to whoring and drinking : there are abundance of them in and about London. One thing is very remarkable of this branch, and that is, there are just as many women as men in it. There was a wicked stick of wood of this name in Harry the Fourth's time, one Sir John Falstaff. As for Tipstaff, the youngest son, he was an honest fellow; but his sons, and his sons' sons, have all of them been the veriest rogues living : it is this unlucky branch that has stocked the nation with that

---

* An allusion to the staff carried, as an ensign of his office, by the First Lord of the Treasury.

† The House of Commons.

swarm of lawyers, attorneys, serjeants, and bailiffs, with which the nation is over-run. Tipstaff, being a seventh son, used to cure the king's-evil; but his rascally descendants are so far from having that healing quality, that by a touch upon the shoulder they give a man such an ill habit of body, that he can never come abroad afterwards. This is all I know of the line of Jacobstaff: his younger brother Isaacstaff, as I told you before, had five sons, and was married twice: his first wife was a Staff (for they did not stand upon false heraldry in those days) by whom he had one son, who, in process of time, being a schoolmaster and well read in the Greek, called himself Distaff, or Twicestaff. He was not very rich, so he put his children out to trades; and the Distaffs have ever since been employed in the woollen and linen manufactures, except myself, who am a genealogist. Pikestaff, the eldest son by the second venter, was a man of business, a downright plodding fellow, and withal so plain, that he became a proverb. Most of this family are at present in the army. Raggedstaff was an unlucky boy, and used to tear his clothes in getting birds' nests, and was always playing with a tame bear his father kept. Mopstaff fell in love with one of his father's maids, and used to help her to clean the house. Broomstaff was a chimney-sweeper. The Mopstaffs and Broomstaffs are naturally as civil people as ever went out of doors; but alas! if they once get into ill hands, they knock down all before them. Pilgrimstaff ran away from his friends, and went strolling about the country: and Pipestaff was a wine-cooper. These two were the unlawful issue of Longstaff.

"N.B. The Canes, the Clubs, the Cudgels, the Wands, the Devil upon two Sticks,* and one Bread, that goes by the name of Staff of Life, are none of our relations.

I am, Dear Cousin,

Your humble servant,

D. DISTAFF."

From the Heralds Office, May 1, 1709.

---

* An allusion to the "Diable Boiteux" of Le Sage.

E

AN ESQUIRE.

No. 19.　TUESDAY, MAY 24, 1709.　[STEELE.]

THERE is nothing can give a man of any consideration greater pain, than to see order and distinction laid aside amongst men, especially when the rank (of which he himself is member) is intruded upon by such as have no pretence to that honour. The appellation of Esquire is the most notoriously abused in this kind, of any class amongst men ; insomuch, that it is become almost the subject of derision : but I will be bold to say, this behaviour towards it proceeds from the ignorance of the people in its true origin. I shall therefore, as briefly as possible, do myself and all true Esquires the justice to look into antiquity upon this subject.*

In the first ages of the world, before the invention of jointures and settlements, when the noble passion of love had possession of the hearts of men, and the fair sex were not yet cultivated into the merciful disposition which they have showed in latter centuries, it was natural for great and heroic spirits to retire to rivulets, woods, and caves, to lament their destiny, and the cruelty of the fair persons who were deaf to their lamentations. The hero in this distress was generally in armour, and in a readiness to fight any man he met with, especially if distinguished by any extraordinary qualifications : it being the nature of heroic love to hate all merit, lest it should come within the observation of the cruel one by whom its own perfections are neglected. A lover of this kind had always about him a person of a second value, and subordinate to him, who could hear his afflictions, carry an inchantment for his wounds, hold his helmet when he was eating (if ever he did eat), or in his absence, when he was retired to his apartment in any king's palace, tell the prince himself, or perhaps his daughter, the birth, parentage, and adventures of his valiant

---

* See Selden's "Titles of Honour," part ii. chap. v, p. 830.

master. This trusty companion was styled his Esquire, and was always fit for any offices about him ; was as gentle and chaste as a gentleman-usher, quick and active as an equerry, smooth and eloquent as the master of the ceremonies. A man thus qualified was the first, as the antients affirm, who was called an Esquire ; and none without these accomplishments ought to assume our order : but, to the utter disgrace and confusion of the heralds, every pretender is admitted into this fraternity, even persons the most foreign to this courteous institution. I have taken an inventory of all within this city, and looked over every letter in the Post-office, for my better information. There are of the Middle Temple, including all in the buttery-books, and in the lists of the house, five thousand. In the Inner, four thousand. In the King's-Bench Walks, the whole buildings are inhabited by Esquires only. The adjacent street of Essex, from Morris's Coffee-house,* and the turning towards the Grecian, you cannot meet one who is not an Esquire, until you take water. Every house in Norfolk and Arundel-streets is also governed by an Esquire, or his Lady : Soho-square, Bloomsbury-square, and all other places where the floors rise above nine feet, are so many universities, where you enter yourselves, and become of our order. However, if this were the worst of the evil, it were to be supported, because they are generally men of some figure, and use ; though I know no pretence they have to an honour which had its rise from chivalry. But if you travel into the counties of Great Britain, we are still more imposed upon by innovation. We are indeed derived from the field : but shall that give title to all that ride mad after foxes, that halloo when they see a hare, or venture their necks full speed after an hawk, immediately to commence Esquires ? No ; our order is temperate, cleanly, sober, and chaste ; but these rural Esquires commit immodesties upon hay-cocks, wear shirts half a week, and are drunk twice a day. These men are also, to the last degree, excessive in their food : an Esquire of Norfolk eats two

---

* Morris's Coffee-house was in the Strand.

pounds of dumplin every meal, as if obliged to it by our order :
an Esquire of Hampshire is as ravenous in devouring hogs
flesh : one of Essex has as little mercy on calves.   But I must
take the liberty to protest against them, and acquaint those
persons, that it is not the quantity they eat, but the manner of
eating, that shews an Esquire.   But, above all, I am most
offended at small quillmen, and transcribing clerks, who
are all come into our order, for no reason that I know of, but
that they can easily flourish at the end of their name.   I will
undertake that, if you read the superscriptions to all the offices
in the kingdom, you will not find three letters directed to any
but Esquires.   I have myself a couple of clerks, and the
rogues make nothing of leaving messages upon each other's
desk : one directs, "To Gregory Goosequill, Esquire ; " to
which the other replies by a note, "To Nehemiah Dashwell,
Esquire, with respect ; " in a word, it is now *Populus
Armigerorum*, a people of Esquires.   And I do not know but,
by the late act of naturalization, foreigners will assume that
title, as part of the immunity of being Englishmen.   All these
improprieties flow from the negligence of the Heralds-office.
Those gentlemen in party-coloured habits do not so rightly, as
they ought, understand themselves ; though they are dressed
cap-a-pee in hieroglyphics, they are inwardly but ignorant men.
I asked an acquaintance of mine, who is a man of wit, but of
no fortune, and is forced to appear as a jack pudding on the
stage to a mountebank : " Pr'ythee, Jack, why is your coat of
so many colours ? " He replied, "I act a fool ; and this
spotted dress is to signify, that every man living has a weak
place about him ; for I am Knight of the Shire, and represent
you all."   I wish the heralds would know as well as this man
does, in his way, that they are to act for us in the case of our
arms and appellations : we should not then be jumbled
together in so promiscuous and absurd a manner.   I design to
take this matter into farther consideration ; and no man shall
be received as an Esquire, who cannot bring a certificate,
that he has conquered some lady's obdurate heart ; that he
can lead up a country dance ; or carry a message between her

and her lover, with address, secrecy, and diligence. A Squire is properly born for the service of the sex, and his credentials shall be signed by three toasts and one prude, before his title shall be received in my office.

DUELLING.

No. 25. TUESDAY, June 7, 1709. [Steele.]

A LETTER from a young lady, written in the most passionate terms, wherein she laments the misfortune of a gentleman, her lover, who was lately wounded in a duel, has turned my thoughts to that subject, and inclined me to examine into the causes which precipitate men into so fatal a folly. And as it has been proposed to treat of subjects of gallantry in the article from hence, and no one point in nature is more proper to be considered by the company who frequent this place than that of duels, it is worth our consideration to examine into this chimerical groundless humour, and to lay every other thought aside, until we have stripped it of all its false pretences to credit and reputation amongst men.

But I must confess, when I consider what I am going about, and run over in my imagination all the endless crowd of men of honour who will be offended at such a discourse ; I am undertaking, methinks, a work worthy an invulnerable hero in romance, rather than a private gentleman with a single rapier : but as I am pretty well acquainted by great opportunities with the nature of man, and know of a truth that all men fight against their will, the danger vanishes, and resolution rises upon this subject. For this reason, I shall talk very freely on a custom which all men wish exploded, though no man has courage enough to resist it.

But there is one unintelligible word, which I fear will extremely perplex my dissertation, and I confess to you I find very hard to explain, which is the term "satisfaction." An honest country gentleman had the misfortune to fall into company with two or three modern men of honour, where he happened to be very ill-treated ; and one of the company, being conscious of his offence, sends a note to him in the morning, and tells him, he was ready to give him satisfaction. " This is fine doing," says the plain fellow ; " last night he sent me away cursedly out of humour, and this morning he fancies it would be a satisfaction to be run through the body."

As the matter at present stands, it is not to do handsome actions denominates a man of honour ; it is enough if he dares to defend ill ones.   Thus you often see a common sharper in competition with a gentleman of the first rank ; though all mankind is convinced, that a fighting gamester is only a pickpocket with the courage of an highway-man.   One cannot with any patience reflect on the unaccountable jumble of persons and things in this town and nation, which occasions very frequently, that a brave man falls by a hand below that of a common hangman, and yet his executioner escapes the clutches of the hangman for doing it.   I shall therefore hereafter consider, how the bravest men in other ages and nations have behaved themselves upon such incidents as we decide by combat ; and shew, from their practice, that this resentment neither has its foundation from true reason or solid fame ; but is an imposture, made of cowardice, falsehood, and want of understanding.   For this work, a good history of quarrels would be very edifying to the public, and I apply myself to the town for particulars and circumstances within their knowledge, which may serve to embellish the dissertation with proper cuts.   Most of the quarrels I have ever known, have proceeded from some valiant coxcomb's persisting in the wrong, to defend some prevailing folly, and preserve himself from the ingenuousness of owning a mistake.

By this means it is called " giving a man satisfaction," to urge your offence against him with your sword ; which puts me in mind of Peter's order to the keeper, in The Tale of a Tub : " if you neglect to do all this, damn you and your generation for ever : and so we bid you heartily farewel."   If the contradiction in

the very terms of one of our challenges were as well explained
and turned into downright English, would it not run after this
manner ?

" Sir,

    " Your extraordinary behaviour last night, and the
liberty you were pleased to take with me, makes me this
morning give you this, to tell you, because you are an ill-bred
puppy, I will meet you in Hyde-park, an hour hence ; and
because you want both breeding and humanity, I desire you
would come with a pistol in your hand, on horseback, and
endeavour to shoot me through the head, to teach you more
manners. If you fail of doing me this pleasure, I shall say,
you are a rascal, on every post in town : and so, sir, if you will
not injure me more, I shall never forgive what you have done
already. Pray, sir, do not fail of getting everything ready ;
and you will infinitely oblige, sir, your most obedient humble
servant, &c."

SNUFF

No. 35. THURSDAY, June 30, 1709. [Steele.]

There is a habit or custom which I have put my patience
to the utmost stretch to have suffered so long, because several
of my intimate friends are in the guilt ; and that is, the humour
of taking snuff, and looking dirty about the mouth by way of
ornament.

  My method is, to dive to the bottom of a sore before I pretend to apply a remedy. For this reason, I sat by an eminent
story-teller and politician, who takes half an ounce in five
seconds, and has mortgaged a pretty tenement near the town,
merely to improve and dung his brains with this prolific powder.
I observed this gentleman, the other day, in the midst of a story,
diverted from it by looking at something at a distance, and I

softly hid his box. But he returns to his tale, and, looking for his box, he cries, " And so, sir—" Then, when he should have taken a pinch, " As I was saying—" says he, " has nobody seen my box ? " His friend beseeches him to finish his narration : then he proceeds : " And so, sir——where can my box be ? " Then turning to me, " Pray, sir, did you see my box ? " " Yes, sir," said I, " I took it to see how long you could live without it." He resumes his tale, and I took notice that his dulness was much more regular and fluent than before. A pinch supplied the place of " As I was saying," and " So, sir ; " and he went on currently enough in that style which the learned call the insipid. This observation easily led me into a philosophic reason for taking snuff, which is done only to supply with sensations the want of reflection. This I take to be an εὕρηκα, a nostrum ; upon which I hope to receive the thanks of this board ; for as it is natural to lift a man's hand to a sore, when you fear anything coming at you ; so when a person feels his thoughts are run out, and he has no more to say, it is as natural to supply his weak brain with powder at the nearest place of access, *viz.* the nostrils. This is so evident that nature suggests the use according to the indigence of the persons who take this medicine, without being prepossessed with the force of fashion or custom. For example ; the native Hibernians, who are reckoned not much unlike the antient Bœotians, take this specific for emptiness in the head, in greater abundance than any other nation under the sun. The learned Sotus, as sparing as he is in his words, would be still more silent if it were not for this powder.

However low and poor the taking of snuff argues a man to be in his own stock of thoughts, or means to employ his brains and his fingers ; yet there is a poorer creature in the world than he, and this is a borrower of snuff ; a fellow that keeps no box of his own, but is always asking others for a pinch. Such poor rogues put me always in mind of a common phrase among school-boys when they are composing their exercise, who run to an upper scholar, and cry, " Pray give me a little sense." But of all things commend me to the ladies who are got into this pretty help to discourse. I have been these three years persuading Sagissa * to leave it off; but she talks so much, and is so learned, that she is above contradiction. However, an accident the other day brought that about, which my eloquence could never accomplish. She had a very pretty fellow in her closet, who ran thither to avoid some company that came to visit her; she made an excuse to go in to him for some implement they were talking of. Her eager gallant snatched a kiss; but, being unused to snuff, some grains from off her upper lip made him sneeze aloud, which alarmed the visitants, and has made a discovery, that profound reading, very much intelligence, and a general knowledge of who and who are together, cannot fill her vacant hours so much, but she is sometimes obliged to descend to entertainments less intellectual.

AN EXERCISE OF ARMS.

No. 41.　THURSDAY, July 14, 1709.　[Steele.]

―― Celebrare domestica facta,

"To celebrate domestic deeds."

THERE is no one thing more to be lamented in our nation, than their general affectation of every thing that is foreign; nay, we carry it so far, that we are more anxious for our own countrymen when they have crossed the seas, than when we see them in the same dangerous condition before our eyes at home: else how is it possible, that on the twenty-ninth of the last month, there should have been a battle fought in our very streets of London, and nobody at this end of the town have heard of it ? I protest, I, who make it my business to enquire after adventures, should never have known this, had not the following account been sent me inclosed in a letter. This, it

* The lady here alluded to, under the name of Sagissa, a diminutive from the word *Sage*, was Mrs. de la Rivicre Manley, who provoked Steele by the liberties she had taken with his character in her " New Atalantis."

seems, is the way of giving out orders in the Artillery-company; and they prepare for a day of action with so little concern, as only to call it, " An Exercise of Arms."

" An Exercise of Arms of the Artillery-company, to be performed on Wednesday, June the twenty-ninth, 1709, under the command of Sir Joseph Woolfe, knight and alderman, general ; Charles Hopson, esquire, present sheriff, lieutenant-general ; Captain Richard Synge, major ; Major John Shorey, captain of grenadiers ; Captain William Grayhust, Captain John Butler, Captain Robert Carellis, captains.

" The body marched from the Artillery-ground, through Moorgate, Coleman Street, Lothbury, Broad Street, Finch Lane, Cornhill, Cheapside, St. Martin's, St. Anne's Lane, halt the pikes under the wall in Noble Street, draw up the firelocks facing the Goldsmiths' Hall, make ready and face to the left, and fire, and so *ditto* three times. Beat to arms, and march round the hall, as up Lad Lane, Gutter Lane, Honey Lane, and so wheel to the right, and make your salute to my lord, and so down St. Ann's Lane, up Aldersgate Street, Barbican, and draw up in Red Cross Street, the right at St. Paul's Alley in the rear. March off lieutenant-general with half the body up Beech Lane : he sends a sub-division up King's Head Court, and takes post in it, and marches two divisions round into Red Lion Market, to defend that pass, and succour the division in King's Head Court ; but keeps in White Cross Street, facing Beech Lane, the rest of the body ready drawn up. Then the general marches up Beech Lane, is attacked, but forces the division in the court into the market, and enters with three divisions while he presses the lieutenant-general's main body ; and at the same time the three divisions force those of the revolters out of the market, and so all the lieutenant-general's body retreats into Chiswell Street, and lodges two divisions in Grub Street : and as the general marches on, they fall on his flank, but soon made to give way : but have a retreating-place in Red Lion Court, but could not hold it, being put to flight through Paul's Alley, and pursued by the general's grenadiers, while he marches up and attacks their main body, but are opposed again by a party of men as lay in Black Raven Court; but they are forced also to retire soon in the utmost confusion, and at the same time, those brave divisions in Paul's Alley ply their rear with grenadoes, that with precipitation they take to the route along Bunhill Row: so the general marches into the Artillery-ground, and being drawn up, finds the revolting party to have found entrance, and makes a show as if for a battle, and both armies soon engage in form, and fire by platoons."

Much might be said for the improvement of this system; which, for its style and invention, may instruct generals and their historians, both in fighting a battle, and describing it when it is over. These elegant expressions, "*ditto*—and so ——but soon——but having——but could not——but are ——but they——finds the party to have found," &c. do certainly give great life and spirit to the relation.

Indeed, I am extremely concerned for the lieutenant-general, who, by his overthrow and defeat, is made a deplorable instance of the fortune of war, and vicissitudes of human affairs. He, alas! has lost, in Beech Lane and Chiswell Street, all the glory he lately gained in and about Holborn and St. Giles's. The art of subdividing first, and dividing afterwards, is new and surprising; and according to this method, the troops are disposed in King's Head Court and Red Lion Market: nor is the conduct of these leaders less conspicuous in their choice of the ground or field of battle. Happy was it, that the greatest part of the achievements of this day was to be performed near Grub Street, that there might not be wanting a sufficient number of faithful historians, who being eye-witnesses of these wonders, should impartially transmit them to posterity! But then it can never be enough regretted, that we are left in the dark as to the name and title of that extraordinary hero, who commanded the divisions in Paul's Alley; especially because those divisions are justly styled brave, and accordingly were to push the enemy along Bunhill Row, and thereby occasion a general battle. But Pallas appeared in the form of a shower of rain, and prevented the slaughter and desolation, which were threatened by these extraordinary preparations.

Hi motus animorum, atque hæc certamina tanta
Pulveris exigui jactu compressa quiescunt.

" Yet all those dreadful deeds, this doubtful fray,
A cast of scatter'd dust will soon allay."

THEATRICAL PROPERTY.

No. 42. SATURDAY, July 16, 1709. [Steele.]

IT is now twelve of the clock at noon, and no mail come in ; therefore, I am not without hopes that the town will allow me the liberty which my brother news-writers take, in giving them what may be for their information in another kind, and indulge me in doing an act of friendship, by publishing the following account of goods and moveables.

This is to give notice, that a magnificent palace, with great variety of gardens, statues, and water-works, may be bought cheap in Drury-lane ; where there are likewise several castles, to be disposed of, very delightfully situated ; as also groves, woods, forests, fountains, and country-seats, with very pleasant prospects on all sides of them ; being the moveables of Christopher Rich,* Esquire, who is breaking up house-keeping, and has many curious pieces of furniture to dispose of, which may be seen between the hours of six and ten in the evening.

THE INVENTORY.

Spirits of right Nantz brandy, for lambent flames and apparitions.

Three bottles and a half of lightning.

One shower of snow in the whitest French paper.

---

* Drury-lane playhouse was shut up about this time by an order from the Lord Chamberlain.

Two showers of a browner sort.

A sea, consisting of a dozen large waves ; the tenth * bigger than ordinary, and a little damaged.

A dozen and half of clouds, trimmed with black, and well-conditioned.

A rainbow, a little faded.

A set of clouds after the French mode, streaked with lightning, and furbelowed.

A new moon, something decayed.

A pint of the finest Spanish wash, being all that is left of two hogsheads sent over last winter.

A coach very finely gilt, and little used, with a pair of dragons, to be sold cheap.

A setting-sun, a pennyworth.

An imperial mantle, made for Cyrus the Great, and worn by Julius Cæsar, Bajazet, king Harry the Eighth, and signor Valentini.

A basket-hilted sword, very convenient to carry milk in.

Roxana's night-gown.

Othello's handkerchief.

The imperial robes of Xerxes, never worn but once.

A wild boar killed by Mrs. Tofts and Dioclesian.

A serpent to sting Cleopatra.

A mustard-bowl to make thunder with.

Another of a bigger sort, by Mr. D——s's † directions, little used.

Six elbow-chairs, very expert in country-dances, with six flower-pots for their partners.

The whiskers of a Turkish Pasha.

The complexion of a murderer in a band-box ; consisting of a large piece of burnt cork, and a coal-black peruke.

A suit of clothes for a ghost, *viz.* a bloody shirt, a doublet curiously pinked, and a coat with three great eyelet-holes upon the breast.

---

* The Latin poets pretend that th tenth wave is the largest and most dangerous.

† John Dennis, the critic.

A bale of red Spanish wool.

Modern plots, commonly known by the name of trap-doors, ladders of ropes, vizard-masques, and tables with broad carpets over them.

Three oak-cudgels, with one of crab-tree ; all bought for the use of Mr. Pinkethman.*

Materials for dancing ; as masques, castanets, and a ladder of ten rounds.

Aurengezebe's scymitar, made by Will Brown in Piccadilly.

A plume of feathers, never used but by Œdipus and the Earl of Essex.

There are also swords, halbards, sheep-hooks, cardinals' hats, turbans, drums, gallipots, a gibbet, a cradle, a rack, a cart-wheel, an altar, an helmet, a back-piece, a breast-plate, a bell, a tub, and a jointed baby.

These are the hard shifts we intelligencers are forced to ; therefore our readers ought to excuse us, if a westerly wind blowing for a fortnight together, generally fills every paper with an order of battle ; when we shew our martial skill in every line, and according to the space we have to fill, we range our men in squadrons and battalions, or draw out company by company, and troop by troop ; ever observing that no muster is to be made, but when the wind is in a cross-point, which often happens at the end of a campaign, when half the men are deserted or killed.† The Courant is sometimes ten deep, his ranks close : the Post-boy is generally in files, for greater exactness ; and the Post-man comes down upon you rather after the Turkish way, sword in hand, pell-mell, without form or discipline ; but sure to bring men enough into the field ; and wherever they are raised, never to lose a battle for want of numbers.

* A low comedy actor and manager of a travelling company.
† A sneer at the ridiculous military articles published in the newspapers of those days, introduced perhaps with a view to insinuate that the news articles in the *Tatler* were most to be relied upon of any then published.

ORLANDO THE FAIR.

No. 50.　THURSDAY, August 4, 1709.　[Steele.]

WHATEVER malicious men may say of our lucubrations, we have no design but to produce unknown merit, or place in a proper light the actions of our contemporaries who labour to distinguish themselves, whether it be by vice or virtue. For we shall never give accounts to the world of anything, but what the lives and endeavours of the persons, of whom we treat, make the basis of their fame and reputation. For this reason, it is to be hoped that our appearance is reputed a public benefit; and though certain persons may turn what we mean for panegyric into scandal, let it be answered once for all, that if our praises are really designed as raillery, such malevolent persons owe their safety from it, only to their being too inconsiderable for history. It is not every man who deals in rats-bane, or is unseasonably amorous, that can adorn story like Æsculapius; nor every stock-jobber of the India company can assume the port, and personate the figure of Aurengezebe. My noble ancestor, Mr. Shakespeare, who was of the race of the Staffs, was not more fond of the memorable Sir John Falstaff, than I am of those worthies; but the Latins have an admirable admonition expressed in three words, to wit, *Ne quid nimis,* which forbids my indulging myself on those delightful subjects, and calls me to do justice to others, who make no less figures in our generation : of such, the first and most renowned is, that eminent hero and lover Orlando * the

---

* Robert Fielding, known then by the name of Beau Fielding. He was tried for felony at the Old Bailey, Dec. 4, 1706. He had married Barbara, Duchess of Cleveland, one of the mistresses of Charles the Second, having a former wife then living. In the course of the evidence on this trial, it appears that sixteen days before, Mrs. Villars, a very bad woman, had artfully drawn him into a marriage with one Mary Wadsworth, a spinster, on the mistaken belief of her being Mrs. Deleau, a widow, with a fortune of £60,000. His marriage with the Duchess was therefore set aside, and her Grace was allowed the liberty of marrying again. Fielding craved the benefit of clergy, and when sentence was given that he should be burnt in his hand, produced the Queen's warrant to suspend execution, and was admitted to bail.

handsome, whose disappointments in love, in gallantry, and in
war, have banished him from public view, and made him
voluntarily enter into a confinement to which the ungrateful
age would otherwise have forced him.   Ten *lustra* * and more
are wholly passed since Orlando first appeared in the
metropolis of this island : his descent noble, his wit humorous,
his person charming.   But to none of these recommendatory
advantages was his title so undoubted, as that of his beauty.
His complexion was fair, but his countenance manly ; his
stature of the tallest, his shape the most exact : and though in
all his limbs he had a proportion as delicate as we see in the
works of the most skilful statuaries, his body had a strength
and firmness little inferior to the marble of which such
images are formed.   This made Orlando the universal flame of
all the fair sex ; innocent virgins sighed for him, as Adonis ;
experienced widows, as Hercules.   Thus did this figure walk
alone the pattern and ornament of our species, but of course
the envy of all who had the same passions without his superior
merit, and pretences to the favour of that enchanting creature,
woman.   However, the generous Orlando believed himself
formed for the world, and not to be engrossed by any particular
affection.   He sighed not for Delia, for Chloris, for Chloe, for
Betty, nor my lady, nor for the ready chamber-maid, nor
distant baroness : woman was his mistress, and the whole sex
his seraglio.   His form was always irresistible ; and if we
consider, that not one of five hundred can bear the least favour
from a lady without being exalted above himself ; if also we
must allow, that a smile from a side-box has made Jack Spruce
half mad : we cannot think it wonderful that Orlando's repeated conquests touched his brain : so it certainly did, and
Orlando became an enthusiast in love ; and in all his address,
contracted something out of the ordinary course of breeding
and civility.   However, powerful as he was, he would still add
to the advantages of his person, that of a profession which the
ladies always favour, and immediately commenced soldier.

* Ten *lustra* amount to half a century.

Thus equipped for love and honour, our hero seeks distant climes and adventures, and leaves the despairing nymphs of Great Britain, to the courtships of beaux and witlings till his return. His exploits in foreign nations and courts have not been regularly enough communicated unto us, to report them with that veracity which we profess in our narrations : but after many feats of arms (which those who were witnesses to them have suppressed out of envy, but which we have had faithfully related from his own mouth in our public streets) Orlando returns home full, but not loaded, with years. Beaux born in his absence made it their business to decry his furniture, his dress, his manner ; but all such rivalry he suppressed (as the philosopher did the sceptic, who argued there was no such thing as motion) by only moving. The beauteous Villaria,* who only was formed for his paramour, became the object of his affection. His first speech to her was as follows :

"MADAM,
      "It is not only that nature has made us two the most accomplished of each sex, and pointed to us to obey her dictates in becoming one ; but that there is also an ambition in following the mighty persons you have favoured. Where kings and heroes, as great as Alexander, or such as could personate Alexander,† have bowed, permit your general to lay his laurels."
      According to Milton ;

> " The Fair with conscious majesty approv'd
> His pleaded reason."——

Fortune having now supplied Orlando with necessaries for his high taste of gallantry and pleasure, his equipage and economy had something in them more sumptuous and gallant than could be received in our degenerate age ; therefore his figure, though highly graceful, appeared so exotic, that it assembled all the Britons under the age of sixteen, who saw

---

* Barbara, daughter and heiress of William Villiers, Viscount Grandison.
† An allusion to Goodman, the player, who was one of the promiscuous rain above mentioned.

his grandeur, to follow chariot with shouts and acclamations ; which he regarded with the contempt which great minds affect in the midst of applauses.   I remember, I had the honour to see him one day stop, and call the youths about him, to whom he spake as follows :

" Good bastards—Go to school, and do not lose your time in following my wheels : I am loth to hurt you, because I know not but you are all my own offspring : hark ye, you sirrah with the white hair, I am sure you are mine : there is half-a-crown.   Tell your mother, this, with the half-crown I gave her when I got you, comes to five shillings.   Thou hast cost me all that, and yet thou art good for nothing.   Why, you young dogs, did you never see a man before ? "   " Never such a one as you, noble general," replied a truant from Westminster. " Sirrah, I believe thee : there is a crown for thee.   Drive on, coachman."

This vehicle, though sacred to love, was not adorned with doves : such an hieroglyphic denoted too languishing a passion. Orlando therefore gave the eagle,* as being of a constitution which inclined him rather to seize his prey with talons, than pine for it with murmurs.

CONTINUATION OF THE HISTORIETTE OF

ORLANDO THE FAIR.

No. 51.   SATURDAY, August 6, 1709.   [Steele.]

Fortune being now propitious to the gay Orlando, he dressed, he spoke, he moved as a man might be supposed to do in a nation of pygmies, and had an equal value for our approbation or dislike.   It is usual for those who profess a contempt for the world, to fly from it and live in obscurity ;

* The Fieldings give the Spread Eagle as Counts of the German Empire.

but Orlando, with a greater magnanimity, contemned it, and appeared in it to tell them so. If, therefore, his exalted mien met with an unwelcome reception, he was sure always to double the cause which gave the distaste. You see our beauties affect a negligence in the ornament of their hair, and adjusting their head-dresses, as conscious that they adorn whatever they wear. Orlando had not only this humour in common with other beauties, but also had a neglect whether things became him, or not, in a world he contemned. For this reason, a noble particularity appeared in all his economy, furniture, and equipage. And to convince the present little race, how unequal all their measures were to an Antediluvian as he called himself, in respect of the insects which now appear for men, he sometimes rode in an open tumbril, of less size than ordinary, to shew the largeness of his limbs, and the grandeur of his personage, to the greater advantage. At other seasons, all his appointments had a magnificence, as if it were formed by the genius of Trimalchio of old, which shewed itself in doing ordinary things with an air of pomp and grandeur. Orlando therefore called for tea by beat of drum ; his valet got ready to shave him by a trumpet to horse ; and water was brought for his teeth, when the sound was changed to boots and saddle.

In all these glorious excesses from the common practice did the happy Orlando live and reign in an uninterrupted tranquillity, until an unlucky accident brought to his remembrance, that one evening he was married before he courted the nuptials of Villaria. Several fatal memorandums were produced to revive the memory of this accident ; and the unhappy lover was for ever banished her presence, to whom he owed the support of his just renown and gallantry. But distress does not debase noble minds ; it only changes the scene, and gives them new glory by that alteration. Orlando therefore now raves in a garret, and calls to his neighbour-skies to pity his dolours, and to find redress for an unhappy lover. All high spirits, in any great agitation of mind, are inclined to relieve themselves by poetry : the renowned porter of

Oliver * had not more volumes around his cell in his college of
Bedlam, than Orlando in his present apartment. And though
inserting poetry in the midst of prose be thought a license
among correct writers not to be indulged, it is hoped the necessity of doing it, to give a just idea of the hero of whom we treat,
will plead for the liberty we shall hereafter take, to print
Orlando's soliloquies in verse and prose, after the manner of
great wits, and such as those to whom they are nearly allied.

DELAMIRA.

No. 52. TUESDAY, AUGUST 9, 1709. [STEELE.]

LONG had the crowd of the gay and young stood in suspense,
as to their fate in their passion *to* the beauteous Delamira;
but all their hopes are lately vanished, by the declaration
that she has made of her choice, to take the happy Archibald †
for her companion for life. Upon her making this known, the
expense of sweet powder and jessamine are considerably
abated; and the mercers and milliners complain of her want of
public spirit, in not concealing longer a secret which was so
much the benefit of trade. But so it has happened; and no
one was in confidence with her in carrying on this treaty, but
the matchless Virgulta, whose despair of ever entering the
matrimonial state made her, some nights before Delamira's
resolution was published to the world, address herself to her
in the following manner :

* Cromwell's porter is said to have been the original from which Caius
Gabriel, father of Colley Cibber, copied one of the lunatic figures on Bedlam
gate.

† Lord Archibald Hamilton, of Motherwell, son of William, third Duke of
Hamilton, was probably the *happy* Archibald here meant. He was member
of Parliament for Lanarkshire, afterwards Governor of Jamaica, and about
this time married Lady Jane Hamilton, youngest daughter of James, Earl of
Abercorn. It seems to follow that Lady Jane Hamilton, who died at Paris in
1752, was the Delamira here celebrated

"Delamira! you are now going into that state of life wherein the use of your charms is wholly to be applied to the pleasing only one man. That swimming air of your body, that janty bearing of your head over one shoulder, and that inexpressible beauty in your manner of playing your Fan, must be lowered into a more confined behaviour ; to shew, that you would rather shun than receive addresses for the future. Therefore, dear Delamira! give me those excellencies you leave off and acquaint me with your manner of charming : for I take the liberty of our friendship to say, that when I consider my own stature, motion, complexion, wit, or breeding, I cannot think myself any way your inferior ; yet do I go through crowds without wounding a man, and all my acquaintance marry round me, while I live a virgin unasked, and I think unregarded."

Delamira heard her with great attention, and, with that dexterity which is natural to her, told her, that "all she had above the rest of her sex and contemporary beauties was wholly owing to a Fan, (that was left her by her mother, and had been long in the family) which whoever had in possession and used with skill, should command the hearts of all her beholders : and since," said she smiling, "I have no more to do with extending my conquests or triumphs, I will make you a present of this inestimable rarity." Virgulta made her expressions of the highest gratitude for so uncommon a confidence in her, and desired she would "show her what was peculiar in the management of that utensil, which rendered it of such general force while she was mistress of it." Delamira replied, "You see, madam, Cupid is the principal figure painted on it ; and the skill in playing this Fan is, in your several motions of it, to let him appear as little as possible ; for honourable lovers fly all endeavours to ensnare them ; and your Cupid must hide his bow and arrow, or he will never be sure of his game. You may observe," continued she, "that in all public assemblies, the sexes seem to separate themselves, and draw up to attack each other with eye-shot : that is the time when the Fan, which is all the armour of a woman, is of

most use in our defence; for our minds are construed by the
waving of that little instrument, and our thoughts appear in
composure or agitation, according to the motion of it.   You
may observe, when Will Peregrine comes into the side-box,
Miss Gatty flutters her fan, as a fly does its wings round a
candle; while her eldest sister, who is as much in love with
him as she is, is as grave as a vestal at his entrance; and the
consequence is accordingly.   He watches half the play for a
glance from her sister, while Gatty is overlooked and
neglected.   I wish you heartily as much success in the management of it as I have had : If you think fit to go on where I
left off, I will give you a short account of the execution I have
made with it.

"Cimon, who is the dullest of mortals, and though a
wonderful great scholar, does not only pause, but seems to
take a nap with his eyes open between every other sentence in
his discourse : him have I made a leader in assemblies; and
one blow on the shoulder as I passed by him has raised him to
a downright impertinent in all conversations.   The airy Will
Sampler is become as lethargic by this my wand, as Cimon is
sprightly.   Take it, good girl, and use it without mercy; for
the reign of beauty never lasted full three years, but it ended
in marriage, or condemnation to virginity.   As you fear therefore, the one, and hope for the other, I expect an hourly
journal of your triumphs; for I have it by certain tradition,
that it was given to the first who wore it, by an enchantress,
with this remarkable power, that it bestows a husband in half
a year on her who does not overlook her proper minute; but
assigns to a long despair the woman who is well offered, and
neglects that proposal.   May occasion attend your charms, and
your charms slip no occasion !   Give me, I say, an account of
the progress of your forces at our next meeting; and you shall
hear what I think of my new condition.   I should meet my
future spouse this moment.   Farewell.   Live in just terror of
the dreadful words, SHE WAS."

THE CIVIL HUSBAND.

No. 53. THURSDAY, August 11, 1709. [Steele.]

The fate and character of the inconstant Osmyn is a just excuse for the little notice taken by his widow of his departure out of this life, which was equally troublesome to Elmira, his faithful spouse, and to himself. That life passed between them after this manner, is the reason the town has just now received a lady with all that gaiety, after having been a relict but three months, which other women hardly assume under fifteen, after such a disaster. Elmira is the daughter of a rich and worthy citizen, who gave her to Osmyn, with a portion which might have obtained her an alliance with our noblest houses, and fixed her in the eye of the world, where her story had not been now to be related : for her good qualities had made her the object of universal esteem among the polite part of mankind, from whom she has been banished and immured until the death of her gaoler. It is now full fifteen years since that beauteous lady was given into the hands of the happy Osmyn, who, in the sense of all the world, received at that time a present more valuable than the possession of both the Indies. She was then in her early bloom, with an understanding and discretion very little inferior to the most experienced matrons. She was not beholden to the charms of her sex, that her company was preferable to any Osmyn could meet with abroad ; for were all she said considered without regard to her being a woman, it might stand the examination of the severest judges. She had all the beauty of her own sex, with all the conversation-accomplishments of ours. But Osmyn very soon grew surfeited with the charms of her person by possession, and of her mind by want of taste ; for he was one of that loose sort of men, who have but one reason for setting any value upon the fair sex ; who consider even brides but as new women, and consequently neglect them when they cease to be such. All the merit of Elmira could not prevent her becoming a mere wife within few months after her nuptials ; and Osmyn had so little relish for her conversation, that he complained of the advantages of it. "My spouse," said he to one of his companions, "is so very discreet, so good, so virtuous, and I know not what, that I think her person is rather the object of esteem than of love ; and there is such a thing as a merit which causes rather distance than passion." But there being no medium in the state of matrimony, their life began to take the usual gradations to become the most irksome of all beings. They grew in the first place very complaisant ; and having at heart a certain knowledge that they were indifferent to each other, apologies were made for every little circumstance which they thought betrayed their mutual coldness. This lasted but few months, when they shewed a difference of opinion in every trifle ; and, as a sign of certain decay of affection, the word "perhaps" was introduced in all their discourse. "I have a mind to go to the park," says she ; "but perhaps, my dear, you will want the coach on some other occasion." He "would very willingly carry her to the play ; but perhaps she had rather go to lady Centaur's * and play at ombre." They were both persons of good discerning, and soon found that they mortally hated each other, by their manner of hiding it. Certain it is, that there are some genio's which are not capable of pure affection, and a man is born with talents for it as much as for poetry or any other science.

Osmyn began too late to find the imperfection of his own heart ; and used all the methods in the world to correct it, and argue himself into return of desire and passion for his wife, by the contemplation of her excellent qualities, his great obligations to her, and the high value he saw all the world except himself did put upon her. But such is man's unhappy condition, that though the weakness of the heart has a prevailing power over the strength of the head, yet the strength of the head has but small force against the weakness of the heart. Osmyn, therefore, struggled in vain to revive departed desire ;

* The name of one of the characters in Ben Jonson's "Silent Woman."

and for that reason resolved to retire to one of his estates in the country, and pass away his hours of wedlock in the noble diversions of the field ; and in the fury of a disappointed lover, made an oath to leave neither stag, fox, or hare living, during the days of his wife. Besides that country-sports would be an amusement, he hoped also, that his spouse would be half-killed by the very sense of seeing this town no more, and would think her life ended as soon as she left it. He communicated his design to Elmira, who received it, as now she did all things, like a person too unhappy to be relieved or afflicted by the circumstance of place. This unexpected resignation made Osmyn resolve to be as obliging to her as possible : and if he could not prevail upon himself to be kind, he took a resolution at least to act sincerely, and communicate frankly to her the weakness of his temper, to excuse the indifference of his behaviour. He disposed his household in the way to Rutland, so as he and his lady travelled only in the coach, for the convenience of discourse. They had not gone many miles out of town, when Osmyn spoke to this purpose :

"My dear, I believe I look quite as silly now I am going to tell you I do not love you, as when I first told you I did. We are now going into the country together, with only one hope of making this life agreeable, survivorship ; desire is not in our power ; mine is all gone for you. What shall we do to carry it with decency to the world, and hate one another with discretion ?"

The lady answered, without the least observation on the extravagance of his speech :

"My dear, you have lived most of your days in a court, and I have not been wholly unacquainted with that sort of life. In courts, you see good-will is spoken with great warmth, ill-will covered with great civility. Men are long in civilities to those they hate, and short in expressions of kindness to those they love. Therefore, my dear, let us be well-bred still ; and it is no matter, as to all who see us, whether we love or hate : and to let you see how much you are beholden to me for my conduct, I have both hated and despised you, my dear, this half year ; and yet neither in language or behaviour has it been visible but that I loved you tenderly. Therefore, as I know you go out of town to divert life in pursuit of beasts, and conversation with men just above them ; so, my life, from this moment, I shall read all the learned cooks who have ever writ ; study broths, plasters, and conserves, until from a fine lady I become a notable woman. We must take our minds a note or two lower, or we shall be tortured by jealousy, or anger. Thus, I am resolved to kill all keen passions, by employing my mind on little subjects, and lessening the easiness of my spirit; while you, my dear, with much ale, exercise, and ill-company, are so good as to endeavour to be as contemptible, as it is necessary for my quiet I should think you."

At Rutland they arrived, and lived with great but secret impatience for many successive years, until Osmyn thought of an happy expedient to give their affairs a new turn. One day he took Elmira aside, and spoke as follows :

" My dear, you see here the air is so temperate and serene ; the rivulets, the groves, and soil, so extremely kind to nature, that we are stronger and firmer in our health since we left the town ; so that there is no hope of a release in this place ; but if you will be so kind as to go with me to my estate in the hundreds of Essex, it is possible some kind damp may one day or other relieve us. If you will condescend to accept of this offer, I will add that whole estate to your jointure in this county."

Elmira, who was all goodness, accepted the offer, removed accordingly, and has left her spouse in that place to rest with his fathers.

This is the real figure in which Elmira ought to be beheld in this town ; and not thought guilty of an indecorum, in not professing the sense, or bearing the habit of sorrow, for one who robbed her of all the endearments of life, and gave her only common civility, instead of complacency of manners, dignity of passion, and that constant assemblage of soft desires and affections which all feel who love, but none can express.

THE DEAN OF ST. PAUL'S.

No. 54. SATURDAY, August 13, 1709. [Steele.]

As we have professed that all the actions of men are our subject, the most solemn are not to be omitted, if there happens to creep into their behaviour anything improper for such occasions. Therefore the offence mentioned in the following epistles, though it may seem to be committed in a place sacred from observation, is such, that it is our duty to remark upon it : for, though he who does it is himself only guilty of an indecorum, he occasions a criminal levity in all others who are present at it.

"St. Paul's Churchyard, *August* 11.

"Mr. Bickerstaff,

"It being mine as well as the opinion of many others, that your papers are extremely well fitted to reform any irregular or indecent practice, I present the following as one which requires your correction. Myself, and a great many good people who frequent the divine service at St. Paul's, have been a long time scandalized by the imprudent conduct of Stentor* in that cathedral. This gentleman, you must know, is always very exact and zealous in his devotion, which I believe nobody blames ; but then he is accustomed to roar and bellow so terribly loud in the responses, that he frightens even us of the congregation who are daily used to him : and one of our petty canons, a punning Cambridge scholar, calls his way of worship a Bull-offering. His harsh untuneable pipe is no more fit than a raven's to join with the music of a choir ; yet, nobody having been enough his friend, I suppose, to inform him of it, he never fails, when present, to drown the harmony of every hymn and anthem, by an inundation of sound beyond that of the bridge at the ebb of the tide, or the neighbouring lions in the anguish of their hunger. This is a grievance,

---

* Dr. William Stanley, Dean of St. Paul's.

which, to my certain knowledge, several worthy people desire to see redressed ; and if by inserting this epistle in your paper, or by representing the matter your own way, you can convince Stentor, that discord in a choir is the same sin that schism is in the church in general, you would lay a great obligation upon us ; and make some atonement for certain of your paragraphs, which have not been highly approved by us.   I am, Sir,

" Your most humble servant,

" JEOFFRY CHANTICLEER."

It is wonderful that there should be such a general lamentation, and the grievance so frequent, and yet the offender never know anything of it.   I have received the following letter from my kinsman at the Heralds-office, near the same place.

" DEAR COUSIN,

     " This office, which has had its share in the impartial justice of your censures, demands at present your vindication of their rights and privileges.   There are certain hours when our young heralds are exercised in the faculties of making proclamation, and other vociferations, which of right belong to us only to utter : but at the same hours Stentor in St. Paul's church, in spite of the coaches, carts, London cries, and all other sounds between us, exalts his throat to so high a key, that the most noisy of our order is utterly unheard.   If you please to observe upon this, you will ever oblige, &c."

There have been communicated to me some other ill consequences from the same cause ; as, the overturning of coaches by sudden starts of the horses as they passed that way, women pregnant frightened, and heirs to families lost ; which are public disasters, though arising from a good intention : but it is hoped, after this admonition, that Stentor will avoid an act of so great supererogation, as singing without a voice.

THE SHARPER.*

No. 56. THURSDAY, August 18, 1709. [Steele.]

There is a young foreigner committed to my care, who puzzles me extremely in the questions he asks about the persons of figure we meet in public places. He has but very little of our language, and therefore I am mightily at a loss to express to him things for which they have no word in that tongue to which he was born. It has been often my answer, upon his asking who such a fine gentleman is? That he is what we call a Sharper: and he wants my explication. I thought it would be very unjust to tell him, he is the same the French call *Coquin*; the Latins, *Nebulo*; or the Greeks, Ράσκαλ: for, as custom is the most powerful of all laws, and that the order of men we call Sharpers are received amongst us, not only with permission, but favour, I thought it unjust to use them like persons upon no establishment; besides that it would be unpardonable dishonour to our country, to let him leave us with an opinion, that our nobility and gentry keep company with common thieves and cheats: I told him, "they were a sort of tame Hussars, that were allowed in our cities, like the wild ones in our camp; who had all the privileges belonging to us, but at the same time were not tied to our discipline or laws." Aletheus, who is a gentleman of too much virtue for the age he lives in, would not let this matter be thus palliated; but told my pupil, "that he was to understand that distinction, quality, merit, and industry, were laid aside among us by the incursions of these civil hussars; who had got so much countenance, that the breeding and fashion of the age turned their way to the ruin of order and economy in all places where they are

---

* This is the first of some excellent papers, in which Steele employed his wit in exposing the gamesters, sharpers, and swindlers of his time, with a view to guard his unwary countrymen from their snares, and "to banish fraud and cozenage from the presence and conversation of gentlemen."

admitted." But Sophronius, who never falls into heat upon any subject, but applies proper language, temper, and skill with which the thing in debate is to be treated, told the youth "that gentleman had spoken nothing but what was literally true ; but fell upon it with too much earnestness to give a true idea of that sort of people he was declaiming against, or to remedy the evil which he bewailed : for the acceptance of these men being an ill which had crept into the conversation-part of our lives, and not into our constitution itself, it must be corrected where it began : and consequently is to be amended only by bringing raillery and derision upon the persons who are guilty, or those who converse with them. " For the Sharpers," continued he, "at present are not as formerly, under the acceptation of pick-pockets ; but are by custom erected into a real and venerable body of men, and have subdued us to so very particular a deference to them, that though they are known to be men without honour or conscience, no demand is called a debt of honour so indisputably as theirs. You may lose your honour to them, but they lay none against you ; as the priesthood in Roman catholic countries can purchase what they please for the church, but they can alienate nothing from it. It is from this toleration, that Sharpers are to be found among all sorts of assemblies and companies ; and every talent amongst men is made use of by some one or other of the society, for the good of their common cause : so that an unexperienced young gentleman is as often ensnared by his understanding as his folly ; for who could be unmoved, to hear the eloquent Dromio explain the constitution, talk in the key of Cato, with the severity of one of the ancient sages, and debate the greatest question of state in a common chocolate or coffee-house ? who could, I say, hear this generous declamator, without being fired at his noble zeal, and becoming his professed follower, if he might be admitted ? Monoculus's* gravity would be no less inviting to a beginner in conversation ; and the snare of his eloquence would equally catch one who had never seen an old gentleman so

---

* Monoculus was supposed to mean Sir Humphrey Moneux.

very wise, and yet so little severe. Many other instances of extraordinary men among the brotherhood might be produced ; but every man, who knows the town, can supply himself with such examples without their being named."—Will Vafer, who is skilful at finding out the ridiculous side of a thing, and placing it in a new and proper light, though he very seldom talks, thought fit to enter into this subject. He has lately lost certain loose sums, which half the income of his estate will bring in within seven years : besides which, he proposes to marry, to set all right. He was, therefore, indolent enough to speak of this matter with great impartiality. " When I look around me," said this easy gentleman, " and consider in a just balance us *bubbles*, elder brothers whose support our dull fathers contrived to depend upon certain acres, with the rooks, whose ancestors left them the wide world ; I cannot but admire their fraternity, and contemn my own. Is not Jack Heyday much to be preferred to the knight he has bubbled ? Jack has his equipage, his wenches, and his followers : the knight, so far from a retinue, that he is almost one of Jack's. However, he is gay, you see, still ; a florid outside.——His habit speaks the man—And since he must unbutton, he would not be reduced outwardly, but is stripped to his upper coat. But though I have great temptation to it, I will not at this time give the history of the losing side ; but speak the effects of my thoughts, since the loss of my money, upon the gaining people. This ill fortune makes most men contemplative and given to reading ; at least it has happened so to me; and the rise and fall of the family of Sharpers in all ages has been my contemplation."

I find, all times have had of this people : Homer, in his excellent heroic poem, calls them Myrmidons, who were a body that kept among themselves, and had nothing to lose ; therefore never spared either Greek or Trojan, when they fell in their way, upon a party. But there is a memorable verse, which gives us an account of what broke that whole body, and made both Greeks and Trojans masters of the secret of their warfare and plunder. There is nothing so pedantic as many quotations ; therefore I shall inform you only, that in this bat-

talion there were two officers called Thersites and Pandarus :
they were both less renowned for their beauty than their wit ;
but each had this particular happiness, that they were plunged
over head and ears in the same water which made Achilles
invulnerable ; and had ever after certain gifts, which the rest
of the world were never to enjoy. Among others, they were
never to know they were the most dreadful to the sight of all
mortals, never to be diffident of their own abilities, never to
blush, or ever to be wounded but by each other. Though some
historians say, gaming began among the Lydians, to divert
hunger, I could cite many authorities to prove it had its rise at
the siege of Troy ; and that Ulysses won the sevenfold shield
at hazard. But be that as it may, the ruin of the corps of the
Myrmidons proceeded from a breach between Thersites and
Pandarus. The first of these was leader of a squadron, wherein
the latter was but a private man ; but having all the good qualities
necessary for a partisan, he was the favourite of his officer. But
the whole history of the several changes in the order of
Sharpers, from those Myrmidons to our modern men of address
and plunder, will require that we consult some ancient manuscripts. As we make these enquiries, we shall diurnally
communicate them to the public, that the Knights of the
Industry may be better understood by the good people of
England. These sort of men, in some ages, were sycophants
and flatterers only, and were endued with arts of life to
capacitate them for the conversation of the rich and great ;
but now the bubble courts the impostor, and pretends at the
utmost to be but his equal. To clear up the reasons and
causes in such revolutions, and the different conduct between
fools and cheats, shall be one of our labours for the good of this
kingdom. How therefore pimps, footmen, fidlers, and lacqueys,
are elevated into companions in this present age, shall be
accounted for from the influence of the planet Mercury * on
this island ; the ascendency of which Sharper over Sol, who is,
a patron of the Muses and all honest professions, has been

* Mercury was the god of thieves.

noted by the learned Job Gadbury,* to be the cause, that "cunning and trick are more esteemed than art and science." It must be allowed also, to the memory of Mr. Partridge, late of Cecil Street, in the Strand, that in his answer to an horary question, At what hour of the night to set a fox-trap in June 1705? he has largely discussed, under the character of Reynard, the manner of surprising all Sharpers as well as him. But of these great points, after more mature deliberation.

HARRY COPPERSMITH.

No. 57. SATURDAY, August 20, 1709. [Steele.]

Since my last, I have received a letter from Tom Trump, to desire that I would do the fraternity of gamesters the justice to own, that there are notorious Sharpers, who are not of their class. Among others he presented me with the picture of Harry Coppersmith, in little, who, he says, is at this day worth half a plum,† by means much more indirect than by false dice. I must confess, there appeared some reason in what he asserted; and he met me since, and accosted me in the following manner: " It is wonderful to me, Mr. Bickerstaff, that you can pretend to be a man of penetration, and fall upon us Knights of the Industry as the wickedest of mortals, when there are so many who live in the constant practice of baser methods unobserved. You cannot, though you know the story of myself and the North Briton, but allow I am an honester man than Will Coppersmith, for all his great credit among the Lombards. I get my money by men's follies, and he gets his by their distresses. The declining merchant communicates his griefs to him, and he augments them by extortion. If, therefore, regard is to be had to the merit of the persons we injure, who is the

---

* Gadbury was an almanack-maker, an astrologer, and a brother conjurer of Partridge, who lived several years after he fell into the hands of Squire Bickerstaff's upholders, and died in reality about the beginning of July, 1715.
† A plum is a term in the City for 100,000*l.*

G

more blameable, he that oppresses an unhappy man, or he that cheats a foolish one ? All mankind are indifferently liable to adverse strokes of fortune ; and he who adds to them, when he might relieve them, is certainly a worse subject than he who unburdens a man whose prosperity is unwieldy to him. Besides all which, he that borrows of Coppersmith does it out of necessity ; he that plays with me does it out of choice."

I allowed Trump there are men as bad as himself, which is the height of his pretensions : and must confess, that Coppersmith is the most wicked and impudent of all Sharpers : a creature that cheats with credit, and is a robber in the habit of a friend. The contemplation of this worthy person made me reflect on the wonderful successes I have observed men of the meanest capacities meet with in the world, and recollect an observation I once heard a sage man make ; which was, " That he had observed, that in some professions, the lower the understand-ing, the greater the capacity." * I remember, he instanced that of a banker, and said, that " the fewer appetites, passions, and ideas a man had, he was the better for his business."

There is little Sir Tristram, without connection in his speech, or so much as common sense, has arrived by his own natural parts at one of the greatest estates amongst us. But honest Sir Tristram knows himself to be but a repository for cash : he is just such an utensil as his iron chest, and may rather be said to hold money, than possess it. There is nothing so pleasant as to be in the conversation of these wealthy proficients. I had lately the honour to drink half a pint with Sir Tristram, Harry Coppersmith, and Giles Twoshoes. These wags gave one another credit in discourse, according to their purses ; they jest by the pound, and make answers as they honour bills. Without vanity, I thought myself the prettiest fellow of the company ; but I had no manner of power over one muscle in their faces, though they smirked at every word spoken by each other. Sir Tristram called for a pipe of tobacco ; and telling

---

* Swift insinuates the same thought, where he bids Lord Bolingbroke take notice, " that the clerks in his lordship's office made use of ivory knives to cut paper with, in preference to penknives."

us " tobacco was a pot-herb," bid the drawer bring him the
other half-pint.   Twoshoes laughed at the knight's wit without
moderation ; I took the liberty to say "it was but a pun."   " A
pun !" said Coppersmith ; "you would be a better man by ten
thousand pounds if you could pun like Sir Tristram."   With
that they all burst out together.   The queer curs maintained
this style of dialogue until we had drunk our quart a-piece by
half-pints.   All I could bring away with me is, that Twoshoes
is not worth twenty thousand pounds : for his mirth, though
he was as insipid as either of the others, had no more effect
upon the company than if he had been a bankrupt.

HARD WORDS.

No. 58.   TUESDAY, August 23, 1709.   [Steele.]

A MAN would be apt to think, in this laughing town, that it
were impossible a thing so exploded as speaking hard words
should be practised by any one that had ever seen good company ; but, as if there were a standard in our minds as well
as bodies, you see very many just where they were twenty years
ago, and more they cannot, will not arrive at.   Were it not
thus, the noble Martius would not be the only man in England
whom nobody can understand, though he talks more than any
man else.

Will Dactyle the epigrammatist, Jack Comma the gram-
marian, Nick Crosse-grain who writes anagrams, and myself,
made a pretty company at a corner of this room ; and entered
very peaceably upon a subject fit enough for us, which was, the
examination of the force of the particle For, when Martius
joined us.   He, being well known to us all, asked " what we
were upon ? for he had a mind to consummate the happiness of
the day, which had been spent among the stars of the first
magnitude, among the men of letters ; and therefore, to put a
period to it as he had commenced it, he should be glad to be

G 2

allowed to participate of the pleasure of our society." I told
him the subject. "Faith, gentlemen," said Martius, "your
subject is humble ; and if you will give me leave to elevate the
conversation, I should humbly offer, that you would enlarge
your enquiries to the word For-as-much ; for though I take it,"
said he, "to be but one word, yet the particle Much implying
quantity, the particle As similitude, it will be greater, and more
like ourselves, to treat of For-as-much." Jack Comma is
always serious, and answered ; "Martius, I must take the
liberty to say, that you have fallen into all this error and profuse manner of speech by a certain hurry in your imagination,
for want of being more exact in the knowledge of the parts of
speech ; and it is so with all men who have not well studied
the particle For. You have spoken For without making any
inference, which is the great use of that particle. There is no
manner of force in your observation of quantity and similitude
in the syllables As and Much. But it is ever the fault of men
of great wit to be incorrect ; which evil they run into by an
indiscreet use of the word For. Consider all the books of controversy which have been written, and I will engage you will
observe, that all the debate lies in this point, Whether they
brought in For in a just manner ; or forced it in for their own
use, rather than as understanding the use of the word itself ?
There is nothing like familiar instances : you have heard the
story of the Irishman, who reading, "Money for live hair,"
took a lodging, and expected to be paid for living at that house.
If this man had known, For was in that place of a quite
different signification from the particle To, he could not have
fallen into the mistake of taking *Live* for what the Latins call
Vivere, or rather *Habitare*."

Martius seemed at a loss ; and, admiring his profound
learning, wished he had been bred a scholar, for he did not take
the scope of his discourse. This wise debate, of which we had
much more, made me reflect upon the difference of their capacities, and wonder that there could be as it were a diversity in
men's genius for nonsense ; that one should bluster, while
another crept, in absurdities. Martius moves like a blind

man, lifting his legs higher than the ordinary way of stepping ; and Comma, like one who is only short-sighted, picking his way when he should be marching on.   Want of learning makes Martius a brisk entertaining fool, and gives him a full scope; but that which Comma has, and calls learning, makes him diffident, and curbs his natural misunderstanding to the great loss of the men of raillery.   This conversation confirmed me in the opinion, that learning usually does but improve in us what nature endowed us with.   He that wants good sense is unhappy in having learning, for he has thereby only more ways of exposing himself; and he that has sense knows that learning is not knowledge, but rather the art of using it.

TOM WILDAIR.

No. 60.   SATURDAY, August 27, 1709.   [Steele.]

To proceed regularly in the history of my worthies, I ought to give an account of what has passed from day to day in this place ; but a young fellow of my acquaintance has so lately been rescued out of the hands of the Knights of the Industry, that I rather choose to relate the manner of his escape from them, and the uncommon way which was used to reclaim him, than to go on in my intended diary.

You are to know then, that Tom Wildair is a student of the Inner Temple, and has spent his time, since he left the university for that place, in the common diversions of men of fashion ; that is to say, in whoring, drinking, and gaming. The two former vices he had from his father ; but was led into the last by the conversation of a partizan of the Myrmidons who had chambers near him.   His allowance from his father was a very plentiful one for a man of sense, but as scanty for a modern fine gentleman.   His frequent losses had reduced him to so necessitous a condition, that his lodgings were always haunted by impatient creditors ; and all his thoughts employed in contriving low methods to support himself in a way of life from which he knew not how to retreat, and in which he wanted means to proceed. There is never wanting some good-natured person to send a man an account of what he has no mind to hear ; therefore many epistles were conveyed to the father of this extravagant, to inform him of the company, the pleasures, the distresses, and entertainments, in which his son passed his time. The old fellow received these advices with all the pain of a parent, but frequently consulted his pillow, to know how to behave himself on such important occasions, as the welfare of his son, and the safety of his fortune. After many agitations of mind, he reflected, that necessity was the usual snare which made men fall into meanness, and that a liberal fortune generally made a liberal and honest mind ; he resolved therefore to save him from his ruin, by giving him opportunities of tasting what it is to be at ease, and inclosed to him the following order upon Sir Tristram Cash.

" Sir,
" Pray pay to Mr. Thomas Wildair, or order, the sum of one thousand pounds, and place it to the account of yours,
" Humphry Wildair."

Tom was so astonished with the receipt of this order, that though he knew it to be his father's hand, and that he had always large sums at Sir Tristram's ; yet a thousand pounds was a trust of which his conduct had always made him appear so little capable, that he kept his note by him, until he writ to his father the following letter :

" Honoured Father,
" I have received an order under your hand for a thousand pounds, in words at length ; and I think I could swear it is your own hand. I have looked it over and over twenty thousand times. There is in plain letters, T,h,o,u,s,a,n,d ; and after it, the letters P,o,u,n,d,s. I have it still by me, and shall, I believe, continue reading it until I hear from you."

The old gentleman took no manner of notice of the receipt of his letter ; but sent him another order for three thousand pounds more. His amazement on this second letter was unspeakable. He immediately double-locked his door, and sat down carefully to reading and comparing both his orders. After he had read them until he was half mad, he walked six or seven turns in his chamber, then opens his door, then locks it again ; and, to examine thoroughly this matter, he locks his door again, puts his table and chairs against it ; then goes into his closet, and, locking himself in, reads his notes over again about nineteen times, which did but increase his astonishment. Soon after, he began to recollect many stories he had formerly heard of persons, who had been possessed with imaginations and appearances which had no foundation in nature, but had been taken with sudden madness in the midst of a seeming clear and untainted reason. This made him very gravely conclude he was out of his wits ; and, with a design to compose himself, he immediately betakes him to his night-cap, with a resolution to sleep himself into his former poverty and senses. To bed therefore he goes at noon-day ; but soon rose again, and resolved to visit Sir Tristram upon this occasion. He did so, and dined with the knight, expecting he would mention some advice from his father about paying him money ; but no such thing being said, " Look you, Sir Tristram," said he, "you are to know, that an affair has happened, which—" " Look you," says Tristram, " I know, Mr. Wildair, you are going to desire me to advance ; but the late call of the bank, where I have not yet made my last payment, has obliged me—" Tom interrupted him, by shewing him the bill of a thousand pounds. When he had looked at it for a convenient time, and as often surveyed Tom's looks and countenance ; " Look you, Mr. Wildair, a thousand pounds—" Before he could proceed, he shews him the order for three thousand more—Sir Tristram examined the orders at the light, and finding at the writing the name, there was a certain stroke in one letter, which the father and he had agreed should be to such directions as he desired might be more immediately honoured, he forthwith pays the money.

The possession of four thousand pounds gave my young gentleman a new train of thoughts : he began to reflect upon his
birth, the great expectations he was born to, and the unsuitable
ways he had long pursued. Instead of that unthinking creature
he was before, he is now provident, generous, and discreet.
The father and son have an exact and regular correspondence,
with mutual and unreserved confidence in each other. The
son looks upon his father as the best tenant he could have in
the country, and the father finds the son the most safe banker
he could have in the city.

FELLOWS OF FIRE.

No. 61.   TUESDAY, August 30, 1709.   [Steele.]

AMONG many phrases which have crept into conversation,
especially of such company as frequent this place, there is not
one which misleads me more, than that of a " Fellow of a great
deal of Fire." This metaphorical term, Fire, has done much
good in keeping coxcombs in awe of one another ; but at the
same time it has made them troublesome to every body else
You see, in the very air of a " Fellow of Fire," something so
expressive of what he would be at, that if it were not for self-
preservation, a man would laugh out.

I had last night the fate to drink a bottle with two of these
Firemen, who were indeed dispersed like the Myrmidons in all
quarters, and to be met with among those of the most different
education. One of my companions was a scholar with Fire ;
and the other a soldier of the same complexion. My learned
man would fall into disputes, and argue without any manner
of provocation or contradiction : the other was decisive without
words, and would give a shrug or an oath to express his
opinion. My learned man was a mere scholar, and my man of
war as mere a soldier. The particularity of the first was
ridiculous, that of the second, terrible. They were relations

by blood, which in some measure moderated their extravagances towards each other : I gave myself up merely as a
person of no note in the company, but as if brought to be convinced that I was an inconsiderable thing, any otherwise than
that they would shew each other to me, and make me spectator
of the triumph they alternately enjoyed.   The scholar has been
very conversant with books, and the other with men, only ;
which makes them both superficial : for the taste of books is
necessary to our behaviour in the best company, and the
knowledge of men is required for a true relish of books : but
they have both Fire, which makes one pass for a man of sense,
and the other for a fine gentleman.   I found, I could easily
enough pass my time with the scholar : for if I seemed not to
do justice to his parts and sentiments, he pitied me, and let
me alone.   But the warrior could not let it rest there ; I must
know all that had happened within his shallow observations of
the nature of the war : to all which he added an air of laziness,
and contempt of those of his companions who were eminent for
delighting in the exercise and knowledge of their duty.   Thus
it is, that all the young fellows of much animal life, and little
understanding, who repair to our armies, usurp upon the conversation of reasonable men, under the notion of having Fire.
    The word has not been of greater use to shallow lovers, to
supply them with chat to their mistresses, than it has been to
pretended men of pleasure, to support them in being pert and
dull, and saying of every fool of their order, " Such a one
has Fire."   There is Colonel Truncheon, who marches with
divisions ready on all occasions ; an hero who never doubted
in his life, but is ever positively fixed in the wrong, not out of
obstinate opinion, but invincible stupidity.
    It is very unhappy for this latitude of London, that it is
possible for such as can learn only fashion, habit, and a set of
common phrases of salutation, to pass with no other accomplishments, in this nation of freedom, for men of conversation
and sense.   All these ought to pretend to is, not to offend ;
but they carry it so far, as to be negligent whether they offend
or not ; " for they have Fire."   But their force differs from

true spirit, as much as a vicious from a mettlesome horse. A man of Fire is a general enemy to all the waiters where you drink ; is the only man affronted at the company's being neglected ; and makes the drawers abroad, his *valet de chambre* and footman at home, know he is not to be provoked without danger.

This is not the Fire that animates the noble Marinus, a youth of good nature, affability, and moderation. He commands his ship as an intelligence moves its orb : he is the vital life, and his officers the limbs of the machine. His vivacity is seen in doing all the offices of life with readiness of spirit, and propriety in the manner of doing them. To be ever active in laudable pursuits, is the distinguishing character of a man of merit ; while the common behaviour of every gay coxcomb of Fire is, to be confidently in the wrong, and dare to persist in it.

CHARMS OF WOMAN.

No. 61.   August 30, 1709.   [Steele.]

There has been lately sent me a much harder question than was ever yet put to me, since I professed astrology ; to wit, how far, and to what age, women ought to make their beauty their chief concern ?   The regard and care of their faces and persons are as variously to be considered, as their complexions themselves differ ; but if one may transgress against the careful practice of the fair sex so much as to give an opinion against it, I humbly presume, that less care, better applied, would increase their empire, and make it last as long as life. Whereas now, from their own example, we take our esteem of their merit from it ; for it is very just that she who values herself only on her beauty, should be regarded by others on no other consideration.

There is certainly a liberal and a pedantic education among

women, as well as men ; and the merit lasts accordingly. She, therefore, that is bred with freedom, and in good company, considers men according to their respective characters and distinctions ; while she, that is locked up from such observations, will consider her father's butler, not as a butler, but as a man. In like manner, when men converse with women, the well-bred and intelligent are looked upon with an observation suitable to their different talents and accomplishments, without respect to their sex ; while a mere woman can be observed under no consideration but that of a woman ; and there can be but one reason for placing any value upon her, or losing time in her company. Wherefore, I am of opinion, that the rule for pleasing long is, to obtain such qualifications as would make them so, were they not women.

Let the beauteous Cleomira then shew us her real face, and know that every stage of life has its peculiar charms, and that there is no necessity for fifty to be fifteen. That childish colouring of her cheeks is now as ungraceful, as that shape would have been when her face wore its real countenance. She has sense, and ought to know, that if she will not follow nature, nature will follow her. Time then has made that person which had, when I visited her grandfather, an agreeable bloom, sprightly air, and soft utterance, now no less graceful in a lovely aspect, an awful manner, and maternal wisdom. But her heart was so set upon her first character, that she neglects and repines at her present ; not that she is against a more stayed conduct in others, for she recommends gravity, circumspection, and severity of countenance to her daughter. Thus, against all chronology, the girl is the sage, the mother the fine lady.

But these great evils proceed from an unaccountable wild method in the education of the better half of the world, the women. We have no such thing as a standard for good breeding. I was the other day at my lady Wealthy's, and asked one of her daughters how she did ? She answered, " She never conversed with men." The same day I visited at Lady Plantwell's, and asked her daughter the same question.

She answers, " What is that to you, you old thief ? " and gives
me a slap on the shoulders.

I defy any man in England, except he knows the family
before he enters, to be able to judge whether he shall be agreeable or not, when he comes into it.   You find either some odd
old woman, who is permitted to rule as long as she lives, in
hopes of her death, and to interrupt all things ; or some
impertinent young woman, who will talk sillily upon the
strength of looking beautifully.   I will not answer for it, but
it may be, that I (like all other old fellows) have a fondness
for the fashions and manners which prevailed when I was
young and in fashion myself.   But certain it is, that the taste
of grace and beauty is very much lowered.   The fine women
they show me now-a-days are at best but pretty girls to me
who have seen Sacharissa,* when all the world repeated the
poems she inspired ; and Villaria,† when a youthful king was
her subject.   The *Things* you follow, and make songs on now,
should be sent to knit or sit down to bobbins or bone-lace :
they are indeed neat, and so are their sempstresses ; they are
pretty, and so are their hand-maids.   But that graceful
motion, that awful mien, and that winning attraction, which
grew upon them from the thoughts and conversations they
met with in my time, are now no more seen.   They tell me I
am old : I am glad I am so : for I do not like your present
young ladies.

Those among us who set up for any thing of decorum, do so
mistake the matter, that they offend on the other side.   Five
young ladies, who are of no small fame for their great severity
of manners, and exemplary behaviour, would lately go no
where with their lovers but to an organ-loft in a church ;
where they had a cold treat, and some few opera songs, to their
great refreshment and edification.   Whether these prudent
persons had not been as much so if this had been done at a

* Lady Dorothy Sidney, daughter of Lord Leicester, and afterwards wife
of the Earl of Sunderland, was celebrated by Waller under the feigned name
of Sacharissa.
† The Duchess of Cleveland.

tavern, is not very hard to determine. It is such silly starts and incoherences as these, which *undervalue* the beauteous sex, and puzzle us in our choice of sweetness of temper and simplicity of manners, which are the only lasting charms of woman.

A PACK OF SWINDLERS.

No. 62. THURSDAY, September 1, 1709. [Steele.]

This place being frequented by persons of condition, I am desired to · recommend a dog-kennel to any who shall want a pack.* It lies not far from Suffolk. Street,† and is kept by two who were formerly dragoons in the French service ; but left plundering for the more orderly life of keeping dogs : besides that, according to their expectation, they find it more profitable, as well as more conducing to the safety of their skin to follow this trade, than the beat of drum. Their residence is very convenient for the dogs to whelp in, and bring up a right breed to follow the scent. The most eminent of the kennel are bloodhounds, which lead the van, and are as follow :

A LIST OF THE DOGS.

Jowler, of a right Irish breed, called Captain.

Rockwood, of French race, with long hair, by the courtesy of England, called also Captain.

Pompey, a tall hound, kennelled in a convent in France, and knows a rich soil.

These two last hunt in couple, and are followed by

Ringwood, a French black whelp of the same breed, a fine

---

* Of the "dogs" that underwent the severe chastisement of this paper, many were hanged soon after the date of it ; and several saved the hangman the exercise of his office.

† Suffolk Street, Pall Mall, was at this time much frequented by papists and foreigners.

open-mouthed dog ; and an old sick hound, always in kennel, but of the true blood, with a good nose, French breed.

There is also an Italian greyhound, with good legs, and knows perfectly the ground from Ghent to Paris.

Ten setting dogs, right English.

Four mongrels of the same nation.

And twenty whelps, fit for any game.

These curs are so extremely hungry, that they are too keen at the sport, and worry their game before the keepers can come in. The other day a wild boar from the north rushed into the kennel, and at first, indeed, defended himself against the whole pack ; but they proved at last too many for him, and tore twenty-five pounds of flesh from off his back, with which they filled their bellies, and made so great a noise in the neighbourhood, that the keepers are obliged to hasten the sale. That quarter of the town where they are kennelled is generally inhabited by strangers, whose blood the hounds have often sucked in such a manner, that many a German count, and other virtuosi, who came from the continent, have lost the intention of their travels, and been unable to proceed on their journey.

If these hounds are not very soon disposed of to some good purchaser, as also those at the kennels nearer Saint James's, it is humbly proposed, that they may be altogether transported to America, where the dogs are few, and the wild beasts many : or that, during their stay in these parts, some eminent justice of the peace may have it in particular direction to visit their harbours ; and that the sheriff of Middlesex may allow him the assistance of the common hangman to cut off their ears, or part of them, for distinction sake, that we may know the bloodhounds from the mongrels and setters. Until these things are regulated, you may enquire at an house belonging to Paris, at the upper-end of Suffolk Street, or an house belonging to Ghent, opposite to the lower end of Pall Mall, and know further.

It were to be wished that these curs were disposed of ; for

it is a very great nuisance to have them tolerated in cities. That of London takes care, that the "Common Hunt," assisted by the serjeants and bailiffs, expel them whenever they are found within the walls; though it is said, some private families keep them, to the destruction of their neighbours: but it is desired, that all who know of any of these curs, or have been bit by them, would send me their marks, and the houses where they are harboured; and I do not doubt but I shall alarm the people so well, as to have them used like mad dogs wherever they appear. In the meantime, I advise all such as entertain this kind of vermin, that if they give me timely notice that their dogs are dismissed, I shall let them go unregarded; otherwise am obliged to admonish my fellow-subjects in this behalf, and instruct them how to avoid being worried, when they are going about their lawful professions and callings. There was lately a young gentleman bit to the bone; who has now indeed recovered his health, but is as lean as a skeleton. It grieved my heart to see a gentleman's son run among the hounds; but he is, they tell me, as fleet and as dangerous as the best of the pack.

SHARPERS AT BATH.

No. 65.　THURSDAY, September 8, 1709.　[Steele.]

The following letters are sent to me from relations; and though I do not know who and who are intended, I publish them. I have only writ nonsense, if there is nothing in them; and done a good action, if they alarm any heedless men against the fraternity of the Knights, whom the Greeks call Ῥάσκαλς.

Bath, *Aug.* 30.

" Mr. Bickerstaff,

　　　" It is taken very ill by several gentlemen here, that you are so little vigilant, as to let the dogs run from their ken-

nels to this place. Had you done your duty, we should have
had notice of their arrival; but the sharpers are now become
so formidable here, that they have divided themselves into
nobles and commons; beau Bogg, beau Pert, Rake, and Tallboy, are of their upper house; broken captains, ignorant
attornies, and such other bankrupts from industrious professions, compose their lower order. Among these two sets of
men, there happened here lately some unhappy differences.
Esquire Humphry came down among us with four hundred
guineas: his raw appearance, and certain signals in the good-
natured muscles of Humphry's countenance, alarmed the
societies; for sharpers are as skilful as beggars in physiognomy,
and know as well where to hope for plunder, as the others to
ask for alms. Pert was the man exactly fitted for taking with
Humphry, as a fine gentleman; for a raw fool is ever enamoured with his contrary, a coxcomb; and a coxcomb is what
the booby, who wants experience, and is unused to company,
regards as the first of men. He ever looks at him with envy,
and would certainly be such, if he were not oppressed by his
rusticity or bashfulness. There arose an entire friendship by
this sympathy between Pert and Humphry, which ended in
stripping the latter. We now could see this forlorn youth for
some days moneyless, without sword, and one day without his
hat, and with secret melancholy pining for his snuff-box; the
jest of the whole town, but most of those who robbed him.

"At last fresh bills came down, when immediately their
countenances cleared up, antient kindnesses and familiarity
renewed, and to dinner he was invited by the fraternity. You
are to know, that while he was in his days of solitude, a commoner, who was excluded from his share of the prey, had
whispered the esquire, that he was bit, and cautioned him of
venturing again. However, hopes of recovering his snuff-box,
which was given him by his aunt, made him fall to play after
dinner; yet, mindful of what he was told, he saw something
that provoked him to tell them, they were a company of
sharpers. Presently Tallboy fell on him, and, being too hard
at fisty-cuffs, drove him out of doors. The valiant Pert fol-

lowed, and kicked him in his turn ; which the esquire resented, as being nearer his match ; so challenged him : but differing about time and place, friends interposed, for he had still money left, and persuaded him to ask pardon for provoking them to beat him, and they asked his for doing it.   The house, consulting whence Humphry could have his information, concluded it must be from some malicious commoner ; and, to be revenged, beau Bogg watched their haunts, and in a shop where some of them were at play with ladies, shewed dice which he found, or pretended to find, upon them ; and, declaring how false they were, warned the company to take care who they played with.   By his seeming candour, he cleared his reputation at least to fools and some silly women ; but it was still blasted by the esquire's story with thinking men : however, he gained a great point by it ; for the next day he got the company shut up with himself and fellow-members, and robbed them at discretion.

" I cannot express to you with what indignation I behold the noble spirit of gentlemen degenerated to that of private cutpurses.   It is in vain to hope a remedy, while so many of the fraternity get and enjoy estates of twenty, thirty, and fifty-thousand pounds, with impunity, creep into the best conversations, and spread the infectious villainy through the nation, while the lesser rogues, that rob for hunger or nakedness, are sacrificed by the blind, and, in this respect, partial and defective law. · Could you open men's eyes against the occasion of all this, the great corrupter of our manners and morality, the author of more bankrupts than the war, and sure bane of all industry, frugality, and good nature ; in a word, of all virtues ; I mean, public or private play at cards or dice ; how willingly would I contribute my utmost, and possibly send you some memoirs of the lives and politics of some of the fraternity of great figure, that might be of use to you in setting this in a clear light against next session ; that all who care for their country or posterity, and see the pernicious effects of such a public vice, may endeavour its destruction by some effectual laws.   In concurrence to this good design, I remain

"Your humble servant, &c."

" Mr. BICKERSTAFF,

" I HEARTILY join with you in your laudable design against the Myrmidons, as well as your late insinuations against Coxcombs of Fire; and I take this opportunity to congratulate you on the success of your labours which I observed yesterday in one of the hottest firemen in town; who not only affects a soft smile, but was seen to be thrice contradicted without shewing any sign of impatience. These, I say, so happy beginnings promise fair, and on this account I rejoice you have undertaken to unkennel the curs; a work of such use, that I admire it so long escaped your vigilance; and exhort you, by the concern you have for the good people of England, to pursue your design : and, that these vermin may not flatter themselves that they pass undiscovered, I desire you would acquaint Jack Haughty, that the whole secret of his bubbling his friend with the Swiss at the Thatched House is well known, as also his sweetening the knight; and I shall acknowledge the favour.

" Your most humble servant, &c."

THE CLERGY AND THEIR DELIVERY.

No. 66. SATURDAY, SEPTEMBER 10, 1709.

[SWIFT AND STEELE.]

THE subject of the discourse this evening was eloquence and graceful action. Lysander, who is something particular in his way of thinking and speaking, told us, " a man could not be eloquent without action : for the deportment of the body, the turn of the eye, and an apt sound to every word that is uttered, must all conspire to make an accomplished speaker. Action in one that speaks in public, is the same thing as a good mien in ordinary life. Thus, as a certain insensibility in the countenance recommends a sentence of humour and jest, so it must be a very lively consciousness that gives grace to great sentiments. The jest is to be a thing unexpected ; therefore your undesigning manner is a beauty in expressions of mirth ; but when you are to talk on a set subject, the more you are moved yourself, the more you will move others.

"There is," said he, " a remarkable example of that kind. Æschines, a famous orator of antiquity, had pleaded at Athens in a great cause against Demosthenes ; but having lost it, retired to Rhodes." Eloquence was then the quality most admired among men ; and the magistrates of that place, having heard he had a copy of the speech of Demosthenes, desired him to repeat both their pleadings. After his own, he recited also the oration of his antagonist. The people expressed their admiration of both, but more of that of Demosthenes. "If you are," said he, "thus touched with hearing only what that great orator said, how would you have been affected had you seen him speak ? For he who hears Demosthenes only, loses much the better part of the oration." Certain it is that they who speak gracefully are very lamely represented in having their speeches read or repeated by unskilful people ; for there is something native to each man, so inherent to his thoughts and sentiments, which it is hardly possible for another to give a true idea of. You may observe in common talk, when a sentence of any man's is repeated, an acquaintance of his shall immediately observe, "that is so like him, methinks I see how he looked when he said it."

But of all the people on the earth, there are none who puzzle me so much as the Clergy of Great Britain, who are, I believe, the most learned body of men now in the world ; and yet this art of speaking, with the proper ornaments of voice and gesture, is wholly neglected among them ; and I will engage, were a deaf man to behold the greater part of them preach, he would rather think they were reading the contents only of some discourse they intended to make, than actually in the body of an oration, even when they are upon matters of such a nature, as one would believe it were impossible to think of without emotion.

H 2

I own there are exceptions to this general observation, and
that the Dean we heard the other day together is an orator.*
He has so much regard to his congregation, that he commits
to his memory what he has to say to them ; and has so soft
and graceful a behaviour, that it must attract your attention.
His person, it is to be confessed, is no small recommendation ;
but he is to be highly commended for not losing that advantage, and adding to the propriety of speech, which might pass
the criticism of Longinus, an action which would have been
approved by Demosthenes.   He has a peculiar force in his way,
and has many of his audience † who could not be intelligent
hearers of his discourse, were there not explanation as well as
grace in his action.   This art of his is used with the most
exact and honest skill : he never attempts your passions until
he has convinced your reason.   All the objections which he
can form are laid open and dispersed before he uses the least
vehemence in his sermon ; but when he thinks he has your
head, he very soon wins your heart ; and never pretends to
shew the beauty of holiness, until he hath convinced you of the
truth of it.

Would every one of our clergymen be thus careful to recommend truth and virtue in their proper figures, and shew so
much concern for them as to give them all the additional
force they were able, it is not possible that nonsense should
have so many hearers as you find it has in dissenting congregations,‡ for no reason in the world, but because it is spoken
extempore : for ordinary minds are wholly governed by their
eyes and ears, and there is no way to come at their hearts, but
by power over their imaginations.

There is my friend and merry companion Daniel.§   He

---

* Dr. Atterbury.
† At the Chapel of Bridewell Hospital, where the Dean was twenty years
minister and preacher.
‡ It was the infelicity of the laity about the time here spoken of, that by
going to church they had no security from hearing nonsense and ribaldry both
read and spoken extempore.
§ Dr. Daniel Burgess, who preached to a congregation of Independents at
the meeting-house in a court adjoining Carey Street, near Lincoln's Inn.

knows a great deal better than he speaks, and can form a
proper discourse as well as any orthodox neighbour.   But he
knows very well, that to bawl out "My beloved!" and the
words "grace!" "regeneration!" "sanctification!" "a new
light!" "the day! the day! ay, my beloved, the day! or
rather the night! the night is coming!" and "judgment will
come, when we least think of it!" and so forth—He knows to
be vehement is the only way to come at his audience.   Daniel,
when he sees my friend Greenhat come in, can give a good
hint, and cry out, "This is only for the saints! the regene-
rated!"   By this force of action, though mixed with all the
incoherence and ribaldry imaginable, Daniel can laugh at his
diocesan, and grow fat by voluntary subscription, while the
parson of the parish goes to law for half his dues.   Daniel will
tell you, "it is not the shepherd, but the sheep with the bell,
which the flock follows."

Another thing very wonderful this learned body should omit
is, learning to read; which is a most necessary part of eloquence in one who is to serve at the altar : for there is no man
but must be sensible, that the lazy tone, and inarticulate
sound of our common readers, depreciates the most proper
form of words that were ever extant, in any nation or language,
to speak our own wants, or his power from whom we ask
relief.

There cannot be a greater instance of the power of action,
than in little parson Dapper, who is the common relief to all
the lazy pulpits in town.   This smart youth has a very good
memory, a quick eye, and a clean handkerchief.   Thus equipped,
he opens his text, shuts his book fairly, shews he has no notes
in his Bible, opens both palms, and shews all is fair there too.
Thus, with a decisive air, my young man goes on without
hesitation ; and though from the beginning to the end of his
pretty discourse he has not used one proper gesture, yet at the
conclusion the churchwarden pulls his gloves from off his
hands : "Pray, who is this extraordinary young man?"   Thus
the force of action is such, that it is more prevalent, even when
improper, than all the reason and argument in the world with-

out it.   This gentleman concluded his discourse by saying, "I
do not doubt but if our preachers would learn to speak, and
our readers to read, within six months' time we should not
have a dissenter within a mile of a church in Great Britain."

A CHAMBER OF FAME.

No. 67.   TUESDAY, September 13, 1709.

[Swift and Steele.]

No man can conceive, until he comes to try it, how great a
pain it is to be a public-spirited person.   I am sure I am
unable to express to the world what great anxiety I have
suffered, to see of how little benefit my lucubrations have been
to my fellow-subjects.   Men will go on in their own way, in
spite of all my labour.   I gave Mr. Didapper a private
reprimand for wearing red-heeled shoes, and at the same time
was so indulgent as to connive at him for fourteen days,
because I would give him the wearing of them out; but, after
all this, I am informed he appeared yesterday with a new pair
of the same sort.   I have no better success with Mr What-
d'ye-call, as to his buttons; Stentor still roars; and box and
dice rattle as loud as they did before I writ against them.
Partridge walks about at noon-day and Æsculapius thinks of
adding a new lace to his livery.   However, I must still go on
in laying these enormities before men's eyes, and let them
answer for going on in their practice.

My province is much larger than at first sight men would
imagine, and I shall lose no part of my jurisdiction, which
extends not only to futurity, but also is retrospect to things
past; and the behaviour of persons, who have long ago acted
their parts, is as much liable to my examination, as that of my
own contemporaries.

In order to put the whole race of mankind in their proper distinctions, according to the opinion their cohabitants conceived of them, I have with very much care, and depth of meditation, thought fit to erect a chamber of Fame, and established certain rules, which are to be observed in admitting members into this illustrious society.

In this chamber of Fame there are to be three tables, but of different lengths : the first is to contain exactly twelve persons ; the second, twenty ; and the third, an hundred. This is reckoned to be the full number of those who have any competent share of Fame. At the first of these tables are to be placed in their order the twelve most famous persons in the world ; not with regard to the things they are famous for, but according to the degree of their Fame, whether in valour, wit, or learning. Thus if a scholar be more famous than a soldier, he is to sit above him. Neither must any preference be given to virtue, if the person be not equally famous.

When the first table is filled, the next in renown must be seated at the second, and so on in like manner to the number of twenty; as also in the same order at the third, which is to hold an hundred. At these tables, no regard is to be had to seniority : for if Julius Cæsar shall be judged more famous than Romulus and Scipio, he must have the precedence. No person who has not been dead an hundred years must be offered to a place at any of these tables : and because this is altogether a lay-society, and that sacred persons move upon greater motives than that of fame, no persons celebrated in holy writ, or any ecclesiastical men whatsoever, are to be introduced here.

At the lower end of the room is to be a side-table for persons of great fame, but dubious existence ; such as Hercules, Theseus, Æneas, Achilles, Hector, and others. But because it is apprehended, that there may be great contention about precedence, the proposer humbly desires the opinion of the learned towards his assistance in placing every person according to his rank, that none may have just occasion of offence.

The merits of the cause shall be judged by plurality of voices.

For the more impartial execution of this important affair, it is desired, that no man will offer his favourite hero, scholar, or poet ; and that the learned will be pleased to send to Mr. Bickerstaff, at Mr. Morphew's° near Stationers' Hall, their several lists for the first table only, and in the order they would have them placed ; after which the proposer will compare the several lists, and make another for the public, wherein every name shall be ranked according to the voices it has had. Under this chamber is to be a dark vault for the same number of persons of evil fame.

It is humbly submitted to consideration, whether the project would not be better if the persons of true fame meet in a middle room, those of dubious existence in an upper room, and those of evil fame in a lower dark room.

It is to be noted, that no historians are to be admitted at any of these tables ; because they are appointed to conduct the several persons to their seats, and are to be made use of as ushers to the assemblies.

I call upon the learned world to send me their assistance towards this design, it being a matter of too great moment for any one person to determine. But I do assure them, their lists shall be examined with great fidelity, and those that are exposed to the public, made with all the caution imaginable.

In the meantime, while I wait for these lists, I am employed in keeping people in a right way, to avoid the contrary to fame and applause, to wit, blame and derision. For this end, I work upon that useful project of the penny post, by the benefit of which it is proposed, that a charitable society be established : from which society there shall go every day circular letters to all parts within the bills of mortality, to tell people of their faults in a friendly and private manner, whereby they may know what the world thinks of them, before it is declared to the world that they are thus faulty. This method cannot fail

---

* The publisher of Steele's lucubrations and of the leading pamphlets of the day.

of universal good consequences : for it is farther added, that
they who will not be reformed by it, must be contented to see
the several letters printed, which were not regarded by them,
that when they will not take private reprehension, they may be
tried farther by a public one.   I am very sorry, I am obliged
to print the following epistles of that kind to some persons,
and the more because they are of the fair sex.

This went on Friday last to a very fine lady.

" MADAM,
        "I am highly sensible, that there is nothing of so tender
a nature as the reputation and conduct of ladies ; and that when
there is the least stain got into their fame, it is hardly ever to
be washed out.   When I have said this, you will believe I am
extremely concerned to hear, at every visit I make, that your
manner of wearing your hair is a mere affectation of beauty, as
well as that your neglect of powder has been a common evil to
your sex.   It is to you an advantage to show that abundance
of fine tresses : but I beseech you to consider, that the force of
your beauty, and the imitation of you, costs Eleonora great
sums of money to her tire-woman for false locks, besides what
is allowed to her maid for keeping the secret, that she is gray.
I must take leave to add to this admonition, that you are not
to reign above four months and odd days longer.   Therefore,
I must desire you to raise and friz your hair a little, for it is
downright insolence to be thus handsome without art ; and
you will forgive me for intreating you to do now out of compassion what you must soon do out of necessity. I am, madam,
                    Your most obedient,
                            and most humble servant."

This person dresses just as she did before I writ ; as does
also the lady to whom I addressed the following billet the
same day :

" MADAM,
        " Let me beg of you to take off the patches at the
lower end of your left cheek, and I will allow two more under

your left eye, which will contribute more to the symmetry of
your face ; except you would please to remove the ten black
atoms on your ladyship's chin, and wear one large patch
instead of them. If so, you may properly enough retain the
three patches above mentioned. I am, &c."

This, I thought, had all the civility and reason in the world
in it ; but whether my letters are intercepted, or whatever it
is, the lady patches as she used to do. It is to be observed by
all the charitable society, as an instruction in their epistles,
that they tell people of nothing but what is in their power to
mend. I shall give another instance of this way of writing :
two sisters in Essex Street are eternally gaping out of the
window, as if they knew not the value of time, or would call in
companions. Upon which I writ the following line :

" Dear Creatures,
        " On the receipt of this, shut your casements."

But I went by yesterday, and found them still at the
window. What can a man do in this case, but go on, and wrap
himself up in his own integrity, with satisfaction only in this
melancholy truth, that virtue is its own reward ; and that if no
one is the better for his admonitions, yet he is himself the
more virtuous in that he gave those advices ?

THE TATLER'S STRICTURES.

No. 71. THURSDAY, SEPTEMBER 22, 1709.

[STEELE AND SWIFT.]

I find here for me the following letter :

" ESQUIRE BICKERSTAFF,
        " Finding your advice and censure to have a good
effect, I desire your admonition to our vicar and schoolmaster,

who, in his preaching to his auditors, stretches his jaws so
wide, that, instead of instructing youth, it rather frightens
them ; likewise in reading prayers, he has such a careless loll,
that people are justly offended at his irreverent posture ;
besides the extraordinary charge they are put to in sending
their children to dance, to bring them off of those ill gestures.
Another evil faculty he has, in making the bowling-green his
daily residence, instead of his church, where his curate reads
prayers every day.   If the weather is fair, his time is spent in
visiting ; if cold or wet, in bed, or least at home, though within a hundred yards of the church.   These, out of many such irregular practices, I write for his reclamation : but, two or three
things more before I conclude ; to wit, that generally when his
curate preaches in the afternoon, he sleeps sotting in the desk,
on a hassock.   With all this he is so extremely proud, that he
will go but once to the sick, except they return his visit."

I was going on in reading my letter, when I was interrupted
by Mr. Greenhat, who has been this evening at the play of Hamlet. " Mr. Bickerstaff," said he, " had you been to-night at the
play-house, you had seen the force of action in perfection : your
admired Mr. Betterton behaved himself so well, that, though
now about seventy, he acted youth ; and by the prevalent power of
proper manner, gesture, and voice, appeared through the whole
drama a young man of great expectation, vivacity, and enterprise.   The soliloquy, where he began the celebrated sentence
of, ' To be, or not to be ! ' the expostulation, where he explains
with his mother in her closet ; the noble ardour after seeing
his father's ghost ; and his generous distress for the death of
Ophelia, are each of them circumstances which dwell strongly
upon the minds of the audience, and would certainly affect
their behaviour on any parallel occasions in their own lives.
Pray, Mr. Bickerstaff, let us have virtue thus represented on
the stage with its proper ornaments, or let these ornaments be
added to her in places more sacred.   As for my part," said he,
" I carried my cousin Jerry, this little boy, with me ; and shall
always love the child for his partiality in all that concerned the
fortune of Hamlet. This is entering youth into the affections and

passions of manhood beforehand, and, as it were, antedating the
effects we hope from a long and liberal education."

I cannot, in the midst of many other things which press,
hide the comfort that this letter from my ingenious kinsman
gives me.

"To my honoured Kinsman, Isaac Bickerstaff, Esquire.

Oxford, Sept. 18.

"Dear Cousin,

"I am sorry, though not surprised, to find that you
have rallied the men of dress in vain; that the amber-headed
cane still maintains its unstable post; that pockets are but a
few inches shortened; and a beau is still a beau, from the
crown of his night-cap to the heels of his shoes. For your comfort, I can assure you, that your endeavours succeed better in
this famous seat of learning. By them, the manners of our
young gentlemen are in a fair way of amendment, and their
very language is mightily refined. To them it is owing, that
not a servitor will sing a catch, nor a senior fellow make a pun,
nor a determining batchelor drink a bumper; and I believe a
gentleman-commoner would as soon have the heels of his shoes
red, as his stockings. When a witling stands at a coffee-house
door, and sneers at those who pass by, to the great improvement of his hopeful audience, he is no longer surnamed 'a
slicer,' but 'a man of fire' is the word. A beauty, whose
health is drunk from Heddington to Hinksey; * who has been
the theme of the Muses, her cheeks painted with roses, and
her bosom planted with orange-boughs; has no more the title
of 'lady,' but reigns an undisputed 'toast.' When to the
plain garb of gown and band a spark adds an inconsistent long
wig, we do not say now 'he bothes,' but 'there goes a smart
fellow.' If a virgin blushes, we no longer cry 'she blues.'
He that drinks until he stares is no more 'tow-row,' but
'honest.' 'A youngster in a scrape,' is a word out of date:
and what bright man says, 'I was joabed by a Dean?'

* Villages in the neighbourhood of Oxford.

' Bamboozling ' is exploded ; ' a shat ' is ' a tatler ; ' and if the muscular motion of a man's face be violent, no mortal says, ' he raises a horse,' but ' he is a merry fellow.'

" I congratulate you, my dear kinsman, upon these conquests ; such as Roman Emperors lamented they could not gain ; and in which you rival your correspondent Louis le Grand, and his dictating academy.

" Be yours the glory to perform, mine to record, as Mr. Dryden has said before me to his kinsman ; and while you enter triumphant into the temple of the Muses, I, as my office requires, will, with my staff on my shoulder, attend and conduct you.

" I am, dear cousin,

" Your most affectionate kinsman,

" BENJAMIN BEADLESTAFF."

JENNY DISTAFF.

No. 75. SATURDAY, OctOBER 1, 1709.

[ADDISON AND STEELE.]

I am called off from public dissertations by a domestic affair of great importance, which is no less than the disposal of my sister Jenny for life. The girl is a girl of great merit, and pleasing conversation ; but I being born of my father's first wife, and she of his third, she converses with me rather like a daughter than a sister. I have indeed told her, that if she kept her honour, and behaved herself in such a manner as became the Bickerstaffs, I would get her an agreeable man for her husband ; which was a promise I made her after reading a passage in Pliny's " Epistles." That polite author had been employed to find out a comfort for his friend's daughter, and gives the following character of the man he had pitched upon. *Aciliano plurimum vigoris & industriæ quanquam in maxima verecundia: est illi facies liberalis, multo sanguine, multo rubore suffusa; est ingenua totius corporis pulchritudo, & quidam senatorius decor, quæ ego nequaquam arbitror negligenda: debet enim hoc castitati puellarum quasi præmium dari.* " Acilianus (for that was the gentleman's name) is a man of extraordinary vigour and industry, accompanied with the greatest modesty : he was very much of the gentleman, with a lively colour, and flush of health in his aspect. His whole person is finely turned, and speakes him a man of quality : which are qualifications that, I think, ought by no means to be over-looked ; and should be bestowed on a daughter as the reward of her chastity."

A woman that will give herself liberties, need not put her parents to so much trouble ; for if she does not possess these ornaments in a husband, she can supply herself elsewhere. But this is not the case of my sister Jenny, who, I may say without vanity, is as unspotted a spinster as any in Great Britain. I shall take this occasion to recommend the conduct of our own family in this particular.

We have in the genealogy of our house, the descriptions and pictures of our ancestors from the time of king Arthur ; in whose days there was one of my own name, a knight of his round table, and known by the name of Sir Isaac Bickerstaff. He was low of stature, and of a very swarthy complexion, not unlike a Portuguese Jew. But he was more prudent than men of that height usually are, and would often communicate to his friends his design of lengthening and whitening his posterity. His eldest son Ralph, for that was his name, was for this reason married to a lady who had little else to recommend her, but that she was very tall and very fair. The issue of this match, with the help of high shoes, made a tolerable figure in the next age ; though the complexion of the family was obscure until the fourth generation from that marriage. From which time, until the reign of William the Conqueror, the females of our house were famous for their needlework and fine skins. In the male line, there happened an unlucky accident in the reign of Richard III., the eldest son of Philip, then chief of the family, being born with an hump-back and very high nose. This was the more astonishing, because none of his forefathers ever had such a blemish ; nor indeed was there any in the neighbourhood of that make, except the butler, who was noted for round shoulders, and a Roman nose : what made the nose the less excusable, was the remarkable smallness of his eyes.

These several defects were mended by succeeding matches ; the eyes were open in the next generation, and the hump fell in a century and an half : but the greatest difficulty was how to reduce the nose ; which I do not find was accomplished until about the middle of the reign of Henry VII. or rather the beginning of that of Henry VIII.

But while our ancestors were thus taken up in cultivating the eyes and nose, the face of the Bickerstaffs fell down insensibly into the chin ; which was not taken notice of, their thoughts being so much employed upon the more noble features, until it became almost too long to be remedied.

But length of time, and successive care in our alliances, have cured this also, and reduced our faces into that tolerable oval, which we enjoy at present. I would not be tedious in this discourse, but cannot but observe, that our race suffered very much about three hundred years ago, by the marriage of one of our heiresses with an eminent courtier, who gave us spindleshanks, and cramps in our bones ; insomuch that we did not recover our health and legs until Sir Walter Bickerstaff married Maud the milk-maid, of whom the then Garter King at Arms, a facetious person, said pleasantly enough, " that she had spoiled our blood, but mended our constitutions."

After this account of the effect our prudent choice of matches has had upon our persons and features, I cannot but observe, that there are daily instances of as great changes made by marriage upon men's minds and humours. One might wear any passion out of a family by culture, as skilful gardeners blot a colour out of a tulip that hurts its beauty. One might produce an affable temper out of a shrew, by grafting the mild upon the choleric ; or raise a jack-pudding from a prude, by inoculating mirth and melancholy.   It is for want of care in the disposing of our children, with regard to our bodies and minds, that we go into an house and see such different complexions and humours in the same race and family.   But to me it is as plain as a pike-staff, from what mixture it is, that this daughter silently lours, the other steals a kind look at you, a third is exactly well-behaved, a fourth a splenetic, and a fifth a coquette.

In this disposal of my sister, I have chosen with an eye to her being a wit, and provided that the bridegroom be a man of a sound and excellent judgment, who will seldom mind what she says when she begins to harangue : for Jenny's only imperfection is an admiration of her parts, which inclines her to be a little, but a very little, sluttish ; and you are ever to remark, that we are apt to cultivate most, and bring into observation, what we think most excellent in ourselves, or most capable of improvement.   Thus, my sister, instead of consulting her glass and her toilet for an hour and a half after her private devotions, sits with her nose full of snuff, and a man's night-cap on her head, reading plays and romances. Her wit she thinks her distinction : therefore knows nothing of the skill of dress, or making her person agreeable.   It would make you laugh to see me often, with my spectacles on, lacing her stays ; for she is so very a wit, that she understands no ordinary thing in the world.

For this reason, I have disposed of her to a man of business, who will soon let her see, that to be well dressed, in good humour, and cheerful in the command of her family, are the arts and sciences of female life.   I could have bestowed her upon a fine gentleman, who extremely admired her wit, and would have given her a coach and six : but I found it absolutely necessary to cross the strain ; for had they met, they had entirely been rivals in discourse, and in continual contention for the superiority of understanding, and brought forth critics, pedants, or pretty good poets.   As it is I expect an offspring fit for the habitation of the city, town, or country ; creatures that are docile and tractable in whatever we put them to.

To convince men of the necessity of taking this method, let any one, even below the skill of an astrologer, behold the turn of faces he meets as soon as he passes Cheapside Conduit, and you see a deep attention and a certain unthinking sharpness in every countenance. They look attentive, but their thoughts are engaged on mean purposes. To me it is very apparent, when I see a citizen pass by, whether his head is upon woollen, silks, iron, sugar, indigo, or stocks. Now this trace of thought appears or lies hid in the race for two or three generations.

I know at this time a person of a vast estate, who is the immediate descendant of a fine gentleman, but the great-grand-son of a broker, in whom his ancestor is now revived. He is a very honest gentleman in his principles, but cannot for his blood talk fairly : he is heartily sorry for it ; but he cheats by constitution, and over-reaches by instinct.

The happiness of the man who marries my sister will be, that he has no faults to correct in her but her own, a little bias of fancy, or particularity of manners, which grew in herself, and can be amended by her. From such an untainted couple, we can hope to have our family rise to its antient splendour of face, air, countenance, manner, and shape, without discovering the product of ten nations in one house. Obadiah Greenhat says, " he never comes into any company in England, but he distinguishes the different nations of which we are composed." There is scarce such a living creature as a true Briton. We sit down indeed all friends, acquaintance, and neighbours ; but after two bottles, you see a Dane start up and swear, " The kingdom is his own." A Saxon drinks up the whole quart, and swears, " He will dispute that with him." A Norman tells them both, " He will assert his liberty :" and a Welchman cries, "They are all foreigners and intruders of yesterday," and beats them out of the room. Such accidents happen frequently among neighbours' children, and cousin-germans. For which reason, I say, study your race ; or the soil of your family will dwindle into cits or esquires, or run up into wits or madmen.

VALETUDINARIANS.

' No. 77. THURSDAY, October 6, 1709. [Steele.]

As bad as the world is, I find by very strict observation upon virtue and vice, that if men appeared no worse than they really are, I should have less work than at present I am obliged to undertake for their reformation. They have generally taken up a kind of inverted ambition, and affect even faults and imperfections of which they are innocent. The other day in a coffee-house I stood by a young heir, with a fresh, sanguine, and healthy look, who entertained us with an account of his diet-drinks ; though, to my knowledge, he is as sound as any of his tenants.

This worthy youth put me into reflections upon that subject ; and I observed the fantastical humour to be so general, that there is hardly a man who is not more or less tainted with it. The first of this order of men are the Valetudinarians, who are never in health ; but complain of want of stomach or rest every day until noon, and then devour all which comes before them. Lady Dainty * is convinced, that it is necessary for a gentlewoman to be out of order ; and, to preserve that character, she dines every day in her closet at twelve, that she may become her table at two, and be unable to eat in public. About five years ago, I remember, it was the fashion to be short-sighted. A man would not own an acquaintance until he had first examined him with his glass. At a lady's entrance into the play-house, you might see tubes immediately levelled at her from every quarter of the pit and side-boxes. However, that mode of infirmity is out, and the age has recovered its sight : but the blind seem to be succeeded by the lame, and a jaunty limp is the present beauty. I think I have formerly observed, a cane is part of the dress of a prig, and always worn upon a button, for fear he should be thought

* The name given to an affected invalid lady by Colley Cibber, in his play of " The Double Gallant, or Sick Lady's Cure."

to have an occasion for it, or be esteemed really, and not genteelly, a cripple. I have considered, but'could never find out, the bottom of this vanity. I indeed have heard of a Gascon general, who, by the lucky grazing of a bullet on the roll of his stocking, took occasion to halt all his life after. But as for our peaceable cripples, I know no foundation for their behaviour, without it may be supposed that, in this war-like age, some think a cane the next honour to a wooden leg. This sort of affectation I have known run from one limb or member to another. Before the limpers came in, I remember a race of lispers, fine persons, who took an aversion to particular letters in our language. Some never uttered the letter H : and others had as mortal an aversion to S. Others have had their fashionable defect in their ears, and would make you repeat all you said twice over. I know an ancient friend of mine, whose table is every day surrounded with flatterers, that makes use of this, sometimes as a piece of grandeur, and at others as an art, to make them repeat their commendations. Such affectations have been indeed in the world in ancient times ; but they fell into them out of politic ends. Alexander the Great had a wry neck, which made it the fashion in his court to carry their heads on one side when they came into the presence. One who thought to outshine the whole court, carried his head so over complaisantly, that this martial prince gave him so great a box on the ear, as set all the heads of the court upright.

This humour takes place in our minds as well as bodies. I know at this time a young gentleman, who talks atheistically all day in coffee-houses, and in his degrees of understanding sets up for a Free-thinker ; though it can be proved upon him, he says his prayers every morning and evening. But this class of modern wits I shall reserve for a chapter by itself.

Of the like turn are all your marriage-haters, who rail at the noose, at the words, " for ever and aye," and at the same time are secretly pining for some young thing or other that makes their hearts ache by her refusal. The next to these, are such as pretend to govern their wives, and boast how ill they use

ɪ 2

them ; when at the same time, go to their houses, and you shall see them step as if they feared making a noise, and as fond as an alderman. I do not know but sometimes these pretences may arise from a desire to conceal a contrary defect than that they set up for. I remember, when I was a young fellow, we had a companion of a very fearful complexion, who, when we sat in to drink, would desire us to take his sword from him when he grew fuddled, for it was his misfortune to be quarrelsome.

There are many, many of these evils, which demand my observation ; but because I have of late been thought somewhat too satirical, I shall give them warning, and declare to the whole world, that they are not true, but false hypocrites ; and make it out that they are good men in their hearts. The motive of this monstrous affectation, in the above-mentioned and the like particulars, I take to proceed from that noble thirst of fame and reputation which is planted in the hearts of all men. As this produces elegant writings and gallant actions in men of great abilities, it also brings forth spurious productions in men who are not capable of distinguishing themselves by things which are really praise-worthy. As the desire of fame in men of true wit and gallantry shews itself in proper instances, the same desire in men who have the ambition without proper faculties, runs wild, and discovers itself in a thousand extravagances, by which they would signalize themselves from others, and gain a set of admirers. When I was a middle-aged man, there were many societies of ambitious young men in England, who, in their pursuits after fame, were every night employed in roasting porters, smoaking coblers, knocking down watchmen, overturning constables, breaking windows, blackening sign-posts, and the like immortal enterprizes, that dispersed their reputation throughout the whole kingdom. One could hardly find a knocker at a door in a whole street after a midnight expedition of these *Beaux Esprits*. I was lately very much surprised by an account of my maid, who entered my bed-chamber this morning in a very great fright, and told me, she was afraid my parlour was haunted ; for that she had found several panes of my windows broken, and the floor strewed with half-pence.* I have not yet a full light into this new way, but am apt to think, that it is a generous piece of wit that some of my contemporaries make use of, to break windows, and leave money to pay for them.

CLAIMANTS FOR THE TABLE OF FAME.

No. 78. SATURDAY, October 8, 1709. [Steele.]

As your painters, who deal in history-pieces, often entertain themselves upon broken sketches, and smaller flourishes of the pencil ; so I find some relief in striking out miscellaneous hints, and sudden starts of fancy, without any order or connection, after having spent myself on more regular and elaborate dissertations. I am at present in this easy state of mind sat down to my scrutoir ; where, for the better disposition of my correspondence, I have writ upon every drawer the proper title of its contents ; as hypocrisy, dice, patches, politics, love, duels, and so forth. My various advices are ranged under such several heads, saving only that I have a particular box for Pacolet, and another for Monoculus. I cannot but observe, that my duel-box, which is filled by the lettered men of honour, is so very ill spelt, that it is hard to decypher their writings. My love-box, though on a quite contrary subject, filled with the works of the fairest hands in Great Britain, is almost as unintelligible. The private drawer, which is sacred to politics, has in it some of the most refined panegyrics and satires that any age has produced.

I have now before me several recommendations for places

---

* Gay's "Trivia" was published about this time ; and from a passage in that poem, we learn, that there were bucks in those days, who took a delight in breaking windows with halfpence, and were distinguished by the name of Nickers.

at my Table of Fame. Three of them are of an extraordinary
nature, in which I find I am misunderstood, and shall, therefore, beg leave to produce them. They are from a quaker, a
courtier, and a citizen.

"ISAAC,

   "Thy lucubrations, as thou lovest to call them, have
been perused by several of our friends, who have taken offence :
forasmuch as thou excludest out of the brotherhood all persons
who are praiseworthy for religion, we are afraid that thou wilt
fill thy table with none but heathens, and cannot hope to spy a
brother there ; for there are none of us who can be placed
among murdering heroes, or ungodly wits ; since we do not
assail our enemies with the arm of flesh, nor our gainsayers
with the vanity of human wisdom. If, therefore, thou wilt
demean thyself on this occasion with a right judgment, according to the gifts that are in thee, we desire thou wilt place
James Nayler * at the upper end of thy table.

                                   "EZEKIEL STIFFRUMP."

   In answer to my good friend Ezekiel, I must stand to it,
that I cannot break my rule for the sake of James Nayler ;
not knowing, whether Alexander the Great, who is a choleric
hero, would not resent his sitting at the upper end of the table
with his hat on.

   But to my courtier.
   "SIR,

   "I am surprised, that you lose your time in compli-
menting the dead, when you may make your court to the
living. Let me only tell you in the ear, Alexander and Cæsar,
as generous as they were formerly, have not now a groat to

---

* This visionary was about eight or nine years in the Parliament's army,
and is said to have been converted by George Fox in 1651. About six years
after, on account of his ravings, he was apprehended at Bristol, and brought
a prisoner, under the charge of blasphemy, before the House of Commons.
He was sentenced to be pilloried, and whipped in London and Bristol, to have
his tongue bored through with a red-hot iron, to be branded with a B in his
forehead, and committed to hard labour in Bridewell.

dispose of. Fill your table with good company : I know a person of quality that shall give you one hundred pounds for a place at it. Be secret, and be rich. Yours,

          " You know my hand."

This gentleman seems to have the true spirit, without the formality, of an under-courtier ; therefore, I shall be plain with him, and let him leave the name of his courtier and one hundred pounds in Morphew's hands : if I can take it, I will.

My citizen writes the following :

" MR. ISAAC BICKERSTAFF,

 " Sir,

  " Your Tatler, of the thirteenth of September, I am now reading, and in your list of famous men, desire you not to forget alderman Whittington, who began the world with a cat, and died worth three hundred and fifty thousand pounds sterling, which he left to an only daughter three years after his mayoralty. If you want any farther particulars of *ditto* alderman, daughter, or cat, let me know, and *per* first will advise the needful : which concludes, your loving friend,

         " LEMUEL LEGER."

I shall have all due regard to this gentleman's recommendation ; but cannot forbear observing how wonderfully this sort of style is adapted for the dispatch of business, by leaving out insignificant particles ; besides that, the dropping of the first person is an artful way to disengage a man from the guilt of rash words or promises. But I am to consider, that a citizen's reputation is credit, not fame ; and am to leave these lofty subjects for a matter of private concern in the next letter before me.

 " Sir,

  " I am just recovered out of a languishing sickness by the care of Hippocrates,* who visited me throughout my

---

* The physician here alluded to was Dr. Garth.

whole illness, and was so far from taking any fee, that he enquired into my circumstances, and would have relieved me
also that way, but I did not want it. I know no method of
thanking him, but recommending it to you to celebrate so
great humanity in the manner you think fit, and to do it with
the spirit and sentiments of a man just relieved from grief,
misery, and pain, to joy, satisfaction, and ease : in which you
will represent the grateful sense of your obedient servant,

"T. B."

I think the writer of this letter has put the matter in as
good a dress as I can for him ; yet I cannot but add my
applause to what this distressed man has said. There is not a
more useful man in a commonwealth than a good physician :
and by consequence no worthier a person than he that uses his
skill with generosity even to persons of condition, and compassion to those who are in want : which is the behaviour of
Hippocrates, who shews as much liberality in his practice, as
he does wit in his conversation, and skill in his profession. A
wealthy doctor, who can help a poor man, and will not without
a fee, has less sense of humanity than a poor ruffian, who kills
a rich man to supply his necessities. It is something
monstrous, to consider a man of a liberal education tearing
out the bowels of a poor family, by taking for a visit what
would keep them a week. Hippocrates needs not the comparison of such extortion to set off his generosity ; but I
mention his generosity to add shame to such extortion.

MARRIAGE OF JENNY DISTAFF.

No. 79.   TUESDAY, October 11, 1709.   [Steele.]

> Felices, ter et amplius,
>   Quos irrupta tenet copula ; nec malis
> Divulsus querimoniis,
>   Supremâ citius solvet amor die.
> > Hor. 1 Od. xiii. 17.

> Thrice happy they, in pure delights
> Whom love in mutual bonds unites,
> Unbroken by complaints or strife
> Even to the latest hours of life.

My sister Jenny's lover, the honest Tranquillus, for that shall be his name, has been impatient with me to dispatch the necessary directions for his marriage ; that while I am taken up with imaginary schemes, as he calls them, he might not burn with real desire, and the torture of expectation.   When I had reprimanded him for the ardour wherein he expressed himself, which I thought had not enough of that veneration with which the marriage-bed is to be ascended, I told him, "the day of his nuptials should be on the Saturday following, which was the eighth instant."   On the seventh in the evening, poor Jenny came into my chamber, and, having her heart full of the great change of life from a virgin condition to that of a wife, she long sat silent.   I saw she expected me to entertain her on this important subject, which was too delicate a circumstance for herself to touch upon ; whereupon I relieved her modesty in the following manner : "Sister," said I, "you are now going from me : and be contented, that you leave the company of a talkative old man, for that of a sober young one : but take this along with you, that there is no mean in the state you are entering into, but you are to be exquisitely happy or miserable, and your fortune in this way of life will be wholly of your own making.   In all the marriages I have ever seen, most of which have been unhappy ones, the great cause of evil has proceeded from slight occasions ; and I take it to be the first maxim in a married condition, that you are to be

above trifles.   When two persons have so good an opinion of
each other as to come together for life, they will not differ in
matters of importance, because they think of each other with
respect ; and in regard to all things of consideration that may
affect them, they are prepared for mutual assistance and relief
in such occurrences.   For less occasions, they form no resolutions, but leave their minds unprepared.

" This, dear Jenny, is the reason that the quarrel between
Sir Harry Willit and his lady, which began about her squirrel,
is irreconcilable.   Sir Harry was reading a grave author ; she
runs into his study, and, in a playing humour, claps the
squirrel upon the folio : he threw the animal in a rage on the
floor ; she snatches it up again, calls Sir Harry a sour pedant,
without good nature or good manners.   This cast him into
such a rage, that he threw down the table before him, kicked
the book round the room ;   then recollected himself : 'Lord,
madam,' said he, ' why did you run into such expressions ? I
was,' said he, ' in the highest delight with that author, when
you clapped your squirrel upon my book ; ' and, smiling, added
upon recollection, ' I have a great respect for your favourite,
and pray let us all be friends.'   My lady was so far from
accepting this apology, that she immediately conceived a
resolution to keep him under for ever ; and, with a serious air,
replied, 'There is no regard to be had to what a man says,
who can fall into so indecent a rage, and such an abject submission, in the same moment, for which I absolutely despise
you.'   Upon which she rushed out of the room.   Sir Harry
staid some minutes behind, to think and command himself ;
after which he followed her into her bed-chamber, where she
was prostrate upon the bed, tearing her hair, and naming
twenty coxcombs who would have used her otherwise.   This
provoked him to so high a degree, that he forbore nothing but
beating her ; and all the servants in the family were at their
several stations listening, whilst the best man and woman, the
best master and mistress, defamed each other in a way that is
not to be repeated even at Billingsgate.   You know this ended
in an immediate separation : she longs to return home, but

knows not how to do it : he invites her home every day, and
lies with every woman he can get. Her husband requires no
submission of her ; but she thinks her very return will argue
she is to blame, which she is resolved to be for ever, rather
than acknowledge it. Thus, dear Jenny, my great advice to
you is, be guarded against giving or receiving little provocations. Great matters of offence I have no reason to fear
either from you or your husband."

After this, we turned our discourse into a more gay style,
and parted : but before we did so, I made her resign her snuff-
box for ever, and half drown herself with washing away the
stench of the musty.*

But the wedding morning arrived, and our family being very
numerous, there was no avoiding the inconvenience of making
the ceremony and festival more public, than the modern way
of celebrating them makes me approve of. The bride next
morning came out of her chamber, dressed with all the art and
care that Mrs. Toilet, the tire-woman, could bestow on her.
She was on her wedding-day three-and-twenty : her person is
far from what we call a regular beauty ; but a certain sweetness in her countenance, an ease in her shape and motion, with
an unaffected modesty in her looks, had attractions beyond
what symmetry and exactness can inspire, without the addition
of these endowments. When her lover entered the room, her
features flushed with shame and joy ; and the ingenuous
manner, so full of passion and of awe, with which Tranquillus
approached to salute her, gave me good omens of his future
behaviour towards her. The wedding was wholly under my
care. After the ceremony at church, I was resolved to entertain the company with a dinner suitable to the occasion, and
pitched upon the Apollo,† at the Old-Devil at Temple-Bar, as
a place sacred to mirth tempered with discretion, where Ben
Jonson and his sons used to make their liberal meetings.

* A sort of snuff.
† A large room at the Devil Tavern bore this name till the house was
finally shut up ; the rules of Ben's club remained till that period in gold
etters over the chimney.

Here the chief of the Staffian race appeared ; and as soon as
the company were come into that ample room, Lepidus Wagstaff began to make me compliments for choosing that place,
and fell into a discourse upon the subject of pleasure and
entertainment, drawn from the rules of Ben's club, which are
in gold letters over the chimney.   Lepidus has a way very uncommon, and speaks on subjects on which any man else would
certainly offend, with great dexterity.   He gave us a large
account of the public meetings of all the well-turned minds
who had passed through this life in ages past, and closed his
pleasing narrative with a discourse on marriage, and a
repetition of the following verses out of Milton.*

> " Hail, wedded love ! mysterious law ! true source
> Of human offspring, sole propriety
> In paradise, of all things common else.
> By thee adult'rous lust was driven from men
> Among the bestial herds to range ; by thee,
> Founded in reason, loyal, just and pure,
> Relations dear, and all the charities
> Of father, son, and brother, first were known.
> Perpetual fountain of domestic sweets,
> Whose bed is undefil'd and chaste pronounc'd,
> Present or past, as saints or patriarchs us'd.
> Here Love his golden shafts employs ; here lights
> His constant lamp, and waves his purple wings :
> Reigns here, and revels not in the bought smile
> Of harlots, loveless, joyless, unendear'd,
> Casual fruition ; nor in court amours,
> Mix'd dance, or wanton mask, or midnight ball,
> Or serenade, which the starv'd lover sings
> To his proud fair, best quitted with disdain."

In these verses, all the images that can come into a young
woman's head on such an occasion are raised ; but that in so
chaste and elegant a manner, that the bride thanked him for
his agreeable talk, and we sat down to dinner.

Among the rest of the company, there was got in a fellow
you call a Wag.   This ingenious person is the usual life of all
feasts and merriments, by speaking absurdities, and putting
everybody of breeding and modesty out of countenance.   As

* Paradise Lost, iv. 750.

soon as we sat down, he drank to the bride's diversion that
night ; and then made twenty double meanings on the word
thing.   We are the best-bred family, for one so numerous, in
this kingdom ; and indeed we should all of us have been as
much out of countenance as the bride, but that we were
relieved by an honest rough relation of ours at the lower end
of the table, who is a lieutenant of marines.   The soldier and
sailor had good plain sense, and saw what was wrong as well
as another ; he had a way of looking at his plate, and speaking
aloud in an inward manner ; and whenever the Wag mentioned the word *thing*, or the words, *that same*, the lieutenant
in that voice cried, " Knock him down."   The merry man,
wondering, angry, and looking round, was the diversion of the
table.   When he offered to recover, and say, " To the bride's
best thoughts," " Knock him down," says the lieutenant, and
so on.   This silly humour diverted, and saved us from the fulsome entertainment of an ill-bred coxcomb ; and the bride
drank the lieutenant's health.   We returned to my lodging,
and Tranquillus led his wife to her apartment, without the
ceremony of throwing the stocking.

A DREAM.

No. 81.   SATURDAY, OctoBER 15, 1709.

[ADDISON AND STEELE.]

Hic manus ob patriam pugnando vulnera passi,——
Quique pii vates, et Phœbo digna locuti ;
Inventas aut qui vitam excoluere per artes,
Quique sui memores alios fecere merendo.
VIRG. ÆN. vi. 660.

Here patriots live, who, for their country's good,
In fighting fields were prodigal of blood ;——
Here poets worthy their inspiring god,
And of unblemish'd life, make their abode :

And searching wits, of more mechanic parts,
Who grac'd their age with new-invented arts :
Those who to worth their bounty did extend ;
And those who knew that bounty to commend.

THERE are two kinds of immortality ; that which the soul
really enjoys after this life, and that imaginary existence by
which men live in their fame and reputation. The best and
greatest actions have proceeded from the prospect of the one
or the other of these ; but my design is to treat only of those
who have chiefly proposed to themselves the latter, as the
principal reward of their labours. It was for this reason that
I excluded from my Tables of Fame all the great founders and
votaries of religion ; and it is for this reason also, that I am
more than ordinary anxious to do justice to the persons of
whom I am now going to speak ; for, since fame was the only
end of all their enterprizes and studies, a man cannot be too
scrupulous in allotting them their due proportion of it. It
was this consideration which made me call the whole body of
the learned to my assistance; to many of whom I must own
my obligations for the catalogues of illustrious persons, which
they have sent me in upon this occasion. I yesterday employed the whole afternoon in comparing them with each
other ; which made so strong an impression upon my imagination, that they broke my sleep for the first part of the following
night, and at length threw me into a very agreeable Vision,
which I shall beg leave to describe in all its particulars.

I dreamed that I was conveyed into a wide and boundless
plain, that was covered with prodigious multitudes of people,
which no man could number. In the midst of it there stood
a mountain, with its head above the clouds. The sides were
extremely steep, and of such a particular structure, that no
creature which was not made in an human figure could possibly
ascend it. On a sudden there was heard from the top of it a
sound like that of a trumpet ; but so exceeding sweet and
harmonious, that it filled the hearts of those who heard it with
raptures, and gave such high and delightful sensations, as
seemed to animate and raise human nature above itself. This

made me very much amazed to find so very few in that innumerable multitude, who had ears fine enough to hear, or relish this music with pleasure : but my wonder abated, when, upon looking round me, I saw most of them attentive to three Syrens, clothed like Goddesses, and distinguished by the names of Sloth, Ignorance, and Pleasure. They were seated on three rocks, amidst a beautiful variety of groves, meadows, and rivulets, that lay on the borders of the mountain.   While the base and groveling multitude of different nations, ranks, and ages were listening to these delusive Deities, those of a more erect aspect, and exalted spirit, separated themselves from the rest, and marched in great bodies towards the mountain from whence they heard the sound, which still grew sweeter, the more they listened to it.

On a sudden methought this select band sprang forward, with a resolution to climb the ascent, and follow the call of that heavenly music. Every one took something with him that he thought might be of assistance to him in his march. Several had their swords drawn, some carried rolls of paper in their hands, some had compasses, others quadrants, others telescopes, and others pencils. Some had laurels on their heads, and others buskins on their legs ; in short, there was scarce any instrument of a mechanic art, or liberal science, which was not made use of on this occasion.   My good Dæmon, who stood at my right hand during the course of this whole vision, observing in me a burning desire to join that glorious company, told me, " he highly approved that generous ardour with which I seemed transported ; but at the same time advised me to cover my face with a mask all the while I was to labour on the ascent." I took his council, without enquiring into his reasons. The whole body now broke into different parties, and began to climb the precipice by ten thousand different paths. Several got into little alleys, which did not reach far up the hill, before they ended, and led no farther ; and I observed, that most of the artizans, which considerably diminished our number, fell into these paths.

We left another considerable body of adventurers behind us,

who thought they had discovered by-ways up the hill, which
proved so very intricate and perplexed, that, after having
advanced in them a little, they were quite lost among the
several turns and windings ; and though they were as active
as any in their motions, they made but little progress in the
ascent.   These, as my guide informed me, were men of subtle
tempers, and puzzled politics, who would supply the place of
real wisdom with cunning and artifice.   Among those who
were far advanced in their way, there were some that by one
false step fell backward, and lost more ground in a moment
than they had gained for many hours, or could be ever able to
recover.   We were now advanced very high, and observed that
all the different paths which ran about the sides of the mountain began to meet in two great roads ; which insensibly
gathered the whole multitude of travellers into two great
bodies.   At a little distance from the entrance of each road
there stood an hideous phantom, that opposed our farther
passage.   One of these apparitions had his right hand filled
with darts, which he brandished in the face of all who came up
that way.   Crowds ran back at the appearance of it, and cried
out, Death.   The spectre that guarded the other road was
Envy.   She was not armed with weapons of destruction, like
the former ; but by dreadful hissings, noises of reproach, and
a horrid distracted laughter, she appeared more frightful than
Death itself, insomuch, that abundance of our company were
discouraged from passing any farther, and some appeared
ashamed of having come so far.   As for myself, I must confess, my heart shrunk within me at the sight of these ghastly
appearances ; but, on a sudden, the voice of the trumpet came
more full upon us, so that we felt a new resolution reviving in
us ; and in proportion as this resolution grew, the terrors
before us seemed to vanish.   Most of the company, who had
swords in their hands, marched on with great spirit, and an
air of defiance, up the road that was commanded by Death ;
while others, who had thought and contemplation in their
looks, went forward in a more composed manner up the road
possessed by Envy.   The way above these apparitions grew

smooth and uniform, and was so delightful, that the travellers went on with pleasure, and in a little time arrived at the top of the mountain. They here began to breathe a delicious kind of æther, and saw all the fields about them covered with a kind of purple light, that made them reflect with satisfaction on their past toils; and diffused a secret joy through the whole assembly, which shewed itself in every look and feature. In the midst of these happy fields there stood a palace of a very glorious structure. It had four great folding-doors, that faced the four several quarters of the world. On the top of it was enthroned the Goddess of the mountain, who smiled upon her votaries, and sounded the silver trumpet which had called them up, and cheered them in their passage to her palace. They had now formed themselves into several divisions; a band of historians taking their stations at each door, according to the persons whom they were to introduce.

On a sudden, the trumpet, which had hitherto sounded only a march, or a point of war, now swelled all its notes into triumph and exultation. The whole fabric shook, and the doors flew open. The first who stepped forward was a beautiful and blooming hero, and as I heard by the murmurs round me, Alexander the Great. He was conducted by a crowd of historians. The person who immediately walked before him was remarkable for an embroidered garment, who, not being well acquainted with the place, was conducting him to an apartment appointed for the reception of fabulous heroes. The name of this false guide was Quintus Curtius. But Arrian and Plutarch, who knew better the avenues of this palace, conducted him into the great hall, and placed him at the upper end of the first table. My good Dæmon, that I might see the whole ceremony, conveyed me to a corner of this room, where I might perceive all that passed, without being seen myself. The next who entered was a charming virgin, leading in a venerable old man that was blind. Under her left arm she bore a harp, and on her head a garland. Alexander, who was very well acquainted with Homer, stood up at his entrance, and placed him on his right hand. The virgin, who it seems was

K

one of the nine sisters that attended on the Goddess of Fame, smiled with an ineffable grace at their meeting, and retired.

Julius Cæsar was now coming forward ; and though most of the historians offered their service to introduce him, he left them at the door, and would have no conductor but himself.

The next who advanced was a man of an homely but cheerful aspect, and attended by persons of greater figure than any that appeared on this occasion. Plato was on his right hand, and Xenophon on his left. He bowed to Homer, and sat down by him. It was expected that Plato would himself have taken a place next to his master Socrates ; but on a sudden there was heard a great clamour of disputants at the door, who appeared with Aristotle at the head of them. That philosopher, with some rudeness, but great strength of reason, convinced the whole table, that a title to the fifth place was his due, and took it accordingly.

He had scarce sat down, when the same beautiful virgin that had introduced Homer brought in another, who hung back at the entrance, and would have excused himself, had not his modesty been overcome by the invitation of all who sat at the table. His guide and behaviour made me easily conclude it was Virgil. Cicero next appeared, and took his place. He had inquired at the door for one Lucceius to introduce him ; but, not finding him there, he contented himself with the attendance of many other writers, who all, except Sallust, appeared highly pleased with the office.

We waited some time in expectation of the next worthy, who came in with a great retinue of historians, whose names I could not learn, most of them being natives of Carthage. The person thus conducted, who was Hannibal, seemed much disturbed, and could not forbear complaining to the board of the affront he had met with among the Roman historians, "who attempted," says he, "to carry me into the subterraneous apartment; and perhaps, would have done it, had it not been for the impartiality of this gentleman," pointing to Polybius, "who was the only person, except my own countrymen, that was willing to conduct me hither."

The Carthaginian took his seat, and Pompey entered with great dignity in his own person, and preceded by several historians. Lucan the poet was at the head of them, who observing Homer and Virgil at the table, was going to sit down himself, had not the latter whispered him, that whatever pretence he might otherwise have had, he forfeited his claim to it, by coming in as one of the historians. Lucan was so exasperated with the repulse, that he muttered something to himself ; and was heard to say, " that since he could not have a seat among them himself, he would bring in one who alone had more merit than their whole assembly :" upon which he went to the door, and brought in Cato of Utica. That great man approached the company with such an air, that showed he contemned the honour which he laid a claim to. Observing the seat opposite to Cæsar was vacant he took possession of it, and spoke two or three smart sentences upon the nature of precedency, which, according to him, consisted not in place, but in intrinsic merit ; to which he added, " that the most virtuous man, wherever he was seated, was always at the upper end of the table." Socrates, who had a great spirit of raillery with his wisdom, could not forbear smiling at a virtue which took so little pains to make itself agreeable. Cicero took the occasion to make a long discourse in praise of Cato, which he uttered with much vehemence. Cæsar answered him with a great deal of seeming temper ; but, as I stood at a great distance from them, I was not able to hear one word of what they said. But I could not forbear taking notice, that, in all the discourse which passed at the table, a word or nod from Homer decided the controversy.

After a short pause, Augustus appeared, looking round him with a serene and affable countenance upon all the writers of his age, who strove among themselves which of them should shew him the greatest marks of gratitude and respect. Virgil rose from the table to meet him ; and though he was an acceptable guest to all, he appeared more such to the learned, than the military worthies.

The next man astonished the whole table with his appearance. He was slow, solemn, and silent in his behaviour.

K 2

and wore a raiment curiously wrought with hieroglyphics.
As he came into the middle of the room, he threw back
the skirt of it, and discovered a golden thigh.   Socrates, at
the sight of it, declared against keeping company with any
who were not made of flesh and blood ; and, therefore, desired
Diogenes the Laertian to lead him to the apartment allotted
for fabulous heroes, and worthies of dubious existence.   At his
going out, he told them, " that they did not know whom they
dismissed ; that he was now Pythagoras, the first of philosophers, and that formerly he had been a very brave man at
the siege of Troy."—" That may be very true," said Socrates ;
"but you forget that you have likewise been a very great
harlot in your time."   This exclusion made way for Archimedes,
who came forward with a scheme of mathematical figures in his
hand ; among which I observed a cone and a cylinder.   Seeing
this table full, I desired my guide, for variety, to lead me to
the fabulous apartment, the roof of which was painted with
Gorgons, Chimæras, and Centaurs, with many other emblema-
tical figures, which I wanted both time and skill to unriddle.
The first table was almost full : at the upper end sat Hercules,
leaning an arm upon his club ; on his right hand were Achilles
and Ulysses, and between them Æneas ; on his left were Hector, Theseus, and Jason : the lower end had Orpheus, Æsop,
Phalaris, and Musæus.   The ushers seemed at a loss for a
twelfth man, when, methought, to my great joy and surprise, I
heard some at the lower end of the table mention Isaac Bickerstaff ; but those of the upper end received it with disdain ; and
said, " if they must have a British worthy, they would have
Robin Hood."

While I was transported with the honour that was done me,
and burning with envy against my competitor, I was awakened
by the noise of the cannon which were then fired for the taking
of Mons.*   I should have been very much troubled at being
thrown out of so pleasing a vision on any other occasion ; but
thought it an agreeable change, to have my thoughts diverted

* The town of Mons surrendered Oct. 21, 1709.

from the greatest among the dead and fabulous heroes, to the most famous among the real and the living.

CRITICISMS ON THE "TABLE OF FAME."

No. 83. THURSDAY, OCTOBER 20, 1709. [STEELE.]

Senilis stultitia, quæ deliratio appellari solet, sonum levium est, non omnium.—M. T. CIC.

That which is usually called dotage is not the foible of all old men, but only of such as are remarkable for their levity and inconstancy.

IT is my frequent practice to visit places of resort in this town where I am least known, to observe what reception my works meet with in the world, and what good effects I may promise myself from my labours: and it being a privilege asserted by monsieur Montaigne, and others, of vain-glorious memory, that we writers of essays may talk of ourselves ; I take the liberty to give an account of the remarks which I find are made by some of my gentle readers upon these my dissertations.

I happened this evening to fall into a coffee-house near the Exchange, where two persons were reading my account of the "Table of Fame."

The one of these was commenting as he read, and explaining who was meant by this and the other worthy as he passed on. I observed the person over against him wonderfully intent and satisfied with his explanation. When he came to Julius Cæsar, who is said to have refused any conductor to the Table ; "No, no," said he, "he is in the right of it, he has money enough to be welcome wherever he comes ;" and then whispered, "he means a certain colonel of the Train-bands." Upon reading that Aristotle made his claim with some rudeness, but great strength of reason ; "Who can that be, so rough and so reasonable ? It must be some Whig, I warrant you. There is nothing but party in these public papers." Where Pythagoras is said to have a golden thigh, "Ay, ay," said "he, he has money enough in his breeches ; that is the alderman of our ward," you must know. Whatever he read, I found he interpreted from his own way of life and acquaintance. I am glad my readers can construe for themselves these difficult points ; but, for the benefit of posterity, I design, when I come to write my last paper of this kind, to make it an explanation of all my former. In that piece, you shall have all I have commended, with their proper names. The faulty characters must be left as they are, because we live in an age wherein vice is very general, and virtue very particular ; for which reason the latter only wants explanation.

But I must turn my present discourse to what is of yet greater regard to me than the care of my writings ; that is to say, the preservation of a lady's heart. Little did I think I should ever have business of this kind on my hands more ; but, as little as any one who knows me would believe it, there is a lady at this time who professes love to me. Her passion and good humour you shall have in her own words.

> "Mr. BICKERSTAFF,
>
> "I HAD formerly a very good opinion of myself ; but it is now withdrawn, and I have placed it upon you, Mr. Bickerstaff, for whom I am not ashamed to declare I have a very great passion and tenderness. It is not for your face, for that I never saw ; your shape and height I am equally a stranger to ; but your understanding charms me, and I am lost if you do not dissemble a little love for me. I am not without hopes ; because I am not like the tawdry gay things that are fit only to make bone-lace. I am neither childish-young, nor beldam-old, but, the world says, a good agreeable woman.
>
> "Speak peace to a troubled heart, troubled only for you ; and in your next paper let me find your thoughts of me.
>
> "Do not think of finding out who I am, for, notwithstanding your interest in dæmons, they cannot help you either to my

name, or a sight of my face ; therefore, do not let them deceive you.

" I can bear no discourse, if you are not the subject ; and believe me, I know more of love than you do of astronomy.

" Pray, say some civil things in return to my generosity, and you shall have my very best pen employed to thank you, and I will confirm it. I am

" Your admirer,
" MARIA."

There is something wonderfully pleasing in the favour of women ; and this letter has put me in so good an humour, that nothing could displease me since I received it. My boy breaks glasses and pipes ; and instead of giving him a knock on the pate, as my way is, for I hate scolding at servants, I only say, " Ah, Jack ! thou hast a head, and so has a pin," or some such merry expression. But, alas ! how am I mortified when he is putting on my fourth pair of stockings on these poor spindles of mine? " The fair-one understands love better than I astronomy !" I am sure, without the help of that art, this poor meagre trunk of mine is a very ill habitation for love. She is pleased to speak civilly of my sense, but *Ingenium malè habitat* is an invincible difficulty in cases of this nature. I had always, indeed, from a passion to please the eyes of the fair, a great pleasure in dress. Add to this, that I have writ songs since I was sixty, and have lived with all the circumspection of an old beau, as I am. But my friend Horace has very well said, " Every year takes something from us ;" and instructed me to form my pursuits and desires according to the stage of my life : therefore, I have no more to value myself upon, than that I can converse with young people without peevishness, or wishing myself a moment younger. For which reason, when I am amongst them, I rather moderate than interrupt their diversions. But though I have this complacency, I must not pretend to write to a lady civil things, as Maria desires. Time was, when I could have told her, " I had received a letter from her fair hands ; and, that if this paper trembled as she read it,

it then best expressed its author," or some other gay conceit.
Though I never saw her, I could have told her, " that good
sense and good humour smiled in her eyes : that constancy and
good-nature dwelt in her heart : that beauty and good 'breeding appeared in all her actions." When I was five-and-twenty,
upon sight of one syllable, even wrong spelt, by a lady I never
saw, I could tell her, " that her height was that which was fit
for inviting our approach, and commanding our respect ; that
a smile sat on her lips, which prefaced her expressions before
she uttered them, and her aspect prevented her speech. All
she could say, though she had an infinite deal of wit, was but
a repetition of what was expressed by her form ; her form !
which struck her beholders with ideas more moving and forcible
than ever were inspired by music, painting, or eloquence." At
this rate I panted in those days ; but, ah ! sixty-three ! I
am very sorry I can only return the agreeable Maria a passion
expressed rather from the head than the heart.

    " DEAR MADAM,
        "You have already seen the best of me, and I so
passionately love you, that I desire we may never meet. If
you will examine your heart, you will find that you join the
man with the philosopher : and if you have that kind opinion
of my sense as you pretend, I question not but you add to it
complexion, air, and shape : but, dear Molly, a man in his
grand climacteric is of no sex. Be a good girl ; and conduct
yourself with honour and virtue, when you love one younger
than myself. I am, with the greatest tenderness,
                        " Your innocent lover,
                                    " I. B."

A MATRIMONIAL QUARREL.

No. 85.   TUESDAY, October 25, 1709.   [Steele.]

My brother Tranquillus, who is a man of business, came to me this morning into my study, and after very many civil expressions in return for what good offices I had done him, told me, " he desired to carry his wife, my sister, that very morning to his own house." I readily told him, " I would wait upon him," without asking why he was so impatient to rob us of his good company. He went out of my chamber, and I thought seemed to have a little heaviness upon him, which gave me some disquiet. Soon after my sister came to me, with a very matronlike air, and most sedate satisfaction in her looks, which spoke her very much at ease ; but the traces of her countenance seemed to discover that she had been lately in a passion, and that air of content to flow from a certain triumph upon some advantage obtained. She no sooner sat down by me, but I perceived she was one of those ladies who begin to be managers within the time of their being brides.—Without letting her speak, which I saw she had a mighty inclination to do, I said, " Here has been your husband, who tells me he has a mind to go home this very morning, and I have consented to it."—" It is well," said she, " for you must know——" " Nay, Jenny," said I, " I beg your pardon, for it is you must know—You are to understand, that now is the time to affix or alienate your husband's heart for ever ; and I fear you have been a little indiscreet in your expressions or behaviour towards him, even here in my house." —"There has," says she, " been some words : but I will be judged by you if he was not in the wrong : nay, I need not be judged by anybody, for he gave it up himself, and said not a word when he saw me grow passionate, but, ' Madam, you are perfectly in the right of it : ' as you shall judge——" " Nay, madam," said I, " I am judge already, and tell you, that you are perfectly in the wrong of it ; for if it was a matter of import-

ance, I know he has better sense than you ; if a trifle, you know
what I told you on your wedding-day, that you were to be
above little provocations." She knows very well I can be sour
upon occasion, therefore gave me leave to go on.

"Sister," said I, "I will not enter into the dispute between
you, which I find his prudence put an end to before it came to
extremity ; but charge you to have a care of the first quarrel,
as you tender your happiness ; for then it is that the mind will
reflect harshly upon every circumstance that has ever passed
between you. If such an accident is ever to happen, which I
hope never will, be sure to keep to the circumstance before
you ; make no allusions to what is passed, or conclusions
referring to what is to come : do not shew an hoard of
matter for dissension in your breast ; but if it is necessary,
lay before him the thing as you understand it, candidly,
without being ashamed of acknowledging an error, or
proud of being in the right. If a young couple be not
careful in this point, they will get into an habit of wrangling :
and when to displease is thought of no consequence, to please
is always of as little moment. There is a play, Jenny, I have
formerly been at when I was a student : we got into a dark
corner with a porringer of brandy, and threw raisins into it,
then set it on fire. My chamber-fellow and I diverted ourselves with the sport of venturing our fingers for the raisins ;
and the wantonness of the thing was, to see each other look
like a demon, as we burnt ourselves, and snatched out the
fruit. This fantastical mirth was called Snap-Dragon. You
may go into many a family, where you see the man and wife at
this sport : every word at their table alludes to some passage
between themselves ; and you see by the paleness and emotion
in their countenances, that it is for your sake, and not their
own, that they forbear playing out the whole game in burning
each other's fingers. In this case, the whole purpose of life is
inverted, and the ambition turns upon a certain contention,
who shall contradict best, and not upon an inclination to excel
in kindness and good offices. Therefore, dear Jenny, remember
me, and avoid Snap-Dragon."

" I thank you, brother," said she, " but you do not know how
he loves me ; I find I can do anything with him."—" If you *can
so*, why should you desire to do anything but please him ? but
I have a word or two more before you go out of the room ; for
I see you do not like the subject I am upon : let nothing pro-
voke you to fall upon an imperfection he cannot help ; for, if
he has a resenting spirit, he will think your aversion as immov-
able as the imperfection with which you upbraid him.   But,
above all, dear Jenny, be careful of one thing, and you will be
something more than woman ; that is, a levity you are almost
all guilty of, which is, to take a pleasure in your power to give
pain.   It is even in a mistress an argument of meanness of
spirit, but in a wife it is injustice and ingratitude.   When a
sensible man once observes this in a woman, he must have a
very great, or very little spirit, to overlook it.   A woman
ought, therefore, to consider very often, how few men there are
who will regard a meditated offence as a weakness of temper."

   I was going on in my confabulation, when Tranquillus
entered.   She cast all her eyes upon him with much shame
and confusion, mixed with great complacency and love, and
went up to him.   He took her in his arms, and looked so many
soft things at one glance, that I could see he was glad I had
been talking to her, sorry she had been troubled, and angry at
himself that he could not disguise the concern he was in an
hour before.   After which he says to me, with an air awkward
enough, but methought not unbecoming, " I have altered my
mind, brother ; we will live upon you a day or two longer."   I
replied, " That is what I have been persuading Jenny to ask of
you, but she is resolved never to contradict your inclination,
and refused me."

   We were going on in that way which one hardly knows how
to express ; as when two people mean the same thing in a nice
case, but come at it by talking as distantly from it as they can ;
when very opportunely came in upon us an honest inconsiderable fellow, Tim Dapper,* a gentleman well known to us both.

---

* The following account of Tim Dapper seems to be given, as a true picture
of the character and dress of a country beau, in 1709.

Tim is one of those who are very necessary, by being very inconsiderable. Tim dropped in at an incident, when we knew not how to fall into either a grave or a merry way. My sister took this occasion to make off, and Dapper gave us an account of all the company he had been in to-day, who was, and who was not at home, where he visited. This Tim is the head of a species : he is a little out of his element in this town ; but he is a relation of Tranquillus, and his neighbour in the country, which is the true place of residence for this species. The habit of a Dapper, when he is at home, is a light broad cloth, with calamanco or red waistcoat and breeches ; and it is remarkable, that their wigs seldom hide the collar of their coats. They have always a peculiar spring in their arms, a wriggle in their bodies, and a trip in their gait. All which motions they express at once in their drinking, bowing, or saluting ladies ; for a distant imitation of a forward fop, and a resolution to overtop him in his way, are the distinguishing marks of a Dapper. These under-characters of men, are parts of the sociable world by no means to be neglected : they are like pegs in a building ; they make no figure in it, but hold the structure together, and are as absolutely necessary as the pillars and columns. I am sure we found it so this morning ; for Tranquillus and I should, perhaps, have looked cold at each other the whole day, but Dapper fell in with his brisk way, shook us both by the hand, rallied the bride, mistook the acceptance he met with amongst us for extraordinary perfection in himself, and heartily pleased, and was pleased, all the while he staid. His company left us all in good humour, and we were not such fools as to let it sink, before we confirmed it by great cheerfulness and openness in our carriage the whole evening.

SIR HARRY QUICKSET.

No. 86.   THURSDAY, October 27, 1709.

[ADDISON AND STEELE.]

WHEN I came home last night, my servant delivered me the following letter :

October 24.

"SIR,

"I have orders from sir Harry Quickset, of Staffordshire, baronet, to acquaint you, that his honour sir Harry himself, sir Giles Wheelbarrow, knight, Thomas Rentfree, esquire, justice of the quorum, Andrew Windmill, esquire, and Mr. Nicholas Doubt, of the Inner Temple, sir Harry's grandson, will wait upon you at the hour of nine to-morrow morning, being Tuesday the twenty-fifth of October, upon business which sir Harry will impart to you by word of mouth. I thought it proper to acquaint you before-hand so many persons of quality came, that you might not be surprised therewith. Which concludes, though by many years absence since I saw you at Stafford, unknown, sir,

"Your most humble servant,
"JOHN THRIFTY."

I received this message with less surprise than I believe Mr. Thrifty imagined ; for I knew the good company too well to feel any palpitations at their approach : but I was in very great concern how I should adjust the ceremonial, and demean myself to all these great men, who perhaps had not seen any-thing above themselves for these twenty years last past. I am sure that is the case of sir Harry. Besides which, I was sen-sible that there was a great point in adjusting my behaviour to the simple squire, so as to give him satisfaction, and not dis-oblige the justice of the quorum.

The hour of nine was come this morning, and I had no sooner set chairs, by the steward's letter, and fixed my tea-equipage, but I heard a knock at my door, which was opened,

but no one entered ; after which followed a long silence, which
was broke at last by, " sir, I beg your pardon ; I think I know
better :" and another voice, " nay, good sir Giles—" I looked
out from my window, and saw the good company all with their
hats off, and arms spread, offering the door to each other.
After many offers, they entered with much solemnity, in the
order Mr. Thrifty was so kind as to name them to me.   But
they are now got to my chamber-door, and I saw my old friend
sir Harry enter.   I met him with all the respect due to so
reverend a vegetable ; for, you are to know, that is my sense of
a person who remains idle in the same place for half a century.
I got him with great success into his chair by the fire, without
throwing down any of my cups.   The knight-bachelor told me,
" he had a great respect for my whole family, and would, with
my leave, place himself next to sir Harry, at whose right hand
he had sat at every quarter sessions these thirty years, unless
he was sick."   The steward in the rear whispered the young
Templar, " That is true, to my knowledge." I had the misfortune, as they stood cheek by jole, to desire the squire to sit
down before the justice of the quorum, to the no small satisfaction of the former, and resentment of the latter.   But I saw
my error too late, and got them as soon as I could into their
seats.   " Well," said I, " gentlemen, after I have told you how
glad I am of this great honour, I am to desire you to drink a
dish of tea."   They answered one and all, " that they never
drank tea in a morning."—" Not in a morning ! " said I, staring
round me.   Upon which the pert jackanapes, Nic Doubt, tipped
me the wink, and put out his tongue at his grandfather.   Here
followed a profound silence, when the steward in his boots and
whip proposed, " that we should adjourn to some public-house,
where everybody might call for what they pleased, and enter
upon the business."   We all stood up in an instant, and sir
Harry filed off from the left, very discreetly, countermarching
behind the chairs towards the door.   After him, sir Giles in
the same manner.   The simple squire made a sudden start to
follow ; but the justice of the quorum whipped between upon
the stand of the stairs.   A maid, going up with coals, made us

halt, and put us into such confusion, that we stood all in a heap, without any visible possibility of recovering our order ; for the young jackanapes seemed to make a jest of this matter, and had so contrived, by pressing amongst us, under pretence of making way, that his grandfather was got into the middle, and he knew nobody was of quality to stir a step, until sir Harry moved first. We were fixed in this perplexity for some time, until we heard a very loud noise in the street ; and sir Harry asking what it was, I, to make them move, said, " it was fire." Upon this, all ran down as fast as they could, without order or ceremony, until we got into the street, where we drew up in very good order, and filed off down Sheer-lane ; the impertinent Templar driving us before him, as in a string, and pointing to his acquaintance who passed by.

I must confess, I love to use people according to their own sense of good breeding, and therefore whipped in between the justice and the simple squire. He could not properly take this ill ; but I overheard him whisper the steward, " that he thought it hard, that a common conjurer should take place of him, though an elder squire." In this order we marched down Sheer-lane, at the upper end of which I lodge. When we came to Temple-bar, sir Harry and sir Giles got over ; but a run of the coaches kept the rest of us on this side of the street ; however, we all at last landed, and drew up in very good order before Ben Tooke's* shop, who favoured our rallying with great humanity ; from whence we proceeded again, until we came to Dick's coffee-house, where I designed to carry them. Here we were at our old difficulty, and took up the street upon the same ceremony. We proceeded through the entry, and were so necessarily kept in order by the situation, that we were now got into the coffee-house itself, where, as soon as we arrived, we repeated our civilities to each other ; after which, we marched up to the high table, which has an ascent to it inclosed in the middle of the room. The whole house was alarmed at this entry, made up of persons of so much state and rusticity. Sir

* Then a celebrated bookseller, in Fleet Street.

Harry called for a mug of ale, and Dyer's Letter.*   The boy
brought the ale in an instant ; but said, "they did not take in
the Letter."—" No!" says sir Harry, "then take back your mug ;
we are like indeed to have good liquor at this house !"   Here
the Templar tipped me a second wink, and, if I had not looked
very grave upon him, I found he was disposed to be very
familiar with me.   In short, I observed after a long pause, that
the gentleman did not care to enter upon business until after
their morning draught, for which reason I called for a bottle
of mum ; and, finding that had no effect upon them, I ordered
a second, and a third, after which sir Harry reached over to
me, and told me in a low voice, "that the place was too public
for business ; but he would call upon me again to-morrow
morning at my own lodgings, and bring some more friends
with him."

A PASTORAL LETTER.

No. 89.   THURSDAY, November 3, 1709.   [Steele.]

Rura mihi placeant, riguique in vallibus amnes,
Flumina amem sylvasque inglorius——
Virg. Georg. ii. 485.

My next desire is, void of care and strife,
To lead a soft, secure, inglorious life :
A country cottage near a crystal flood,
A winding valley, and a lofty wood.

I HAVE received this short epistle from an unknown hand.

" SIR,

" I have no more to trouble you with, than to desire
you would in your next help me to some answer to the inclosed

---

* Dyer, the publisher of a written newspaper, under the title of " Dyer's
Letter," is humorously said by Addison to be " justly looked upon by all the
fox-hunters in the nation, as the greatest statesman our country has produced."

concerning yourself. In the mean time I congratulate you upon the increase of your fame, which you see has extended itself beyond the bills of mortality."

" Sir,
"That the country is barren of news has been the excuse, time out of mind, for dropping a correspondence with our friends in London ; as if it were impossible out of a coffee-house to write an agreeable letter. I am too ingenuous to endeavour at the covering of my negligence with so common an excuse. Doubtless, amongst friends, bred, as we have been, to the knowledge of books as well as men, a letter dated from a garden, a grotto, a fountain, a wood, a meadow, or the banks of a river, may be more entertaining than one from Tom's, Will's, White's, or Saint James's. I promise, therefore, to be frequent for the future in my rural dates to you. But.for fear you should, from what I have said, be induced to believe I shun the commerce of men, I must inform you, that there is a fresh topic of discourse lately arisen amongst the ingenious in our part of the world, and is become the more fashionable for the ladies giving into it. This we owe to Isaac Bickerstaff, who is very much censured by some, and as much justified by others. Some criticise his style, his humour, and his matter ; others admire the whole man. Some pretend, from the informations of their friends in town, to decypher the author ; and others confess they are lost in their guesses. For my part, I must own myself a professed admirer of the paper, and desire you to send me a complete set, together with your thoughts of the squire and his lucubrations."

There is no pleasure like that of receiving praise from the praise-worthy ; and I own it a very solid happiness, that these my lucubrations are approved by a person of so fine a taste as the author of this letter, who is capable of enjoying the world in the simplicity of its natural beauties. This pastoral letter, if I may so call it, must be written by a man who carries his entertainment wherever he goes, and is undoubtedly one of those happy men who appear far otherwise to the vulgar. I dare say, he is not envied by the vicious, the vain, the frolic, and the loud ; but is continually blessed with that strong and serious delight, which flows from a well-taught and liberal mind. With great respect to country sports, I may say, this gentleman could pass his time agreeably, if there were not a hare or a fox in his county. That calm and elegant satisfaction which the vulgar call melancholy is the true and proper delight of men of knowledge and virtue. What we take for diversion, which is a kind of forgetting ourselves, is but a mean way of entertainment, in comparison of that which is considering, knowing, and enjoying ourselves. The pleasures of ordinary people are in their passions ; but the seat of this delight is in the reason and understanding. Such a frame of mind raises that sweet enthusiasm, which warms the imagination at the sight of every work of nature, and turns all round you into a picture and landscape. I shall be ever proud of advices from this gentleman ; for I profess writing news from the learned, as well as the busy world.

As for my labours, which he is pleased to inquire after, if they can but wear one impertinence out of human life, destroy a single vice, or give a morning's cheerfulness to an honest mind ; in short, if the world can be but one virtue the better, or in any degree less vicious, or receive from them the smallest addition to their innocent diversions ; I shall not think my pains, or indeed my life, to have been spent in vain.

Thus far as to my studies. It will be expected I should in the next place give some account of my life. I shall therefore, for the satisfaction of the present age, and the benefit of posterity, present the world with the following abridgement of it.

It is remarkable, that I was bred by hand, and eat nothing but milk until I was a twelve-month old ; from which time, to the eighth year of my age, I was observed to delight in pudding and potatoes ; and indeed I retain a benevolence for that sort of food to this day. I do not remember that I distinguished myself in any thing at those years, but by my great skill at taw, for which I was so barbarously used, that it has ever since given me an aversion to gaming. In my twelfth year, I suffered very much for two or three false concords. At fifteen I was sent to the university, and staid there for some time ; but a drum passing by, being a lover of music, I inlisted myself for a soldier. As years came on, I began to examine things, and grew discontented at the times. This made me quit the sword, and take to the study of the occult sciences, in which I was so wrapped up, that Oliver Cromwell had been buried, and taken up again, five years before I heard he was dead. This gave me first the reputation of a conjurer, which has been of great disadvantage to me ever since, and kept me out of all public employments. The greater part of my later years has been divided between Dick's coffee-house, the Trumpet in Sheer-lane, and my own lodgings.

LOVE.

No. 90.   SATURDAY, November 5, 1709.

[Steele and Addison.]

—— Amoto quæramus seria ludo.
HOR. 1 Sat. i. 27.

Let us now ——
With graver air our serious theme pursue,
And yet preserve our moral full in view.

The passion of love happened to be the subject of discourse between two or three of us at the table of the poets this evening ; and, among other observations, it was remarked, " that the same sentiment on this passion had run through all languages and nations." Memmius, who has a very good taste, fell into a little sort of dissertation on this occasion. " It is," said he, " remarkable, that no passion has been treated, by all who have touched upon it, with the same bent of design but this. The poets, the moralists, the painters, in all their descriptions, allegories, and pictures, have represented it as a

L 2

soft torment, a bitter sweet, a pleasing pain, or an agreeable distress; and have only expressed the same thought in a different manner."

The joining of pleasure and pain together in such devices, seems to me the only pointed thought I ever read which is natural; and it must have proceeded from its being the universal sense and experience of mankind, that they have all spoken of it in the same manner. I have, in my own reading, remarked an hundred and three epigrams, fifty odes, and ninety-one sentences, tending to this sole purpose.

It is certain, there is no other passion which does produce such contrary effects in so great a degree. But this may be said for love, that if you strike it out of the soul, life would be insipid, and our being but half-animated. Human nature would sink into deadness and lethargy, if not quickened with some active principle; and as for all others, whether ambition, envy, or avarice, which are apt to possess the mind in the absence of this passion, it must be allowed that they have greater pains, without the compensation of such exquisite pleasures as those we find in love. The great skill is to heighten the satisfactions, and deaden the sorrows of it; which has been the end of many of my labours, and shall continue to be so, for the service of the world in general, and in particular of the fair sex, who are always the best or the worst part of it. It is a pity that a passion, which has in it a capacity of making life happy, should not be cultivated to the utmost advantage. Reason, prudence, and good-nature, rightly applied, can thoroughly accomplish this great end, provided they have always a real and constant love to work upon. But this subject I shall treat more at large in the history of my married sister, and in the mean time shall conclude my reflection on the pains and pleasures which attend this passion, with one of the finest allegories which I think I have ever read. It is invented by the divine Plato, and, to show the opinion he himself had of it, ascribed by him to his admired Socrates, whom he represents as discoursing with his friends, and giving the history of Love in the following manner.

"At the birth of Beauty," says he, "there was a great feast made, and many guests invited. Among the rest, was the god Plenty, who was the son of the goddess Prudence, and inherited many of his mother's virtues. After a full entertainment, he retired into the garden of Jupiter, which was hung with a great variety of ambrosial fruits, and seems to have been a very proper retreat for such a guest. In the mean time, an unhappy female called Poverty, having heard of this great feast, repaired to it, in hopes of finding relief. The first place she lights upon was Jupiter's garden, which generally stands open to people of all conditions. Poverty enters, and by chance finds the god Plenty asleep in it. She was immediately fired with his charms, laid herself down by his side, and managed matters so well, that she conceived a child by him. The world was very much in suspense upon the occasion, and could not imagine to themselves what would be the nature of an infant that was to have its original from two such parents. At the last, the child appears ; and who should it be but Love. This infant grew up, and proved in all his behaviour, what he really was, a compound of opposite beings. As he is the son of Plenty, who was the offspring of Prudence, he is subtle, intriguing, full of stratagems and devices : as the son of Poverty, he is fawning, begging, serenading, delighting to lie at a threshold, or beneath a window. By the father, he is audacious, full of hopes, conscious of merit, and therefore quick of resentment. By the mother, he is doubtful, timorous, mean-spirited, fearful of offending, and abject in submissions. In the same hour you may see him transported with raptures, talking of immortal pleasures, and appearing satisfied as a god ; and immediately after, as the mortal mother prevails in his composition, you behold him pining, languishing, despairing, dying."

I have been always wonderfully delighted with fables, allegories, and the like inventions, which the politest and the best instructors of mankind have always made use of. They take off from the severity of instruction, and inforce it at the same time that they conceal it. The supposing Love to be conceived immediately after the birth of Beauty ; the parentage

of Plenty; and the inconsistency of this passion with its self
so naturally derived to it, are great master-strokes in this fable;
and if they fell into good hands, might furnish out a more
pleasing canto than any in Spenser.

A TOP TOAST'S VISIT.

No. 91.   TUESDAY, November 8, 1709.   [Steele.]

I was very much surprised this evening with a visit from
one of the top toasts of the town, who came privately in a
chair, and bolted into my room, while I was reading a chapter
of Agrippa upon the occult sciences; but, as she entered with
all the air and bloom that nature ever bestowed on woman, I
threw down the conjuror, and met the charmer. I had no
sooner placed her at my right hand by the fire, but she opened
to me the reason of her visit. "Mr. Bickerstaff," said the fine
creature, "I have been your correspondent some time, though
I never saw you before; I have writ by the name of Maria.
You have told me, you were too far gone in life to think of
love. Therefore, I am answered as to the passion I spoke of;
and," continued she, smiling, "I will not stay until you grow
young again, as you men never fail to do in your dotage; but
am come to consult you about disposing of myself to another.
My person you see; my fortune is very considerable; but I
am at present under much perplexity how to act in a great
conjuncture. I have two lovers, Crassus and Lorio: Crassus
is prodigiously rich, but has no one distinguishing quality;
though at the same time he is not remarkable on the defective
side. Lorio has travelled, is well bred, pleasant in discourse,
discreet in his conduct, agreeable in his person; and with all
this, he has a competency of fortune without superfluity.
When I consider Lorio, my mind is filled with an idea of the
great satisfactions of a pleasant conversation. When I think

of Crassus, my equipage, numerous servants, gay liveries, and various dresses, are opposed to the charms of his rival. In a word, when I cast my eyes upon Lorio, I forget and despise fortune ; when I behold Crassus, I think only of pleasing my vanity, and enjoying an uncontrolled expence in all the pleasures of life, except love." She paused here.

"Madam," said I, "I am confident you have not stated your case with sincerity, and there is some secret pang which you have concealed from me : for I see by your aspect the generosity of your mind ; and that open ingenuous air lets me know, that you have too great a sense of the generous passion of love, to prefer the ostentation of life in the arms of Crassus, to the entertainments and conveniences of it in the company of your beloved Lorio ; for so he is indeed, madam ; you speak his name with a different accent from the rest of your discourse. The idea his image raises in you gives new life to your features, and new grace to your speech. Nay, blush not, madam ; there is no dishonour in loving a man of merit ; I assure you, I am grieved at this dallying with yourself, when you put another in com-petition with him, for no other reason but superior wealth."— "To tell you, then," said she, "the bottom of my heart, there is Clotilda lies by, and plants herself in the way of Crassus, and I am confident will snap him if I refuse him. I cannot bear to think that she will shine above me. When our coaches meet, to see her chariot hung behind with *four footmen*, and mine with but *two :* hers, *powdered*, gay, and saucy, kept only for show ; mine, a couple of careful rogues that are good for something : I own, I cannot bear that Clotilda should be in all the pride and wantonness of wealth, and I only in the case and affluence of it."

Here I interrupted : "Well, madam, now I see your whole affliction ; you could be happy, but that you fear another would be happier. Or rather, you could be solidly happy, but that another is to be happy in appearance. This is an evil which you must get over, or never know happiness. We will put the case, madam, that you married Crassus, and she Lorio." She answered, "Speak not of it. I could tear her eyes out at the mention of it."—" Well then, I pronounce Lorio to be the man; but I must tell you, that what we call settling in the world is, in a kind, leaving it ; and you must at once resolve to keep your thoughts of happiness within the reach of your fortune, and not measure it by comparison with others——— But, indeed, madam, when I behold that beauteous form of yours, and consider the generality of your sex, as to their disposal of themselves in marriage, or their parents doing it for them without their own approbation, I cannot but look upon all such matches as the most impudent prostitutions. Do but observe, when you are at a play, the *familiar wenches* that sit laughing among the men. These appear detestable to you in the boxes. Each of them would give up her person for a guinea ; and some of you would take the worst there for life for twenty thousand. If so, how do you differ but in price ? As to the circumstance of marriage, I take that to be hardly an alteration of the case ; for wedlock is but a more solemn prostitution, where there is not an union of minds. You would hardly believe it, but there have been designs even upon me.

"A neighbour in this very lane, who knows I have, by leading a very wary life, laid up a little money, had a great mind to marry me to his daughter. I was frequently invited to their table : the girl was always very pleasant and agreeable. After dinner, miss Molly would be sure to fill my pipe for me, and put more sugar than ordinary into my coffee ; for she was sure I was good-natured. If I chanced to hem, the mother would applaud my vigour; and has often said on that occasion, ' I wonder, Mr. Bickerstaff, you do not marry, I am sure you would have children.' Things went so far, that my mistress presented me with a *wrought* night-cap and a *laced band* of her own working. I began to think of it in earnest ; but one day, having an occasion to ride to Islington, as two or three people were lifting me upon my pad, I spied her at a convenient distance laughing at her lover, with a parcel of romps of her acquaintance. One of them, who I suppose had the same design upon me, told me she said, " Do

you see how briskly my old gentleman mounts ? "   This made
me cut off my amour, and to reflect with myself, that no
married life could be so unhappy, as where the wife proposes
no other advantage from her husband, than that of making
herself fine, and keeping her out of the dirt."

My fair client burst out a laughing at the account I gave
her of my escape, and went away seemingly convinced of the
reasonableness of my discourse to her.

FALSE PRAISE.

No. 92.   THURSDAY, November 10, 1709.   [Steele.]

Falsus honor juvat, et mendax infamia terret
Quem nisi mendosum et mendacem ?————
                                        Hor. 1 Ep. xvi.

False praise can please, and calumny affright,
None but the vicious and the hypocrite.

I know no manner of speaking so offensive as that of giving
praise, and closing it with an exception ; which proceeds (where
men do not do it to introduce malice, and make calumny more
effectual) from the common error of considering man as a perfect creature.   But, if we rightly examine things, we shall find
that there is a sort of œconomy in Providence, that one shall
excel where another is defective, in order to make men more
useful to each other, and mix them in society.   This man having this talent, and that man another, is as necessary in
conversation, as one professing one trade, and another another, is
beneficial in commerce.   The happiest climate does not produce all things ; and it was so ordered, that one part of the
earth should want the product of another, for uniting mankind
in a general correspondence and good understanding.   It is,
therefore, want of good sense as well as good nature, to say
Simplicius has a better judgment, but not so much wit as
Latius ; for that these have not each other's capacities is no
more a diminution to either, than if you should say, Simplicius

is not Latius; or Latius not Simplicius. The heathen world had so little notion that perfection was to be expected amongst men, that among them any one quality or endowment in an heroic degree made a God. Hercules had strength; but it was never objected to him that he wanted wit. Apollo presided over wit, and it was never asked whether he had strength. We hear no exceptions against the beauty of Minerva, or the wisdom of Venus. These wise heathens were glad to immortalize any one serviceable gift, and overlook all imperfections in the person who had it. But with us it is far otherwise, for we reject many eminent virtues, if they are accompanied with one apparent weakness.

The reflecting after this manner made me account for the strange delight men take in reading lampoons and scandal, with which the age abounds, and of which I receive frequent complaints. Upon mature consideration, I find it is principally for this reason, that the worst of mankind, the libellers, receive so much encouragement in the world. The low race of men take a secret pleasure in finding an eminent character levelled to their condition by a report of its defects; and keep themselves in countenance, though they are excelled in a thousand virtues, if they believe they have in common with a great person any one fault. The libeller falls in with this humour, and gratifies this baseness of temper, which is naturally an enemy to extraordinary merit. It is from this, that libel and satire are promiscuously joined together in the notions of the vulgar, though the satirist and libeller differ as much as the magistrate and the murderer. In the consideration of human life, the satirist never falls upon persons who are not glaringly faulty, and the libeller on none but who are conspicuously commendable. Were I to expose any vice in a good or great man, it should certainly be by correcting it in some one where that crime was the most distinguishing part of the character; as pages are chastised for the admonition of princes.* When it is performed otherwise, the

* This alludes to a practice long prevalent in England of whipping the royal children by proxy. The curious may find an account of this custom in Sir John Hawkins's "History of Music," vol. iii. p. 252.

vicious are kept in credit, by placing men of merit in the same
accusation. But all the pasquils, lampoons, and libels we meet
with now-a-days, are a sort of playing with the four-and-twenty
letters, and throwing them into names and characters, without
sense, truth, or wit. In this case, I am in great perplexity to
know whom they mean, and should be in distress for those
they abuse, if I did not see their judgment and ingenuity in
those they commend. This is the true way of examining a
libel ; and when men consider, that no one man living thinks
the better of their heroes and patrons for the panegyric given
them, none can think themselves lessened by their invective.
The hero or patron in a libel is but a scavenger to carry off the
dirt, and by that very employment is the filthiest creature in
the street. Dedications and panegyrics are frequently ridiculous, let them be addressed where they will ; but at the front,
or in the body of a libel, to commend a man, is saying to the
persons applauded, "My lord, or sir, I have pulled down all
men that the rest of the world think great and honourable, and
here is a clear stage ; you may, as you please, be valiant or
wise ; you may choose to be on the military or civil list ; for
there is no one brave who commands, or just who has power.
You may rule the world now it is empty, which exploded you
when it was full : I have knocked out the brains of all whom
mankind thought good for anything ; and I doubt not but you
will reward that invention, which found out the only expedient
to make your lordship, or your worship, of any consideration."
    Had I the honour to be in a libel, and had escaped the ap-
probation of the author, I should look upon it exactly in this
manner. But though it is a thing thus perfectly indifferent
who is exalted or debased in such performances, yet it is not
so with relation to the authors of them ; therefore, I shall, for
the good of my country, hereafter take upon me to punish
these wretches. What is already passed may die away according to its nature, and continue in its present oblivion ; but, for
the future, I shall take notice of such enemies to honour and
virtue, and preserve them to immortal infamy. Their names
shall give fresh offence many ages hence, and be detested a

thousand years after the commission of their crime. It shall
not avail, that these children of infamy publish their works
under feigned names, or under none at all ; for I am so perfectly well acquainted with the styles of all my contemporaries,
that I shall not fail of doing them justice, with their proper
names, and at their full length. Let these miscreants, therefore, enjoy their present act of oblivion, and take care how they
offend hereafter.

But, to avert our eyes from such objects, it is methinks but
requisite to settle our opinion in the case of praise and blame.
I believe, the only true way to cure that sensibility of reproach,
which is a common weakness with the most virtuous men, is to
fix their regard firmly upon only what is strictly true, in relation to their advantage, as well as diminution. For if I am
pleased with commendation which I do not deserve, I shall
from the same temper be concerned at scandal I do not deserve.
But he that can think of false applause with as much contempt as false detraction, will certainly be prepared for all
adventures, and will become all occasions. *Undeserved praise
can please only those who want merit, and undeserved reproach
frighten only those who want sincerity.* I have thought of this
with so much attention, that I fancy there can be no other
method in nature found for the cure of that delicacy which
gives good men pain under calumny, but placing satisfaction
no where but in a just sense of their own integrity, without
regard to the opinion of others. If we have not such a foundation as this, there is no help against scandal, but being in
obscurity, which to noble minds is not being at all. The
truth of it is, this love of praise dwells most in great and
heroic spirits ; and those who best deserve it have generally
the most exquisite relish of it. Methinks I see the renowned
Alexander, after a painful and laborious march, amidst the
heats of a parched soil and a burning climate, sitting over the
head of a fountain, and, after a draught of water, pronounce
that memorable saying, " Oh! Athenians! How much do I
suffer, that you may speak well of me ? " The Athenians were
at that time the learned of the world, and their libels against

Alexander were written, as he was a professed enemy of their state. But how monstrous would such invectives have appeared in Macedonians !

As love of reputation is a darling passion in great men, so the defence of them in this particular is the business of every man of honour and honesty. We should run on such an occasion, as if a public building was on fire, to their relief; and all who spread or publish such detestable pieces as traduce their merit should be used like incendiaries. It is the common cause of our country to support the reputation of those who preserve it against invaders; and every man is attacked in the person of that neighbour who deserves well of him.

A MONITOR.

No. 95.   THURSDAY, November 17, 1709.   [Steele.]

Interea dulces pendent circum oscula nati,
Casta pudicitiam servat domus ——
                                    Virg. Georg. ii. 523.

His cares are eas'd with intervals of bliss ;
His little children, climbing for a kiss,
Welcome their father's late return at night ;
His faithful bed is crown'd with chaste delight.

THERE are several persons who have many pleasures and entertainments in their possession, which they do not enjoy. It is, therefore, a kind and good office to acquaint them with their own happiness, and turn their attention to such instances of their good fortune as they are apt to overlook. Persons in the married state often want such a monitor; and pine away their days, by looking upon the same condition in anguish and murmur, which carries with it in the opinion of others a complication of all the pleasures of life, and a retreat from its inquietudes.

I am led into this thought by a visit I made an old friend,

who was formerly my schoolfellow. He came to town last
week with his family for the winter, and yesterday morning
sent me word his wife expected me to dinner. I am as it were
at home at that house, and every member of it knows me for
their well-wisher. I cannot indeed express the pleasure it is,
to be met by the children with so much joy as I am when I go
thither. The boys and girls strive who shall come first, when
they think it is I that am knocking at that door ; and that child
which loses the race to me runs back again to tell the father it
is Mr. Bickerstaff. This day I was led in by a pretty girl, that
we all thought must have forgot me ; for the family has been
out of town these two years. Her knowing me again was a
mighty subject with us, and took up our discourse at the first
entrance. After which, they began to rally me upon a thousand little stories they heard in the country, about my marriage to one of my neighbour's daughters. Upon which the
gentleman, my friend said, "Nay, if Mr. Bickerstaff marries a
child of any of his old companions, I hope mine shall have the
preference ; there is Mrs. Mary is *now sixteen*, and would make
him as fine a widow as the best of them. But I know him too
well ; he is so enamoured with the very memory of those who
flourished in our youth, that he will not so much as look upon
the modern beauties. I remember, old gentleman, how often
you went home in a day to refresh your countenance and dress,
when Teraminta reigned in your heart. As we came up in the
coach, I repeated to my wife some of your verses on her."
   With such reflections on little passages which happened long
ago, we passed our time, during a cheerful and elegant meal.
After dinner, his lady left the room, as did also the children.
As soon as we were alone, he took me by the hand ; "Well, my
good friend," says he, " I am heartily glad to see thee ; I was
afraid you would never have seen all the company that dined
with you to-day again. Do not you think the good woman of
the house a little altered, since you followed her from the play-
house, to find out who she was, for me ?" I perceived a tear
fall down his cheek as he spoke, which moved me not a little.
But, to turn the discourse, I said, "She is not indeed quite that

creature she was, when she returned me the letter I carried
from you ; and told me, 'she hoped, as I was a gentleman, I
would be employed no more to trouble her, who had never offended me ; but would be so much the gentleman's friend, as
to dissuade him from a pursuit, which he could never succeed
in.' You may remember, I thought her in earnest ; and you
were forced to employ your cousin Will, who made his sister
get acquainted with her, for you. You cannot expect her to
be for ever fifteen."—" Fifteen !" replied my good friend :
"Ah you little understand, you that have lived a bachelor,
how great, how exquisite a pleasure there is, in being really
beloved ! It is impossible, that the most beauteous face in
nature should raise in me such pleasing ideas, as when I look
upon that excellent woman. That fading in her countenance
is chiefly caused by her watching with me, in my fever. This
was followed by a fit of sickness, which had like to have carried her off last winter. I tell you sincerely, I have so many
obligations to her, that I cannot, with any sort of moderation,
think of her present state of health. But as to what you say
of fifteen, she gives me every day pleasures beyond what I ever
knew in the possession of her beauty, when I was in the vigour
of youth. Every moment of her life brings me fresh instances
of her complacency to my inclinations, and her prudence in
regard to my fortune. Her face is to me much more beautiful
than when I first saw it ; there is no decay in any feature,
which I cannot trace, from the very instant it was occasioned
by some anxious concern for my welfare and interests. Thus,
at the same time, methinks, the love I conceived towards her
for what she was is heightened by my gratitude for what she
is. The love of a wife is as much above the idle passion commonly called by that name, as the loud laughter of buffoons is
inferior to the elegant mirth of gentlemen. Oh ! she is an
inestimable jewel. In her examination of her household affairs,
she shews a certain fearfulness to find a fault, which makes her
servants obey her like children ; and the meanest we have has
an ingenuous shame for an offence, not always to be seen in
children in other families. I speak freely to you, my old friend ;

ever since her sickness, things that gave me the quickest joy
before turn now to a certain anxiety. As the children play in
the next room, I know the poor things by their steps, and am
considering what they must do, should they lose their mother
in their tender years. The pleasure I used to take in telling
my boy stories of battles, and asking my girl questions about
the disposal of her baby, and the gossiping of it, is turned into
inward reflection and melancholy."

He would have gone on in this tender way, when the good
lady entered, and with an inexpressible sweetness in her countenance told us, " she had been searching her closet for something very good, to treat such an old friend as I was." Her
husband's eyes sparkled with pleasure at the cheerfulness of her
countenance ; and I saw all his fears vanish in an instant. The
lady observing something in our looks which shewed we had
been more serious than ordinary, and seeing her husband
receive her with great concern under a forced cheerfulness, immediately guessed at what we had been talking of; and applying herself to me, said, with a smile, " Mr. Bickerstaff, do not
believe a word of what he tells you ; I shall still live to have
you for my second, as I have often promised you, unless he
takes more care of himself than he has done since his coming to
town. You must know, he tells me that he finds London is a
much more healthy place than the country ; for he sees several
of his old acquaintance and schoolfellows are here *young fellows
with fair full-bottomed periwigs.* I could scarce keep him this
morning from going out *open breasted.*" My friend, who is
always extremely delighted with her agreeable humour, made
her sit down with us. She did it with that easiness which is
peculiar to women of sense ; and, to keep up the good humour
she had brought in with her, turned her raillery upon me.
" Mr. Bickerstaff, you remember you followed me one night
from the play-house ; suppose you should carry me thither to-
morrow night, and lead me into the front-box." This put us
into a long field of discourse about the beauties, who were
mothers to the present, and shined in the boxes twenty years
ago. I told her, " I was glad she had transferred so many of

her charms, and I did not question but her eldest daughter was within half a year of being a Toast."

We were pleasing ourselves with this fantastical preferment of the young lady, when on a sudden we were alarmed with the noise of a drum, and immediately entered my little godson to give me a point of war. His mother, between laughing and chiding, would have put him out of the room ; but I would not part with him so. I found upon conversation with him, though he was a little noisy in his mirth, that the child had excellent parts, and was a great master of all the learning on the other side eight years old. I perceived him a very great historian in Æsop's Fables ; but he frankly declared to me his mind, "that he did not delight in that learning, because he did not believe they were true ; " for which reason I found he had very much *turned* his studies, for about a twelve-month past, into the lives and adventures of don Bellianis of Greece, Guy of Warwick, the Seven Champions, and other historians of that age. I could not but observe the satisfaction the father took in the forwardness of his son ; and that these diversions might turn to some profit, I found the boy had made remarks, which might be of service to him during the course of his whole life. He would tell you the mismanagements of John Hickathrift, find fault with the passionate temper in Bevis of Southampton, and loved Saint George for being the champion of England ; and by this means had his thoughts insensibly moulded into the notions of discretion, virtue, and honour. I was extolling his accomplishments, when the mother told me, "that the little girl who led me in this morning was in her way a better scholar than he. Betty, says she, "deals chiefly in fairies and sprights ; and sometimes in a winter-night will terrify the maids with her accounts, until they are afraid to go up to bed."

I sat with them until it was very late, sometimes in merry, sometimes in serious discourse, with this particular pleasure, which gives the only true relish to all conversation, a sense that every one of us liked each other. I went home, considering the different conditions of a married life and that of a bachelor ; and I must confess it struck me with a secret concern, to reflect, that whenever I go off I shall leave no traces behind me.

DEAD MEN.

No. 96. SATURDAY, November 19, 1709. [Addison.]

Is mihi demum vivere et frui animâ videtur, qui aliquo negotio intentus, præclari facinoris aut artis bonæ famam querit.—SALL. Bell. Cat.

In my opinion, he only may be truly said to live, and enjoy his being, who is engaged in some laudable pursuit, and acquires a name by some illustrious action, or useful art.

IT has cost me very much care and thought to marshal and fix the people under their proper denominations, and to range them according to their respective characters. These my endeavours have been received with unexpected success in one kind, but neglected in another : for though I have many readers, I have but few converts. This must certainly proceed from a false opinion, that what I write is designed rather to amuse and entertain, than convince and instruct. I entered upon my Essays with a declaration that I should consider mankind in quite another manner than they had hitherto been represented to the ordinary world ; and asserted, that none but an useful life should be, with me, any life at all. But, lest this doctrine should have made this small progress towards the conviction of mankind, because it may have appeared to the unlearned light and whimsical, I must take leave to unfold the wisdom and antiquity of my first proposition in these my Essays, to wit, that "every worthless man is a dead man." This notion is as old as Pythagoras, in whose school it was a point of discipline, that if among the ʼΑκδѕικοί, or probationers, there were any who grew weary of studying to be useful, and returned to an idle life, they were to regard them as dead ; and, upon their departing, to perform their obsequies, and raise them tombs, with inscriptions to warn others of the like mortality, and quicken them to resolutions of refining their souls above that wretched state.   It is upon a like supposition, that young ladies, at this very time, in Roman Catholic countries, are received into some nunneries with their coffins, and with the pomp of a formal funeral, to signify, that hence-forth they are to be of no farther use, and consequently dead. Nor was Pythagoras himself the first author of this symbol, with whom, and with the Hebrews, it was generally received. Much more might be offered in illustration of this doctrine from sacred authority, which I recommend to my reader's own reflection ; who will easily recollect, from places which I do not think fit to quote here, the forcible manner of applying the word *dead* and *living*, to men as they are good or bad.

I have, therefore, composed the following scheme of existence for the benefit both of the living and the dead ; though chiefly for the latter, whom I must desire to read it with all possible attention.   In the number of the dead I comprehend all per-sons, of what title or dignity soever, who bestow most of their time in eating and drinking, to support that imaginary exist-ence of theirs, which they call life ; or in dressing and adorn-ing those shadows and apparitions, which are looked upon by the vulgar as real men and women.   In short, whoever resides in the world without having any business in it, and passes away an age without ever thinking on the errand for which he was sent hither, is to me a dead man to all intents and purposes ; and I desire that he may be so reputed.   The living are only those that are some way or other laudably employed in the improvement of their own minds, or for the advantage of others ; and even amongst these, I shall only reckon into their lives that part of their time which has been spent in the manner above mentioned.   By these means, I am afraid, we shall find the longest lives not to consist of many months, and the greatest part of the earth to be quite unpeopled.   Accord-ing to this system we may observe, that some men are born at twenty years of age, some at thirty, some at threescore, and some not above an hour before they die : nay, we may observe

multitudes that die without ever being born, as well as many
dead persons that fill up the bulk of mankind, and make a
better figure in the eyes of the ignorant, than those who are
alive, and in their proper and full state of health.   However,
since there may be many good subjects, that pay their taxes,
and live peaceably in their habitations, who are not yet born,
or have departed this life several years since, my design is, to
encourage both to join themselves as soon as possible to the
number of the living.

AN ALLEGORY.

No. 97.   TUESDAY, November 22, 1709.   [Addison.]

Illud maximè rarum genus est eorum, qui aut excellente ingenii magni-
tudine, aut præclarâ eruditione atque doctrinâ, aut utrâque re ornati, spatium
deliberandi habuerunt,   quem   potissimùm   vitæ   cursum   sequi   vellent.—
Tull. Offic.

There are very few persons of extraordinary genius, or eminent for learning
and other noble endowments, who have had sufficient time to consider what
particular course of life they ought to pursue.

Having swept away prodigious multitudes in my last
paper, and brought a great destruction upon my own species, I
must endeavour in this to raise fresh recruits, and, if possible,
to supply the places of the unborn and the deceased.   It is
said of Xerxes, that when he stood upon a hill, and saw the
whole country round him covered with his army, he burst out
into tears, to think that not one of that multitude would be
alive an hundred years after.   For my part, when I take a
survey of this populous city, I can scarce forbear weeping, to
see how few of its inhabitants are now living.   It was with
this thought that I drew up my last bill of mortality, and
endeavoured to set out in it the great number of persons who
have perished by a distemper, commonly known by the name
of idleness, which has long raged in the world, and destroys

more in every great town than the plague has done at Dant-
zick.* To repair the mischief it has done, and stock the world
with a better race of mortals, I have more hopes of bringing to
life those that are young, than of reviving those that are old.
For which reason, I shall here set down that noble allegory
which was written by an old author called Prodicus, but recommended and embellished by Socrates. It is the description
of Virtue and Pleasure, making their court to Hercules under
the appearance of two beautiful women.

When Hercules, says the divine moralist, was in that part of
his youth, in which it was natural for him to consider what
course of life he ought to pursue, he one day retired into a
desert, where the silence and solitude of the place very much
favoured his meditations. As he was musing on his present
condition, and very much perplexed in himself on the state of
life he should choose, he saw two women of a larger stature
than ordinary approaching towards him. One of them had a
very noble air, and graceful deportment ; her beauty was
natural and easy, her person clean and unspotted, her eyes cast
towards the ground with an agreeable reserve, her motion and
behaviour full of modesty, and her raiment as white as snow.
The other had a great deal of health and floridness in her
countenance, which she had helped with an artificial white and
red ; and endeavoured to appear more graceful than ordinary
in her mien, by a mixture of affectation in all her gestures.
She had a wonderful confidence and assurance in her looks, and
all the variety of colours in her dress that she thought were
most proper to shew her complexion to an advantage. She
cast her eyes upon herself, then turned them on those that
were present, to see how they liked her, and often looked on
the figure she made in her own shadow. Upon her nearer
approach to Hercules, she stepped before the other lady, who
came forward with a regular composed carriage, and running
up to him, accosted him after the following manner :

" My dear Hercules," says she, " I find you are very much

* In 1709 Dantzic was visited by the plague, which swept off above 40,000
of its inhabitants.

divided in your own thoughts, upon the way of life that you ought to choose. Be my friend, and follow me ; I will lead you into the possession of pleasure, and out of the reach of pain, and remove you from all the noise and disquietude of business. The affairs of either war or peace shall have no power to disturb you. Your whole employment shall be, to make your life easy, and to entertain every sense with its proper gratification. Sumptuous tables, beds of roses, clouds of perfumes, concerts of music, crowds of beauties, are all in readiness to receive you. Come along with me into this region of delights, this world of pleasure, and bid farewell for ever to care, to pain, to business."

Hercules, hearing the lady talk after this manner, desired to know her name ; to which she answered, " My friends, and those who are well acquainted with me, call me Happiness ; but my enemies, and those who would injure my reputation, have given me the name of Pleasure."

By this time the other lady was come up, who addressed herself to the young hero in a very different manner.

"Hercules," says she, " I offer myself to you, because I know you are descended from the Gods, and give proofs of that descent by your love to virtue, and application to the studies proper for your age. This makes me hope you will gain both for yourself and me an immortal reputation. But, before I invite you into my society and friendship, I will be open and sincere with you, and must lay down this as an established truth, That *there is nothing truly valuable, which can be purchased without pains and labour*. The Gods have set a price upon every real and noble pleasure. If you would gain the favour of the Deity, you must be at the pains of worshipping him ; if the friendship of good men, you must study to oblige them ; if you would be honoured by your country, you must take care to serve it. In short, if you would be eminent in war or peace, you must become master of all the qualifications that can make you so. These are the only terms and conditions upon which I can propose happiness." The Goddess of Pleasure here broke in upon her discourse. " You see,"

said she, " Hercules, by her own confession, the way to her
pleasure is long and difficult, whereas that which I propose is
short and easy."—"Alas !" said the other lady, whose visage
glowed with a passion made up of scorn and pity, "what are
the pleasures you propose ?　To eat before you are hungry,
drink before you are a-thirst, sleep before you are a-tired, to
gratify appetites before they are raised, and raise such appetites
as nature never planted.　You never heard the most delicious
music, which is the praise of one's self ; nor saw the most
beautiful object, which is the work of one's own hands.　Your
votaries pass away their youth in a dream of mistaken
pleasures, while they are hoarding up anguish, torment, and
remorse for old age.

" As for me, I am the friend of the Gods and of good men,
an agreeable companion to the artizan, an household guardian
to the fathers of families, a patron and protector of servants,
an associate in all true and generous friendships.　The banquets
of my votaries are never costly, but always delicious ; for none
eat or drink at them who are not invited by hunger and thirst.
Their slumbers are sound, and their wakings cheerful.　My young
men have the pleasure of hearing themselves praised by those
who are in years ; and those who are in years, of being honoured
by those who are young.　In a word, my followers are favoured
by the Gods, beloved by their acquaintance, esteemed by
their country, and, after the close of their labours, honoured by
posterity."

We know by the life of this memorable hero, to which of
these two ladies he gave up his heart ; and I believe, every
one who reads this will do him the justice to approve his
choice.

I very much admire the speeches of these ladies, as containing in them the chief arguments for a life of virtue, or a life of
pleasure, that could enter into the thoughts of an heathen ;
but am particularly pleased with the different figures he gives
the two Goddesses.　Our modern authors have represented
Pleasure or Vice with an alluring face, but ending in snakes
and monsters.　Here she appears in all the charms of beauty,

though they are all false and borrowed ; and by that means composes a vision entirely natural and pleasing.

I have translated this allegory for the benefit of the youth of Great Britain ; and particularly of those who are still in the deplorable state of non-existence, and whom I most earnestly intreat to come into the world. Let my embrios shew the least inclination to any single virtue, and I shall allow it to be a struggling towards birth. I do not expect of them that, like the hero in the foregoing story, they should go about as soon as they are born, with a club in their hands, and a lion's skin on their shoulders, to root out monsters, and destroy tyrants ; but, as the finest author of all antiquity has said upon this very occasion, though a man has not the abilities to distinguish himself in the most shining parts of a great character, he has certainly the capacity of being just, faithful, modest, and temperate.

A VISION.

No. 100. TUESDAY, November 29, 1709. [Addison.]

Jam redit et Virgo, redeunt Saturnia regna.—Virg. Ecl. iv. ver. 6.
Returning justice brings a golden age.

I was last week taking a solitary walk in the garden of Lincoln's-Inn (a favour that is indulged me by several of the benchers, who are my intimate friends, and grown old with me in this neighbourhood) when, according to the nature of men in years, who have made but little progress in the advancement of their fortune or their fame, I was repining at the sudden rise of many persons who are my juniors, and indeed at the unequal distribution of wealth, honour, and all other blessings of life. I was lost in this thought, when the night came upon me, and drew my mind into a far more agreeable contemplation. The heaven above me appeared in all its glories, and presented me with such an hemisphere of stars, as made the most agreeable prospect imaginable to one who delights in the study of nature. It happened to be a freezing night, which had purified the whole body of air into such a bright transparent æther, as made every constellation visible ; and at the same time gave such a particular glowing to the stars, that I thought it the richest sky I had ever seen. I could not behold a scene so wonderfully adorned and lighted up, if I may be allowed that expression, without suitable meditations on the author of such illustrious and amazing objects : for on these occasions, philosophy suggests motives to religion, and religion adds pleasure to philosophy.

As soon as I had recovered my usual temper and serenity of soul, I retired to my lodgings, with the satisfaction of having passed away a few hours in the proper employments of a reasonable creature ; and promising myself that my slumbers would be sweet, I no sooner fell into them, but I dreamed a dream, or saw a vision, for I know not which to call it, that seemed to rise out of my evening-meditation, and had something in it so solemn and serious, that I cannot forbear communicating it ; though, I must confess, the wildness of imagination, which in a dream is always loose and irregular, discovers itself too much in several parts of it.

Methought I saw the same azure sky diversified with the same glorious luminaries which had entertained me a little before I fell asleep. I was looking very attentively on that sign in the heavens which is called by the name of the Balance,* when on a sudden there appeared in it an extraordinary light, as if the sun should rise at midnight. By its increasing in breadth and lustre, I soon found that it approached towards the earth ; and at length could discern something like a shadow hovering in the midst of a great glory, which in a little time

---

* Libra, or the Balance, is next to the sign Virgo, into which Astræa, the goddess of justice, was translated, when she could no longer stay on earth.

after I distinctly perceived to be the figure of a woman. I fancied at first it might have been the angel, or intelligence that guided the constellation from which it descended ; but, upon a nearer view, I saw about her all the emblems with which the goddess of justice is usually described. Her countenance was unspeakably awful and majestic, but exquisitely beautiful to those whose eyes were strong enough to behold it ; her smiles transported with rapture, her frowns terrified to despair. She held in her hand a mirror, endowed with the same qualities as that which the painters put into the hand of truth.

There streamed from it a light, which distinguished itself from all the splendours that surrounded her, more than a flash of lightning shines in the midst of day-light. As she moved it in her hand, it brightened the heavens, the air, or the earth. When she had descended so low as to be seen and heard by mortals, to make the pomp of her appearance more supportable, she threw darkness and clouds about her, that tempered the light into a thousand beautiful shades and colours, and multiplied that lustre, which was before too strong and dazzling, into a variety of milder glories.

In the meantime, the world was in an alarm, and all the inhabitants of it gathered together upon a spacious plain ; so that I seemed to have the whole species before my eyes. A voice was heard from the clouds, declaring the intention of this visit, which was to restore and appropriate to every one living what was his due. The fear and hope, joy and sorrow, which appeared in that great assembly, after this solemn declaration, are not to be expressed. The first edict was then pronounced, " That all titles and claims to riches and estates, or to any part of them, should be immediately vested in the rightful owner." Upon this, the inhabitants of the earth held up the instruments of their tenure, whether in parchment, paper, wax, or any other form of conveyance ; and as the goddess moved the mirror of truth which she held in her hand, so that the light which flowed from it fell upon the multitude, they examined the several instruments by the beams of it. The rays of this mirror had a particular quality of setting fire to all forgery and falsehood. The blaze of papers, the melting of seals, and crackling of parchments, made a very odd scene. The fire very often ran through two or three lines only, and then stopped. Though I could not but observe that the flames chiefly broke out among the interlineations and codicils ; the light of the mirror, as it was turned up and down, pierced into all the dark corners and recesses of the universe, and by that means detected many writings and records which had been hidden or buried by time, chance, or design. This occasioned a wonderful revolution among the people. At the same time, the spoils of extortion, fraud, and robbery, with all the fruits of bribery and corruption, were thrown together into a prodigious pile, that almost reached to the clouds, and was called " The mount of restitution ; " to which all injured persons were invited, to receive what belonged to them.

One might see crowds of people in tattered garments come up, and change cloaths with others that were dressed with lace and embroidery. Several who were *Plums,* or very near it, became men of moderate fortunes ; and many others, who were overgrown in wealth and possessions, had no more left than what they usually spent. What moved my concern most was, to see a certain street of the greatest credit in Europe.* from one end to the other become bankrupt.

The next command was, for the whole body of mankind to separate themselves into their proper families ; which was no sooner done, but an edict was issued out, requiring all children " to repair to their true and natural fathers." This put a great part of the assembly in motion ; for as the mirror was moved over them, it inspired everyone with such a natural instinct, as directed them to their real parents. It was a very melancholy spectacle to see the fathers of very large families become childless, and bachelors undone by a charge of sons and daughters. You might see a presumptive heir of a great estate ask blessing of his coachman, and a celebrated toast paying her duty to a *valet de chambre.* Many, under vows of celibacy, appeared

---

* Alluding to the bankers in Lombard Street.

surrounded with a numerous issue. This change of parentage
would have caused great lamentation, but that the calamity was
pretty common ; and that generally those who lost their
children, had the satisfaction of seeing them put into the
hands of their dearest friends. Men were no sooner settled in
their right to their possessions and their progeny, but there
was a third order proclaimed, "That all the posts of dignity
and honour in the universe should be conferred on persons of
the greatest merit, abilities, and perfection." The handsome,
the strong, and the wealthy, immediately pressed forward ; but,
not being able to bear the splendour of the mirror, which
played upon their faces, they immediately fell back among the
crowd : but as the goddess tried the multitude by her glass, as
the eagle does its young ones by the lustre of the sun, it was
remarkable, that everyone turned away his face from it, who
had not distinguished himself either by virtue, knowledge, or
capacity in business, either military or civil. This select
assembly was drawn up in the centre of a prodigious multitude,
which was diffused on all sides, and stood observing them, as
idle people use to gather about a regiment that are exercising
their arms. They were drawn up in three bodies : in the first,
were the men of virtue ; in the second, men of knowledge ; and
in the third, the men of business. It was impossible to look
at the first column without a secret veneration, their aspects
were so sweetened with humanity, raised with contemplation,
emboldened with resolution, and adorned with the most agreeable airs, which are those that proceed from secret habits of
virtue. I could not but take notice, that there were many faces
among them which were unknown, not only to the multitude,
but even to several of their own body.

In the second column, consisting of the men of knowledge,
there had been great disputes before they fell into the ranks,
which they did not do at last without the positive command of
the goddess who presided over the assembly. She had so
ordered it, that men of the greatest genius and strongest sense
were placed at the head of the column. Behind these were
such as had formed their minds very much on the thoughts

and writings of others. In the rear of the column were men who had more wit than sense, or more learning than understanding. All living authors of any value were ranged in one of these classes ; but, I must confess, I was very much surprised to see a great body of editors, critics, commentators, and grammarians, meet with so very ill a reception. They had formed themselves into a body, and with a great deal of arrogance demanded the first station in the column of knowledge ; but the goddess, instead of complying with their request, clapped them all into liveries, and bid them know themselves for no other but lacquies of the learned.

The third column were men of business, and consisting of persons in military and civil capacities. The former marched out from the rest, and placed themselves in the front ; at which the others shook their heads at them, but did not think fit to dispute the post with them. I could not but make several observations upon this last column of people ; but I have certain private reasons why I do not think fit to communicate them to the public. In order to fill up all the posts of honour, dignity, and profit, there was a draught made out of each column of men, who were masters of all three qualifications in some degree, and were preferred to stations of the first rank. The second draught was made out of such as were possessed of any two of the qualifications, who were disposed of in stations of a second dignity. Those who were left, and were endowed only with one of them, had their suitable posts. When this was over, there remained many places of trust and profit unfilled, for which there were fresh draughts made out of the surrounding multitude, who had any appearance of these excellences, or were recommended by those who possessed them in reality.

All were surprised to see so many new faces in the most eminent dignities ; and for my own part, I was very well pleased to see that all my friends either kept their present posts, or were advanced to higher.

Having filled my paper with those particulars of my vision which concern the male part of mankind, I must reserve for another occasion the sequel of it, which relates to the fair sex.

A CONTINUATION OF

THE VISION.

No. 102. SATURDAY, December 3, 1709. [Addison.]

The male world were dismissed by the goddess of justice,
and disappeared, when on a sudden the whole plain was
covered with women. So charming a multitude filled my
heart with unspeakable pleasure ; and as the celestial light of
the mirror shone upon their faces, several of them seemed
rather persons that descended in the train of the goddess, than
such who were brought before her to their trial. The clack of
tongues, and confusion of voices, in this new assembly, were
so very great, that the goddess was forced to command silence
several times, and with some severity, before she could make
them attentive to her edicts. They were all sensible that the
most important affair among woman-kind was then to be
settled, which every one knows to be the point of *place*. This
had raised innumerable disputes among them, and put the
whole sex into a tumult. Every one produced her claim, and
pleaded her pretensions. *Birth, beauty, wit*, or *wealth*, were
words that rung in my ears from all parts of the plain. Some
boasted of the merit of their husbands ; others of their own
power in governing them. Some pleaded their unspotted
virginity ; others their numerous issue. Some valued themselves as they were the mothers, and others as they were the
daughters, of considerable persons. There was not a single
accomplishment unmentioned, or unpractised. The whole
congregation was full of singing, dancing, tossing, ogling,
squeaking, smiling, fighting, fanning, frowning, and all those
irresistible arts which women put in practice, to captivate the
hearts of reasonable creatures. The goddess, to end this
dispute, caused it to be proclaimed, " that everyone should
take place according as she was more or less beautiful." This
declaration gave great satisfaction to the whole assembly,

which immediately bridled up, and appeared in all its beauties. Such as believed themselves graceful in their motion found an occasion of falling back, advancing forward, or making a false step, that they might show their persons in the most becoming air. Such as had fine necks and bosoms were wonderfully curious to look over the heads of the multitude, and observe the most distant parts of the assembly. Several clapt their hands on their foreheads, as helping their sight to look upon the glories that surrounded the goddess, but in reality to shew fine hands and arms. The ladies were yet better pleased, when they heard "that, in the decision of this great controversy, each of them should be her own judge, and take her place according to her own opinion of herself, when she consulted her looking-glass."

The goddess then let down the mirror of truth in a golden chain, which appeared larger in proportion as it descended and approached nearer to the eyes of the beholders. It was the particular property of this looking-glass, to banish all false appearances, and shew people what they are. The whole woman was represented, without regard to the usual external features, which were made entirely conformable to their real characters. In short, the most accomplished, taking in the whole circle of female perfections, were the most beautiful; and the most defective, the most deformed. The goddess so varied the motion of the glass, and placed it in so many different lights, that each had an opportunity of seeing herself in it.

It is impossible to describe the rage, the pleasure, or astonishment, that appeared in each face upon its representation in the mirror ; multitudes started at their own form, and would have broke the glass if they could have reached it. Many saw their blooming features wither as they looked upon them, and their self-admiration turned into a loathing and abhorrence. The lady who was thought so agreeable in her anger, and was so often celebrated for a woman of fire and spirit, was frighted at her own image, and fancied she saw a Fury in the glass. The interested mistress beheld a Harpy, and the subtle

jilt a Sphinx.   I was very much troubled in my own heart, to
see such a destruction of fine faces ; but at the same time had
the pleasure of seeing several improved, which I had before
looked upon as the greatest master-piece of nature. I observed,
that some few were so humble as to be surprised at their own
charms, and that many a one, who had lived in the retirement
and severity of a Vestal, shined forth in all the graces and
attractions of a Siren.   I was ravished at the sight of a particular image in the mirror, which I think the most beautiful
object that my eyes ever beheld.   There was something more
than human in her countenance ; her eyes were so full of light,
that they seemed to beautify everything they looked upon.
Her face was enlivened with such a florid bloom, as did not so
properly seem the mark of health, as of immortality.   Her
shape, her stature, and her mien, were such as distinguished
her even there, where the whole fair sex was assembled.

I was impatient to see the lady represented by so divine an
image, whom I found to be the person that stood at my right
hand, and in the same point of view with myself.   This was a
little old woman, who in her prime had been about five feet
high, though at present shrunk to about three quarters of
that measure.   Her natural aspect was puckered up with
wrinkles, and her head covered with gray hairs.   I had
observed all along an innocent cheerfulness in her face, which
was now heightened into rapture, as she beheld herself in the
glass.   It was an odd circumstance in my dream, but I cannot
forbear relating it, I conceived so great an inclination towards
her, that I had thoughts of discoursing her upon the point of
marriage, when on a sudden she was carried from me ; for the
word was now given, that all who were pleased with their own
images should separate, and place themselves at the head of
their sex.

This detachment was afterwards divided into three bodies,
consisting of maids, wives, and widows; the wives being
placed in the middle, with the maids on the right, and widows
on the left, though it was with difficulty that these two last
bodies were hindered from falling into the centre.   This

separation of those who liked their real selves not having
lessened the number of the main body so considerably as it
might have been wished, the goddess, after having drawn up
her mirror, thought fit to make new distinctions among those
who did not like the figure which they saw in it. She made
several wholesome edicts, which are slipped out of my mind ;
but there were two which dwelt upon me, as being very extraordinary in their kind, and executed with great severity
Their design was, to make an example of two extremes in the
female world ; of those who are very severe on the conduct of
others, and of those who are very regardless of their own. The
first sentence, therefore, the goddess pronounced was, that all
females addicted to censoriousness and detraction should lose
the use of speech ; a punishment which would be the most
grievous to the offender, and, what should be the end of all
punishments, effectual for rooting out the crime. Upon this
edict, which was as soon executed as published, the noise of
the assembly very considerably abated. It was a melancholy
spectacle, to see so many who had the reputation of rigid virtue
struck dumb. A lady who stood by me, and saw my concern,
told me, " she wondered how I could be concerned for such a
pack of ——." I found, by the shaking of her head, she was
going to give me their characters ; but, by her saying no more,
I perceived she had lost the command of her tongue. This
calamity fell very heavy upon that part of women who are
distinguished by the name of Prudes, a courtly word for female
hypocrites, who have a short way to being virtuous, by showing
that others are vicious. The second sentence was then pronounced against the loose part of the sex, that all should
immediately be pregnant, who in any part of their lives had
run the hazard of it. This produced a very goodly appearance, and revealed so many misconducts, that made those who
were lately struck dumb repine more than ever at their want
of utterance ; though at the same time, as afflictions seldom
come single, many of the mutes were also seized with this new
calamity. The ladies were now in such a condition, that they
would have wanted room, had not the plain been large enough

N

to let them divide their ground, and extend their lines on all
sides.   It was a sensible affliction to me, to see such a multitude of fair ones, either dumb or big-bellied.   But I was something more at ease, when I found that they agreed upon several
regulations to cover such misfortunes.   Among others, that it
should be an established maxim in all nations, that a woman's
first child might come into the world within six months after
her acquaintance with her husband ; and that grief might
retard the birth of her last until fourteen months after his
decease.

This vision lasted until my usual hour of waking, which I
did with some surprise, to find myself alone, after having been
engaged almost a whole night in so prodigious a multitude.   I
could not but reflect with wonder at the partiality and
extravagance of my vision ; which, according to my thoughts,
has not done justice to the sex.   If virtue in men is more
venerable, it is in women more lovely ; which Milton has very
finely expressed in his Paradise Lost, where Adam, speaking of
Eve, after having asserted his own pre-eminence, as being first
in creation and internal faculties, breaks out into the following
rapture :

—— Yet when I approach
Her loveliness, so absolute she seems,
And in herself compleat, so well to know
Her own, that what she wills, or do, or say,
Seems wisest, virtuousest, discreetest, best.
All higher knowledge in her presence falls
Degraded, wisdom in discourse with her
Loses discountenanc'd, and like folly shews.
Authority and reason on her wait,
As one intended first, not after made
Occasionally.   And, to consummate all,
Greatness of mind, and nobleness, their seat
Build in her loveliest, and create an awe
About her, as a guard angelic plac'd.

MRS. TRANQUILLUS.

No. 104. THURSDAY, December 8, 1709. [Steele.]

—— Garrit aniles
Ex re fabellas————.   Hor. 2 Sat. vi. 78.

He tells an old wife's tale very pertinently.

My brother Tranquillus being gone out of town for some
days, my sister Jenny sent me word she would come and dine
with me, and therefore desired me to have no other company.
I took care accordingly, and was not a little pleased to see her
enter the room with a decent and matron-like behaviour, which
I thought very much became her. I saw she had a great deal
to say to me, and easily discovered in her eyes, and the air of
her countenance, that she had abundance of satisfaction in her
heart, which she longed to communicate. However, I was
resolved to let her break into her discourse her own way, and
reduced her to a thousand little devices and intimations to
bring me to the mention of her husband. But, finding I was
resolved not to name him, she began of her own accord. "My
husband," said she, "gives his humble service to you ; " to
which I only answered, "I hope he is well ; " and, without
waiting for a reply, fell into other subjects. She at last was
out of all patience, and said, with a smile and manner that I
thought had more beauty and spirit than I had ever observed
before in her, "I did not think, brother, you had been so ill-
natured. You have seen, ever since I came in, that I had a
mind to talk of my husband, and you will not be so kind as to
give me an occasion."—"I did not know," said I, "but it might
be a disagreeable subject to you. You do not take me for so
old-fashioned a fellow as to think of entertaining a young
lady with the discourse of her husband. I know, nothing is
more acceptable than to speak of one who is to be so ; but to
speak of one who is so ! indeed, Jenny, I am a better bred man
than you think me." She shewed a little dislike at my raillery ; and, by her bridling up, I perceived she expected to be

N 2

treated hereafter not as Jenny Distaff, but Mrs. Tranquillus. I was very well pleased with this change in her humour; and, upon talking with her on several subjects, I could not but fancy that I saw a great deal of her husband's way and manner in her remarks, her phrases, the tone of her voice, and the very air of her countenance. This gave me an unspeakable satisfaction, not only because I had found her an husband, from whom she could learn many things that were laudable, but also because I looked upon her imitation of him as an infallible sign that she entirely loved him.

This is an observation that I never knew fail, though I do not remember that any other has made it. The natural shyness of her sex hindered her from telling me the greatness of her own passion; but I easily collected it from the representation she gave me of his. "I have everything," says she, "in Tranquillus, that I can wish for; and enjoy in him, what indeed you have told me were to be met with in a good husband, the fondness of a lover, the tenderness of a parent, and the intimacy of a friend." It transported me to see her eyes swimming in tears of affection when she spoke. "And is there not, dear sister," said I, "more pleasure in the possession of such a man, than in all the little impertinences of balls, assemblies, and equipage, which it cost me so much pains to make you contemn?" She answered, smiling, "Tranquillus has made me a sincere convert in a few weeks, though I am afraid you could not have done it in your whole life. To tell you truly, I have only one fear hanging upon me, which is apt to give me trouble in the midst of all my satisfactions: I am afraid, you must know, that I shall not always make the same amiable appearance in his eye that I do at present. You know, brother Bickerstaff, that you have the reputation of a conjurer; and if you have any one secret in your art to make your sister always beautiful, I should be happier than if I were mistress of all the worlds you have shown me in a starry night."—"Jenny," said I, "without having recourse to magic, I shall give you one plain rule, that will not fail of making you always amiable to a man who has so great a passion for you, and is of so equal and reasonable a temper as Tranquillus. Endeavour to please, and you must please ; be always in the same disposition as you are when you ask for this secret, and you may take my word, you will never want it. An inviolable fidelity, good humour, and complacency of temper, out-live all the charms of a fine face, and make the decays of it invisible."

We discoursed very long upon this head, which was equally agreeable to us both ; for I must confess, as I tenderly love her, I take as much pleasure in giving her instructions for her welfare, as she herself does in receiving them. I proceeded, therefore, to inculcate these sentiments, by relating a very particular passage that happened within my own knowledge.

There were several of us making merry at a friend's house in a country village, when the sexton of the parish church entered the room in a sort of surprise, and told us, " that as he was digging a grave in the chancel, a little blow of his pick-axe opened a decayed coffin, in which there were several written papers." Our curiosity was immediately raised, so that we went to the place where the sexton had been at work, and found a great concourse of people about the grave. Among the rest, there was an old woman, who told us, the person buried there was a lady whose name I do not think fit to mention, though there is nothing in the story but what tends very much to her honour. This lady lived several years an exemplary pattern of conjugal love, and, dying soon after her husband, who every way answered her character in virtue and affection, made it her death-bed request, " that all the letters which she had received from him both before and after her marriage should be buried in the coffin with her." These, I found upon examination, were the papers before us. Several of them had suffered so much by time, that I could only pick out a few words ; as *my soul! lilies! roses! dearest angel!* and the like. One of them, which was legible throughout, ran thus :

" MADAM,

" If you would know the greatness of my love, con-sider that of your own beauty. That blooming countenance, that snowy bosom, that graceful person, return every moment to my imagination : the brightness of your eyes hath hindered me from closing mine since I last saw you. You may still add to your beauties by a smile. A frown will make me the most wretched of men, as I am the most passionate of lovers."

It filled the whole company with a deep melancholy, to compare the description of the letter with the person that occasioned it, who was now reduced to a few crumbling bones and a little mouldering heap of earth. With much ado I decyphered another letter, which began with, "My dear, dear wife." This gave me a curiosity to see how the style of one written in marriage differed from one written in courtship. To my surprise, I found the fondness rather augmented than lessened, though the panegyric turned upon a different accomplishment. The words were as follows :

"Before this short absence from you, I did not know that I loved you so much as I really do ; though, at the same time, I thought I loved you as much as possible. I am under great apprehension, lest you should have any uneasiness whilst I am defrauded of my share in it, and cannot think of tasting any pleasures that you do not partake with me. Pray, my dear, be careful of your health, if for no other reason, but because you know I could not outlive you. It is natural in absence to make professions of an inviolable constancy ; but towards so much merit, it is scarce a virtue, especially when it is but a bare return to that of which you have given me such continued proofs ever since our first acquaintance. I am, &c."

It happened that the daughter of these two excellent persons was by when I was reading this letter. At the sight of the coffin, in which was the body of her mother, near that of her father, she melted into a flood of tears. As I had heard a great character of her virtue, and observed in her this instance of filial piety, I could not resist my natural inclination of giving advice to young people, and therefore addressed myself to her. "Young lady," said I, "you see how short is the possession of that beauty, in which nature has been so liberal to you. You find the melancholy sight before you is a contradiction to the first letter that you heard on that subject; whereas you may observe, the second letter, which celebrates your mother's constancy, is itself, being found in this place, an argument of it. But, madam, I ought to caution you, not to think the bodies that lie before you your father and your mother. Know, their constancy is rewarded by a nobler union than by this mingling of their ashes, in a state where there is no danger or possibility of a second separation."

SELF RESPECT.

No. 108.   SATURDAY, December 17, 1709.   [ADDISON.]

Pronaque cùm spectent animalia cætera terram,
Os homini sublime dedit : Cœlûmque tueri
Jussit————.   OVID. Met. i. 85.

Thus, while the mute creation downward bend
Their sight, and to their earthly mother tend,
Man looks aloft, and with erected eyes
Beholds his own hereditary skies.

IT is not to be imagined how great an effect well-disposed lights, with proper forms and orders in assemblies, have upon some tempers. I am sure I feel it in so extraordinary a manner, that I cannot in a day or two get out of my imagination any very beautiful or disagreeable impression which I receive on such occasions. For this reason I frequently look in at the playhouse, in order to enlarge my thoughts, and warm my mind with some new ideas, that may be serviceable to me in my Lucubrations.

In this disposition I entered the theatre the other day, and placed myself in a corner of it very convenient for seeing, without being myself observed. I found the audience hushed in a very deep attention, and did not question but some noble tragedy was just then in its crisis, or that an incident was to be unravelled, which would determine the fate of a hero. While

I was in this suspense, expecting every moment to see my old friend Mr. Betterton appear in all the majesty of distress, to my unspeakable amazement there came up a monster with a face between his feet ; and as I was looking on, he raised himself on one leg in such a perpendicular posture, that the other grew in a direct line above his head. It afterwards twisted itself into the motions and wreathings of several different animals, and after great variety of shapes and transformations, went off the stage in the figure of a human creature. The admiration, the applause, the satisfaction of the audience, during this strange entertainment, is not to be expressed. I was very much out of countenance for my dear countrymen, and looked about with some apprehension, for fear any foreigner should be present. Is it possible, thought I, that human nature can rejoice in its disgrace, and take pleasure in seeing its own figure turned to ridicule, and distorted into forms that raise horror and aversion ? There is something disingenuous and immoral in the being able to bear such a sight. Men of elegant and noble minds are shocked at seeing the characters of persons who deserve esteem for their virtue, knowledge, or services to their country, placed in wrong lights and by misre-presentation made the subject of buffoonery. Such a nice abhorrence is not indeed to be found among the vulgar ; but methinks it is wonderful, that those who have nothing but the outward figure to distinguish them as men should delight in seeing humanity abused, vilified, and disgraced.

I must confess, there is nothing that more pleases me, in all that I read in books, or see among mankind, than such passages as represent human nature in its proper dignity. As man is a creature made up of different extremes, he has something in him very great and very mean. A skilful artist may draw an excellent picture of him in either of these views. The finest authors of antiquity have taken him on the more advantageous side. They cultivate the natural grandeur of the soul, raise in her a generous ambition, feed her with hopes of immortality and perfection, and do all they can to widen the partition between the virtuous and the vicious, by making the difference betwixt them as great as between gods and brutes. In short, it is impossible to read a page in Plato, Tully, and a thousand other ancient moralists, without being a greater and a better man for it. On the contrary, I could never read any of our modish French authors, or those of our own country, who are the imitators and admirers of that trifling nation, without being for some time out of humour with myself, and at every thing about me. Their business is, to depreciate human nature, and consider it under its worst appearances. They give mean interpretations and base motives to the worthiest actions : they resolve virtue and vice into constitution. In short, they endeavour to make no distinction between man and man, or between the species of men and that of brutes. As an instance of this kind of authors, among many others, let any one examine the celebrated Rochefoucault, who is the great philosopher for administering of consolation to the idle, the envious, and worthless part of mankind.

I remember a young gentleman of moderate understanding, but great vivacity, who by dipping into many authors of this nature, had got a little smattering of knowledge, just enough to make an atheist or a free-thinker, but not a philosopher or a man of sense. With these accomplishments, he went to visit his father in the country, who was a plain, rough, honest man, and wise, though not learned. The son, who took all opportunities to shew his learning, began to establish a new religion in the family, and to enlarge the narrowness of their country notions ; in which he succeeded so well, that he had seduced the butler by his table-talk, and staggered his eldest sister. The old gentleman began to be alarmed at the schisms that arose among his children, but did not yet believe his son's doctrine to be so pernicious as it really was, until one day talking of his setting-dog, the son said, "he did not question but Trey was as immortal as any one of the family ;" and in the heat of the argument told his father, "that, for his own part, he expected to die like a dog." Upon which, the old man starting up in a very great passion, cried out, "Then, sirrah, you shall live like one ;" and taking his cane in his hand, cud-

gelled him out of his system.   This had so good an effect upon
him, that he took up from that day, fell to reading good books,
and is now a bencher in the Middle Temple.

I do not mention this cudgelling part of the story with a
design to engage the secular arm in matters of this nature ;
but certainly, if it ever exerts itself in affairs of opinion and
speculation, it ought to do it on such shallow and despicable
pretenders to knowledge, who endeavour to give man dark and
uncomfortable prospects of his being, and destroy those principles which are the support, happiness, and glory of all public
societies, as well as private persons.

I think it is one of Pythagoras's golden sayings, " That a
man should take care above all things to have a due respect
for himself."   And it is certain, that this licentious sort of
authors, who are for depreciating mankind, endeavour to
disappoint and undo what the most refined spirits have been
labouring to advance since the beginning of the world.   The
very design of dress, good-breeding, outward ornaments, and
ceremony, were to lift up human nature, and set it off to an
advantage. Architecture, painting, and statuary, were invented
with the same design ; as indeed every art and science contributes to the embellishment of life, and to the wearing off and
throwing into shades the mean and low parts of our nature.
Poetry carries on this great end more than all the rest, as may
be seen in the following passage taken out of sir Francis
Bacon's " Advancement of Learning," which gives a truer and
better account of this art than all the volumes that were ever
written upon it.

" Poetry, especially heroical, seems to be raised altogether
from a noble foundation, which makes much for the dignity of
man's nature.   For seeing this sensible world is in dignity
inferior to the soul of man, poesy seems to endow human
nature with that which history denies ; and to give satisfaction
to the mind, with at least the shadow of things, where the
substance cannot ¡be had.   For if the matter be thoroughly
considered, a strong argument may be drawn from poesy, that a
more stately greatness of things, a more perfect order, and a

more beautiful variety, delights the soul of man, than any way can be found in nature since the fall. Wherefore, seeing the acts and events, which are the subjects of true history, are not of that amplitude as to content the mind of man ; poesy is ready at hand to feign acts more heroical. Because true history reports the successes of business not proportionable to the merit of virtues and vices, poesy corrects it, and presents events and fortunes according to desert, and according to the law of Providence : because true history, through the frequent satiety and similitude of things, works a distaste and misprision in the mind of man ; poesy cheareth and refresheth the soul, chanting things rare and various, and full of vicissitudes. So as poesy serveth and conferreth to delectation, magnanimity, and morality ; and, therefore, it may seem deservedly to have some participation of divineness, because it doth raise the mind, and exalt the spirit with high raptures, by proportioning the shews of things to the desires of the mind, and not submitting the mind to things, as reason and history do. And by these allurements and congruities, whereby it cherisheth the soul of man, joined also with consort of music, whereby it may more sweetly insinuate itself, it hath won such access, that it hath been in estimation even in rude times, and barbarous nations, when other learning stood excluded."

But there is nothing which favours and falls in with this natural greatness and dignity of human nature so much as religion, which does not only promise the entire refinement of the mind, but the glorifying of the body, and the immortality of both.

SIR HANNIBAL.

No. 115.　MONDAY, JANUARY 2, 1709–10.　[STEELE.]

I CAME in here [White's Chocolate-house] to-day at an hour when only the dead appear in places of resort and gallantry, and saw *hung up the escutcheon* of Sir Hannibal,* a gentleman who used to frequent this place, and was taken up and interred by the company of upholders, as having been seen here at an unlicensed hour. The coat of the deceased is, three bowls and a jack in a green field ; the crest, a dice-box, with the king of clubs and pam for supporters. Some days ago the body was carried out of town with great pomp and ceremony, in order to be buried with his ancestors at the *Peak*. It is a maxim in morality, that we are to speak nothing but truth of the living, nothing but good of the dead. As I have carefully observed the first during his lifetime, I shall acquit myself as to the latter now he is deceased.

He was knighted very young, not in the ordinary form, but by the common consent of mankind. He was in his person between round and square; in the motion and gesture of his body he was unaffected and free, as not having too great a respect for superiors. He was in his discourse bold and intrepid ; and as every one has an excellence, as well as a failing, which distinguishes him from other men, eloquence was his predominant quality, which he had to so great perfection, that it was easier to him to speak, than to hold his tongue. This sometimes exposed him to the derision of men who had much less parts than himself : and indeed his great volubility, and inimitable manner of speaking, as well as the great courage he shewed on those occasions, did sometimes betray him into that figure of speech which is commonly distinguished by the name of *gasconade*. To mention no other, he professed in this very place, some days before he died, "that he would be one of the six that would undertake to assault me ; " for which reason I have had his figure upon my wall until the hour of his death : and am resolved for the future to bury every one forthwith who I hear has an intention to kill me.

Since I am upon the subject of my adversaries, I shall here publish a short letter, which I have received from a well-wisher, and is as follows :—

* Sir James Baker, commonly called the Knight of the Peak.

"SAGE SIR,

"You cannot but know, there are many scribblers, and others, who revile you and your writings. It is wondered that you do not exert yourself, and crush them at once. I am, sir, with great respect,

         "Your most humble admirer and disciple."

In answer to this, I shall act like my predecessor Æsop, and give him a fable instead of a reply.

It happened one day, as a stout and honest mastiff, that guarded the village where he lived against thieves and robbers, was very gravely walking, with one of his puppies by his side, all the little dogs in the street gathered about him, and barked at him. The little puppy was so offended at this affront done to his sire, that he asked him why he would not fall upon them, and tear them to pieces? To which the sire answered, with great composure of mind, "If there were no curs, I should be no mastiff."

THE PETTICOAT.

No. 116.   THURSDAY, JANUARY 5, 1709-10.   [ADDISON.]

—— Pars minima est ipsa puella sui.   OVID.

The young lady is the least part of herself.

THE court being prepared for proceeding on the cause of the petticoat, I gave orders to bring in a criminal, who was taken up as she went out of the puppet-shew about three nights ago, and was now standing in the street, with a great concourse of people about her. Word was brought me, that she had endeavoured twice or thrice to come in, but could not do it by reason of her petticoat, which was too large for the entrance of my house, though I had ordered both the folding doors to be thrown open for its reception. Upon this, I desired the jury of matrons, who stood at my right-hand, to inform themselves of her condition, and know whether there were any private reasons why she might not make her appearance separate from her petticoat. This was managed with great discretion, and had such an effect, that upon the return of the verdict from the bench of matrons, I issued out an order forthwith, "that the criminal should be stripped of her incumbrances, until she became little enough to enter my house." I had before given directions for an engine of several legs, that could contract or open itself like the top of an *umbrella*, in order to place the petticoat upon it, by which means I might take a leisurely survey of it, as it should appear in its proper dimensions. This was all done accordingly; and forthwith, upon the closing of the engine, the petticoat was brought into court. I then directed the machine to be set upon the table, and dilated in such a manner as to shew the garment in its utmost circumference; but my great hall was too narrow for the experiment; for before it was half unfolded, it described so immoderate a circle, that the lower part of it brushed upon my face as I sat in my chair of judicature. I then inquired for the person that belonged to the petticoat; and, to my great surprise, was directed to a very beautiful young damsel, with so pretty a face and shape, that I bid her come out of the crowd, and seated her upon a little crock at my left hand. "My pretty maid," said I, "do you own yourself to have been the inhabitant of the garment before us?" The girl, I found, had good sense, and told me with a smile, that, "notwithstanding it was her own petticoat, she should be very glad to see an example made of it; and that she wore it for no other reason, but that she had a mind to look as big and burly as other persons of her quality; that she had kept out of it as long as she could, and until she began to appear little in the eyes of her acquaintance; that, if she laid it aside, people would think she was not made like other women." I always give great allowances to the fair sex upon account of the fashion, and, therefore, was not displeased with the defence of my pretty criminal. I then ordered the vest which stood before us to be drawn up by a pulley to the top of my great hall, and afterwards to be spread open by the engine it was placed upon, in such a manner, that it formed a very splendid and ample canopy over our heads, and covered the whole court of judicature with a kind of silken rotunda, in its form not unlike the cupola of Saint Paul's. I entered upon the whole cause with great satisfaction as I sat under the shadow of it.

The counsel for the petticoat were now called in, and ordered to produce what they had to say against the popular cry which was raised against it. They answered the objections with great strength and solidity of argument, and expatiated in very florid harangues, which they did not fail to set off and furbelow, if I may be allowed the metaphor, with many periodical sentences and turns of oratory. The chief arguments for their client were taken, first, from the great benefit that might arise to our woollen manufactory from this invention, which was calculated as follows. The common petticoat has not above four yards in the circumference; whereas this over our heads had more in the semi-diameter; so that, by allowing it twenty-four yards in the circumference, the five millions of woollen petticoats which, according to Sir William Petty, supposing what ought to be supposed in a well-governed state, that all petticoats are made of that stuff, would amount to thirty millions of those of the ancient mode. A prodigious improvement of the woollen trade! and what could not fail to sink the power of France in a few years.

To introduce the second argument, they begged leave to read a petition of the ropemakers, wherein it was represented, "that the demand for cords, and the price of them, were much risen since this fashion came up." At this, all the company who were present lifted up their eyes into the vault; and I must confess, we did discover many traces of cordage, which were interwoven in the stiffening of the drapery.

A third argument was founded upon a petition of the Greenland trade, which likewise represented the great consumption of whalebone which would be occasioned by the present fashion, and the benefit which would thereby accrue to that branch of the British trade.

To conclude, they gently touched upon the weight and un-wieldiness of the garment, which, they insinuated, might be of great use to preserve the honour of families.

These arguments would have wrought very much upon me, as I then told the company in a long and elaborate discourse, had I not considered the great and additional expense which such fashions would bring upon fathers and husbands ; and, therefore, by no means to be thought of until some years after a peace. I farther urged, that it would be a prejudice to the ladies themselves, who could never expect to have any money in the pocket, if they laid out so much on the petticoat. To this I added, the great temptation it might give to virgins, of acting in security like married women, and by that means give a check to matrimony, an institution always encouraged by wise societies.

At the same time, in answer to the several petitions pro-duced on that side, I shewed one subscribed by the women of several persons of quality, humbly setting forth, " that, since the introduction of this mode, their respective ladies had, instead of bestowing on them their cast gowns, cut them into shreds, and mixed them with the cordage and buckram, to complete the stiffening of their under petticoats." For which, and sundry other reasons, I pronounced the petticoat a for-feiture : but, to shew that I did not make that judgment for the sake of filthy lucre, I ordered it to be folded up, and sent it as a present to a widow-gentlewoman, who has five daughters ; desiring she would make each of them a petticoat out of it, and send me back the remainder, which I design to cut into stomachers, caps, facings of my waistcoat-sleeves, and other garnitures suitable to my age and quality.

I would not be understood, that, while I discard this mon-strous invention, I am an enemy to the proper ornaments of the fair sex. On the contrary, as the hand of nature has poured on them such a profusion of charms and graces, and sent them into the world more amiable and finished than the

rest of her works ; so I would have them bestow upon themselves all the additional beauties that art can supply them with,
provided it does not interfere with, disguise, or pervert those
of nature.

I consider woman as a beautiful romantic animal, that may
be adorned with furs and feathers, pearls and diamonds, ores
and silks.   The lynx shall cast its skin at her feet to make
her a tippet ; the peacock, parrot, and swan shall pay contributions to her muff ; the sea shall be searched for shells,
and the rocks for gems ; and every part of nature furnish out
its share towards the embellishment of a creature that is the
most consummate work of it.   All this I shall indulge them
in ; but as for the petticoat I have been speaking of, I neither
can nor will allow it.

ON DELIVERANCE FROM DANGER.

No. 117.   SATURDAY, JANUARY 7, 1709–10.   [ADDISON.]

Durate, et vosmet rebus servate secundus.
VIRG. Æn. i. 211.

Endure the hardships of your present state,
Live, and reserve yourselves for better fate.

WHEN I look into the frame and constitution of my own
mind, there is no part of it which I observe with greater
satisfaction, than that tenderness and concern which it bears
for the good and happiness of mankind.   My own circumstances are indeed so narrow and scanty, that I should taste
but very little pleasure, could I receive it only from those
enjoyments which are in my own possession ; but by this
great tincture of humanity, which I find in all my thoughts
and reflections, I am happier than any single person can be,
with all the wealth, strength, beauty, and success, that can
be conferred upon a mortal, if he only relishes such a propor-

tion of these blessings as is vested in himself, and in his own private property. By this means, every man that does himself any real service does me a kindness. I come in for my share in all the good that happens to a man of merit and virtue, and partake of many gifts of fortune and power that I was never born to. There is nothing in particular in which I so much rejoice as the deliverance of good and generous spirits out of dangers, difficulties, and distresses. And because the world does not supply instances of this kind to furnish out sufficient entertainments for such an humanity and benevolence of temper, I have ever delighted in reading the history of ages past, which draws together into a narrow compass the great occurrences and events that are but thinly sown in those tracts of time, which lie within our own knowledge and observation. When I see the life of a great man, who has deserved well of his country, after having struggled through all the oppositions of prejudice and envy, breaking out with lustre, and shining forth in all the splendour of success, I close my book, and am an happy man for a whole evening.

But since in history events are of a mixed nature, and often happen alike to the worthless and the deserving, insomuch that we frequently see a virtuous man dying in the midst of disappointments and calamities, and the vicious ending their days in prosperity and peace ; I love to amuse myself with the accounts I meet with in fabulous histories and fictions : for in this kind of writing we have always the pleasure of seeing vice punished, and virtue rewarded. Indeed, were we able to view a man in the whole circle of his existence, we should have the satisfaction of seeing it close with happiness or misery, according to his proper merit : but though our view of him is interrupted by death before the finishing of his adventures, if I may so speak, we may be sure that the conclusion and catastrophe is altogether suitable to his behaviour. On the contrary, the whole being of a man, considered as an hero or a knight-errant, is comprehended within the limits of a poem or romance, and, therefore always ends to our satisfaction ; so that inventions of this kind are like food and exercise to a good-natured disposition, which they please and gratify at the same time that they nourish and strengthen. The greater the affliction is in which we see our favourites in these relations engaged, the greater is the pleasure we take in seeing them relieved.

Among the many feigned histories which I have met with in my reading, there is none in which the hero's perplexity is greater, and the winding out of it more difficult, than that in a French author whose name I have forgot. It so happens, that the hero's mistress was the sister of his most intimate friend, who for certain reasons, was given out to be dead, while he was preparing to leave his country in quest of adventures. The hero having heard of his friend's death, immediately repaired to his mistress, to condole with her, and comfort her. Upon his arrival in her garden, he discovered at a distance a man clasped in her arms, and embraced with the most endearing tenderness. What should he do? It did not consist with the gentleness of a knight-errant either to kill his mistress, or the man whom she was pleased to favour. At the same time, it would have spoiled a romance, should he have laid violent hands on himself. In short, he immediately entered upon his adventures; and after a long series of exploits, found out by degrees that the person he saw in his mistress's arms was her own brother, taking leave of her before he left his country, and the embrace she gave him nothing else but the affectionate farewell of a sister : so that he had at once the two greatest satisfactions that could enter into the heart of man, in finding his friend alive, whom he thought dead ; and his mistress faithful, whom he had believed inconstant.

There are indeed some disasters so very fatal, that it is impossible for any accidents to rectify them. Of this kind was that of poor Lucretia ; and yet we see Ovid has found an expedient even in this case. He describes a beautiful and royal virgin walking on the sea-shore, where she was discovered by Neptune, and violated after a long and unsuccessful importunity. To mitigate her sorrow, he offers her whatever she could wish for.   Never certainly was the wit of woman more puzzled in finding out a stratagem to retrieve her honour. Had she desired to be changed into a stock or stone, a beast, fish, or fowl, she would have been a loser by it : or had she desired to have been made a sea-nymph, or a goddess, her immortality would but have perpetuated her disgrace.   " Give me, therefore," said she, " such a shape as may make me incapable of suffering again the like calamity, or of being reproached for what I have already suffered."   To be short, she was turned into a man, and, by that only means, avoided the danger and imputation she so much dreaded.

I was once myself in agonies of grief that are unutterable, and in so great a distraction of mind, that I thought myself even out of the possibility of receiving comfort.   The occasion was as follows.   When I was a youth in a part of the army which was then quartered at Dover, I fell in love with an agreeable young woman, of a good family in those parts, and had the satisfaction of seeing my addresses kindly received, which occasioned the perplexity I am going to relate.

We were in a calm evening diverting ourselves upon the top of the cliff with the prospect of the sea, and trifling away the time in such little fondnesses as are most ridiculous to people in business, and most agreeable to those in love.

In the midst of these our innocent endearments, she snatched a paper of verses out of my hand, and ran away with them. I was following her, when on a sudden the ground, though at a considerable distance from the verge of the precipice, sunk under her, and threw her down from so prodigious an height upon such a range of rocks, as would have dashed her into ten thousand pieces, had her body been made of adamant.   It is much easier for my reader to imagine my state of mind upon such an occasion, than for me to express it.   I said to myself, it is not in the power of heaven to relieve me ! when I awaked, equally transported and astonished, to see myself drawn out of an affliction which, the very moment before, appeared to me altogether inextricable.

The impressions of grief and horror were so lively on this

occasion, that while they lasted they made me more miserable than I was at the real death of this beloved person, which happened a few months after, at a time when the match between us was concluded ; inasmuch as the imaginary death was untimely, and I myself in a sort an accessary ; whereas her real decease had at least these alleviations, of being natural and inevitable.

PENELOPE PRIM.

No. 118. TUESDAY, January 10, 1709–10. [Steele.]

When I came home this evening, a very tight middle-aged woman presented to me the following petition :—

"To the Worshipful Isaac Bickerstaff,
    Esquire, Censor of Great Britain.

"The humble Petition of Penelope Prim, Widow,
    "Sheweth,

"That your petitioner was bred a clear-starcher and sempstress, and for many years worked to the Exchange, and to several aldermen's wives, lawyers' clerks, and merchants' apprentices.

"That through the scarcity caused by regrators of bread corn, of which starch is made, and the gentry's immoderate frequenting the operas, the ladies, to save charges, have their heads washed at home, and the beaux put out their linen to common laundresses. So that your petitioner has little or no work at her trade : for want of which, she is reduced to such necessity, that she and her seven fatherless children must inevitably perish, unless relieved by your worship.

"That your petitioner is informed, that in contempt of your judgment pronounced on Tuesday the third instant against the new-fashioned petticoat, or old-fashioned fardingal, the ladies design to go on in that dress. And since it is presumed your worship will not suppress them by force, your petitioner humbly desires you would order, that ruffs may be added to the dress ; and that she may be heard by her counsel, who has assured your petitioner, he has such cogent reasons to offer to your court, that ruffs and fardingals are inseparable, that he questions not but two-thirds of the greatest beauties about town will have cambric collars on their necks before the end of Easter term next. He farther says, that the design of our great grandmothers in this petticoat, was to appear much bigger than the life ; for which reason they had false shoulder-blades, like wings, and the ruff above mentioned, to make the upper and lower parts of their bodies appear proportionable ; whereas the figure of a woman in the present dress bears, as he calls it, the figure of a cone, which as he advises, is the same with that of an extinguisher, with a little knob at the upper end, and widening downward, until it ends in a basis of a most enormous circumference.

"Your petitioner, therefore, most humbly prays, that you would restore the ruff to the fardingal, which in their nature ought to be as inseparable as the two Hungarian twins.*

"And your petitioner shall ever pray."

I have examined into the allegations of this petition, and find, by several antient pictures of my own predecessors, particularly that of dame Deborah Bickerstaff, my great grandmother, that the ruff and fardingal are made use of as absolutely necessary to preserve the symmetry of the figure ; and Mrs. Pyramid Bickerstaff, her second sister, is recorded in our family-book, with some observations to her disadvantage, as the first female of our house that discovered, to any besides her nurse and her husband, an inch below her chin, or above her instep. This convinces me of the reasonableness of

* Helen and Judith, two united twin-sisters, were born at Tzoni, in Hungary, October 26th, 1701 ; lived to the age of twenty-one, and died in a convent at Presburgh, February 23rd, 1723. These twins were exhibited at a house in the Strand, near Charing Cross, in 1708.

Mrs. Prim's demand; and, therefore, I shall not allow the reviving of any one part of that antient mode, except the whole is complied with.   Mrs. Prim, is therefore, hereby impowered to carry home ruffs to such as she shall see in the above-mentioned petticoats, and require payment on demand.

A DREAM OF HUMAN LIFE.

No. 120.   SATURDAY, January 14, 1709-10.   [Addison.]

—— Velut silvis, ubi passim
Palantes error certo de tramite pellit ;
Ille sinistrorsum, hic dextrorsum abit.
> Hor. 2 Sat. iii. 48.

When, in a wood, we leave the certain way,
One error fools us, though we various stray,
Some to the left, and some to t'other side.

INSTEAD of considering any particular passion or character in any one set of men, my thoughts were last night employed on the contemplation of human life in general ; and truly it appears to me, that the whole species are hurried on by the same desires, and engaged in the same pursuits, according to the different stages and divisions of life.   Youth is devoted to lust, middle age to ambition, old age to avarice.   These are the three general motives and principles of action both in good and bad men ; though it must be acknowledged, but they change their names, and refine their natures, according to the temper of the person whom they direct and animate.   For with the good, lust becomes virtuous love ; ambition true honour ; and avarice, the care of posterity.   This scheme of thought amused me very agreeably until I retired to rest, and after-wards formed itself into a pleasing and regular vision, which I shall describe in all its circumstances, as the objects presented themselves, whether in a serious or ridiculous manner.

I dreamed that I was in a wood, of so prodigious an extent,

and cut into such a variety of walks and alleys, that all mankind were lost and bewildered in it. After having wandered
up and down some time, I came into the centre of it, which
opened into a wide plain, filled with multitudes of both sexes.
I here discovered three great roads, very wide and long, that
led into three different parts of the forest. On a sudden, the
whole multitude broke into three parts, according to their
different ages, and marched in their respective bodies into the
three great roads that lay before them. As I had a mind to
know how each of these roads terminated, and whither they
would lead those who passed through them, I joined myself
with the assembly that were in the flower and vigour of their
age, and called themselves " the band of lovers." I found, to
my great surprise, that several old men besides myself had
intruded into this agreeable company ; as I had before
observed, there were some young men who had united themselves to " the band of misers," and were walking up the path
to avarice ; though both made a very ridiculous figure, and
were as much laughed at by those they joined, as by those they
forsook. The walk which we marched up, for thickness of
shades, embroidery of flowers, and melody of birds, with the
distant purling of streams, and falls of water, was so wonderfully delightful, that it charmed our senses, and intoxicated
our minds with pleasure. We had not been long here, before
every man singled out some woman, to whom he offered his
addresses, and professed himself a lover ; when on a sudden
we perceived this delicious walk to grow more narrow as we
advanced into it, until it ended in many intricate thickets,
mazes, and labyrinths, that were so mixed with roses and
brambles, brakes of thorns, and beds of flowers, rocky paths,
and pleasing grottos, that it was hard to say, whether it gave
greater delight or perplexity to those who travelled in it.

It was here that the lovers began to be eager in their pursuits. Some of their mistresses, who only seemed to retire for
the sake of form and decency, led them into plantations that
were disposed into different walks ; where, after they had
wheeled about in some turns and windings, they suffered them-

selves to be overtaken, and gave their hands to those who
pursued them.   Others withdrew from their followers, into
little wildernesses, where there were so many paths interwoven
with each other in so much confusion and irregularity, that
several of the lovers quitted the pursuit, or broke their hearts
in the chase.   It was sometimes very odd to see a man pursuing a fine woman that was following another, whose eye was
fixed upon a fourth, that had her own game in view in some
other part of the wilderness.   I could not but observe two
things in this place which I thought very particular.   That
several persons, who stood only at the end of the avenues, and
cast a careless eye upon the nymphs during their whole flight,
often catched them ; when those who pressed them the most
warmly, through all their turns and doubles, were wholly unsuccessful : and that some of my own age, who were at first
looked upon with aversion and contempt, by being well
acquainted with the wilderness, and by dodging their women in
the particular corners and alleys of it, catched them in their arms,
and took them from those whom they really loved and admired.

  There was a particular grove, which was called " the labyrinth
of coquettes : " where many were enticed to the chase, but few
returned with purchase.   It was pleasant enough to see a celebrated beauty, by smiling upon one, casting a glance upon another,
beckoning to a third, and adapting her charms and graces to
the several follies of those that admired her, drawing into the
labyrinth a whole pack of lovers, that lost themselves in the
maze, and never could find their way out of it.   However, it
was some satisfaction to me, to see many of the fair ones, who
had thus deluded their followers, and left them among the
intricacies of the labyrinth, obliged, when they came out of it,
to surrender to the first partner that offered himself.   I now
had crossed over all the difficult and perplexed passages that
seemed to bound our walk, when on the other side of them I
saw the same great road running on a little way until it was
terminated by two beautiful temples.   I stood here for some
time, and saw most of the multitude who had been dispersed
amongst the thickets, coming out two by two, and marching

up in pairs towards the temples that stood before us. The
structure on the right hand was, as I afterwards found, consecrated to virtuous love, and could not be entered but by such
as received a ring, or some other token, from a person who
was placed as a guard at the gate of it. He wore a garland of
roses and myrtles on his head, and on his shoulders a robe
like an imperial mantle, white and unspotted all over, excepting only, that where it was clasped at his breast, there were
two golden turtle-doves that buttoned it by their bills, which
were wrought in rubies. He was called by the name of
Hymen, and was seated near the entrance of the temple, in a
delicious bower, made up of several trees, that were embraced
by woodbines, jasmines, and amaranths, which were as so many
emblems of marriage, and ornaments to the trunks that supported them. As I was single and unaccompanied, I was not
permitted to enter the temple, and for that reason am a
stranger to all the mysteries that were performed in it.

I had, however, the curiosity to observe how the several
couples that entered were disposed of; which was after the
following manner. There were two great gates on the backside
of the edifice, at which the whole crowd was let out. At one
of these gates were two women, extremely beautiful though in a
different kind, the one having a very careful and composed
air, the other a sort of smile and ineffable sweetness in her
countenance. The name of the first was Discretion, and of
the other Complacency. All who came out of this gate, and
put themselves under the direction of these two sisters, were
immediately conducted by them into gardens, groves, and
meadows, which abounded in delights, and were furnished
with everything that could make them the proper seats of
happiness. The second gate of this temple let out all the
couples that were unhappily married, who came out linked
together with chains, which each of them strove to break, but
could not. Several of these were such as had never been
acquainted with each other before they met in the great walk,
or had been too well acquainted in the thicket. The entrance
to this gate was possessed by three sisters, who joined them-

selves with these wretches, and occasioned most of their miseries. The youngest of these sisters was known by the name of Levity, who, with the innocence of a virgin, had the dress and behaviour of a harlot. The name of the second was Contention, who bore on her right arm a muff made of the skin of a porcupine; and on her left carried a little lap dog, that barked and snapped at every one that passed by her.

The eldest of the sisters, who seemed to have an haughty and imperious air, was always accompanied with a tawny Cupid, who generally marched before her with a little mace on his shoulder, the end of which was fashioned into the horns of a stag. Her garments were yellow, and her complexion pale. Her eyes were piercing, but had odd casts in them, and that particular distemper, which makes persons who are troubled with it, see objects double. Upon inquiry, I was informed that her name was Jealousy.

Having finished my observations upon this temple and its votaries, I repaired to that which stood on the left hand, and was called "the temple of lust." The front of it was raised on Corinthian pillars, with all the meretricious ornaments that accompany that order; whereas that of the other was composed of the chaste and matron-like Ionic. The sides of it were adorned with several grotesque figures of goats, sparrows, heathen gods, satyrs, and monsters made up of half man half beast. The gates were unguarded, and open to all that had a mind to enter. Upon my going in, I found the windows were blinded, and let in only a kind of twilight, that served to discover a prodigious number of dark corners and apartments, into which the whole temple was divided. I was here stunned with a mixed noise of clamour and jollity. On one side of me I heard singing and dancing; on the other brawls and clashing of swords. In short, I was so little pleased with the place, that I was going out of it; but found I could not return by the gate where I entered, which was barred against all that were come in, with bolts of iron, and locks of adamant. There was no going back from this temple through the paths of pleasure which led to it. All who passed through the ceremonies of the place, went out at an iron wicket, which was kept by a dreadful giant, called Remorse, that held a scourge of scorpions in his hand, and drove them into the only outlet from that temple. This was a passage so rugged, so uneven, and choked with so many thorns and briars, that it was a melancholy spectacle to behold the pains and difficulties which both sexes suffered who walked through it. The men, though in the prime of their youth, appeared weak and enfeebled with old age. The women wrung their hands, and tore their hair; and several lost their limbs before they could extricate themselves out of the perplexities of the path in which they were engaged. The remaining part of this vision, and the adventures I met with in the two great roads of Ambition and Avarice, must be the subject of another Paper.

PETS.

No. 121.   TUESDAY, JANUARY 17, 1709-10.   [ADDISON.]

—— Similis tibi, Cynthia, vel tibi, cujus
Turbavit nitidos extinctus passer ocellos.
Juv. Sat. vi. 7.

Like Cynthia, or the Lesbias of our years,
Who for a sparrow's death dissolve in tears.

I WAS recollecting the remainder of my vision, when my maid came to me, and told me " there was a gentlewoman below who seemed to be in great trouble, and pressed very much to see me." When it lay in my power to remove the distress of an unhappy person, I thought I should very ill employ my time in attending to matters of speculation, and therefore desired the lady would walk in. When she entered, I saw her eyes full of tears. However, her grief was not so great as to make her omit rules ; for she was very long and exact in her civilities, which gave me time to view and consider her. Her

cloaths were very rich, but tarnished ; and her words very fine,
but ill applied. These distinctions made me, without hesitation, though I had never seen her before, ask her, " if her lady
had any commands for me ? " She then began to weep afresh,
and with many broken sighs told me, " that their family was in
great affliction."—I beseeched her " to compose herself, for
that I might possibly be capable of assisting them."—She then
cast her eye upon my little dog, and was again transported
with too much passion to proceed ; but, with much ado, she at
last gave me to understand, " that Cupid, her lady's lap-dog,
was dangerously ill, and in so bad a condition, that her lady
neither saw company, nor went abroad, for which reason she
did not come herself to consult me ; that, as I had mentioned
with great affection my own dog," (here she courtesied, and
looking first at the cur, and then on me, said, " indeed I had
reason, for he was very pretty) her lady sent to me rather than
to any other doctor, and hoped I would not laugh at her
sorrow, but send her my advice."

I must confess, I had some indignation to find myself treated
like something below a farrier ; yet well knowing that the best,
as well as most tender way of dealing with a woman, is to fall
in with her humours, and by that means to let her see the
absurdity of them ; I proceeded accordingly. " Pray, madam,"
said I, " can you give me any methodical account of this illness,
and how Cupid was first taken ? " " Sir," said she, " we have a
little ignorant country girl, who is kept to tend him ; she was
recommended to our family by one that my lady never saw but
once, at a visit ; and you know, persons of quality are always
inclined to strangers ; for I could have helped her to a cousin of
my own, but "—" Good madam," said I, " you neglect the account
of the sick body, while you are complaining of this girl."—" No,
no, sir," said she, " begging your pardon : but it is the general
fault of physicians, they are so in haste, that they never hear
out the case. I say, this silly girl, after washing Cupid, let
him stand half an hour in the window without his collar,
where he catched cold, and in an hour after, began to bark
very hoarse. He had, however, a pretty good night, and we

hoped the danger was over ; but for these two nights last past, neither he nor my lady have slept a wink." "Has he," said I, "taken anything ?" "No," said she ; "but my lady says, he shall take anything that you prescribe, provided you do not make use of *Jesuit's Powder*, or the *cold bath*. Poor Cupid," continued she, "has always been phthisical ; and as he lies under something like a chin-cough, we are afraid it will end in a consumption.

Upon this, I paused a little without returning any answer, and after some short silence, I proceeded in the following manner: "I have considered the nature of the distemper, and the constitution of the patient ; and by the best observation that I can make on both, I think it is safest to put him into a course of kitchen physic. In the meantime, to remove his hoarseness, it will be the most natural way to make Cupid his own druggist ; for which reason I shall prescribe to him, three mornings successively, as much powder as will lie on a groat, of that noble remedy which the apothecaries call *Album Græcum*." Upon hearing this advice, the young woman smiled, as if she knew how ridiculous an errand she had been employed in ; and I found by the sequel of her discourse, that she was an arch baggage, and of a character that is frequent enough in persons of her employment ; who are so used to concern themselves in everything to the humours and passions of their mistresses, that they sacrifice superiority of sense to superiority of condition, and are insensibly betrayed into the passions and prejudices of those whom they serve, without giving themselves leave to consider that they are extravagant and ridiculous. However, I thought it very natural, when her eyes were thus open, to see her give a new turn to her discourse, and from sympathising with her mistress in her follies, to fall a-railing at her. "You cannot imagine," said she, "Mr. Bickerstaff, what a life she makes us lead, for the sake of this little ugly cur. If he dies, we are the most unhappy family in town. She chanced to lose a parrot last year, which, to tell you truly, brought me into her service ; for she turned off her woman upon it, who had lived with her ten years, because she neglected to give him water, though every one of the family says she was innocent of the bird's death, as the babe that is unborn; nay, she told me this very morning, that if Cupid should die, she would send the poor innocent wench I was telling you of to Bridewell, and have the milk-woman tried for her life at the Old Bailey, for putting water into his milk. In short, she talks like any distracted creature."

"Since it is so, young woman," said I, "I will by no means let you offend her, by staying on this message longer than is absolutely necessary;" and so forced her out.

While I am studying to cure those evils and distresses that are necessary or natural to human life, I find my task growing upon me, since by these accidental cares, and acquired calamities, if I may so call them, my patients contract distempers to which their constitution is of itself a stranger. But this is an evil I have for many years remarked in the fair sex; and as they are by nature very much formed for affection and dalliance, I have observed, that when by too obstinate a cruelty, or any other means, they have disappointed themselves of the proper objects of love, as husbands, or children, such virgins have, exactly at such a year, grown fond of lap-dogs, parrots or other animals. I know at this time a celebrated toast, whom I allow to be one of the most agreeable of her sex, that, in the presence of her admirers, will give a torrent of kisses to her cat, any one of which a Christian would be glad of. I do not at the same time deny, but there are as great enormities of this kind committed by our sex as theirs. A Roman emperor had so very great an esteem for an horse of his, that he had thought of making him a *Consul*; and several moderns of that rank of men whom we call Country Esquires, would not scruple to kiss their hounds before all the world, and declare in the presence of their wives, that they would rather salute a favourite of the pack, than the finest woman in England. These voluntary friendships, between animals of different species, seem to arise from instinct; for which reason, I have always looked upon the mutual goodwill between the esquire and the hound, to be of the same nature with that between the lion and the jackall.

The only extravagance of this kind which appears to me excusable, is one that grew out of an excess of gratitude, which I have somewhere met with in the life of a Turkish emperor. His horse had brought him safe out of a field of battle, and from the pursuit of a victorious enemy. As a reward for such his good and faithful service, his master built him a stable of marble, shod him with gold, fed him in an ivory manger, and made him a rack of silver. He annexed to the stable several fields and meadows, lakes and running streams. At the same time he provided for him a seraglio of mares, the most beautiful that could be found in the whole Ottoman empire. To these were added a suitable train of domestics, consisting of grooms, farriers, rubbers, &c., accommodated with proper liveries and pensions. In·short, nothing was omitted.that could contribute to the ease and happiness of his life, who had preserved the emperor's.

CONTINUATION OF

THE DREAM OF HUMAN LIFE.

No. 123.   SATURDAY, JANUARY 21, 1709–10.   [ADDISON.]

Audire, atque togam jubeo componere, quisquis
Ambitione malâ, aut argenti pallet amore.
Hor. 2 Sat. iii. 77.

Come all, whose breasts with bad ambition rise,
Or the pale passion, that for money dies,——
Compose your robes——.

WITH much labour and difficulty I passed through the first part of my vision, and recovered the centre of the wood from whence I had the prospect of the three great roads. I here joined myself to the middle-aged party of mankind, who marched behind the standard of Ambition. The great road lay in a direct line, and was terminated by the "Temple of Virtue." It was planted on each side with laurels, which were intermixed with marble trophies, carved pillars, and statues of lawgivers, heroes, statesmen, philosophers, and poets. The persons who travelled up this great path were such whose thoughts were bent upon doing eminent services to mankind, or promoting the good of their country. On each side of this great road were several paths, that were also laid out in strait lines, and ran parallelled with it. These were most of them covered walks, and received into them men of retired virtue, who proposed to themselves the same end of their journey, though they chose to make it in shade and obscurity. The edifices at the extremity of the walk were so contrived, that we could not see the "Temple of Honour" by reason of the "Temple of Virtue," which stood before it. At the gates of this temple we were met by the goddess of it, who conducted us into that of Honour, which was joined to the other edifice by a beautiful triumphal arch, and had no other entrance into it. When the deity of the inner structure had received us, she presented us in a body to a figure that was placed over the high-altar, and was the emblem of eternity. She sat on a globe in the midst of a golden zodiac, holding the figure of a sun in one hand, and a moon in the other. Her head was veiled, and her feet covered. Our hearts glowed within us, as we stood amidst the sphere of light which this image cast on every side of it.

Having seen all that happened to this band of adventurers, I repaired to another pile of building that stood within view of the "Temple of Honour," and was raised in imitation of it, upon the very same model; but at my approach to it, I found, that the stones were laid together without mortar, and that the whole fabric stood upon so weak a foundation, that it shook with every wind that blew. This was called the "Temple of Vanity." The goddess of it sat in the midst of a great many tapers, that burned day and night, and made her appear much better than she would have done in open daylight. Her whole art was, to shew herself more beautiful and majestic than she really was. For which reason she had painted her face, and wore a cluster of false jewels upon her breast : but what I more particularly observed was, the breadth of her petticoat, which was made altogether in the fashion of a

P

modern *fardingal.* This place was filled with hypocrites, pedants, free-thinkers, and prating politicians ; with a rabble of those who have only titles to make them great men. Female votaries crowded the temple, choked up the avenues of it, and were more in number than the sand upon the sea-shore. I made it my business, in my return towards that part of the wood from whence I first set out, to observe the walk which led to this temple; for I met in it several who had begun their journey with the band of virtuous persons, and travelled some time in their company : but upon examination I found, that there were several paths which led out of the great road into the sides of the wood, and ran into so many crooked turns and windings, that those who travelled through them, often turned their backs upon the "Temple of Virtue; " then crossed the strait road, and sometimes marched in it for a little space, until the crooked path which they were engaged in, again led them into the wood. The several alleys of these wanderers had their particular ornaments. One of them I could not but take notice of in the walk of the mischievous pretenders to politics, which had at every turn the figure of a person, whom by the inscription I found to be Machiavel, pointing out the way with an extended finger, like a Mercury.

I was now returned in the same manner as before, with a design to observe carefully every thing that passed in the region of Avarice, and the occurrences in that assembly, which was made up of persons of my own age. This body of travellers had not gone far in the third great road, before it led them insensibly into a deep valley, in which they journeyed several days with great toil and uneasiness, and without the necessary refreshments of food and sleep. The only relief they met with, was in a river that ran through the bottom of the valley on a bed of golden sand. They often drank of this stream, which had such a particular quality in it, that though it refreshed them for a time, it rather inflamed than quenched their thirst. On each side of the river was a range of hills full of precious ore ; for where the rains had washed off the earth, one might see in several parts of them long veins of gold, and rocks that

looked like pure silver. We were told, that the deity of the
place had forbidden any of his votaries to dig into the bowels
of these hills, or convert the treasures they contained to any
use, under pain of starving. At the end of the valley stood
the "Temple of Avarice," made after the manner of a fortifi-
cation, and surrounded with a thousand triple-headed dogs,
that were placed there to keep off beggars. At our approach,
they all fell a barking, and would have very much terrified us,
had not an old woman, who called herself by the forged name
of Competency, offered herself for our guide. She carried
under her garment a golden bough, which she no sooner held
up in her hand, but the dogs lay down, and the gates flew
open for our reception. We were led through an hundred
iron doors before we entered the temple. At the upper end of
it sat the god of Avarice, with a long filthy beard, and a
meagre starved countenance ; inclosed with heaps of ingots, and
pyramids of money, but half naked and shivering with cold.
On his right hand was a fiend called Rapine, and on his left
a particular favourite, to whom he had given the title of Par-
simony. The first was his collector, and the other his cashier.

There were several long tables placed on each side of the
temple, with respective officers attending behind them. Some
of these I inquired into. At the first table was kept the
"Office of Corruption." Seeing a solicitor extremely busy, and
whispering every body that passed by ; I kept my eye upon
him very attentively, and saw him often going up to a person
that had a pen in his hand, with a multiplication table and an
almanack before him, which, as I afterwards heard, was all the
learning he was master of. The solicitor would often apply
himself to his ear, and at the same time convey money into his
hand, for which the other would give him out a piece of paper
or parchment, signed and sealed in form. The name of this
dexterous and successful solicitor was Bribery. At the next
table was the "Office of Extortion." Behind it sat a person in
a bob-wig, counting over great sums of money. He gave out
little purses to several ; who after a short tour brought him, in
return, sacks full of the same kind of coin. I saw at the same

time a person called Fraud, who sat behind a counter with false scales, light weights, and scanty measures; by the skilful application of which instruments, she had got together an immense heap of wealth. It would be endless to name the several officers, or describe the votaries that attend this temple. There were many old men panting and breathless, reposing their heads on bags of money; nay, many of them actually dying, whose very pangs and convulsions, which rendered their purses useless to them, only made them grasp them the faster. There were some tearing with one hand all things, even to the garments and flesh of many miserable persons who stood before them; and with the other hand, throwing away what they had seized, to harlots, flatterers, and panders, that stood behind them.

On a sudden the whole assembly fell a trembling; and upon inquiry, I found that the great room we were in was haunted with a spectre, that many times a day appeared to them, and terrified them to distraction.

In the midst of their terror and amazement, the apparition entered, which I immediately knew to be Poverty. Whether it were by my acquaintance with this phantom, which had rendered the sight of her more familiar to me, or however it was, she did not make so indigent or frightful a figure in my eye, as the god of this loathsome temple. The miserable votaries of this place were, I found, of another mind. Every one fancied himself threatened by the apparition as she stalked about the room, and began to lock their coffers, and tie their bags, with the utmost fear and trembling.

I must confess, I look upon the passion which I saw in this unhappy people, to be of the same nature with those unaccountable antipathies which some persons are born with, or rather as a kind of phrenzy, not unlike that which throws a man into terrors and agonies, at the sight of so useful and innocent a thing as water. The whole assembly was surprised, when, instead of paying my devotions to the deity whom they all adored, they saw me address myself to the phantom.

"O Poverty!" said I, "my first petition to thee is, that thou wouldest never appear to me hereafter ; but if thou wilt not grant me this, that then thou wouldest not bear a form more terrible than that in which thou appearest to me at present. Let not thy threats and menaces betray me to anything that is ungrateful, or unjust.   Let me not shut my ears to the cries of the needy.   Let me not forget the person that has deserved well of me.   Let me not, for any fear of thee, desert my friend, my principles, or my honour.   If Wealth is to visit me, and to come with her usual attendants, Vanity and Avarice, do thou, O Poverty ! hasten to my rescue ; but bring along with thee the two sisters, in whose company thou art always cheerful Liberty and Innocence."

A WHEEL OF CHANCE.

No. 124.   TUESDAY, January 24, 1709–10   [Steele.]

—— Ex humili summa ad fastigia rerum
Extollit, quoties voluit Fortuna jocari.
                              Juv. Sat. iii. 39.

Fortune can, for her pleasure, fools advance,
And toss them on the wheels of Chance.

I WENT on Saturday last to make a visit in the city ; and as I passed through Cheapside, I saw crowds of people turning down towards the Bank, and struggling who should first get their money into the *new-erected lottery.* *   It gave me a great notion of the credit of our present government and administration, to find people press as eagerly to pay money, as they would to receive it ; and, at the same time, a due respect for that body

---

* The words of Steele seem to imply, that this was the first public lottery. The earliest lottery however was in 1569, consisting of 40,000 lots, at 10s. each lot.   The prizes were plate, and the profits were to go towards repairing the havens of the kingdom.   It was drawn at the west-door of St. Paul's Cathedral ; and the drawing, which began January 11, continued incessantly, day and night, till May 6.   There were then only three lottery offices in London.

of men who have found out so pleasing an expedient for carrying on the common cause, that they have turned a tax into a diversion. The cheerfulness of spirit, and the hopes of success, which this project has occasioned in this great city, lightens the burden of the war, and puts me in mind of some games which, they say, were invented by wise men, who were lovers of their country, to make their fellow-citizens undergo the tediousness and fatigues of a long siege. I think there is a kind of homage due to fortune, if I may call it so, and that I should be wanting to myself, if I did not lay in my pretences to her favour, and pay my compliments to her by recommending a ticket to her disposal. For this reason, upon my return to my lodgings, I sold off *a couple of globes and a telescope*, which, with the cash I had by me, raised the sum that was requisite for that purpose. I find by my calculations, that it is but *an hundred and fifty thousand to one*, against my being worth a thousand pounds *per annum* for thirty-two years; and if any *Plumb* in the city will lay me an hundred and fifty thousand pounds to twenty shillings, which is an even bet, that I am not this fortunate man, I will take the wager, and shall look upon him as a man of singular courage and fair-dealing; having given orders to Mr. Morphew to subscribe such a policy in my behalf, if any person accepts of the offer. I must confess, I have had such private intimations from the twinkling of a certain star in some of my astronomical observations, that I should be unwilling to take fifty pounds a year for my chance, unless it were to oblige a particular friend.

My chief business at present is, to prepare my mind for this change of fortune : for as Seneca, who was a greater moralist, and a much richer man than I shall be with this addition to my present income, says, *Munera ista Fortunæ putatis? Insidiæ sunt.* "What we look upon as gifts and presents of fortune, are traps and snares which she lays for the unwary." I am arming myself against her favours with all my philosophy; and that I may not lose myself in such a redundance of unnecessary and superfluous wealth, I have determined to settle an annual pension out of it upon a family of Palatines, and by that means give these unhappy strangers a taste of British property. At the same time, as I have an excellent servant-maid, whose diligence in attending me has increased in proportion to my infirmities, I shall settle upon her the revenue arising out of the ten pounds, and amounting to fourteen shillings *per annum ;* with which she may retire into Wales, where she was born a gentlewoman, and pass the remaining part of her days in a condition suitable to her birth and quality. It was impossible for me to make an inspection into my own fortune on this occasion, without seeing, at the same time, the fate of others who are embarked in the same adventure. And indeed it was a great pleasure to me to observe, that the war, which generally impoverishes those who furnish out the expense of it, will by this means give estates to some, without making others the poorer for it. I have lately seen several in liveries, who will give as good of their own very suddenly ; and took a particular satisfaction in the sight of a young country-wench, whom I this morning passed by as she was whirling her mop, with her petticoats tucked up very agreeably, who, if there is any truth in my art, is within ten months of being the handsomest great fortune in town. I must confess, I was so struck with the foresight of what she is to be, that I treated her accordingly, and said to her, " Pray, young lady, permit me to pass by." I would for this reason advise all masters and mistresses, to carry it with great moderation and condescension towards their servants until next Michaelmas, lest the superiority at that time should be inverted.

I must likewise admonish all my brethren and fellow-adventurers, to fill their minds with proper arguments for their support and consolation in case of ill success. It so happens in this paticular, that though the gainers will have reason to rejoice, the losers will have no reason to complain. I remember, the day after the *thousand pound prize* was drawn in the Penny-lottery, I went to visit a splenetic acquaintance of mine, who was under much dejection, and seemed to me to have suffered some great disappointment. Upon inquiry, I found he had put *two-pence* for himself and his son into the lottery, and that neither of them had drawn the thousand pounds. Hereupon this unlucky person took occasion to enumerate the misfortunes of his life, and concluded with telling me, "that he never was successful in any of his undertakings." I was forced to comfort him with the common reflection upon such occasions, "that men of the greatest merit are not always men of the greatest success, and that persons of his character must not expect to be as happy as fools." I shall proceed in the like manner with my rivals and competitors for the *thousand pounds a year*, which we are now in pursuit of; and that I may give general content to the whole body of candidates, I shall allow all that draw prizes to be fortunate, and all that miss them to be wise.

I must not here omit to acknowledge, that I have received several letters upon this subject, but find one common error running through them all, which is, that the writers of them believe their fate in these cases depends upon the astrologer, and not upon the stars; as in the following letter from one, who, I fear, flatters himself with hopes of success which are altogether groundless, since he does not seem to me so great a fool as he takes himself to be.

"SIR,

"COMING to town, and finding my friend Mr. Partridge dead and buried, and you the only conjurer in repute, I am under a necessity of applying myself to you for a favour, which nevertheless I confess it would better become a friend to ask, than one who is, as I am, altogether a stranger to you; but poverty, you know, is impudent; and as that gives me the occasion, so that alone could give me the confidence to be thus importunate.

"I am, sir, very poor, and very desirous to be otherwise: I have got ten pounds, which I design to venture in the lottery now on foot. What I desire of you is, that by your art, you will choose such a ticket for me as shall arise a benefit sufficient to maintain me. I must beg leave to inform you, that I am good for nothing, and must therefore insist upon a larger lot than would satisfy those who are capable, by their own abilities, of adding something to what you should assign them ; whereas I must expect an absolute independent maintenance, because, as I said, I can do nothing.   It is possible, after this free confession of mine, you may think I do not deserve to be rich ; but I hope you will likewise observe, I can ill afford to be poor. My own opinion is, that I am well qualified for an estate, and have a good title to luck in a lottery ; but I resign myself wholly to your mercy, not without hopes that you will consider, the less I deserve, the greater the generosity in you.   If you reject me, I have agreed with an acquaintance of mine to bury me for my ten pounds.   I once more recommend myself to your favour, and bid you adieu ! "

THE PRUDE AND THE COQUETTE.

No. 126.   SATURDAY, January 28, 1709–10.   [Steele.]

Anguillam caudâ tenes.—T. D'Urfey.

You have got an eel by the tail.

There is no sort of company so agreeable as that of women who have good sense without affectation, and can converse with men without any private design of imposing chains and fetters. Belvidera, whom I visited this evening, is one of these.   There is an invincible prejudice in favour of all she says, from her being a beautiful woman ; because she does not consider herself as such when she talks to you.   This amiable temper gives a certain tincture to all her discourse, and made it very agreeable to me until we were interrupted by Lydia, a creature who has all the charms that can adorn a woman.   Her attractions would indeed be irresistible, but that she thinks them so, and is always employing them in stratagems and conquests.   When I turned my eye upon her as she sat down, I saw she was a person of that character, which, for the farther information of my country correspondents, I had long wanted an opportunity

of explaining. Lydia is a finished coquette, which is a sect
among women of all others the most mischievous, and makes
the greatest havoc and disorder in society.   I went on in the
discourse I was in with Belvidera, without shewing that I had
observed anything extraordinary in Lydia : upon which, I
immediately saw her look me over as some very ill-bred fellow ;
and, casting a scornful glance on my dress, give a shrug at
Belvidera.   But, as much as she despised me, she wanted my
admiration, and made twenty offers to bring my eyes her way :
but I reduced her to a restlessness in her seat, and impertinent
playing of her fan, and many other motions and gestures, before
I took the least notice of her.   At last I looked at her with a
kind of surprise, as if she had before been unobserved by reason
of an ill light where she sat.   It is not to be expressed what a
sudden joy I saw arise in her countenance, even at the approbation of such a very old fellow : but she did not long enjoy
her triumph without a rival ; for there immediately entered
Castabella, a lady of a quite contrary character, that is to say,
as eminent a prude as Lydia is a coquette.   Belvidera gave me
a glance, which methought intimated, that they were both
curiosities in their kind, and worth remarking.   As soon as we
were again seated, I stole looks at each lady, as if I was comparing their perfections.   Belvidera observed it, and began to
lead me into a discourse of them both to their faces, which is to
be done easily enough ; for one woman is generally so intent
upon the faults of another, that she has not reflection enough
to observe when her own are represented.   "I have taken
notice, Mr. Bickerstaff," said Belvidera, "that you have, in
some parts of your writings, drawn characters of our sex, in
which you have not, to my apprehension, been clear enough
and distinct ; particularly in those of a Prude and a Coquette."
Upon the mention of this, Lydia was roused with the expectation of seeing Castabella's picture, and Castabella, with the
hopes of that of Lydia. " Madam," said I to Belvidera, " when
we consider nature, we shall often find very contrary effects
flow from the same cause.   The Prude and Coquette, as different
as they appear in their behaviour, are in reality the same kind

of women.   The motive of action in both is the affectation of pleasing men.   They are sisters of the same blood and constitution ; only one chooses a grave, and the other a light dress. The Prude appears more virtuous, the Coquette more vicious than she really is.   The distant behaviour of the Prude tends to the same purpose as the advances of the Coquette ; and you have as little reason to fall into despair from the severity of the one, as to conceive hopes from the familiarity of the other. What leads you into a clear sense of their character is, that you may observe each of them has the distinction of sex in all her thoughts, words, and actions.   You can never mention any assembly you were lately in, but one asks you with a rigid, the other with a sprightly air, " Pray, what men were there ? " As for Prudes, it must be confessed, that there are several of them who, like hypocrites, by long practice of a false part become sincere; or at least delude themselves into a belief that they are so."

For the benefit of the society of ladies, I shall propose one rule to them as a test of their virtue.   I find in a very celebrated modern author, that the great foundress of Pietists, madam de Bourignon,* who was no less famous for the sanctity of her life than for the singularity of some of her opinions, used to boast, that she had not only the spirit of continency in herself, but that she had also the power of communicating it to all who beheld her. This the scoffers of those days called, " The gift of infrigidation," and took occasion from it to rally her face, rather than admire her virtue.   I would therefore advise the Prude, who has a mind to know the integrity of her own heart, to lay her hand seriously upon it, and to examine herself, whether she could sincerely rejoice in such a gift of conveying chaste thoughts to all her male beholders.   If she has any aversion to the power of inspiring so great a virtue, whatever notion she may have of her perfection, she deceives her own heart, and is

---

* Antoinette Bourignon was born at Lisle in 1616, so deformed, that it was debated for some days in the family, whether it was not proper to stifle her as a monster.   She pretended to inspiration, and boasted of extraordinary communications with God,

still in the state of prudery. Some perhaps will look upon the boast of madam de Bourignon, as the utmost ostentation of a Prude.

If you would see the humour of a Coquette pushed to the last excess, you may find an instance of it in the following story : which I will set down at length, because it pleased me when I read it, though I cannot recollect in what author.

"A young coquette widow in France having been followed by a Gascon of quality, who had boasted among his companions of some favours which he had never received ; to be revenged of him, sent for him one evening, and told him, "it was in his power to do her a very particular service." The Gascon, with much profession of his readiness to obey her commands, begged to hear in what manner she designed to employ him. "You know," said the widow, "my friend Belinda ; and must often have heard of the jealousy of that impotent wretch her husband. Now it is absolutely necessary, for the carrying on a certain affair, that his wife and I should be together a whole night. What I have to ask of you is, to dress yourself in her night-cloaths, and lie by him a whole night in her place, that he may not miss her while she is with me." The Gascon, though of a very lively and undertaking complexion, began to startle at the proposal. "Nay," says the widow, "if you have not the courage to go through what I ask of you, I must employ some-body else that will." "Madam," says the Gascon, "I will kill him for you if you please ; but for lying with him !——How is it possible to do it without being discovered ? " "If you do not discover yourself," says the widow, "you will lie safe enough, for he is past all curiosity. He comes in at night while she is asleep, and goes out in a morning before she awakes ; and is in pain for nothing, so he knows she is there." "Madam," replied the Gascon, "how can you reward me for passing a night with this old fellow ? " The widow answered with a laugh, "Per-haps by admitting you to pass a night with one you think more agreeable." He took the hint ; put on his night-cloaths ; and had not been a-bed above an hour before he heard a knocking at the door, and the treading of one who approached the other

side of the bed, and who he did not question was the good man
of the house.   I do not know, whether the story would be better
by telling you in this place, or at the end of it, that the person
who went to bed to him was our young coquette widow.   The
Gascon was in a terrible fright every time she moved in the
bed, or turned towards him ; and did not fail to shrink from
her, until he had conveyed himself to the very ridge of the bed.
I will not dwell upon the perplexity he was in the whole night,
which was augmented, when he observed that it was now broad
day, and that the husband did not yet offer to get up and go about
his business.   All that the Gascon had for it, was to keep his
face turned from him, and to feign himself asleep, when, to his
utter confusion, the widow at last puts out her arm, and pulls
the bell at her bed's head.   In came her friend, and two or
three companions to whom the Gascon had boasted of her
favours.   The widow jumped into a wrapping gown, and
joined with the rest in laughing at this man of intrigue.

PRIDE.

No. 127.   TUESDAY, January 31, 1709–10.   [Steele.]

Nimirum insanus paucis videatur, eò quod
Maxima pars hominum morbo jactatur eodem.
                                        Hor. 2 Sat. iii. 120.

By few, forsooth, a madman he is thought,
For half mankind the same disease have caught.

There is no affection of the mind so much blended in human
nature, and wrought into our very constitution, as Pride.   It
appears under a multitude of disguises, and breaks out in ten
thousand different symptoms.   Every one feels it in himself, and
yet wonders to see it in his neighbour.   I must confess, I met
with an instance of it the other day, where I should very little
have expected it.   Who would believe the proud person I am
going to speak of is a *cobbler upon Ludgate Hill?*   This artist

being naturally a lover of respect, and considering that his circumstances are such that no man living will give it him, has contrived the figure of a beau in wood ; who stands before him in a bending posture, with his hat under his left arm, and his right hand extended in such a manner as to hold a thread, a piece of wax, or an awl, according to the particular service in which his master thinks fit to employ him. When I saw him, he held a candle in this obsequious posture. I was very well pleased with the cobbler's invention, that had so ingeniously contrived an inferior, and stood a little while contemplating this inverted idolatry, wherein the image did homage to the man. When we meet with such a fantastic vanity in one of this order, it is no wonder if we may trace it through all degrees above it, and particularly through all the steps of greatness. We easily see the absurdity of Pride, when it enters into the heart of a cobbler ; though in reality it is altogether as ridiculous and unreasonable, wherever it takes possession of an human creature. There is no temptation to it from the reflection upon our being in general, or upon any comparative perfection, whereby one man may excel another. The greater a man's knowledge is, the greater motive he may seem to have for Pride ; but in the same proportion as the one rises, the other sinks, it being the chief office of wisdom to discover to us our weaknesses and imperfections.

As folly is the foundation of Pride, the natural superstructure of it is madness. If there was an occasion for the experiment, I would not question to make a proud man a lunatic in three weeks time ; provided I had it in my power to ripen his phrenzy with proper applications. It is an admirable reflection in Terence, where it is said of a parasite, *Hic homines ex stultis facit insanos.* "This fellow," says he, "has an art of converting fools into madmen." When I was in France, the reason of complaisance and vanity, I have often observed, that a great man who has entered a levee of flatterers humble and temperate, has grown so insensibly heated by the court which was paid him on all sides, that he has been quite distracted before he could get into his coach.

If we consult the collegiates of Moorfields,* we shall find most of them beholden to their Pride for their introduction into that magnificent palace. I had, some years ago, the curiosity to inquire into the particular circumstances of these whimsical freeholders ; and learned from their own mouths the condition and character of each of them. Indeed, I found that all I spoke to were persons of quality. There were at that time five duchesses, three earls, two heathen gods, an emperor, and a prophet. There were also a great number of such as were locked up from their estates, and others who concealed their titles. A leather-seller of Taunton whispered me in the ear, that he was " the duke of Monmouth ; " but begged me not to betray him. At a little distance from him sat a taylor's wife, who asked me, as I went, if I had seen the swordbearer ? upon which I presumed to ask her, who she was ? and was answered, " My Lady Mayoress."

I was very sensibly touched with compassion towards these miserable people ; and, indeed, extremely mortified to see human nature capable of being thus disfigured. However, I reaped this benefit from it, that I was resolved to guard myself against a passion which makes such havoc in the brain, and produces so much disorder in the imagination. For this reason I have endeavoured to keep down the secret swellings of resentment, and stifle the very first suggestions of self-esteem ; to establish my mind in tranquillity, and over value nothing in my own or in another's possession.

For the benefit of such whose heads are a little turned, though not to so great a degree as to qualify them for the place of which I have been now speaking, I shall assign one of the sides of the college which I am erecting, for the cure of this dangerous distemper.

The most remarkable of the persons, whose disturbance arises from Pride, and whom I shall use all possible diligence to cure, are such as are hidden in the appearance of quite contrary habits and dispositions. Among such, I shall, in the

---

* A lunatic Asylum.

first place, take care of one who is under the most subtle species
of Pride that I have observed in my whole experience.

This patient is a person for whom I have a great respect, as
being an old courtier, and a friend of mine in my youth.   The
man has but a bare subsistence, just enough to pay his reckoning with us at the Trumpet * : but by having spent the beginning
of his life in the hearing of great men, and persons of power,
he is always promising to do good offices, to introduce every
man he converses with into the world ; will desire one of ten
times his substance to let him see him sometimes, and hints to
him, that he does not forget him.   He answers to matters of
no consequence with great circumspection ; but, however,
maintains a general civility in his words and actions, and an
insolent benevolence to all whom he has to do with.   This he
practises with a grave tone and air ; and though I am his senior
by twelve years, and richer by forty pounds *per annum*, he had
yesterday the impudence to commend me to my face, and tell
me, " he should be always ready to encourage me."   In a word,
he is a very insignificant fellow, but exceedingly gracious.
The best return I can make him for his favours is, to carry
him myself to Bedlam, and see him well taken care of.

The next person I shall provide for is of a quite contrary
character ; that has in him all the stiffness and insolence of
quality, without a grain of sense or good nature, to make it
either respected or beloved.   His Pride has infected every
muscle of his face ; and yet, after all his endeavours to show
mankind that he contemns them, he is only neglected by all
that see him, as not of consequence enough to be hated.

For the cure of this particular sort of madness, it will be
necessary to break through all forms with him, and familiarize
his carriage by the use of a good cudgel.   It may likewise be
of great benefit to make him jump over a stick half a dozen
times every morning.

A third, whom I have in my eye, is a young fellow, whose
lunacy is such, that he boasts of nothing but what he ought to

* The tavern in Sheer Lane.

be ashamed of. He is vain of being rotten, and talks publicly of having committed crimes which he ought to be hanged for by the laws of his country.

There are several others whose brains are hurt with Pride, and whom I may hereafter attempt to recover; but shall conclude my present list with an old woman, who is just dropping into her grave, that talks of nothing but her birth. Though she had not a tooth in her head, she expects to be valued for the blood in her veins; which she fancies is much better than that which glows in the cheeks of Belinda,* and sets half the town on fire.

PASQUIN'S LETTER.

No. 129. SATURDAY, February 4, 1709–10. [Steele.]

Ingenio manus est et cervix cæsa.——
Juv. Sat. x. 120.

His wit's rewarded with the fatal loss
Of hand and head ————

When my paper for to-morrow was prepared for the press, there came in this morning a mail from Holland, which brought me several advices from foreign parts, and took my thoughts off domestic affairs. Among others, I have a letter from a burgher of Amsterdam, who makes me his compliments, and tells me he has sent me several draughts of humorous and satirical pictures by the best hands of the Dutch nation. They are a trading people, and in their very mind mechanics. They express their wit in manufacture, as we do in manuscript. He informs me, that a very witty hand has lately represented the

---

* Steele alludes to certain ladies celebrated at this time for their beauty. Among these, a daughter of Baron Spanheim, the Bavarian Ambassador at St. James's, was not the least eminent. After the death of her father, which happened here, she married the Marquis de Montandre, who bore a commission in the British army. "As beautiful as Madam Spanheim," was a proverbial expression. This lady is mentioned as a distinguished beauty, under her real maiden name, in the "Spectator."

present posture of public affairs in a landskip, or rather a sea-piece, wherein the potentates of the alliance are figured as their interests correspond with, or affect each other, under the appearance of commanders of ships.   These vessels carry the colours of the respective nations concerned in the present war. The whole design seems to tend to one point, which is, that several squadrons of British and Dutch ships are battering a French man-of-war, in order to make her deliver up a long boat with Spanish colours.   My correspondent informs me, that a man must understand the compass perfectly well, to be able to comprehend the beauty and invention of this piece; which is so skilfully drawn, that the particular views of every prince in Europe are seen according as the ships lie to the main figure in the picture, and as that figure may help or retard their sailing. It seems this curiosity is now on board a ship bound for England, and, with other rarities, made a present to me.   As soon as it arrives, I design to expose it to public view at my secretary Mr. Lillie's, who shall have an explication of all the terms of art; and I doubt not but it will give as good content as the moving picture in Fleet Street.*

But, above all the honours I have received from the learned world abroad, I am most delighted with the following epistle from Rome.

> " PASQUIN OF ROME to ISAAC BICKERSTAFF, of Great Britain, greeting.

> "SIR,

> " Your reputation has passed the Alps, and would have come to my ears by this time, if I had any.   In short, sir, you are looked upon here as a northern droll, and the greatest virtuoso among the Tramontanes.   Some indeed say, that Mr. Bickerstaff and Pasquin are only names invented to

---

* To be seen daily, at the Duke of Marlborough's Head in Fleet Street, a new moving figure, drawn by the best hand, with a great variety of curious motions and figures, which form a most agreeable prospect.   It has the general approbation of all who see it, and far exceeds the original formerly shown at the same place.   This picture was never exposed to public view before the beginning of the present year, 1710.—*Advertisement.*

father compositions which the natural parent does not care for owning. But, however that is, all agree, that there are several persons, who, if they durst attack you, would endeavour to leave you no more limbs than I have. I need not tell you that my adversaries have joined in a confederacy with Time to demolish me, and that, if I were not a very great wit, I should make the worst figure in Europe, being abridged of my legs, arms, nose, and ears. If you think fit to accept of the correspondence of so facetious a cripple, I shall from time to time send you an account of what happens at Rome. You have only heard of it from Latin and Greek authors; nay, perhaps, have read no accounts from hence, but of a triumph, ovation, or *apotheosis*,* and will, doubtless, be surprised to see the description of a profession, jubilee, or canonization. I shall, however, send you what the place affords, in return to what I shall receive from you. If you will acquaint me with your next promotion of general officers, I will send you an account of our next advancement of saints. If you will let me know who is reckoned the bravest warrior in Great Britain, I will tell you who is the best fiddler in Rome. If you will favour me with an inventory of the riches that were brought into your nation by admiral Wager,† I will not fail giving you an account of a pot of medals that has been lately dug up here, and are now under the examination of our ministers of state.

" There is one thing, in which I desire you would be very particular. What I mean is an exact list of all the religions in Great Britain, as likewise the habits, which are said here to

---

* An ovation was a lesser sort of triumph or honour granted by the Romans to their victorious generals. At the ovation the general entered the city on foot or on horseback, whereas in the triumph he rode in a chariot. Apotheosis signifies their deification of a great man after his death, or reckoning him among the gods.

† Charles Wager, a man of great skill in his profession, was first made a Captain at the battle of La Hogue by Admiral Russel. He was sent Commodore to the West Indies in 1707, where he attacked the Spanish galleons, May 28, 1708, with three ships, though they were fourteen in number drawn up in line of battle, and defeated them. His services Queen Anne distinguished by sending him a flag as Vice-Admiral of the Blue, intended for him before this engagement, and by honouring him at his return with knighthool. His share of prize money amounted to £100,000.

be the great points of conscience in England; whether they are made of serge or broad-cloth, of silk or linen. I should be glad to see a model of the most conscientious dress among you, and desire you will send me a hat of each religion; as likewise, if it be not too much trouble, a cravat. It would also be very acceptable here to receive an account of those two religious orders, which are lately sprung up amongst you, the Whigs and the Tories, with the points of doctrine, severities in discipline, penances, mortifications, and good works, by which they differ one from another. It would be no less kind, if you would explain to us a word, which they do not understand even at our English monastery, Toasts, and let us know whether the ladies so called are nuns or lay-sisters. In return, I will send you the secret history of several cardinals, which I have by me in manuscript, with the gallantries, amours, politics, and intrigues, by which they made their way to the holy purple.

But, when I propose a correspondence, I must not tell you what I intend to advise you of hereafter, and neglect to give you what I have at present. The pope has been sick for this fortnight of a violent tooth-ache, which has very much raised the French faction, and put the Conclave into a great ferment. Every one of the pretenders to the succession is grown twenty years older than he was a fortnight ago. Each candidate tries who shall cough and stoop most; for these are at present the great gifts, that recommend to the great Apostolical seat; which he stands the fairest for, who is likely to resign it the soonest. I have known the time, when it used to rain *Louis d'ors* on such occasions; but, whatever is the matter, there are very few of them to be seen, at present, at Rome, insomuch, that it is thought a man might purchase infallibility at a very reasonable rate. It is nevertheless hoped, that his holiness may recover, and bury these his imaginary successors.

"There has lately been found an human tooth in a catacomb, which has engaged a couple of convents in law suit; each of them pretending that it belonged to the jaw-bone of a saint, who was of their order. The college have sat upon it thrice; and I find there is a disposition among them to take it out of the possession of both the contending parties, by reason of a speech, which was made by one of the cardinals, who, by reason of its being found out of the company of any other bones, asserted, that it might be one of the teeth, which was coughed out by Ælia, an old woman, whose loss is recorded in Martial.

"I have nothing remarkable to communicate to you of state affairs, excepting only, that the Pope has lately received a horse from the German ambassador, as an acknowledgment for the kingdom of Naples, which is a fief of the church. His holiness refused this horse from the Germans ever since the duke of Anjou has been possessed of Spain ; but as they lately took care to accompany it with a body of ten thousand more, they have at last overcome his holiness's modesty, and prevailed upon him to accept the present. I am, sir, your most obedient, humble servant,

"PASQUIN."

THE PRESENT AGE.

No. 130. TUESDAY, FEBRUARY 7, 1709–10. [STEELE.]

—— Tamen me
Cum magnis vixisse invita fatebitur usque
Invidia —— Hor. 2 Sat. i. 75.

Spite of herself ev'n Envy must confess,
That I the friendship of the great possess.

I FIND some of the most polite Latin authors, who wrote at a time when Rome was in its glory, speak with a certain noble vanity of the brightness and splendour of the age in which they lived. Pliny often compliments his emperor Trajan upon this head ; and when he would animate him to anything great, or dissuade him from anything that was improper, he insinuates, that it is befitting or unbecoming the *claritas et nitor seculi*, that period of time which was made illustrious by his reign. When we cast our eyes back on the history of mankind, and trace them through their several successions to their first original, we sometimes see them breaking out in great and memorable actions, and towering up to the utmost heights of virtue and knowledge ; when, perhaps, if we carry our observations to a little distance, we see them sunk into sloth and ignorance, and altogether lost in darkness and obscurity. Sometimes the whole species is asleep for two or three generations, and then again awakens into action ; flourishes in heroes, philosophers, and poets ; who do honour to human nature, and leave such tracks of glory behind them, as distinguish the years in which they acted their part from the ordinary course of time.

Methinks a man cannot, without a secret satisfaction, consider the glory of the present age, which will shine as bright as any other in the history of mankind. It is still big with great events, and has already produced changes and revolutions, which will be as much admired by posterity, as any that have happened in "the days of our fathers, or in the old times before them." We have seen kingdoms divided and united, monarchs erected and deposed, nations transferred from one sovereign to another ; conquerors raised to such a greatness, as has given a terror to Europe, and thrown down by such a fall, as has moved their pity.

But it is still a more pleasing view to an Englishman, to see his own country give the chief influence to so illustrious an age, and stand in the strongest point of light amidst the diffused glory that surround it.

If we begin with learned men, we may observe, to the honour of our country, that those who make the greatest figure in most arts and sciences, are universally allowed to be of the British nation ; and, what is more remarkable, that men of the greatest learning, are among the men of the greatest quality.

A nation may indeed abound with persons of such uncommon parts and worth, as may make them rather a misfortune than a blessing to the public. Those, who singly might have been of infinite advantage to the age they live in, may, by rising up together in the same crisis of time, and by interfering in their pursuits of honour, rather interrupt, than promote the service of their country. Of this we have a famous instance in the republic of Rome, when Cæsar, Pompey, Cato, Cicero, and Brutus, endeavoured to recommend themselves at the same time to the admiration of their contemporaries. Mankind was not able to provide for so many extraordinary persons at once, or find out posts suitable to their ambition and abilities. For this reason they were all as miserable in their deaths, as they were famous in their lives, and occasioned not only the ruin of each other, but also that of the commonwealth.

It is therefore a particular happiness to a people, when the men of superior genius and character are so justly disposed in the high places of honour, that each of them moves in a sphere which is proper to him, and requires those particular qualities in which he excels.

If I see a general commanding the forces of his country, whose victories are not to be paralleled in story, and who is as famous for his negotiations as his victories;* and at the same time see the management of a nation's treasury in the hand of one, who has always distinguished himself by a generous contempt of his own private wealth, and an exact frugality of that which belongs to the public; † I cannot but think a people under such an administration may promise themselves conquests abroad, and plenty at home. If I were to wish for a proper person to preside over the public councils, it should certainly be one as much admired for his universal knowledge of men and things, as for his eloquence, courage, and integrity, in the exerting of such extraordinary talents.‡

Who is not pleased to see a person in the highest station in the law, who was the most eminent in his profession, and the most accomplished orator at the bar? § Or at the head of the fleet a commander, under whose conduct the common enemy received such a blow, as he has never been able to recover? ‖

---

* Steele here takes occasion to pay his compliments to some of the principal people in the higher departments of the State ; and first to the Duke of Marlborough, Commander-in-Chief of her Majesty's forces.

† Sidney Lord Godolphin was then Lord High-Treasurer of England.

‡ Lord Somers was at this time Lord President of the Council.

§ Lord Chancellor Cowper is here alluded to.

‖ Edward Russel, Earl of Orford, First Lord Commissioner of the Admiralty. He defeated the French at La Hogue.

Were we to form to ourselves the idea of one, whom we should think proper to govern a distant kingdom, consisting chiefly of those who differ from us in religion, and are influenced by foreign politics; would it not be such a one, as had signalized himself by an uniform and unshaken zeal for the Protestant interest, and by his dexterity in defeating the skill and artifice of its enemies?* In short, if we find a great man popular for his honesty and humanity, as well as famed for his learning and great skill in all the languages of Europe; or a person eminent for those qualifications, which make men shine in public assemblies, or for that steadiness, constancy, and good sense, which carry a man to the desired point through all the opposition of tumult and prejudice, we have the happiness to behold them in all posts suitable to their characters.

Such a constellation of great persons, if I may so speak, while they shine out in their own distinct capacities, reflect a lustre upon each other, but in a more particular manner on their Sovereign, who has placed them in those proper situations, by which their virtues become so beneficial to all her subjects. It is the anniversary of the birthday of this glorious Queen, which naturally led me into this field of contemplation, and, instead of joining in the public exaltations that are made on such occasions, to entertain my thoughts with the more serious pleasure of ruminating upon the glories of her reign.

While I behold her surrounded with triumphs, and adorned with all the prosperity and success which heaven ever shed on a mortal, and still considering herself as such; though the person appears to me exceeding great, that has these just honours paid to her; yet I must confess, she appears much greater in that she receives them with a such glorious humility, and shows she has no farther regard for them, than as they arise from these great events, which have made her subjects happy. For my own part, I must confess, when I see private virtues in so high a degree of perfection, I am not astonished

---

* Thomas, Earl of Wharton, had recently been appointed Lord-Lieutenant of Ireland. Addison was his secretary.

at any extraordinary success that attends them, but look upon public triumphs as the natural consequences of religious retirements.

ADULTERATION OF WINES.

No. 131.   THURSDAY, February 9, 1709–10.   [Addison.]

Scelus est jugulare Falernum,
Et dare Campano toxica sæva mero.   Mart. i. 19.

How great the crime, how flagrant the abuse !
T' adulterate generous wine with noxious juice.

THERE is in this city a certain fraternity of chemical operators, who work underground in holes, caverns, and dark retirements, to conceal their mysteries from the eyes and observation of mankind. These subterraneous philosophers are daily employed in the transmutation of liquors, and, by the power of magical drugs and incantations, raising under the streets of London the choicest products of the hills and valleys of France. They can squeeze Bordeaux out of the sloe, and draw Champagne from an apple. Virgil, in that remarkable prophecy,

Incultisque rubens pendebit sentibus uva.
VIRG. Ecl. iv. 29.

The ripening grape shall hang on every thorn,

seems to have hinted at this art, which can turn a plantation of northern hedges into a vineyard. These adepts are known among one another by the name of Wine-brewers ; and, I am afraid, do great injury, not only to her majesty's customs, but to the bodies of many of her good subjects.

Having received sundry complaints against these invisible workmen, I ordered the proper officer of my court to ferret them out of their respective caves, and bring them before me, which was yesterday executed accordingly.

The person who appeared against them was a merchant, who had by him a great magazine of wines, that he had laid in before the war : but these gentlemen, as he said, had so vitiated the nation's palate, that no man could believe his to be French, because it did not taste like what they sold for such." As a man never pleads better than where his own personal interest is concerned, he exhibited to the court, with great eloquence, " that this new corporation of druggists had inflamed the bills of mortality, and puzzled the college of physicians with diseases, for which they neither knew a name or cure. He accused some of giving all their customers colics and megrims ; and mentioned one who had boasted, he had a tun of claret by him, that in a fortnight's time should give the gout to a dozen of the healthfulest men in the city, provided that their constitutions were prepared for it by wealth and idleness. He then enlarged, with a great show of reason, upon the prejudice, which these mixtures and compositions had done to the brains of the English nation ; as is too visible, said he, from many late pamphlets, speeches, and sermons, as well as from the ordinary conversations of the youth of this age. He then quoted an ingenious person, who would undertake to know by a man's writings the wine he most delighted in ; and on that occasion named a certain satirist, whom he had discovered to be the author of a lampoon, by a manifest taste of the sloe, which showed itself in it, by much roughness, and little spirit.

In the last place, he ascribed to the unnatural tumults and fermentations which these mixtures raise in our blood, the divisions, heats, and animosities, that reign among us ; and, in particular, asserted most of the modern enthusiasms and agitations to be nothing else but the effects of adulterated Port.

The counsel for the Brewers had a face so extremely inflamed, and illuminated with carbuncles, that I did not wonder to see him an advocate for these sophistications. His rhetoric was likewise such as I should have expected from the common draught, which I found he often drank to a great excess.   Indeed, I was so surprised at his figure and parts, that I ordered him to give me a taste of his usual liquor ; which I had no sooner drunk, but I found a pimple rising in my forehead ; and felt such a terrible decay in my under-standing, that I would not proceed in the trial until the fume of it was entirely dissipated.

This notable advocate had little to say in the defence of his clients, but that they were under a necessity of making claret, if they keep open their doors ; it being the nature of mankind to love everything that is prohibited.   He farther pretended to reason, that it might be as profitable to the nation to make French wine as French hats ; and concluded with the great advantage that this practice had already brought to part of the kingdom.   Upon which he informed the court, that the lands in Herefordshire were raised two years purchase since the beginning of the war.

When I had sent out my summons to these people, I gave, at the same time, orders to each of them to bring the several ingredients he made use of in distinct phials, which they had done accordingly, and ranged them into two rows on each side of the court.   The workmen were drawn up in ranks behind them.   The merchant informed me, "that in one row of phials were the several colours they dealt in, and in the other, the tastes."   He then showed me, on the right-hand, one who went by the name of Tom Tintoret, who, as he told me, " was the greatest master in his colouring of any vintner in London." To give me a proof of his art, he took a glass of fair water ; and, by the infusion of three drops out of one of his phials, converted it into a most beautiful pale Burgundy.   Two more of the same kind heightened it into a perfect Languedoc : from thence it passed into a florid Hermitage : and after having gone through two or three other changes, by the addition of a single drop, ended in a very deep Pontac.   This ingenious virtuoso, seeing me very much surprised at his art, told me, that he had not an opportunity of showing it in perfection, having only made use of water for the ground-work of his colouring ; but that, if I were to see an operation upon liquors of stronger bodies, the art would appear to a much greater advantage. He added, that he doubted not but it would please my curiosity to see the cyder of one apple take only a vermilion, when another, with a less quantity of the same infusion, would rise into a dark purple, according to the different texture of parts in the liquor. He informed me also, that he could hit the different shades and degrees of red, as they appear in the pink and the rose, the clove and the carnation, as he had Rhenish or Moselle, Perry or White Port, to work in.

I was so satisfied with the ingenuity of this virtuoso, that, after having advised him to quit so dishonest a profession, I promised him, in consideration of his great genius, to recommend him as a partner to a friend of mine, who has heaped up great riches, and is a scarlet-dyer.

The artists on my other hand were ordered, in the second place, to make some experiments of their skill before me : upon which the famous Harry Sippet stepped out, and asked me, "what I would be pleased to drink?" At the same time he filled out three or four white liquors in a glass, and told me, "that it should be what I pleased to call for;" adding very learnedly, "That the liquor before him was as the naked substance, or first matter of his compound, to which he and his friend, who stood over-against him, could give what accidents, or form they pleased." Finding him so great a philosopher, I desired he would convey into it the qualities and essence of right Bordeaux. "Coming, coming, sir," said he, with the air of a drawer ; and, after having cast his eye on the several tastes and flavours that stood before him, he took up a little cruet, that was filled with a kind of inky juice, and pouring some of it out into the glass of white wine, presented it to me ; and told me, "this was the wine, over which most of the business of the last term had been dispatched." I must confess, I looked upon that sooty drug, which he held up in his cruet, as the quintessence of English Bordeaux ; and therefore desired him to give me a glass of it by itself, which he did with great unwillingness. My cat at that time sat by me upon the elbow of my chair ; and as I did not care for making the experiment upon myself, I reached it to her to sip of it, which had like to have cost her her life; for, notwithstanding it flung her at first into freakish tricks, quite contrary to her usual gravity, in less than a quarter of an hour she fell into convulsions ; and, had it not been a creature more tenacious of life than any other, would certainly have died under the operation.

I was so incensed by the tortures of my innocent domestic, and the unworthy dealings of these men, that I told them, if each of them had as many lives as the injured creature before them, they deserved to forfeit them for the pernicious arts which they used for their profit. I therefore bid them look upon themselves as no better than as a kind of assassins and murderers within the law. However, since they had dealt so clearly with me, and laid before me their whole practice, I dismissed them for that time ; with a particular request, that they would not poison any of my friends and acquaintance, and take to some honest livelihood without loss of time.

For my own part, I have resolved hereafter to be very careful in my liquors ; and have agreed with a friend of mine in the army, upon their next march, to secure me two hogsheads of the best stomach-wine in the cellars of Versailles, for the good of my Lucubrations, and the comfort of my old age.

OUR CLUB.

No. 132.　SATURDAY, February 11, 1709–10.　[Steele.]

Habeo senectuti magnam gratiam, quæ mihi sermonis aviditatem auxit, potionis et cibi sustulit.—Tull. de Sen.

I am much beholden to old age, which has increased my eagerness for conversation in proportion as it has lessened my appetites of hunger and thirst.

After having applied my mind with more than ordinary attention to my studies, it is my usual custom to relax and unbend it in the conversation of such, as are rather easy than shining companions. This I find particularly necessary for me before I retire to rest, in order to draw my slumbers upon me by degrees, and fall asleep insensibly. This is the particular use I make of a set of heavy honest men, with whom I have passed many hours with much indolence, though not with great pleasure. Their conversation is a kind of preparative for sleep : it takes the mind down from its abstractions, leads it into the familiar traces of thought, and lulls it into that state of tranquillity, which is the condition of a thinking man, when he is but half awake. After this, my reader will not be surprised to hear the account, which I am about to give of a club of my own contemporaries, among whom I pass two or three hours every evening. This I look upon as taking my first nap before I go to bed. The truth of it is, I should think myself unjust to posterity, as well as to the society at the Trumpet,* of which I am a member, did not I in some part of my writings give an account of the persons among whom I have passed almost a sixth part of my time for these last forty years. Our club consisted originally of fifteen ; but, partly by the severity of the law in arbitrary times, and partly by the natural effects of old age, we are at present reduced to a third part of that number : in which, however, we hear this consolation, that the best company is said to consist of five persons. I must confess, besides the aforementioned benefit which I meet with in the conversation of this select society, I am not the less pleased with the company, in that I find myself the greatest wit among them, and am heard as their oracle in all points of learning and difficulty.

Sir Jeoffrey Notch, who is the oldest of the club, has been in possession of the right-hand chair time out of mind, and is the only man among us that has the liberty of stirring the fire. This our foreman is a gentleman of an ancient family, that came to a great estate some years before he had discretion, and run it out in hounds, horses, and cock-fighting ; for which

* A tavern in Sheer Lane.

reason he looks upon himself as an honest, worthy gentleman, who has had misfortunes in the world, and calls every thriving man a pitiful upstart.

Major Matchlock is the next senior, who served in the last civil wars, and has all the battles by heart. He does not think any action in Europe worth talking of since the fight of Marston Moor ; * and every night tells us of his having been knocked off his horse at the rising of the London apprentices ; † for which he is in great esteem among us.

Honest old Dick Reptile is the third of our society. He is a good-natured indolent man, who speaks little himself, but laughs at our jokes ; and brings his young nephew along with him, a youth of eighteen years old, to shew him good company, and give him a taste of the world. This young fellow sits generally silent ; but whenever he opens his mouth, or laughs at anything that passes, he is constantly told by his uncle, after a jocular manner, "Ay, ay, Jack, you young men think us fools ; but we old men know you are."

The greatest wit of our company, next to myself, is a Bencher of the neighbouring Inn, who in his youth frequented the ordinaries about Charing Cross, and pretends to have been intimate with Jack Ogle. He has about ten distichs of Hudibras without book, and never leaves the club until he has applied them all. If any modern wit be mentioned, or any town-frolic spoken of, he shakes his head at the dulness of the present age, and tells us a story of Jack Ogle.

For my own part, I am esteemed among them, because they see I am something respected by others ; though at the same time I understand by their behaviour, that I am considered by them as a man of a great deal of learning, but no knowledge of the world ; insomuch, that the Major sometimes, in the height of his military pride, calls me the Philosopher : and Sir Jeoffrey, no longer ago than last night, upon a dispute what

---

* Marston Moor was fought July 2, 1644.

† July 14, 1647, the London Apprentices presented a petition signed by above 10,000 hands ; and on the 26th they forced their way into the house, threatening members until their demands were satisfied.

day of the month it was then in Holland, pulled his pipe out
of his mouth, and cried, "What does the scholar say to it?"

Our club meets precisely at *six o'clock in the evening;* * but
I did not come last night until half an hour after seven, by
which means I escaped the battle of Naseby, which the Major
usually begins at about three-quarters after six : I found also,
that my good friend the Bencher had already spent three of
his distichs ; and only waited an opportunity to hear a sermon
spoken of, that he might introduce the couplet where "a
stick" rhymes to "ecclesiastic." At my entrance into the
room, they were naming a red petticoat and a cloak, by which
I found that the Bencher had been diverting them with a story
of Jack Ogle.†

I had no sooner taken my seat, but Sir Jeoffrey, to show his
good-will towards me, gave me a pipe of his own tobacco, and
stirred up the fire. I look upon it as a point of morality, to be
obliged by those who endeavour to oblige me ; and therefore,
in requital for his kindness, and to set the conversation
a-going, I took the best occasion I could to put him upon
telling us the story of old Gantlett, which he always does with
very particular concern. He traced up his descent on both
sides for several generations, describing his diet and manner of
life, with his several battles, and particularly that in which he
fell. This Gantlett was a gamecock, upon whose head the
knight, in his youth, had won five hundred pounds, and lost
two thousand. This naturally set the Major upon the account
of Edge Hill fight,‡ and ended in a duel of Jack Ogle's.

---

* Clubs at the Universities met at six till 1730.

† Jack Ogle was a man of great extravagance, and a noted gamester. He
had an only sister, who was mistress to the Duke of York. This sister Ogle
laid under very frequent contributions to supply his wants and support his
extravagance. It is said that by the interest of her royal keeper, Ogle was
placed as a private gentleman in the first troop of Foot Guards, at that time
under the command of the Duke of Monmouth. To this era of Ogle's life, the
story of the red petticoat refers. He had pawned his trooper's cloak, and to
save appearances at a review, had borrowed his landlady's red petticoat, which
he carried rolled up *en croupe* behind him. The Duke of Monmouth noticed
it, and willing to enjoy the confusion of a detection, gave order to *cloak all*,
with which Ogle, after some hesitation, was obliged to comply. Although he
could not *cloak*, he said he would *petticoat* with the best of them.

‡ The battle of Edge Hill was fought October 23, 1642.

Old Reptile was extremely attentive to all that was said, though it was the same he had heard every night for these twenty years, and, upon all occasions, winked upon his nephew to mind what passed.

This may suffice to give the world a taste of our innocent conversation, which we spun out until about ten of the clock, when my maid came with a lantern to light me home. I could not but reflect with myself, as I was going out, upon the talkative humour of old men, and the little figure which that part of life makes in one who cannot employ his natural propensity in discourses which would make him venerable. I must own, it makes me very melancholy in company, when I hear a young man begin a story ; and have often observed, that one of a quarter of an hour long in a man of five-and-twenty, gathers circumstances every time he tells it, until it grows into a long Canterbury tale of two hours by that time he is threescore.

The only way of avoiding such a trifling and frivolous old age is, to lay up in our way to it such stores of knowledge and observation, as may make us useful and agreeable in our declining years. The mind of man in a long life will become a magazine of wisdom or folly, and will consequently discharge itself in something impertinent or improving. For which reason, as there is nothing more ridiculous than an old trifling story-teller, so there is nothing more venerable, than one who has turned his experience to the entertainment and advantage of mankind.

In short, we, who are in the last stage of life, and are apt to indulge ourselves in talk, ought to consider, if what we speak be worth being heard, and endeavour to make our discourse like that of Nestor, which Homer compares to the flowing of honey for its sweetness.

ON SILENCE.

No. 133. TUESDAY, February 14, 1709. [Addison.]

Dum tacent, clamant.   Tull.

Their Silence pleads aloud.

Silence is sometimes more significant and sublime, than the most noble and most expressive eloquence, and is on many occasions the indication of a great mind. Several authors have treated of Silence, as a part of duty and discretion ; but none of them have considered it in this light. Homer compares the noise and clamour of the Trojans advancing towards the enemy, to the cackling of cranes, when they invade an army of pigmies. On the contrary, he makes his countrymen and favourites, the Greeks, move forward in a regular and determined march, and in the depth of Silence. I find in the accounts, which are given us of some of the more Eastern nations, where the inhabitants are disposed by their constitutions and climates to higher strains of thought, and more elevated raptures than what we feel in the Northern regions of the world, that Silence is a religious exercise among them. For when their public devotions are in the greatest fervour, and their hearts lifted up as high as words can raise them, there are certain suspensions of sound and motion for a time, in which the mind is left to itself, and supposed to swell with such secret conceptions, as are too big for utterance. I have myself been wonderfully delighted with a master-piece of music, when in the very tumult and ferment of their harmony, all the voices and instruments have stopped short on a sudden ; and after a little pause recovered themselves again as it were, and renewed the concert in all its parts. This short interval of Silence has had more music in it, than any the same space of time before or after it. There are two instances of Silence in the two greatest poets that ever wrote, which have something in them as sublime, as any of the speeches in their whole works. The first is that of Ajax, in the eleventh book of the Odyssey. Ulysses, who had been the rival of this great man in his life, as well as the occasion of his death, upon meeting his shade in the region of departed heroes, makes his submission to him with an humility next to adoration, which the other passes over with dumb, sullen majesty, and such a Silence, as to use the words of Longinus, had more greatness in it than any thing he could have spoken.

The next instance I shall mention is in Virgil, where the poet doubtless imitates this Silence of Ajax in that of Dido ; though I do not know that any of his commentators have taken notice of it. Æneas, finding among the shades of despairing lovers the ghost of her who had lately died for him, with the wound still fresh upon her, addresses himself to her with expanded arms, floods of tears, and the most passionate professions of his own innocence, as to what had happened ; all which Dido receives with the dignity and disdain of a resenting lover and an injured queen ; and is so far from vouchsafing him an answer, that she does not give him a single look. The poet represents her as turning away her face from him while he spoke to her ; and, after having kept her eyes some time upon the ground, as one that heard and contemned his protestations, flying from him into the grove of myrtle, and into the arms of another, whose fidelity had deserved her love.

I have often thought our writers of tragedy have been very defective in this particular, and that they might have given great beauty to their works, by certain stops and pauses in the representation of such passions as it is not in the power of language to express. There is something like this in the last act of " Venice Preserved," where Pierre is brought to an infamous execution, and begs of his friend, as a reparation for past injuries, and the only favour he could do him, to rescue him from the ignominy of the wheel by stabbing him. As he is going to make this dreadful request, he is not able to communicate it ; but withdraws his face from his friend's ear, and bursts into tears. The melancholy Silence that

follows hereupon, and continues until he has recovered himself
enough to reveal his mind to his friend, raises in the spectators
a grief that is inexpressible, and an idea of such a complicated
distress in the actor, as words cannot utter. It would look
as ridiculous to many readers, to give rules and directions
for proper Silences, as for "penning a Whisper," but it is
certain, that in the extremity of most passions, particularly
surprise, admiration, astonishment, nay, rage itself, there is
nothing more graceful than to see the play stand still for a
few moments, and the audience fixed in an agreeable suspense,
during the Silence of a skilful actor.

But Silence never shews itself to so great an advantage, as
when it is made the reply to calumny and defamation, provided
that we give no just occasion for them. We might produce
an example of it in the behaviour of one, in whom it appeared
in all its majesty, and one, whose silence, as well as his person,
was altogether divine. When one considers this subject only
in its sublimity, this great instance could not but occur to
me; and since I only make use of it to shew the highest
example of it, I hope I do not offend in it. To forbear reply-
ing to an unjust reproach, and overlook it with a generous,
or, if possible, with an entire neglect of it, is one of the most
heroic acts of a great mind: and I must confess, when I reflect
upon the behaviour of some of the greatest men in antiquity,
I do not so much admire them, that they deserved the praise
of the whole age they lived in, as because they contemned the
envy and detraction of it.

All that is incumbent on a man of worth, who suffers under
so ill a treatment, is to lie by for some time in silence and
obscurity, until the prejudice of the times be over, and his
reputation cleared. I have often read, with a great deal of
pleasure, a legacy of the famous Lord Bacon, one of the
greatest geniuses that our own or any country has produced.
After having bequeathed his soul, body, and estate, in the
usual form, he adds, "My name and memory I leave to foreign
nations, and to my countrymen after some time be passed over."
At the same time that I recommend this philosophy to others,

I must confess, I am so poor a proficient in it myself, that if in the course of my Lucubrations it happens, as it has done more than once, that my paper is duller than in conscience it ought to be, I think the time an age until I have an opportunity of putting out another, and growing famous again for two days.

CRUELTY TO ANIMALS.

No. 134. THURSDAY, February 16, 1709-10. [Steele.]

——— Quis talia fando
Myrmidonum, Dolopumve, aut duri miles Ulyssei,
Temperet à lacrymis ? Virg. Æn. ii. 8.

——— Such woes
Not even the hardest of our foes could hear,
Nor stern Ulysses tell without a tear.

I WAS awakened very early this morning by the distant crowing of a cock, which I thought had the finest pipe I ever heard. He seemed to me to strain his voice more than ordinary, as if he designed to make himself heard to the remotest corner of this lane. Having entertained myself a little before I went to bed with a discourse on the transmigration of men into other animals, I could not but fancy that this was the soul of some drowsy bell-man who used to sleep upon his post, for which he was condemned to do penance in feathers, and distinguish the several watches of the night under the outside of a cock. While I was thinking of the condition of this poor bell-man in masquerade, I heard a great knocking at my door, and was soon after told by my maid, that my worthy friend the tall black gentleman, who frequents the coffee-houses hereabouts, desired to speak to me. This antient *Pythagorean*, who has as much honesty as any man living, but good nature to an excess, brought me the following petition ; which I am apt to believe he penned himself, the petitioner not being able to express his mind on paper under his present form, however famous he might have been for writing verses when he was in his original shape.

"To Isaac Bickerstaff, Esquire, Censor of Great-Britain.

"The humble petition of Job Chanticleer in behalf of himself, and many other poor sufferers in the same condition,

From my Coop in Clare Market, *February* 13, 1709.

"Sheweth,

"That whereas your petitioner is truly descended of the antient family of the Chanticleers, at Cock-hall near Rumford in Essex, it has been his misfortune to come into the mercenary hands of a certain ill-disposed person, commonly called an higler, who, under the close confinement of a pannier, has conveyed him and many others up to London ; but hearing by chance of your worship's great humanity towards Robin-red-breasts and Tom-tits, he is emboldened to beseech you to take his deplorable condition into your tender consideration, who otherwise must suffer, with many thousands more as innocent as himself, that inhuman barbarity of a *Shrove-Tuesday* persecution. We humbly hope, that our courage and vigilance may plead for us on this occasion.

"Your poor petitioner most earnestly implores your immediate protection from the insolence of the rabble, the batteries of cat-sticks, and a painful lingering death.

"And your petitioner, &c."

Upon delivery of this petition, the worthy gentleman, who presented it, told me the customs of many wise nations of the East, through which he had travelled ; that nothing was more frequent than to see a Dervise lay out a whole year's income in the redemption of larks or linnets, that had unhappily fallen into the hands of bird-catchers : that it was also usual to run between a dog and a bull to keep them from hurting one another, or to lose the use of a limb in parting a couple of furious mastiffs. He then insisted upon the ingratitude and disingenuity of treating in this manner a necessary and

domestic animal, that has made the whole house keep good
hours, and called up the cook-maid for five years together.
" What would a Turk say," continued he, " should he hear,
that it is a common entertainment in a nation, which pretends
to be one of the most civilized of Europe, to tie an innocent
animal to a stake, and put him to an ignominious death, who
has perhaps been the guardian and proveditor of a poor family,
as long as he was able to get eggs for his mistress ? "

I thought what this gentleman said was very reasonable ;
and have often wondered, that we do not lay aside a custom,
which makes us appear barbarous to nations much more rude
and unpolished than ourselves. Some French writers have
represented this diversion of the common people much to our
disadvantage, and imputed it to natural fierceness and cruelty
of temper ; as they do some other entertainments peculiar to
our nation : I mean those elegant diversions of bull-baiting
and prize-fighting, with the like ingenious recreations of the
Bear-garden. I wish I knew how to answer this reproach
which is cast upon us, and excuse the death of so many innocent cocks, bulls, dogs, and bears, as have been set together
by the ears, or died untimely deaths, only to make us sport.

It will be said, that these are the entertainments of common
people. It is true ; but they are the entertainments of no
other common people. Besides, I am afraid, there is a tincture
of the same savage spirit in the diversions of those of higher
rank, and more refined relish. Rapin observes, that the
English theatre very much delights in bloodshed, which he
likewise represents as an indication of our tempers. I must
own, there is something very horrid in the public executions
of an English tragedy. Stabbing and poisoning, which are
performed behind the scenes in other nations, must be done
openly among us, to gratify the audience.

When poor Sandford* was upon the stage, I have seen him

---

* Sandford was an excellent actor in disagreeable characters ; he had a
low and crooked person, and such bodily defects as were too strong to be
admitted into great or amiable characters, so that he was the stage villain, not
by choice, but from necessity.

groaning upon a wheel, stuck with daggers, impaled alive, calling his executioners, with a dying voice, " cruel dogs and villains ! " and all this to please his judicious spectators, who were wonderfully delighted with seeing a man in torment so well acted.   The truth of it is, the politeness of our English stage, in regard to decorum, is very extraordinary.   We act murders, to shew our intrepidity ; and adulteries, to shew our gallantry : both of them are frequent in our most taking plays, with this difference only, that the former are done in the sight of the audience, and the latter wrought up to such an height upon the stage, that they are almost put in execution before the actors can get behind the scenes.

I would not have it thought, that there is just ground for those consequences which our enemies draw against us from these practices ; but methinks one would be sorry for any manner of occasion for such misrepresentations of us.   The virtues of tenderness, compassion, and humanity, are those by which men are distinguished from brutes, as much as by reason itself; and it would be the greatest reproach to a nation to distinguish itself from all others by any defect in these particular virtues.   For which reasons, I hope that my dear countrymen will no longer expose themselves by an effusion of blood, whether it be of theatrical heroes, cocks, or any other innocent animals, which we are not obliged to slaughter for our safety, convenience, or nourishment.   When any of these ends are not served in the destruction of a living creature, I cannot but pronounce it a great piece of cruelty, if not a kind of murder.

MINUTE PHILOSOPHERS.

No. 135. SATURDAY, FEBRUARY 18, 1709-10. [STEELE.]

Quòd si in hoc erro, quòd animos hominum immortales esse credam, libenter erro ; nec mihi hunc errorem, quo delector, dum vivo, extorqueri volo : sin mortuus, ut quidam minuti philosophi censent, nihil sentiam ; non vereor, ne hunc errorem meum *mortui* philosophi irrideant.—CICERO, De Senect. cap. ult.

But if I err in believing that the souls of men are immortal, I willingly err ; nor while I live would I wish to have this delightful error extorted from me : and if after death I shall feel nothing, as some minute philosophers think, I am not afraid lest dead philosophers should laugh at me for the error.

SEVERAL letters, which I have lately received, give me information, that some well-disposed persons have taken offence at my using the word *free-thinker* as a term of reproach. To set, therefore, this matter in a clear light, I must declare, that no one can have a greater veneration than myself for the free-thinkers of antiquity ; who acted the same part in those times, as the great men of the reformation did in several nations of Europe, by exerting themselves against the idolatry and superstition of the times in which they lived. It was by this noble impulse that Socrates and his disciples, as well as all the philosophers of note in Greece, and Cicero, Seneca, with all the learned men of Rome, endeavoured to enlighten their contemporaries amidst the darkness and ignorance in which the world was then sunk and buried.

The great points, which these free-thinkers endeavoured to establish and inculcate into the minds of men, were the formation of the universe, the superintendency of Providence, the perfection of the Divine Nature, the immortality of the soul, and the future state of rewards and punishments. They all complied with the religion of their country, as much as possible, in such particulars as did not contradict and pervert these great and fundamental doctrines of mankind. On the contrary, the persons who now set up for Free-thinkers, are such as endeavour, by a little trash of words and sophistry, to weaken and destroy those very principles, for the vindication of which, freedom of thought at first became laudable and heroic. These apostates from reason and good sense can look at the glorious frame of nature, without paying an adoration to Him that raised it; can consider the great revolutions in the universe, without lifting up their minds to that superior Power which hath the direction of it; can presume to censure the Deity in his ways towards men; can level mankind with the beasts that perish; can extinguish in their own minds all the pleasing hopes of a future state, and lull themselves into a stupid security against the terrors of it. If one were to take the word *priestcraft* out of the mouths of these shallow monsters, they would be immediately struck dumb. It is by the help of this single term that they endeavour to disappoint the good works of the most learned and venerable order of men, and harden the hearts of the ignorant against the very light of nature, and the common received notions of mankind. We ought not to treat such miscreants as these upon the foot of fair disputants; but to pour out contempt upon them, and speak of them with scorn and infamy, as the pests of society, the revilers of human nature, and the blasphemers of a Being, whom a good man would rather die than hear dishonoured. Cicero, after having mentioned the great heroes of knowledge that recommended this divine doctrine of the immortality of the soul, calls those small pretenders to wisdom, who declared against it, certain *minute philosophers*, using a diminutive even of the word *Little*, to express the despicable opinion he had of them. The contempt he throws upon them in another passage, is yet more remarkable; where, to shew the mean thoughts he entertains of them, he declares " he would rather be in the wrong with Plato, than in the right with such company." There is indeed nothing in the world so ridiculous as one of these grave philosophical Free-thinkers, that hath neither passions nor appetites to gratify, no heats of blood, nor vigour of constitution, that can turn his systems of infidelity to his advantage, or raise pleasures out of them which are inconsistent with the belief of an hereafter. One that has neither wit, gallantry, mirth, or youth, to indulge by these notions, but only a poor, joyless, uncomfortable vanity of distinguishing himself from the rest of mankind, is rather to be regarded as a mischievous lunatic, than a mistaken philosopher. A chaste infidel, a speculative libertine, is an animal that I should not believe to be in nature, did I not sometimes meet with this species of men, that plead for the indulgence of their passions in the midst of a severe studious life, and talk against the immortality of the soul over a dish of coffee.

I would fain ask a minute philosopher, what good he proposes to mankind by the publishing of his doctrines? Will they make a man a better citizen, or father of a family; a more endearing husband, friend, or son? will they enlarge his public or private virtues, or correct any of his frailties or vices? What is there either joyful or glorious in such opinions? do they either refresh or enlarge our thoughts? do they contribute to the happiness, or raise the dignity, of human nature? The only good, that I have ever heard pretended to, is, that they banish terrors, and set the mind at ease. But whose terrors do they banish? It is certain, if there were any strength in their arguments, they would give great disturbance to minds that are influenced by virtue, honour, and morality, and take from us the only comforts and supports of affliction, sickness, and old age. The minds, therefore, which they set at ease, are only those of impenitent criminals and malefactors, and which, to the good of mankind, should be in perpetual terror and alarm.

I must confess, nothing is more useful than for a Freethinker, in proportion as the insolence of scepticism is abated in him by years and knowledge, or humbled and beaten down by sorrow or sickness, to reconcile himself to the general conceptions of reasonable creatures; so that we frequently see the apostates turning from their revolt towards the end of their lives, and employing the refuse of their parts in promoting those truths which they had before endeavoured to invalidate.

The history of a gentleman in France * is very well known,

---

* No one appears to know who this "gentleman in France" was.

who was so zealous a promoter of infidelity, that he had got together a select company of disciples, and travelled into all parts of the kingdom to make converts. In the midst of his fantastical success he fell sick, and was reclaimed to such a sense of his condition, that after he had passed some time in great agonies and horrors of mind, he begged those who had the care of burying him, to dress his body in the habit of a capuchin, that the devil might not run away with it ; and, to do farther justice upon himself, desired them to tie an halter about his neck, as a mark of that ignominious punishment, which, in his own thoughts, he had so justly deserved.

I would not have persecution so far disgraced, as to wish these vermin might be animadverted on by any legal penalties ; though I think it would be highly reasonable, that those few of them who die in the professions of their infidelity, should have such tokens of infamy fixed upon them, as might distinguish those bodies which are given up by the owners to oblivion and putrefaction, from those which rest in hope, and shall rise in glory. But at the same time that I am against doing them the honour of the notice of our laws, which ought not to suppose there are such criminals in being, I have often wondered, how they can be tolerated in any mixed conversations, while they are venting these absurd opinions ; and should think, that if, on any such occasions, half a dozen of the most robust Christians in the company would lead one of these gentlemen to a pump, or convey him into a blanket, they would do very good service both to church and state. I do not know how the laws stand in this particular ; but I hope, whatever knocks, bangs, or thumps, might be given with such an honest intention, would not be construed as a breach of the peace. I dare say, they would not be returned by the person who receives them ; for whatever these fools may say in the vanity of their hearts, they are too wise to risque their lives upon the uncertainty of their opinions.

When I was a young man about this town, I frequented the ordinary of the Black-horse in Holborn, where the person that usually presided at the table was a rough old-fashioned gentle-

man, who, according to the customs of those times, had been
the major and preacher of a regiment. It happened one day
that a noisy young officer, bred in France, was venting some
new-fangled notions, and speaking, in the gaiety of his humour,
against the dispensations of Providence. The major, at first,
only desired him to talk more respectfully of one for whom all
the company had an honour ; but, finding him run on in his
extravagance, began to reprimand him after a more serious
manner. "Young man," said he, "do not abuse your benefactor whilst you are eating his bread. Consider whose air
you breathe, whose presence you are in, and who it is that gave
you the power of that very speech, which you make use of to
his dishonour." The young fellow, who thought to turn
matters into a jest, asked him "if he was going to preach ?"
but at the same time desired him "to take care what he said
when he spoke to a man of honour." "A man of honour !"
says the major ; "thou art an infidel and a blasphemer, and I
shall use thee as such." In short, the quarrel ran so high, that
the major was desired to walk out. Upon their coming into
the garden, the old fellow advised his antagonist to consider the
place into which one pass might drive him ; but, finding him
grow upon him to a degree of scurrility, as believing the advice
proceeded from fear ; " Sirrah," says he, " if a thunderbolt does
not strike thee dead before I come at thee, I shall not fail to
chastise thee for thy profaneness to thy Maker, and thy sauci-
ness to his servant." Upon this he drew his sword, and cried
out with a loud voice, "The sword of the Lord and of
Gideon !" which so terrified his antagonist, that he was
immediately disarmed, and thrown upon his knees. In this
posture he begged his life ; but the major refused to grant it,
before he had asked pardon for his offence in a short ex-
temporary prayer, which the old gentleman dictated to him
upon the spot, and which his proselyte repeated after him in
the presence of the whole ordinary, that were now gathered
about him in the garden.

TOM VARNISH.

No. 136. TUESDAY, February 21, 1709–10. [Steele.]

Deprendi miserum est : Fabio vel judice vincam.
Hor. 1 Sat. ii. ver. ult.

To be surpris'd, is, sure a wretched tale,
And for the truth to Fabius I appeal.

Because I have a professed aversion to long beginnings of stories, I will go into this at once, by telling you, that there dwells near the Royal Exchange as happy a couple as ever entered into wedlock. These live in that mutual confidence of each other, which renders the satisfaction of marriage even greater than those of friendship, and makes wife and husband the dearest appellations of human life. Mr. Balance is a merchant of good consideration, and understands the world, not from speculation, but practice. His wife is the daughter of an honest house, ever bred in a family-way ; and has, from a natural good understanding, and great innocence, a freedom which men of sense know to be the certain sign of virtue, and fools take to be an encouragement to vice.

Tom Varnish, a young gentleman of the Middle-Temple, by the bounty of a good father, who was so obliging as to die, and leave him, in his twenty-fourth year, besides a good estate, a large sum which lay in the hands of Mr. Balance, had by *this means* an intimacy at his house ; and being one of those hard students who read plays for the improvement in the law, took his rules of life from thence. Upon mature delibera-tion, he conceived it very proper, that he, as a man of wit and pleasure of the town, should have an intrigue with *his merchant's* wife. He no sooner thought of this adventure, but he began it by an amorous epistle to the lady, and a faithful promise to wait upon her at a certain hour the next evening, when he knew her husband was to be absent.

The letter was no sooner received, but it was communicated to the husband, and produced no other effect in him, than that he

joined with his wife to raise all the mirth they could out of
this fantastical piece of gallantry. They were so little concerned at this dangerous man of mode, that they plotted ways
to perplex him without hurting him. Varnish comes exactly
at his hour ; and the lady's well-acted confusion at his entrance
gave him opportunity to repeat some couplets very fit for the
occasion with very much grace and spirit. His theatrical
manner of making love was interrupted by an alarm of the
husband's coming ; and the wife, in a personated terror,
beseeched him, " if he had any value for the honour of a woman
that loved him, he would jump out of the window." He did
so, and fell upon feather-beds placed on purpose to receive
him.

It is not to be conceived how great the joy of an amorous
man is, when he has suffered for his mistress, and is never the
worse for it. Varnish the next day writ a most elegant billet,
wherein he said all that imagination could form upon the
occasion. He violently protested, "going out of the window
was no way terrible, but as it was going from her ; " with
several other kind expressions, which procured him a second
assignation. Upon his second visit, he was conveyed by a
faithful maid into her bed chamber, and left there to expect the
arrival of her mistress. But the wench, according to her
instructions, ran in again to him, and locked the door after
her to keep out her master. She had just time enough to
convey the lover into a chest before she admitted the husband
and his wife into the room.

You may be sure that trunk was absolutely necessary to be
opened ; but upon her husband's ordering it, she assured him,
"she had taken all the care imaginable in packing up the
things with her own hands, and he might send the trunk
abroad as soon as he thought fit." The easy husband believed
his wife, and the good couple went to bed ; Varnish having the
happiness to pass the night in his mistress's bedchamber without molestation. The morning arose, but our lover was not
well situated to observe her blushes ; so that all we know of
his sentiments on this occasion is, that he heard Balance ask

for the key, and say, "he would himself go with this chest, and have it opened before the captain of the ship, for the greater safety of so valuable a lading."

The goods were hoisted away ; and Mr. Balance, marching by his chest with great care and diligence, omitted nothing that might give his passenger perplexity. But, to consummate all, he delivered the chest, with strict charge, "in case they were in danger of being taken, to throw it overboard, for there were letters in it, the matter of which might be of great service to the enemy."

EXCRESCENCES OF DISCOURSE.

No. 137.   THURSDAY, February 23, 1709–10.   [Steele.]

Ter centum tonat ore Deos, Erebúmque, Chaósque,
Tergeminámque Hecaten ——
                              Virg. Æn. iv. 510.

He thrice invokes th' infernal powers profound
Of Erebus and Chaos ; thrice he calls
On Hecate's triple form ——

DICK REPTILE and I sat this evening later than the rest of the club : and as some men are better company when only with one friend, others when there is a larger number, I found Dick to be of the former kind. He was bewailing to me, in very just terms, the offences which he frequently met with in the abuse of speech : some use ten times more words than they need ; some put in words quite foreign to their purpose ; and others adorn their discourses with oaths and blasphemies, by way of tropes and figures. What my good friend started dwelt upon me after I came home this evening, and led me into an inquiry with myself, Whence should arise such strange excrescences in discourse ? whereas it must be obvious to all reasonable beings, that the sooner a man speaks his mind, the more complaisant he is to the man with whom he talks : but, upon mature deliberation, I am come to this resolution, that for one man who speaks to be understood, there are ten who talk only to be admired.

The antient Greeks had little independent syllables called expletives, which they brought into their discourses both in verse and prose, for no other purpose but for the better grace and sound of their sentences and periods. I know no example but this, which can authorize the use of more words than are necessary. But whether it be from this freedom taken by that wise nation, or however it arises, Dick Reptile hit upon a very just and common cause of offence in the generality of people of all orders. We have one here in our lane, who speaks nothing without quoting an authority ; for it is always with him, so and so, "as the man said." He asked me this morning, how I did, " as the man said ? " and hoped I would come now and then to see him, " as the man said." I am acquainted with another, who never delivers himself upon any subject, but he cries, " he only speaks his poor judgment; this is his humble opinion ; as for his part, if he might presume to offer any thing on that subject."—But of all persons who add elegances and superfluities to their discourses, those who deserve the foremost rank are the swearers ; and the lump of these may, I think, be very aptly divided into the common distinction of *High* and *Low*. Dulness and barrenness of thought is the original of it in both these *sects*, and they differ only in constitution : The *Low* is generally a phlegmatic, and the *High* a choleric cox-comb. The man of phlegm is sensible of the emptiness of his discourse, and will tell you, that, " I'fackins," such a thing is true : or if you warm him a little, he may run into a passion, and cry, " Odsbodikins, you do not say right." But the *High* affects a sublimity in dulness, and invokes " hell and damna-tion " at the breaking of a glass, or the slowness of a drawer.

I was the other day trudging along Fleet-street on foot, and an old army-friend came up with me. We were both going towards Westminster ; and, finding the streets were so crowded that we could not keep together, we resolved to club for a coach. This gentleman I knew to be the first of the order of the choleric. I must confess, were there no crime in it, nothing

could be more diverting than the impertinence of the *High*
juror : for whether there is remedy or not against what offends
him, still he is to shew he is offended ; and he must, sure, not
omit to be magnificently passionate, by falling on all things in
his way.   We were stopped by a train of coaches at Temple-
bar.   " What the devil ! " says my companion, " cannot you
drive on, coachman ? D—n you all, for a set of sons of whores ;
you would stop here to be paid by the hour !   There is not
such a set of confounded dogs as the coachmen, unhanged !
But these rascally cits——'Ounds, why should there not be a
tax to make these dogs widen their gates ?   Oh ! but the hell-
hounds move at last."   " Ay," said I, " I knew you would
make them whip on, if once they heard you "——" No," says
he " but would it not fret a man to the devil, to pay for
being carried slower than he can walk ?   Look'ye ! there is for
ever a stop at this hole by St. Clement's church.   Blood, you
dog !   Hark'ye, sirrah !——Why, and be d——d to you, do
not you drive over that fellow ?——Thunder, furies, and dam-
nation !   I will cut your ears off, you fellow before there——
Come hither, you dog you, and let me wring your neck round
your shoulders."   We had a repetition of the same eloquence
at the Cockpit, and the turning into Palace-yard.

This gave me a perfect image of the insignificancy of the
creatures who practise this enormity ; and make me conclude,
that it is ever want of sense makes a man guilty in this *kind.*
It was excellently well said, " that this folly had no temptation to excuse it, no man being born of a swearing constitution."   In a word, a few rumbling words and consonants
clapped together without any sense, will make an accomplished
swearer.   It is needless to dwell long upon this blustering
impertinence, which is already banished out of the society of
well-bred men, and can be useful only to bullies and *ill* tragic
writers, who would have sound and noise pass for courage and
sense.

IMAGINARY PRE-EMINENCE.

No. 139. TUESDAY, February 28, 1709–10. [Steele.]

—— Nihil est quod credere de se
Non possit, cum laudatur Diis æqua potestas.
Juv. Sat. iv. 70.

Nothing so monstrous can be said or feign'd,
But with belief and joy is entertain'd
When to her face a giddy girl is prais'd,
By ill-judg'd flattery to an angel rais'd.

WHEN I reflect upon the many nights I have sat up for some months last past, in the greatest anxiety for the good of my neighbours and contemporaries, it is no small discouragement to me, to see how slow a progress I make in the reformation of the world.   But indeed I must do my female readers the justice to own, that their tender hearts are much more susceptible of good impressions, than the minds of the other sex.   Business and ambition take up men's thoughts too much to leave room for philosophy : but if you speak to women in a style and manner proper to approach them, they never fail to improve by your counsels.   I shall, therefore, for the future, turn my thoughts more particularly to their service ; and study the best methods to adorn their persons, and inform their minds in the justest methods to make them what nature designed them, the most beauteous objects of our eyes, and the most agreeable companions of our lives.   But, when I say this, I must not omit at the same time to look into their errors and mistakes, that being the readiest way to the intended end of adorning and instructing them.   It must be acknowledged, that the very inadvertences of this sex are owing to the other ; for if men were not flatterers, women could not fall into that general cause of all their follies, and our misfortunes, their love of flattery.   Were the commendation of these agreeable creatures built upon its proper foundation, the higher we raised their opinion of themselves, the greater would be the advantage to our sex ; but all the topic of praise is drawn from very senseless and extravagant ideas we pretend to have of their beauty and perfection. Thus, when a young man falls in love with a young woman, from that moment she is no more *Mrs.* Alice such-a-one, born of such a father, and educated by such a mother; but from the first minute that he casts his eyes upon her with desire, he conceives a doubt in his mind, what heavenly power gave so unexpected a blow to an heart that was ever before untouched. But who can resist fate and destiny, which are lodged in *Mrs.* Alice's eyes? after which he desires orders accordingly, whether he is to live or die; the smile or frown of his goddess is the only thing that can now either save or destroy him. By this means, the well-humoured girl, that would have romped with him before she had received this declaration, assumes a state suitable to the majesty he has given her, and treats him as the vassal he calls himself. The girl's head is immediately turned by having the power of life and death, and takes care to suit every motion and air to her new sovereignty. After he has placed himself at this distance, he must never hope to recover familiarity, until she has had the addresses of another, and found them less sincere.

If the application to women were justly turned, the address of flattery, though it implied at the same time an admonition, would be much more likely to succeed. Should a captivated lover, in a billet, let his mistress know, that her piety to her parents, her gentleness of behaviour, her prudent œconomy with respect to her own little affairs in a virgin condition, had improved the passion which her beauty had inspired him with, into so settled an esteem for her, that of all women breathing he wished her his wife; though his commending her for qualities she knew she had as a virgin, would make her believe he expected from her an answerable conduct in the character of a matron; I will answer for it, his suit would be carried on with less perplexity.

Instead of this, the generality of our young women, taking all their notions of life from gay writings, or letters of love, consider themselves as goddesses, nymphs, and shepherdesses.

By this romantic sense of things, all the natural relations

and duties of life are forgotten ; and our female part of mankind are bred and treated, as if they were designed to inhabit
the happy fields of Arcadia, rather than be wives and mothers
of old England.   It is, indeed, long since I had the happiness
to converse familiarly with this sex, and therefore have been
fearful of falling into the error which recluse men are very
subject to, that of giving false representations of the world,
from which they have retired, by imaginary schemes drawn
from their own reflections.   An old man cannot easily gain
admittance into the dressing-room of ladies : I therefore
thought it time well-spent, to turn over Agrippa, and use all
my Occult Art, to give my old Cornelian ring the same force
with that of Gyges, which I have lately spoken of.   By the
help of this I went unobserved to a friend's house of mine, and
followed the chamber-maid invisibly about twelve of the clock
into the bed-chamber of the beauteous Flavia, his fine daughter,
just before she got up.

I drew the curtains ; and being wrapped up in the safety of
my old age, could with much pleasure, without passion, behold
her sleeping with Waller's poems, and a letter fixed in that
part of him where every woman thinks herself described.
The light flashing upon her face, awakened her : she opened
her eyes, and her lips too, repeating that piece of false wit in
that admired poet,

> " Such Helen was : and who can blame the boy,
>   That in so bright a flame consum'd his Troy ? "

This she pronounced with a most bewitching sweetness ; but
after it fetched a sigh, that methought had more desire than
languishment : then took out her letter ; and read aloud, for
the pleasure, I suppose, of hearing soft words in praise of herself, the following epistle :

" MADAM,
       " I sat near you at the opera last night ; but knew no
entertainment from the vain show and noise about me, while I
waited wholly intent upon the motion of your bright eyes, in

hopes of a glance, that might restore me to the pleasures of sight and hearing in the midst of beauty and harmony. It is said, the hell of the accursed in the next life arises from an incapacity to partake the joys of the blessed, though they were to be admitted to them. Such, I am sure, was my condition all that evening; and if you, my Deity, cannot have so much mercy, as to make me by your influence capable of tasting the satisfactions of life, my being is ended, which consisted only in your favour."

The letter was hardly read over, when she rushed out of bed in her wrapping gown, and consulted her glass for the truth of his passion. She raised her head, and turned it to a profile, repeating the last lines, "My being is ended, which consisted only in your favour." The goddess immediately called her maid, and fell to dressing that mischievous face of hers, without any manner of consideration for the mortal who had offered up his petition. Nay, it was so far otherwise, that the whole time of her woman's combing her hair was spent in discourse of the impertinence of his passion, and ended in declaring a resolution, "if she ever had him, to make him wait." She also frankly told the favourite gipsy that was prating to her, "that her passionate lover had put it out of her power to be civil to him, if she were inclined to it; for," said she, "if I am thus celestial to my lover, he will certainly so far think himself disappointed, as I grow into the familiarity and form of a mortal woman."

I came away as I went in, without staying for other remarks than what confirmed me in the opinion, that it is from the notions the men inspire them with, that the women are so fantastical in the value of themselves. This imaginary pre-eminence which is given to the fair sex, is not only formed from the addresses of people of condition; but it is the fashion and humour of all orders to go regularly out of their wits, as soon as they begin to make love. I know at this time three goddesses in the New Exchange; and there are two shepherdesses that sell gloves in Westminster hall.

MISPLACED ATTENTIONS.

No. 20. [*Extra Tatler.*] TUESDAY, March 6, 1710.
[Swift.] *

—— Ingenuas didicisse fideliter artes
Emollit mores.—Ovid.

To have learnt the ingenuous arts
faithfully softens the manners.

THOSE inferior duties of life which the French call *les petites morales*, or the smaller morals, are with us distinguished by the name of good manners, or breeding. This I look upon, in the general notion of it, to be a sort of artificial good sense, adapted to the meanest capacities, and introduced to make mankind easy in their commerce with each other. Low and little understandings, without some rules of this kind, would be perpetually wandering into a thousand indecencies and irregularities in behaviour, and in their ordinary conversation fall into the same boisterous familiarities, that one observes amongst them, when a debauch has quite taken away the use of their reason. In other instances, it is odd to consider, that, for want of common discretion, the very end of good breeding is wholly perverted, and civility, intended to make us easy, is employed in laying chains and fetters upon us, in debarring us of our wishes, and in crossing our most reasonable desires and inclinations.

This abuse reigns chiefly in the country, as I found to my vexation, when I was last there, in a visit I made to a neighbour, about two miles from my cousin. As soon as I entered the parlour, they forced me into the great chair that stood close by a huge fire, and kept me there, by force, till I was almost stifled. Then a boy came in great hurry to pull off my boots, which I in vain opposed, urging that I must return soon after dinner. In the meantime the good lady whispered

* This paper should be hung up in every Squire's hall in England.—
Orrery.

her eldest daughter, and slipped a key into her hand. She returned instantly with a beer glass half full of *aqua mirabilis*, and syrup of gillyflowers. I took as much as I had a mind for, but Madam vowed I should drink it off (for she was sure it would do me good, after coming out of the cold air), and I was forced to obey, which absolutely took away my stomach. When dinner came in, I had a mind to sit at a distance from the fire ; but they told me, it was as much as my life was worth, and set me with my back just against it. Though my appetite was quite gone, I resolved to force down as much as I could, and desired the leg of a pullet. "Indeed, Mr. Bickerstaff," says the lady, "you must eat a wing to oblige me," and so put a couple upon my plate. I was persecuted at this rate, during the whole meal. As often as I called for small-beer, the master tipped the wink, and the servant brought me a brimmer of October. Some time after dinner, I ordered my cousin's man, who came with me, to get ready the horses ; but it was resolved I should not stir that night ; and when I seemed pretty much bent upon going, they ordered the stable door to be locked, and the children hid away my cloak and boots. The next question was, "what I would have for supper ? " I said I never ate anything at night : but was at last, in my own defence, obliged to name the first thing that came into my head. After three hours spent chiefly in apology for my entertainment, insinuating to me, "that this was the worst time of the year for provisions, that they were at a great distance from any market, that they were afraid I should be starved, and they knew they kept me to my loss," the lady went, and left me to her husband, (for they took special care I should never be alone). As soon as her back was turned, the little misses ran backwards and forwards every moment, and constantly as they came in, or went out, made a courtesy directly at me, which in good manners I was forced to return with a bow, and "your humble servant, pretty miss." Exactly at eight, the mother came up, and discovered by the redness of her face, that supper was not far off. It was twice as large as the dinner, and my persecution doubled in proportion. I

desired, at my usual hour, to go to my repose, and was conducted to my chamber, by the gentleman, his lady, and the
whole train of children. They importuned me to drink something before I went to-bed, and upon my refusing, at last left
a bottle of stingo, as they called it, for fear I should wake, and
be thirsty in the night. I was forced in the morning, to rise,
and dress myself, in the dark, because, they would not suffer
my kinsman's servant to disturb me at the hour I had desired
to be called. I was now resolved to break through all
measures, to get away, and, after sitting down to a monstrous
breakfast, of cold beef, mutton, neats' tongues, venison pasty,
and stale beer, took leave of the family ; but the gentleman
would needs see me part of my way, and carry me a short cut
through his own grounds, which, he told me, would save half
a mile's riding. This last piece of civility had like to have
cost me dear, being once or twice in danger of my neck, by
leaping over his ditches, and at last forced me to alight in the
dirt, when my horse having slipped his bridle, ran away, and
took us up more than an hour to recover him again.

It is evident, that none of the absurdities I met with in this
visit, proceeded from an ill intention, but from a wrong judgment of complaisance, and a misapplication of the rules of it.
I cannot so easily excuse the more refined critics upon behaviour,
who having professed no other study, are yet infinitely defective, in the most material parts of it. Ned Fashion has been
bred all his life about court, and understands to a tittle all the
punctilios of a drawing-room. He visits most of the fine women
near St. James's, and, upon all occasions, says the civilest and
softest things to them of any man breathing. To Mr. Isaac *
he owes an easy slide in his bow, and a graceful manner of
coming into a room. But in some other cases, he is very far
from being a well-bred person : he laughs at men of far
superior understanding to his own, for not being so well-
dressed as himself, despises all his acquaintance that are not
quality, and in public places has, on that account, often

* An eminent dancing master at this time.

avoided taking notice of some of the best speakers in the
House of Commons. He rails strenuously at both universities,
before the members of either, and never is heard to swear an
oath, or break in upon morality, or religion, but in the company of divines. On the other hand, a man of right sense,
has all the essentials of good breeding, though he may be
wanting in the forms of it. Horatio has spent most of his
time at Oxford. He has a great deal of learning, an agreeable
wit, and as much modesty, as serves to adorn, without concealing his other good qualities. In that retired way of living, he
seems to have formed a notion of human nature, as he has
found it described in the writings of the greatest men, not as
he is like to meet with it in the common course of life. Hence
it is, that he gives no offence, that he converses with great
deference, candour, and humanity. His bow, I must confess,
is somewhat aukward ; but then he has an extensive, universal,
and unaffected knowledge, which makes some amends for it.
He would make no extraordinary figure at a ball ; but I can
assure the ladies in his behalf, and for their own consolation,
that he has writ better verses to the sex, than any man now
living, and is preparing such a poem for the press, as will
transmit their praises, and his own, to many generations.

EQUIPAGES.

No. 144.   SATURDAY, March 11, 1709-10.   [Steele.]

In a nation of liberty, there is hardly a person in the whole
mass of the people more absolutely necessary than a Censor.
It is allowed, that I have no authority for assuming this important appellation, and that I am Censor of these nations just
as one is chosen king at the game of " Questions and Commands : " but if, in the execution of this fantastical dignity, I
observe upon things which do not fall within the cognizance of
real authority, I hope it will be granted, that an idle man

could not be more usefully employed. Among all the irregularities of which I have taken notice, I know none so proper to be presented to the world by a Censor, as that of the general expense and affectation in equipage. I have lately hinted, that this extravagance must necessarily get footing where we have no sumptuary laws, and where every man may be dressed, attended, and carried, in what manner he pleases. But my tenderness to my fellow-subjects will not permit me to let this enormity go unobserved.

As the matter now stands, every man takes it in his head that he has a liberty to spend his money as he pleases. Thus, in spite of all order, justice, and decorum, we, the greater number of the queen's loyal subjects, for no reason in the world but because we want money, do not share alike in the division of her majesty's high road. The horses and slaves of the rich take up the whole street; while we peripatetics are very glad to watch an opportunity to whisk across a passage, very thankful that we are not run over for interrupting the machine, that carries in it a person neither more handsome, wise, or valiant, than the meanest of us. For this reason, were I to propose a tax, it should certainly be upon coaches and chairs : for no man living can assign a reason, why one man should have half a street to carry him at his ease, and perhaps only in pursuit of pleasures, when as good a man as himself wants room for his own person to pass upon the most necessary and urgent occasion. Until such an acknowledgment is made to the public, I shall take upon me to vest certain rights in the scavengers of the cities of London and Westminster, to take the horses and servants of all such as do not become or deserve such distinctions, into their peculiar custody. The offenders themselves I shall allow safe conduct to their places of abode in the carts of the said scavengers, but their horses shall be mounted by their footmen, and sent into the service abroad : and I take this opportunity, in the first place, to recruit the regiment of my good old friend the brave and honest Sylvius,*

---

* The person here alluded to was Cornelius Wood, a gentleman of an excellent character and very distinguished military merit.

that they may be as well taught as they are fed. It is to me most miraculous, so unreasonable an usurpation, as this I am speaking of, should so long have been tolerated. We hang a poor fellow for taking any trifle from us on the road, and bear with the rich for robbing us of the road itself. Such a tax as this would be of great satisfaction to us who walk on foot ; and since the distinction of riding in a coach is not to be appointed according to a man's merit or service to his country, nor that liberty given as a reward for some eminent virtue, we should be highly contented to see them pay something for the insult they do us, in the state they take upon them while they *are drawn by* us.

Until they have made us some reparation of this kind, we the Peripatetics of Great Britain cannot think ourselves well treated, while every one that is able, is allowed to set up an Equipage.

As for my part, I cannot but admire how persons, conscious to themselves of no manner of superiority above others, can out of mere pride or laziness expose themselves at this rate to public view, and put us all upon pronouncing those three terrible syllables, " Who is that ? " When it comes to that question, our method is, to consider the mien and air of the passenger, and comfort ourselves for being dirty to the ankles, by laughing at his figure and appearance who overlooks us. I must confess, were it not for the solid injustice of the thing, there is nothing could afford a discerning eye greater occasion for mirth, than this licentious huddle of qualities and characters in the equipages about this town. The overseers of the highways and constables have so little skill or power to rectify this matter, that you may often see the equipage of a fellow, whom all the town knows to deserve hanging, make a stop that shall interrupt the lord high chancellor and all the judges in their way to Westminster.

For the better understanding of things and persons in this general confusion, I have given directions to all the coachmakers and coach-painters in town, to bring me in lists of their several customers ; and doubt not, but with comparing the orders of each man, in the placing his arms on the door of his chariot, as well as the words, devices, and cyphers, to be fixed upon them, to make a collection which shall let us into the nature, if not the history, of mankind, more usefully than the curiosities of any medalist in Europe.

But this evil of vanity in our figure, with many others, proceeds from a certain gaiety of heart, which has crept into men's very thoughts and complexions. The passions and adventures of heroes, when they enter the lists for the tournament in romances, are not more easily distinguishable by their palfreys and their armour, than the secret springs and affections of the several pretenders to show amongst us are known by their equipages in ordinary life. The young bridegroom with his gilded cupids and winged angels, has some excuse in the joy of his heart to launch out into something that may be significant of his present happiness. But to see men, for *no reason upon earth* but that they are rich, ascend triumphant chariots, and ride through the people, has *at the bottom* nothing else in it but an insolent transport, arising only from the distinction of fortune.

It is therefore high time that I call in such coaches as are in their embellishments improper for the character of their owners. But if I find I am not obeyed herein, and that I cannot pull down those equipages already erected, I shall take upon me to prevent the growth of this evil for the future, by enquiring into the pretensions of the persons, who shall hereafter attempt to make public entries with ornaments and decorations of their own appointment. If a man, who believed he had the handsomest leg in this kingdom, should take a fancy to adorn so deserving a limb with a blue garter, he would justly be punished for offending against the Most Noble Order: and, I think, the general prostitution of equipage and retinue is as destructive to all distinction, as the impertinence of one man, if permitted, would certainly be to that illustrious fraternity.

THE OGLERS.

No. 145.   TUESDAY, March 14, 1709–10.   [Steele.]

Nescio quis teneros oculus mihi fascinat agnos
                              Virg. Ecl. iii. 103.

Ah ! What ill eyes bewitch my tender lambs ?

This evening was allotted for taking into consideration a
late request of two indulgent parents, touching the care of a
young daughter, whom they design to send to a boarding-
school, or keep at home, according to my determination ; but
I am diverted from that subject by letters which I have received from several ladies, complaining of a certain *sect* of
professed enemies to the repose of the fair sex, called Oglers.
These are, it seems, gentlemen who look with deep attention on
one object at the play-houses, and are ever staring all round
them in churches. It is urged by my correspondents, that
they do all that is possible to keep their eyes off these in-
snarers ; but that, by what power they know not, both their
diversions and devotions are interrupted by them in such a
manner, as that they cannot attend to either, without stealing
looks at the persons whose eyes are fixed upon them. By this
means, my petitioners say, they find themselves grow insensibly
less offended, and in time enamoured of these their enemies.
What is required of me on this occasion is, that as I love and
study to preserve the better part of mankind, the females, I
would give them some account of this dangerous way of
assault ; against which there is so little defence, that it lays
ambush for the sight itself, and makes them seeingly, know-
ingly, willingly, and forcibly, go on to their own captivity.

This representation of the present state of affairs between
the two sexes gave me very much alarm ; and I had no more
to do, but to recollect what I had seen at any one assembly for
some years last past, to be convinced of the truth and justice
of this remonstrance. If there be not a stop put to this evil

art, all the modes of address, and the elegant embellishments of life, which arise out of the noble passion of love, will of necessity decay. Who would be at the trouble of rhetoric, or study the *bon mien*, when his introduction is so much easier obtained by a sudden reverence in a down-cast look at the meeting the eye of a fair lady, and beginning again to *ogle* her as soon as she glances another way ? I remember very well, when I was last at an opera, I could perceive the eyes of the whole audience cast into particular cross angles one upon another, without any manner of regard to the stage, though king Latinus was himself present when I made that observation. It was then very pleasant to look into the hearts of the whole company ; for the balls of sight are so formed, that one man's eyes are spectacles to another to read his heart with. The most ordinary beholder can take notice of any violent agitation in the mind, any pleasing transport, or any inward grief, in the person he looks at ; but one of these Oglers can see a studied indifference, a concealed love, or a smothered resentment, in the very glances that are made to hide those dispositions of thought. The naturalists tell us, that the rattle-snake will fix himself under a tree where he sees a squirrel playing ; and, when he has once got the exchange of a glance from the pretty wanton, will give it such a sudden stroke on its imagination that though it may play from bough to bough, and strive to avert its eyes from it for some time, yet it comes nearer and nearer by little intervals of looking another way, until it drops into the jaws of the animal, which it knew gazed at it for no other reason but to ruin it. I did not believe this piece of philosophy until that night I was just now speaking of ; but I then saw the same thing pass between an ogler and a coquette. Mirtillo, the most learned of the former, had for some time discontinued to visit Flavia, no less eminent among the latter. They industriously avoided all places where they might probably meet, but chance brought them together to the play-house, and seated them in a direct line over-against each other, she in a front *box*, he in the *pit* next the stage. As soon as Flavia had received the looks of the whole crowd

below her with that air of insensibility, which is necessary at
the first entrance, she began to look round her, and saw the
vagabond Mirtillo, who had so long absented himself from her
circle ; and when she first discovered him, she looked upon
him with that glance, which in the language of Oglers is called
the *scornful*, but immediately turned her observation another
way, and returned upon him with the *indifferent*. This gave
Mirtillo no small resentment ; but he used her accordingly.
He took care to be ready for her next glance. She found his
eyes full in the *indolent*, with his lips crumpled up, in the posture of one whistling. Her anger at this usage immediately
appeared in every muscle of her face ; and after many emotions,
which glistened in her eyes, she cast them round the whole
house, and gave them softnesses in the face of every man she
had ever seen before. After she thought she had reduced all
she saw to her obedience, the play began, and ended their
dialogue. As soon as the first act was over, she stood up with
a visage full of dissembled alacrity and pleasure, with which
she overlooked the audience, and at last came to him ; he was
then placed in a side-way, with his hat slouched over his eyes,
and gazing at a wench in the side-box, as talking of that gypsy
to the gentleman who sat by him. But, as she fixed upon him,
he turned suddenly with a full face upon her, and, with all the
respect imaginable, made her the most obsequious bow in the
presence of the whole theatre. This gave her a pleasure not to
be concealed ; and she made him the recovering, or second
courtsy, with a smile that spoke a perfect reconciliation.
Between the ensuing acts, they talked to each other with gestures and glances so significant, that they ridiculed the whole
house in this silent speech, and made an appointment that
Mirtillo should lead her to her coach.

The peculiar language of one eye, as it differs from another
as much as the tone of one voice from another, and the fascina-
tion or enchantment, which is lodged in the optic nerves of the
persons concerned in these dialogues, is, I must confess, too
nice a subject for one who is not an adept in these speculations ;
but I shall, for the good and safety of the fair sex, call my

learned friend Sir William Read to my assistance, and, by the help of his observations on this organ,* acquaint them when the eye is to be believed, and when distrusted. On the contrary, I shall conceal the true meaning of the looks of ladies, and indulge in them all the art they can acquire in the management of their glances : all which is but too little against creatures who triumph in falsehood, and begin to forswear with their eyes, when their tongues can be no longer believed.

THE COMPLAINERS.

No. 146.　THURSDAY, March 16, 1709-10.　[Addison.]

> Permittes ipsis expendere numinibus, quid
> Conveniat nobis, rebusque sit utile nostris.
> Nam pro jucundis aptissima quæque dabunt Dii.
> Carior est illis homo, quam sibi.　Nos animorum
> Impulsu, et cæca magnâque cupidine ducti,
> Conjugium petimus, partumque uxoris ; at illis
> Notum, qui pueri, qualisque futura sit uxor.
>
> Juv. Sat. x. 347, et seq.

> Intrust thy fortune to the Powers above ;
> Leave them to manage for thee, and to grant
> What their unerring wisdom sees thee want ;
> In goodness as in greatness they excel :
> Ah ! that we lov'd ourselves but half so well !
> We, blindly by our headstrong passions led,
> Are hot for action, and desire to wed ;
> Then wish for heirs, but to the gods alone
> Our future offspring and our wives are known.

Among the various sets of correspondents who apply to me for advice, and send up their cases from all parts of Great Britain, there are none who are more importunate with me, and whom I am inclined to answer, than the Complainers. One of them dates his letter to me from the banks of a

---

* "A short but exact Account of all the Diseases incident to the Eyes, with the Causes, Symptoms, and Cures.　Also practical Observations upon some extraordinary Diseases of the Eyes." By Sir William Read, her Majesty's oculist, and operator in the eyes in ordinary.

purling stream, where he used to ruminate in solitude upon the divine Clarissa, and where he is now looking about for a convenient leap, which he tells me he is resolved to take, unless I support him under the loss of that charming perjured woman. Poor Lavinia presses as much for consolation on the other side, and is reduced to such an extremity of despair by the inconstancy of Philander, that she tells me she writes her letter with her pen in one hand, and her garter in the other. A gentleman of an ancient family in Norfolk is almost out of his wits upon the account of a greyhound, that, after having been his inseparable companion for ten years, is at last run mad. Another, who I believe is serious, complains to me, in a very moving manner, of the loss of a wife ; and another, in terms still more moving, of a purse of money that was taken from him on Bagshot-heath, and which, he tells me, would not have troubled him, if he had given it to the poor. In short, there is scarce a calamity in human life that has not produced me a letter.

It is indeed wonderful to consider, how men are able to raise affliction to themselves out of every thing. Lands and houses, sheep and oxen, can convey happiness and misery into the hearts of reasonable creatures. Nay, I have known a muff, a scarf, or a tippet, become a solid blessing or misfortune. A lap-dog has broke the hearts of thousands. Flavia, who had buried five children and two husbands, was never able to get over the loss of her parrot. How often has a divine creature been thrown into a fit by a neglect at a ball or an assembly ? Mopsa has kept her chamber ever since the last masquerade, and is in greater danger of her life upon being left out of it, than Clarinda from the violent cold which she caught at it. Nor are these dear creatures the only sufferers by such imaginary calamities. Many an author has been dejected at the censure of one whom he ever looked upon as an idiot : and many an hero cast into a fit of melancholy, because the rabble have not hooted at him as he passed through the streets. Theron places all his happiness in a running horse, Suffenus in a gilded chariot, Fulvius in a blue string, and Florio in a tulip-root. It would be endless to enumerate the many fantastical afflictions that disturb mankind; but as a misery is not to be measured from the nature of the evil, but from the temper of the sufferer, I shall present my readers, who are unhappy either in reality or imagination, with an allegory, for which I am indebted to the great father and prince of poets.

As I was sitting after dinner in my elbow-chair, I took up Homer, and dipped into that famous speech of Achilles to Priam,* in which he tells him, that Jupiter has by him two great vessels, the one filled with Blessings, and the other with Misfortunes: out of which he mingles a composition for every man that comes into the world. This passage so exceedingly pleased me, that, as I fell insensibly into my afternoon's slumber, it wrought my imagination into the following dream.

When Jupiter took into his hands the government of the world, the several parts of nature with the presiding deities did homage to him. One presented him with a mountain of winds, another with a magazine of hail, and a third with a pile of thunder-bolts. The stars offered up their influences; Ocean gave in his trident, Earth her fruits, and the Sun his seasons. Among the several deities who came to make their court on this occasion, the Destinies advanced with two great tuns carried before them, one of which they fixed at the right hand of Jupiter, as he sat upon his throne, and the other on his left. The first was filled with all the blessings, and the other with all the calamities of human life. Jupiter, in the beginning of his reign, finding the world much more innocent than it is in this iron age, poured very plentifully out of the tun that stood at his right-hand; but, as mankind degenerated, and became

---

* Two urns by Jove's high throne have ever stood,
The source of evil one, and one of good;
From thence the cup of mortal man he fills,
Blessings to those, to those distributes ills;
To most he mingles both: the wretch decreed
To taste the bad, unmix'd, is curst indeed;
Pursu'd by wrongs, by meagre famine driven,
He wanders, outcast both of earth and heaven.
      POPE's Hom. Il. xiv. ver. 863.

unworthy of his blessings, he set abroach the other vessel, that filled the world with pain and poverty, battles and distempers, jealousy and falsehood, intoxicating pleasures and untimely deaths.

He was at length so very much incensed at the great depravation of human nature, and the repeated provocations which he received from all parts of the earth, that, having resolved to destroy the whole species, except Deucalion and Pyrrha, he commanded the Destinies to gather up the blessings which he had thrown away upon the sons of men, and lay them up until the world should be inhabited by a more virtuous and deserving race of mortals.

The *three* Sisters immediately repaired to the earth, in search of the several blessings that had been scattered on it ; but found the task which was enjoined them, to be much more difficult than they imagined. The first places they resorted to, as the most likely to succeed in, were cities, palaces, and courts ; but, instead of meeting with what they looked for here, they found nothing but envy, repining, uneasiness, and the like bitter ingredients of the left-hand vessel. Whereas, to their great surprise, they discovered content, cheerfulness, health, innocence, and other the most substantial blessings of life, in cottages, shades, and solitudes.

There was another circumstance no less unexpected than the former, and which gave them very great perplexity in the discharge of the trust which Jupiter had committed to them. They observed, that several blessings had degenerated into calamities, and that several calamities had improved into blessings, according as they fell into the possession of wise or foolish men. They often found power, with so much insolence and impatience cleaving to it, that it became a misfortune to the person on whom it was conferred. Youth had often distempers growing about it, worse than the infirmities of old age. Wealth was often united to such a sordid avarice, as made it the most uncomfortable and painful kind of poverty. On the contrary, they often found pain made glorious by fortitude, poverty lost in content, deformity beautified with virtue. In a word, the blessings were often like good fruits planted in a bad soil, that by degrees fall off from their natural relish, into tastes altogether insipid or unwholesome ; and the calamities, like harsh fruits, cultivated in a good soil, and enriched by proper grafts and inoculations, until they swell with generous and delightful juices.

There was still a third circumstance that occasioned as great a surprise to the *three* Sisters as either of the foregoing, when they discovered several blessings and calamities which had never been in either of the tuns that stood by the throne of Jupiter, and were nevertheless as great occasions of happiness or misery as any there. These were that spurious crop of blessings and calamities which were never sown by the hand of the Deity, but grow of themselves out of the fancies and dispositions of human creatures. Such are dress, titles, place, equipage, false shame, and groundless fear, with the like vain imaginations, that shoot up in trifling, weak, and irresolute minds.

The Destinies finding themselves in so great a perplexity, concluded that it would be impossible for them to execute the commands that had been given them, according to their first intention ; for which reason they agreed to throw all the blessings and calamities together into one large vessel, and in that manner offer them up at the feet of Jupiter.

This was performed accordingly ; the *Eldest Sister* presenting herself before the vessel, and introducing it with an apology for what they had done :

' O Jupiter,' says she, ' we have gathered together all the good and evil, the comforts and distresses of human life, which we thus present before thee in one promiscuous heap. We beseech thee, that thou thyself wilt sort them out for the future as in thy wisdom thou shalt think fit. For we acknowledge, that there is none besides thee that can judge what will occasion grief or joy in the heart of a human creature, and what will prove a blessing or a calamity to the person on whom it is bestowed.'

KICKSHAWS.

No. 148. TUESDAY, MARCH 21, 1709-10. [ADDISON.]

—— Gustus elementa per omnia quærunt,
Nunquam animo pretiis obstantibus——.
Juv. Sat. xi. 14.

They ransack every element for choice
Of every fish and fowl, at any price.

HAVING intimated in my last paper, that I design to take under my inspection the diet of this great city, I shall begin with a very earnest and serious exhortation to all my well-disposed readers, that they would return to the food of their forefathers, and reconcile themselves to beef and mutton. This was the diet which bred that hardy race of mortals who won the fields of Cressy and Agincourt. I need not go up so high as the history of Guy, earl of Warwick, who is well known to have eaten up a dun cow of his own killing. The renowned king Arthur is generally looked upon as the first who ever sat down to a whole roasted ox, which was certainly the best way to preserve the gravy ; and it is farther added, that he and his knights sat about it at his round table, and usually consumed it to the very bones before they would enter upon any debate of moment. The Black Prince was a professed lover of the Brisket ; not to mention the history of the Surloin, or the institution of the order of Beef-eaters ; which are all so many evident and undeniable marks of the great respect, which our warlike predecessors have paid to this excellent food. The tables of the ancient gentry of this nation were covered thrice a day with hot roast beef ; and I am credibly nformed, by an antiquary who has searched the registers in which the bills of fare of the court are recorded, that instead of tea and bread and butter, which have prevailed of late years, the maids of honour in Queen Elizabeth's time were allowed three rumps of beef for their breakfast. Mutton has likewise been in great repute among our valiant countrymen ; but was formerly observed to be the food rather of men of nice and delicate appetites, than those of strong and robust constitutions. For which reason, even to this day, we use the word *Sheep-biter* as a term of reproach, as we do *Beef-eater* in a respectful and honourable sense. As for the flesh of lamb, veal, chicken, and other animals under age, they were the invention of sickly and degenerate palates, according to that wholesome remark of Daniel the historian ; who takes notice, that in all taxes upon provisions, during the reigns of several of our kings, there is nothing mentioned besides the flesh of such fowl and cattle as were arrived at their full growth, and were mature for slaughter. The common people of this kingdom do still keep up the taste of their ancestors ; and it is to this that we, in a great measure, owe the unparalleled victories that have been gained in this reign : for I would desire my reader to consider, what work our countrymen would have made at Blenheim and Ramillies, if they had been fed with fricassees and ragoûts.

For this reason, we at present see the florid complexion, the strong limb, and the hale constitution, are to be found chiefly among the meaner sort of people, or in the wild gentry who have been educated among the woods or mountains. Whereas many great families are insensibly fallen off from the athletic constitution of their progenitors, and are dwindled away into a pale, sickly, spindle-legged generation of valetudinarians.

I may perhaps, be thought extravagant in my notion ; but I must confess, I am apt to impute the dishonours that some-times happen in great families, to the inflaming kind of diet which is so much in fashion. Many dishes can excite desire without giving strength, and heat the body without nourishing it ; as physicians observe, that the poorest and most dispirited blood is most subject to fevers. I look upon a French ragoût to be as pernicious to the stomach as a glass of spirits ; and when I have seen a young lady swallow all the instigations of high soups, seasoned sauces, and forced meats, I have wondered at the despair or tedious fighting of her lovers.

The rules among these false Delicates are, to be as contra-dictory as they can be to nature.

Without expecting the return of hunger, they eat for an appetite, and prepare dishes, not to allay, but to excite it.

They admit of nothing at their tables in its natural form, or without a disguise.

They are to eat of everything before it comes in season, and to leave it off as soon as it is good to be eaten.

They are not to approve anything that is agreeable to ordinary palates ; and nothing is to gratify their senses, but what would offend those of their inferiors.

I remember I was last summer invited to a friend's house, who is a great admirer of the French cookery, and, as the phrase is, ' eats well.'   At our sitting down, I found the table covered with a great variety of unknown dishes.   I was mightily at a loss to learn what they were, and therefore did not know where to help myself.   That which stood before me I took to be a roasted porcupine, however did not care for asking questions ; and have since been informed, that it was only a larded turkey.   I afterwards passed my eye over several hashes, which I do not know the names of to this day ; and, hearing that they were delicacies, did not think fit to meddle with them.

Among other dainties, I saw something like a pheasant, and, therefore desired to be helped to a wing of it ; but, to my great surprise, my friend told me it was a rabbit, which is a sort of meat I never cared for.   At last I discovered, with some joy, a pig at the lower end of the table, and begged a gentleman that was near it to cut me a piece of it.   Upon which the gentleman of the house said, with great civility, "I am sure you will like the pig, for it was whipped to death."   I must confess, I heard him with horror, and could not eat of an animal that had died so tragical a death.   I was now in great hunger and confusion, when methought I smelled the agreeable savour of roast beef ; but could not tell from which dish it arose, though I did not question but it lay disguised in one of them.   Upon turning my head, I saw a noble surloin on the side-table smoking in the most delicious manner.   I had recourse to it more than once, and could not see without some indignation that substantial English dish banished in so ignominious a manner, to make way for French kickshaws.

The desert was brought up at last, which in truth was as extraordinary as anything that had come before it. The whole, when ranged in its proper order, looked like a very beautiful winter-piece. There were several pyramids of candied sweet-meats, that hung like icicles, with fruits scattered up and down, and hid in an artificial kind of frost. At the same time there were great quantities of cream beaten up into a snow, and near them little plates of sugar-plums, disposed like so many heaps of hail-stones, with a multitude of congelations in jellies of various colours. I was indeed so pleased with the several objects which lay before me, that I did not care for displacing any of them ; and was half angry with the rest of the company, that, for the sake of a piece of lemon-peel, or a sugar-plum, would spoil so pleasing a picture. Indeed, I could not but smile to see several of them cooling their mouths with lumps of ice which they had just before been burning with salts and peppers.

As soon as this show was over, I took my leave, that I might finish my dinner at my own house. For as I in everything love what is simple and natural, so particularly in my food ; two plain dishes, with two or three good-natured, cheerful, in-genious friends, would make me more pleased and vain, than all that pomp and luxury can bestow. For it is my maxim that " he keeps the greatest table who has the most valuable company at it."

PRIVATE TYRANTS.

No. 149.   THURSDAY, March 23, 1709–10.   [Steele.]

It has often been a solid grief to me, when I have reflected on this glorious nation, which is the scene of public happiness and liberty, that there are still crowds of private tyrants, against whom there neither is any law now in being, nor can there be invented any by the wit of man. These cruel men are ill-natured husbands. The commerce in the conjugal state is so delicate, that it is impossible to prescribe rules for the conduct of it, so as to fit ten thousand nameless pleasures and disquietudes which arise to people in that condition. But it is in this as in some other nice cases, where touching upon the malady tenderly is half way to the cure ; and there are some faults which need only to be observed, to be amended. I am put into this way of thinking by a late conversation, which I am going to give an account of.

I made a visit the other day to a family for which I have a great honour, and found the father, the mother, and two or three of the younger children drop off designedly to leave me alone with the eldest daughter; who was but a visitant there as well as myself, and is the wife of a gentleman of a very fair character in the world. As soon as we were alone, I saw her eyes full of tears, and methought she had much to say to me, for which she wanted encouragement. "Madam," said I, "you know I wish you all as well as any friend you have : speak freely what I see you are oppressed with ; and you may be sure, if I cannot relieve your distress, you may at least reap so much present advantage, as safely to give yourself the ease of uttering it." She immediately assumed the most becoming composure of countenance, and spoke as follows: "It is an aggravation of affliction in a married life, that there is a sort of guilt in communicating it : for which reason it is, that a lady of your and my acquaintance, instead of speaking to you herself, desired me, the next time I saw you, as you are a professed friend to our sex, to turn your thoughts upon the reciprocal complaisance which is the duty of a married state.

"My friend was neither in birth, fortune, nor education below the gentleman whom she married. Her person, her age, and her character, are also such as he can make no exception to. But so it is, that from the moment the marriage ceremony was over, the obsequiousness of a lover was turned into the haughtiness of a master. All the kind endeavours which she uses to please him, are at best but so many instances of her duty.   This insolence takes away that secret satisfaction, which does not only excite to virtue, but also rewards it.   It abates the fire of a free and generous love, and imbitters all the pleasures of a social life." The young lady spoke all this with such an air of resentment, as discovered how nearly she was concerned in the distress.

When I observed she had done speaking, " Madam," said I, " the affliction you mention is the greatest that can happen in human life ; and I know but one consolation in it, if that be a consolation, that the calamity is a pretty general one.   There is nothing so common as for men to enter into marriage, without so much as expecting to be happy in it.   They seem to propose to themselves a few holidays in the beginning of it ; after which they are to return at best to the usual course of their life ; and for aught they know, to constant misery and uneasiness.   From this false sense of the state they are going into, proceed the immediate coldness and indifference, or hatred and aversion, which attend ordinary marriages, or rather bargains to cohabit."   Our conversation was here interrupted by company which came in upon us.

The humour of affecting a superior carriage, generally rises from a false notion of the weakness of a female understanding in general, or an over-weening opinion that we have of our own ; for when it proceeds from a natural ruggedness and brutality of temper, it is altogether incorrigible, and not to be amended by admonition.   Sir Francis Bacon, as I remember, lays it down as a maxim, that no marriage can be happy in which the wife has no opinion of her husband's wisdom ; but, without offence to so great an authority, I may venture to say, that a sullen wise man is as bad as a good-natured fool. Knowledge, softened with complacency and good-breeding, will make a man equally beloved and respected ; but when joined with a severe, distant, and unsociable temper, it creates rather fear than love.   I, who am a bachelor, have no other notions of conjugal tenderness but what I learn from books ; and shall therefore produce three letters of Pliny, who was

not only one of the greatest, but the most learned man in the
whole Roman empire.   At the same time I am very much
ashamed, that on such occasions I am obliged to have recourse
to heathen authors ; and shall appeal to my readers, if they
would not think it a mark of a narrow education in a man of
quality, to write such passionate letters to any woman but a
mistress.   They were all three written at a time when she was
at a distance from him.   The first of them puts me in mind of
a married friend of mine, who said, " Sickness itself is pleasant
to a man that is attended in it by one whom he dearly loves."

"PLINY TO CALPHURNIA.

" I never was so much offended at business, as when it
hindered me from going with you into the country, or following
you thither : for I more particularly wish to be with you at
present, that I might be sensible of the progress you make in
the recovery of your strength and health ; as also of the entertainment and diversions you can meet with in your retirement.
Believe me, it is an anxious state of mind to live in ignorance
of what happens to those whom we passionately love.   I am
not only in pain for your absence, but also for your indisposition.   I am afraid of every thing, fancy every thing, and,
as it is the nature of man in fear, I fancy those things most,
which I am most afraid of.   Let me therefore earnestly desire
you to favour me, under these my apprehensions, with one
letter every day, or, if possible, with two ; for I shall be a
little at ease while I am reading your letters, and grow
anxious again as soon as I have read them."

SECOND LETTER.

" You tell me, that you are very much afflicted at my
absence, and that you have no satisfaction in any thing but my
writings, which you often lay by you upon my pillow.   You
oblige me very much in wishing to see me, and making me
your comforter in my absence.   In return, I must let you

know, I am no less pleased with the letters which you *writ* to me, and read them over a thousand times with new pleasure. If your letters are capable of giving me so much pleasure, what would your conversation do ? Let me beg of you to write to me often ; though at the same time I must confess, your letters give me anguish whilst they give me pleasure."

THIRD LETTER.

" It is impossible to conceive how much I languish for you in your absence ; the tender love I bear you is the chief cause of this my uneasiness ; which is still the more insupportable, because absence is wholly a new thing to us. I lie awake most part of the night in thinking of you, and several times of the day go as naturally to your apartment as if you were there to receive me ; but when I miss you, I come away dejected, out of humour, and like a man that had suffered a repulse. There is but one part of the day in which I am relieved from this anxiety, and that is when I am engaged in public affairs.

" You may guess at the uneasy condition of one who has no rest but in business, no consolation but in trouble."

I shall conclude this paper with a beautiful passage out of Milton, and leave it as a lecture to those of my own sex, who have a mind to make their conversation agreeable, as well as instructive, to the fair partners who are fallen into their care. Eve having observed, that Adam was entering into some deep disquisitions with the Angel, who was sent to visit him, is described as retiring from their company, with a design of learning what should pass there from her husband.

> " So spake our sire, and by his countenance seem'd
> Entering on studious thoughts abstruse, which Eve
> Perceiving where she sat retir'd in sight,
> With lowliness majestic from her seat
> Rose, and went forth among her fruits and flowers.
> Yet went she not, as not with such discourse
> Delighted, or not capable her ear
> Of what was high. Such pleasures she reserv'd,
> Adam relating, she sole auditress ;
> Her husband the relater she preferr'd

Before the angel, and of him to ask
Chose rather. He, she knew, would intermix
Grateful digressions, and solve high dispute
With conjugal caresses ; from his lip
Not words alone pleas'd her. O ! when meet now
Such pairs, in love and mutual honour join'd ! " *

BEAUTY UNADORNED.

No. 151. TUESDAY, March 28, 1710. [Steele.]

—— Ni vis boni
In ipsa inesset forma, hæc formam extinguerent.   Ter.

These things would extinguish beauty, if there were not an innate pleasure-giving energy in beauty itself.

When artists would expose their diamonds to an advantage, they usually set them to show in little cases of black velvet. By this means the jewels appear in their true and genuine lustre, while there is no colour that can infect their brightness, or give a false cast to the water. When I was at the opera the other night, the assembly of ladies in mourning † made me consider them in the same kind of view. A dress wherein there is so little variety shews the face in all its natural charms, and makes one differ from another only as it is more or less beautiful. Painters are ever careful of offending against a rule which is so essential in all just representations. The chief figure must have the strongest point of light, and not be injured by any gay colourings, that may draw away the attention to any less considerable part of the picture. The present fashion obliges every body to be dressed with propriety, and

---

* Milton's " Paradise Lost," Book viii. l. 39.
† In allusion to the long-continued mourning on the decease of the Queen's husband, George, Prince of Denmark, who died October 21, 1708. Lewis, Duke of Bourbon, eldest son to the Dauphin of France, died on the 3rd of March, about three weeks before the date of this Paper. A month before, in consequence of a petition presented by the Mercers, &c., complaining of their sufferings from the length and frequency of public mournings, leave was given to bring in a bill for ascertaining and limiting the time of them.

makes the ladies' faces the principal objects of sight. Every
beautiful person shines out in all the excellence with which
nature has adorned her ; gaudy ribbands and glaring colours
being now out of use, the sex has no opportunity given them
to disfigure themselves, which they seldom fail to do whenever it lies in their power. When a woman comes to her
glass, she does not employ her time in making herself look
more advantageously what she really is ; but endeavours to be
as much another creature as she possibly can. Whether this
happens because they stay so long, and attend their work so
diligently, that they forget the faces and persons which they
first sat down with, or whatever it is, they seldom rise from
the toilet the same women they appeared when they began to
dress. What jewel can the charming Cleora place in her ears,
that can please her beholders so much as her eyes ? The
cluster of diamonds upon the breast can add no beauty to the
fair chest of ivory which supports it. It may indeed tempt a
man to steal a woman, but never to love her. Let Thalestris
change herself into a motley, party-coloured animal : the pearl
necklace, the flowered stomacher, the artificial nosegay, and
shaded furbelow, may be of use to attract the eye of her
beholder, and turn it from the imperfections of her features
and shape. But if ladies will take my word for it (and as
they dress to please men, they ought to consult our fancy
rather than their own in this particular), I can assure them,
there is nothing touches our imagination so much as a
beautiful woman in a plain dress. There might be more
agreeable ornaments found in our own manufacture, than any
that rise out of the looms of Persia.

This, I know, is a very harsh doctrine to woman-kind, who
are carried away with every thing that is showy, and with
what delights the eye, more than any other species of living
creatures whatsoever. Were the minds of the sex laid open,
we should find the chief idea in one to be a tippet, in another a
muff, in a third a fan, and in a fourth a fardingal. The
memory of an old visiting lady is so filled with gloves, silks,
and ribbands, that I can look upon it as nothing else but a

toy-shop. A matron of my acquaintance, complaining of her daughter's vanity, was observing, that she had all of a sudden held up her head higher than ordinary, and *taken an air* that shewed a secret satisfaction in herself, mixed with a scorn of others. " I did not know," says my friend, " what to make of the carriage of this fantastical girl, until I was informed by her eldest sister, that she had a pair of striped garters on." This odd turn of mind makes the sex unhappy, and disposes them to be struck with every thing that makes a show, however trifling and superficial.

Many a lady has fetched a sigh at the *toss* of a wig, and been ruined by the tapping of a snuff-box. It is impossible to describe all the execution that was done by *the shoulder-knot*, while that fashion prevailed, or to reckon up all the virgins that have fallen a sacrifice to a pair of *fringed gloves*. A sincere heart has not made half so many conquests as an *open waistcoat* * ; and I should be glad to see an able head make so good a figure in a woman's company as a pair of *red heels*. A Grecian hero, when he was asked whether he could play upon the lute, thought he had made a very good reply, when he answered, "No ; but I can make a great city of a little one." Notwithstanding his boasted wisdom, I appeal to the heart of any Toast in town, whether she would not think the *lutenist* preferable to the statesman ? I do not speak this out of any aversion that I have to the sex : on the contrary, I have always had a tenderness for them ; but, I must confess, it troubles me very much, to see the generality of them place their affections on improper objects, and give up all the pleasures of life for gewgaws and trifles.

Mrs. Margery Bickerstaff, my great aunt, had a thousand pounds to her portion, which our family was desirous of keeping among themselves, and therefore used all possible means to

* One of the Princes of Orange, who had many French refugees among his officers, observed to them that they ought to consider they were in a colder country, and dress accordingly. Says one of them, "We have a remedy against cold ; does your Highness know anything so warm as two shirts ?" " Yes," replied the Prince, " three."

turn off her thoughts from marriage. The method they took was, in any time of danger, to throw a new gown or petticoat in her way. When she was about twenty-five years of age, she fell in love with a man of an agreeable temper and equal fortune, and would certainly have married him, had not my grandfather, Sir Jacob, dressed her up in a suit of flowered satin; upon which she set so immoderate a value upon herself, that the lover was contemned and discarded. In the fortieth year of her age, she was again smitten; but very luckily transferred her passion to a *tippet*, which was presented to her by another relation who was in the plot. This, with a *white sarsenet hood*, kept her safe in the family until fifty. About sixty, which generally produces a kind of latter spring in amorous constitutions, my aunt Margery had again a colt's tooth in her head; and would certainly have eloped from the mansion-house, had not her brother Simon, who was a wise man and a scholar, advised to dress her in *cherry-coloured ribbands*, which was the only expedient that could have been found out by the wit of man to preserve the thousand pounds in our family, part of which I enjoy at this time.

This discourse puts me in mind of an humourist mentioned by Horace, called Eutrapelus, who, when he designed to do a man a mischief, made him a present of a gay suit; and brings to my memory another passage of the same author, when he describes the most ornamental dress that a woman can appear in with two words, *Simplex Munditiis*, which I have quoted for the benefit of my female readers.

- - - - - - -

IMMORTALITY OF THE SOUL.

No. 152. THURSDAY, March 30, 1710. [Addison.]

Dii, quibus imperium est animarum, umbræque silentes,
Et Chaos, et Phlegethon, loca nocte silentia late,
Sit mihi fas audita loqui ; sit numine vestro
Pandere res altâ terrâ et caligine mersas.

VIRG. Æn. vi. 264.

Infernal gods, who rule the shades below,
Chaos and Phlegethon, the realms of woe ;
Grant what I've heard I may to light expose,
Secrets which earth, and night, and hell inclose !

A MAN who confines his speculations to the time present, has but a very narrow province to employ his thoughts in. For this reason, persons of studious and contemplative natures often entertain themselves with the history of past ages, or raise schemes and conjectures upon futurity. For my own part, I love to range through that half of eternity which is still to come, rather than look on that which is already run out ; because I know I have a real share and interest in the one, whereas all that was transacted in the other can be only matter of curiosity to me.

Upon this account, I have been always very much delighted with meditating on the soul's immortality, and in reading the several notions which the wisest of men, both antient and modern, have entertained on that subject. What the opinions of the greatest philosophers have been, I have several times hinted at, and shall give an account of them from time to time as occasion requires. It may likewise be worth while to consider, what men of the most exalted genius and elevated imagination have thought of this matter. Among these, Homer stands up as a prodigy of mankind, that looks down upon the rest of human creatures as a species beneath him. Since he is the most antient heathen author, we may guess from his relation, what were the common opinions in his time concerning the state of the soul after death.

Ulysses, he tells us, made a voyage to the regions of the

dead, in order to consult Tiresias how he should return to his own country, and recommend himself to the favour of the gods. The poet scarce introduces a single person who doth not suggest some useful precept to his reader, and designs his description of the dead for the amendment of the living.

Ulysses, after having made a very plenteous sacrifice, *sat him down* by the pool of holy blood, which attracted a prodigious assembly of ghosts of all ages and conditions, that hovered about the hero, and feasted upon the steams of his oblation. The first he knew was the shade of Elpenor, who, to shew the activity of a spirit above that of body, is represented as arrived there long before Ulysses, notwithstanding the winds and seas had contributed all their force to hasten his voyage thither. This Elpenor, to inspire the reader with a detestation of drunkenness, and at the same time with a religious care of doing proper honours to the dead, describes himself as having broken his neck in a debauch of wine ; and begs Ulysses, that for the repose of his soul, he would build a monument over him, and perform funereal rites to his memory. Ulysses, with great sorrow of heart, promises to fulfil his request, and is immediately diverted to an object much more moving than the former. The ghost of his own mother Anticlea, whom he still thought living, appears to him among the multitudes of shades that surrounded him ; and sits down at a small distance from him by the lake of blood, without speaking to him, or knowing who he was. Ulysses was exceedingly troubled at the sight, and could not forbear weeping as he looked upon her : but being all along set forth as a pattern of consummate wisdom, he makes his affection give way to prudence ; and therefore, upon his seeing Tiresias, does not reveal himself to his mother, until he had consulted that great prophet, who was the occasion of this his descent into the empire of the dead. Tiresias having cautioned him to keep himself and his companions free from the guilt of sacrilege, and to pay his devotions to all the gods, promises him a safe return to his kingdom and family, and a happy old age in the enjoyment of them.

The poet, having thus with great art kept the curiosity of his reader in suspense, represents his wise man, after the dispatch of his business with Tiresias, as yielding himself up to the calls of natural affection, and making himself known to his mother. Her eyes are no sooner opened, but she cries out in tears, "Oh my son!" and inquires into the occasions that brought him thither, and the fortune that attended him.

Ulysses, on the other hand, desires to know what the sickness was that had sent her into those regions, and the condition in which she had left his father, his son, and more particularly his wife. She tells him, "they were all three inconsolable for his absence. As for myself," says she, "that was the sickness of which I died. My impatience for your return, my anxiety for your welfare, and my fondness for my dear Ulysses, were the only distempers that preyed upon my life, and separated my soul from my body." Ulysses was melted with these expressions of tenderness, and thrice endeavoured to catch the apparition in his arms, that he might hold his mother to his bosom, and weep over her.

This gives the poet occasion to describe the notion the heathens at that time had of an unbodied soul, in the excuse which the mother makes for seeming to withdraw herself from her son's embraces. "The soul," says she, "is composed neither of bones, flesh, nor sinews; but leaves behind her all those incumbrances of mortality to be consumed on the funeral pile. As soon as she has thus cast her burden, she makes her escape, and flies away from it like a dream."

When this melancholy conversation is at an end, the poet draws up to view as charming a vision as could enter into man's imagination. He describes the next who appeared to Ulysses, to have been the shades of the finest women that had ever lived upon the earth, and who had either been the daughters of kings, the mistresses of gods, or mothers of heroes; such as Antiope, Alcmena, Leda, Ariadne, Iphimedia, Eriphyle, and several others, of whom he gives a catalogue, with a short history of their adventures. The beautiful assembly of apparitions were all gathered together about the blood.

"Each of them," says Ulysses, as a gentle satire upon female vanity, "giving me an account of her birth and family." This scene of extraordinary women, seems to have been designed by the poet as a lecture of mortality to the whole sex, and to put them in mind of what they must expect, notwithstanding the greatest perfections, and highest honours, they can arrive at.

The circle of beauties at length disappeared, and was succeeded by the shades of several Grecian heroes, who had been engaged with Ulysses in the siege of Troy. The first that approached was Agamemnon, the generalissimo of that great expedition, who, at the appearance of his old friend, wept very bitterly, and, without saying anything to him, endeavoured to grasp him by the hand. Ulysses, who was much moved at the sight, poured out a flood of tears, and asked him the occasion of his death, which Agamemnon related to him in all its tragical circumstances ; how he was murdered at a banquet by the contrivance of his own wife, in confederacy with her adulterer : from whence he takes occasion to reproach the whole sex, after a manner which would be inexcusable in a man who had not been so great a sufferer by them. "My wife," says he, "has disgraced all the women that shall ever be born into the world, even those who hereafter shall be innocent. Take care how you grow too fond of your wife. Never tell her all you know. If you reveal some things to her, be sure you keep others concealed from her. You, indeed, have nothing to fear from your Penelope, she will not use you as my wife has treated me ; however, take care how you trust a woman." The poet, in this and other instances, according to the system of many heathen as well as Christian philosophers, shews, how anger, revenge, and other habits which the soul had contracted in the body, subsist, and grow in it under its state of separation.

I am extremely pleased with the companions which the poet in the next description assigns to Achilles. "Achilles," says the hero, "came up to me with Patroclus and Antilochus." By which we may see that it was Homer's opinion, and probably that of the age he lived in, that the friendships which are made among the living, will likewise continue among the dead. Achilles enquires after the welfare of his son, and of his father, with a fierceness of the same character that Homer has everywhere expressed in the actions of his life. The passage relating to his son is so extremely beautiful, that I must not omit it. Ulysses, after having described him as wise in council, and active in war, and mentioned the foes whom he had slain in battle, adds an observation that he himself had made of his behaviour, whilst he lay in the wooden horse. "Most of the generals," says he, "that were with us, either wept or trembled : as for your son, I never saw him wipe a tear from his cheeks, or change his countenance. On the contrary, he would often lay his hand upon his sword, or grasp his spear, as impatient to employ them against the Trojans." He then informs his father of the great honour and rewards which he had purchased before Troy, and of his return from it without a wound. "The shade of Achilles," says the poet, "was so pleased with the account he received of his son, that he enquired no farther, but stalked away with more than ordinary majesty over the green meadow that lay before them."

This last circumstance, of a deceased father's rejoicing in the behaviour of his son, is very finely contrived by Homer, as an incentive to virtue, and made use of by none that I know besides himself.

The description of Ajax, which follows, and his refusing to speak to Ulysses, who had won the armour of Achilles from him, and by that means occasioned his death, is admired by every one that reads it. When Ulysses relates the sullenness of his deportment, and considers the greatness of the hero, he expresses himself with generous and noble sentiments. "Oh ! that I had never gained a prize which cost the life of so brave a man as Ajax ! who, for the beauty of his person, and greatness of his actions, was inferior to none but the divine Achilles." The same noble condescension, which never dwells but in truly great minds, and such as Homer would represent that of Ulysses to have been, discovers itself likewise in the speech which he made to the ghost of Ajax on that occasion. "Oh,

Ajax !" says he, "will you keep your resentments even after death ? What destructions hath this fatal armour brought upon the Greeks, by robbing them of you, who were their bulwark and defence ? Achilles is not more bitterly lamented among us than you. Impute not then your death to any one but Jupiter, who, out of his anger to the Greeks, took you away from among them : let me entreat you to approach me ; restrain the fierceness of your wrath, and the greatness of your soul, and hear what I have to say to you." Ajax, without making a reply, turned his back upon him, and retired into a crowd of ghosts.

Ulysses, after all these visions, took a view of those impious wretches who lay in tortures for the crimes they had committed upon the earth, whom he describes under all the varieties of pain, as so many marks of divine vengeance, to deter others from following their example. He then tells us, that notwith-standing he had a great curiosity to see the heroes that lived in the ages before him, the ghosts began to gather about him in such prodigious multitudes, and with such a confusion of voices, that his heart trembled as he saw himself amidst so great a scene of horrors. He adds, that he was afraid lest some hideous spectre should appear to him, that might terrify him to distraction ; and therefore withdrew in time.

I question not but my reader will be pleased with this description of a future state, represented by such a noble and fruitful imagination, that had nothing to direct it besides the light of nature, and the opinions of a dark and ignorant age.

A MUSICAL INTERPRETATION OF TALK.

No. 153. SATURDAY, April 1, 1710. [Addison.]

Bombalio, clangor, stridor, taratantara, murmur.
FARN. Rhet.

Rend with tremendous sounds your ears asunder,
With gun, drum, trumpet, blunderbuss, and thunder.

I HAVE heard of a very valuable picture, wherein all the painters of the age in which it was drawn, are represented sitting together in a circle, and joining in a *consort* of music. Each of them plays upon such a particular instrument as is the most suitable to his character, and expresses that style and manner of painting which is peculiar to him. The famous cupola-painter of those times, to shew the grandeur and boldness of his figures, hath a horn in his mouth, which he seems to wind with great strength and force. On the contrary, an eminent artist, who wrought up his pictures with the greatest accuracy, and gave them all those delicate touches which are apt to please the nicest eye, is represented as tuning a Theorbo. The same kind of *humour* runs through the whole piece.

I have often, from this hint, imagined to myself, that different talents in discourse might be shadowed out after the same manner by different kinds of music ; and that the several conversable parts of mankind in this great city, might be cast into proper characters and divisions, as they resemble several instruments that are in use among the masters of harmony. Of these therefore in their order ; and first of the Drum.

Your Drums are the blusterers in conversation, that, with a loud laugh, unnatural mirth, and a torrent of noise, domineer in public assemblies ; over-bear men of sense ; stun their companions ; and fill the place they are in with a rattling sound, that hath seldom any wit, humour, or good breeding in it. The Drum notwithstanding, by this boisterous vivacity, is very proper to impose upon the ignorant ; and in conversation with ladies who are not of the finest taste, often passes for a man of mirth and wit, and for wonderful pleasant company. I need not observe, that the emptiness of the Drum very much contributes to its noise.

The Lute is a character directly opposite to the Drum, that sounds very finely by itself, or in a very small *consort*. Its notes are exquisitely sweet, and very low, easily drowned in a multitude of instruments, and even lost among a few, unless you give a particular attention to it. A Lute is seldom heard in a company of more than five, whereas a Drum will shew itself to advantage in an assembly of five hundred. The Lutenists therefore are men of a fine genius, uncommon reflection, great affability, and esteemed chiefly by persons of a good taste, who are the only proper judges of so delightful and soft a melody.

The Trumpet is an instrument that has in it no compass of music, or variety of sound, but is notwithstanding very agreeable, so long as it keeps within its pitch. It has not above four or five notes, which are however very pleasing, and capable of exquisite turns and modulations. The gentlemen who fall under this denomination, are your men of the most fashionable education, and refined breeding, who have learned a certain smoothness of discourse, and sprightliness of air, from the polite company they have kept; but at the same time have shallow parts, weak judgments, and a short reach of understanding. A play-house, a drawing-room, a ball, a visiting-day, or a Ring at Hyde-park, are the few notes they are masters of, which they touch upon in all conversations. The Trumpet, however, is a necessary instrument about a court, and a proper enlivener of a *consort*, though of no great harmony by itself.

Violins are the lively, forward, importunate wits, that distinguish themselves by the flourishes of imagination, sharpness of repartee, glances of satire, and bear away the upper part in every *consort*. I cannot however but observe, that when a man is not disposed to hear music, there is not a more disagreeable sound in harmony than that of a violin.

There is another musical instrument which is more frequent

in this nation than any other ; I mean your Bass-viol, which grumbles in the bottom of the *consort*, and with a surly masculine sound strengthens the harmony, and tempers the sweetness of the several instruments that play along with it. The Bass-viol is an instrument of a quite different nature to the Trumpet, and may signify men of rough sense and unpolished parts ; who do not love to hear themselves talk, but sometimes break out with an agreeable bluntness, unexpected wit, and surly pleasantries, to the no small diversion of their friends and companions. In short, I look upon every sensible true-born Briton to be naturally a Bass-viol.

As for your rural wits, who talk with great eloquence and alacrity of foxes, hounds, horses, quickset hedges, and six-bar gates, double ditches, and broken necks, I am in doubt, whether I should give them a place in the conversable world. However, if they will content themselves with being raised to the dignity of Hunting-horns, I shall desire for the future, that they may be known by that name.

I must not here omit the Bag-pipe *species*, that will entertain you from morning to night with the repetition of a few notes, which are played over and over, with the perpetual humming of a drone running underneath them. These are your dull, heavy, tedious story-tellers, the load and burden of conversations, that set up for men of importance, by knowing secret history, and giving an account of transactions, that whether they ever passed in the world or not, doth not signify an half-penny to its instruction, or its welfare. Some have observed, that the Northern parts of this island are more particularly fruitful in Bag-pipes.

There are so very few persons who are masters in every kind of conversation, and can talk on all subjects, that I do not know whether we should make a distinct species of them. Nevertheless, that my scheme may not be defective, for the sake of those few who are endowed with such extraordinary talents, I shall allow them to be Harpsichords, a kind of music which every one knows is a *consort* by itself.

As for your Passing-bells, who look upon mirth as criminal,

and talk of nothing but what is melancholy in itself, and mortifying to human nature, I shall not mention them.

I shall likewise pass over in silence all the rabble of mankind, that crowd our streets, coffee-houses, feasts, and public tables. I cannot call their discourse conversation, but rather something that is practised in imitation of it. For which reason, if I would describe them by any musical instrument, it should be by those modern inventions of the bladder and string, tongs and key, marrow-bone and cleaver.

My reader will doubtless observe, that I have only touched here upon male instruments, having reserved my female *consort* to another occasion. If he has a mind to know where these several characters are to be met with, I could direct him to a whole club of Drums ; not to mention another of Bagpipes, which I have before given some account of in my description of our nightly meetings in Sheer-lane. The Lutes may often be met with in couples upon the banks of a crystal stream, or in the retreats of shady woods, and flowery meadows ; which, for different reasons, are likewise the great resort of your Hunting-horns. Bass-viols are frequently to be found over a glass of stale-beer, and a pipe of tobacco ; whereas those who set up for Violins, seldom fail to make their appearance at Will's once every evening. You may meet with a Trumpet any where on the other side of Charing-cross.

That we may draw something for advantage in life out of the foregoing discourse, I must intreat my reader to make a narrow search into his life and conversation, and, upon his leaving any company, to examine himself seriously, whether he has behaved himself in it like a Drum or a Trumpet, a Violin or a Bass-viol ; and accordingly endeavour to mend his music for the future. For my own part, I must confess, I was a Drum for many years ; nay, and a very noisy one, until, having polished myself a little in good company, I threw as much of the Trumpet into my conversation, as was possible for a man of an impetuous temper, by which mixture of different musics I look upon myself, during the course of many years, to have resembled a Tabor and Pipe. I have since very much endeavoured at the sweetness of the Lute ; but, in spite of all my resolutions, I must confess, with great confusion, that I find myself daily degenerating into a Bag-pipe ; whether it be the effect of my old age, or of the company I keep, I know not. All that I can do, is to keep a watch over my conversation, and to silence the Drone as soon as I find it begin to hum in my discourse, being determined rather to hear the notes of others, than to play out of time, and encroach upon their parts in the *consort* by the noise of so tiresome an instrument.

THE POLITICAL UPHOLSTERER.

No. 155. THURSDAY, April 6, 1710. [Addison.]

—— Aliena negotia curat,
Excussus propriis.   Hor. 3 Sat. ii. 19.

When he had lost all business of his own,
He ran in quest of news through all the town.

There lived some years since, within my neighbourhood, a very grave person, an upholsterer,* who seemed a man of more than ordinary application to business. He was a very early riser, and was often abroad two or three hours before any of his neighbours. He had a particular carefulness in the knitting of his brows, and a kind of impatience in all his motions, that plainly discovered he was always intent on matters of importance. Upon my inquiry into his life and conversation, I found him to be the greatest newsmonger in our quarter; that he rose before day to read the Post-man ; and that he would take two or three turns to the other end of the town before his neighbours were up, to see if there were any Dutch mails come in. He had a wife and several children ; but was much more inquisitive to know what passed in Poland than in his own family, and was in greater pain and anxiety of

---

* Arne, an upholsterer in Covent Garden, was, it is said, the original of the politician exposed in this Paper.

mind for King Augustus's welfare, than that of his nearest relations.*   He looked extremely thin in a dearth of news, and never enjoyed himself in a westerly wind.   This indefatigable kind of life was the ruin of his shop ; for, about the time that his favourite prince left the crown of Poland, he broke and disappeared.

This man and his affairs had been long out of my mind, until about three days ago, as I was walking in St. James's Park, I heard somebody at a distance hemming after me : and who should it be but my old neighbour the upholsterer ?   I saw he was reduced to extreme poverty, by certain shabby superfluities in his dress ; for, notwithstanding that it was a very sultry day for the time of the year, he wore a loose great-coat and a *muff,* with a *long campaign wig* out of curl ; to which he had added the ornament of a pair of *black garters buckled under the knee.*†   Upon his coming to me, I was going to inquire into his present circumstances ; but was prevented by his asking me, with a whisper, " whether the last letters brought any accounts that one might rely upon from Bender ? " ‡   I told him, " None that I heard of ; " and asked him, " whether he had yet married his eldest daughter ? "   He told me, " no.   But pray," says he, " tell me sincerely, what are your thoughts of the king of Sweden ? "   For though his wife and children were starving, I found his chief concern at present was for this great monarch.   I told him, " that I looked upon him as one of the first heroes of the age."   " But pray," says he, " do you think there is any truth in the story of his wound ? "   And finding me surprised at the question, " Nay," says he, " I only propose it to you."   I answered, " that I thought there was no reason to doubt of it."   " But why in the heel," says he, " more than in any other part of the body ? "   " Because," said I, " the bullet chanced to light there."

* By the defeat of the King of Sweden by Russia at Pultowa, Frederick Augustus was restored to his throne of Poland.
† Black garters were then very unfashionable.
‡ After his defeat at Pultowa, Charles XII. of Sweden escaped with difficulty to Bender.

This extraordinary dialogue was no sooner ended, but he began to launch out into a long dissertation upon the affairs of the North ; and after having spent some time on them, he told me, " he was in a great perplexity how to reconcile "The Supplement" with "The English-Post," and had been just now examining what the other papers say upon the same subject. "'The Daily Courant,'" says he, "has these words : ' We have advices from very good hands, that a certain prince has some matters of great importance under consideration.' This is very mysterious ; but the Post-boy leaves us more in the dark ; for he tells us, ' That there are private intimations of measures taken by a certain prince, which time will bring to light.' Now the ' Post-man '," says he, " who uses to be very clear, refers to the same news in these words ; ' The late conduct of a certain prince affords great matter of speculation.' This certain prince," says the upholsterer, " whom they are all so cautious of naming, I take to be ——." Upon which, though there was nobody near us, he whispered something in my ear, which I did not hear, or think worth my while to make him repeat.

We were now got to the upper end of the Mall, where were three or four very odd fellows sitting together upon the bench. These I found were all of them politicians, who used to sun themselves in that place every day about dinner-time. Observing them to be curiosities in their kind, and my friend's acquaintance, I sat down among them.

The chief politician of the bench was a great asserter of paradoxes. He told us, with a seeming concern, " that, by some news he had lately read from Muscovy, it appeared to him that there was a storm gathering in the Black Sea, which might in time do hurt to the naval forces of this nation." To this he added, " that, for his part, he could not wish to see the Turk driven out of Europe, which he believed could not but be prejudicial to our woollen manufacture." He then told us, "that he looked upon those extraordinary revolutions which had lately happened in those parts of the world, to have risen chiefly from two persons who were not much talked of ; and those," says he, " are Prince Menzikoff, and the Duchess of Mirandola." He backed his assertions with so many broken hints, and such a show of depth and wisdom, that we gave ourselves up to his opinions.

The discourse at length fell upon a point which seldom escapes a knot of true-born Englishmen, whether, in case of a religious war, the Protestants would not be too strong for the Papists ? This we unanimously determined on the Protestant side. One who sat on my right-hand, and, as I found by his discourse, had been in the West Indies, assured us, "that it would be a very easy matter for the Protestants to beat the Pope at sea ; " and added, "that whenever such a war does break out, it must turn to the good of the Leeward Islands." Upon this, one who sat at the end of the bench, and as I afterwards found, was the geographer of the company, said, " that in case the Papists should drive the Protestants from these parts of Europe, when the worst came to the worst, it would be impossible to beat them out of Norway and Greenland, provided the Northern crowns hold together, and the czar of Muscovy stand neuter."

He farther told us, for our comfort, "that there were vast tracks of lands about the pole, inhabited neither by Protestants nor Papists, and of greater extent than all the Roman-Catholic dominions in Europe."

When we had fully discussed this point, my friend the upholsterer began to exert himself upon the present negotiations of peace ; in which he deposed princes, settled the bounds of kingdoms, and balanced the power of Europe, with great justice and impartiality.

I at length took my leave of the company, and was going away ; but had not gone thirty yards, before the upholsterer hemmed again after me. Upon his advancing towards me with a whisper, I expected to hear some secret piece of news, which he had not thought fit to communicate to the bench ; but, instead of that, he desired me in my ear to lend him half a crown. In compassion to so needy a statesman, and to dissipate the confusion I found he was in, I told him, " if he pleased, I would give him five shillings, to receive five pounds of him when the great Turk was driven out of Constantinople ; " which he very readily accepted, but not before he had laid down to me the impossibility of such an event, as the affairs of Europe now stand.

This paper I design for the particular benefit of those worthy citizens who live more in a coffee-house than in their shops, and whose thoughts are so taken up with the affairs of the allies, that they forget their customers.

TOM FOLIO.

No. 158.   THURSDAY, April 13, 1710.   [Addison.]

Faciunt næ intelligendo, ut nihil intelligant.   Ter.

While they pretend to know more than others, they know nothing in reality.

Tom Folio * is a broker in learning, employed to get together good editions, and stock the libraries of great men. There is not a sale of books begins until Tom Folio is seen at the door. There is not an auction where his name is not heard, and that too in the very nick of time, in the critical moment, before the last decisive stroke of the hammer. There is not a subscription goes forward in which Tom is not privy to the first rough draught of the proposals ; nor a catalogue printed, that doth not come to him wet from the press. He is an universal scholar, so far as the title-page of all authors ; knows the manuscripts in which they were discovered, the editions through which they have passed, with the praises or censures which they have received from the several members of the learned world. He has a greater esteem for Aldus and Elzevir, than for Virgil and Horace. If you talk of Herodotus,

---

* The person supposed to be alluded to here was Thomas Rawlinson, the eldest son of Sir Thomas Rawlinson, Lord Mayor of London in 1706. He collected a great stock of books, which were sold by auction after his decease.

he breaks out into a panegyric upon Harry Stephens. He thinks he gives you an account of an author, when he tells you the subject he treats of, the name of the editor, and the year in which it was printed. Or if you draw him into farther particulars, he cries up the goodness of the paper, extols the diligence of the corrector, and is transported with the beauty of the letter. This he looks upon to be' sound learning, and substantial criticism. As for those who talk of the fineness of style, and the justness of thought, or describe the brightness of any particular passages ; nay, though they themselves write in the genius and spirit of the author they admire ; Tom looks upon them as men of superficial learning, and flashy parts.

I had yesterday morning a visit from this learned *ideot*, for *that* is the light in which I consider every pedant, when I discovered in him some little touches of the coxcomb, which I had not before observed. Being very full of the figure which he makes in the republic of letters, and wonderfully satisfied with his great stock of knowledge, he gave me broad intimations, that he did not believe in all points as his forefathers had done. He then communicated to me a thought of a certain author upon a passage of Virgil's account of the dead, which I made the subject of a late paper. This thought hath taken very much among men of Tom's pitch and understanding, though universally exploded by all that know how to construe Virgil, or have any relish of antiquity. Not to trouble my reader with it, I found, upon the whole, that Tom did not believe a future state of rewards and punishments, because Æneas, at his leaving the empire of the dead, passed through the gate of ivory, and not through that of horn. Knowing that Tom had not sense enough to give up an opinion which he had once received, that I might avoid wrangling, I told him "that Virgil possibly had his oversights as well as another author." "Ah ! Mr. Bickerstaff," says he, "you would have another opinion of him, if you would read him in Daniel Heinsius's edition. I have perused him myself several times in that edition," continued he ; "and after the strictest and most malicious examination, could find but two faults in him ; one of them is

x

in the Æneids, where there are two commas instead of a
parenthesis ; and another in the third Georgic, where you may
find a semicolon turned upside down." " Perhaps," said I,
" these were not Virgil's faults, but those of the transcriber."
" I do not design it," says Tom, "as a reflection on Virgil ; on
the contrary, I know that all the manuscripts declaim against
such a punctuation. Oh ! Mr. Bickerstaff," says he, " what
would a man give to see one simile of Virgil writ in his own
hand ? " I asked him which was the simile he meant ; but
was answered, any simile in Virgil. He then told me all the
secret history in the commonwealth of learning ; of modern
pieces that had the names of ancient authors annexed to them ;
of all the books that were now writing or printing in the
several parts of Europe ; of many amendments which are
made, and not yet published, and a thousand other particulars,
which I would not have my memory burdened with for a
Vatican.*

At length, being fully persuaded that I thoroughly admired
him, and looked upon him as a prodigy of learning, he took his
leave. I know several of Tom's class, who are professed
admirers of Tasso, without understanding a word of Italian :
and one in particular, that carries a *Pastor Fido* in his pocket,
in which, I am sure, he is acquainted with no other beauty but
the clearness of the character.

There is another kind of pedant, who, with all Tom Folio's
impertinences, hath greater superstructures and embellishments
of Greek and Latin ; and is still more insupportable than the
other, in the same degree as he is more learned. Of this kind very
often are editors, commentators, interpreters, scholiasts, and
critics ; and, in short, all men of deep learning without common
sense. These persons set a greater value on themselves for
having found out the meaning of a passage in Greek, than
upon the author for having written it ; nay, will allow the
passage itself not to have any beauty in it, at the same time
that they would be considered as the greatest men of the age,
for having interpreted it. They will look with contempt on

* For all the books in the Vatican library.

the most beautiful poems that have been composed by any of
their contemporaries; but will lock themselves up in their
studies for a twelvemonth together, to correct, publish, and
expound such trifles of antiquity, as a modern author would be
contemned for.   Men of the strictest morals, severest lives, and
the gravest professions, will write volumes upon an idle sonnet,
that is originally in Greek or Latin ; give editions of the most
immoral authors ; and spin out whole pages upon the various
readings of a lewd expression.   All that can be said in excuse
for them is, that their works sufficiently shew they have no
taste of their authors ; and that what they do in this kind, is
out of their great learning, and not out of any levity or lascivi-
ousness of temper.

A pedant of this nature is wonderfully well described in six
lines of Boileau, with which I shall conclude his character :

> Un Pedant enyvré de sa vaine science,
> Tout herissé de Grec, tout bouffi d'arrogance.
> Et qui de mille auteurs retenus mot pour mot,
> Dans sa tête entassez n'a souvent fait qu'un sot,
> Croit qu'un livre fait tout, and que sans Aristote
> La raison ne voit goute, and le bon sens radote.

> Brim-full of learning see that pedant stride,
> Bristling with horrid Greek, and puff'd with pride !
> A thousand authors he in vain has read,
> And with their maxims stuff'd his empty head ;
> And thinks that, without Aristotle's rule,
> Reason is blind, and common sense a fool.

THE GODDESS OF LIBERTY.

No. 161.   THURSDAY, April 20, 1710.   [Addison.]

—— Nunquam Libertas gratior extat
Quàm sub rege pio.

Never does Liberty appear more amiable than under the government of a
pious and good prince.

I was walking two or three days ago in a very pleasant
retirement, and amusing myself with the reading of that

ancient and beautiful allegory, called "The Table of Cebes."
I was at last so tired with my walk, that I sat down to rest
myself upon a bench that stood in the midst of an agreeable
shade. The music of the birds, that filled all the trees about
me, lulled me asleep before I was aware of it; which was
followed by a dream, that I impute in some measure to the
foregoing author, who had made an impression upon my
imagination, and put me into his own way of thinking.

I fancied myself among the Alps, and, as it is natural in a
dream, seemed every moment to bound from one summit to
another, until at last, having made this airy progress over the
tops of several mountains, I arrived at the very centre of those
broken rocks and precipices. I here, methought, saw a prodigious circuit of hills, that reached above the clouds, and
encompassed a large space of ground, which I had a great
curiosity to look into. I thereupon continued my former way
of travelling through a great variety of winter scenes, until I
had gained the top of these white mountains, which seemed
another Alps of snow. I looked down from hence into a
spacious plain, which was surrounded on all sides by this
mound of hills, and which presented me with the most agreeable prospect I had ever seen. There was a greater variety of
colours in the embroidery of the meadows, a more lively green
in the leaves and grass, a brighter crystal in the streams, than
what I ever met with in any other region. The light itself
had something more shining and glorious in it, than that of
which the day is made in other places. I was wonderfully
astonished at the discovery of such a paradise amidst the
wildness of those cold, hoary landskips which lay about it ;
but found at length, that this happy region was inhabited by
the goddess of Liberty ; whose presence softened the rigours
of the climate, enriched the barrenness of the soil, and more
than supplied the absence of the sun. The place was covered
with a wonderful profusion of flowers, that, without being
disposed into regular borders and parterres, grew promiscuously ; and had a greater beauty in their natural luxuriancy
and disorder, than they could have received from the checks

and restraints of art. There was a river that arose out of the south-side of the mountain, that, by an infinite number of turnings and windings, seemed to visit every plant, and cherish the several beauties of the spring, with which the. fields abounded. After having run to and fro in a wonderful variety of meanders, as unwilling to leave so charming a place, it at last throws itself into the hollow of a mountain ; from whence it passes under a long range of rocks, and at length rises in that part of the Alps where the inhabitants think *is* the first source of the Rhône. This river, after having made its progress through those free nations, stagnates in a huge lake at the leaving of them ; and no sooner enters into the regions of slavery, but *it* runs through them with an incredible rapidity, and takes its shortest way to the sea.

I descended into the happy fields that lay beneath me, and in the midst of them beheld the goddess sitting upon a throne. She had nothing to enclose her but the bounds of her own dominions, and nothing over her head but the heavens. Every glance of her eye cast a track of light where it fell, that revived the spring, and made all things smile about her. My heart grew cheerful at the sight of her ; and as she looked upon me, I found a certain confidence growing in me, and such an inward resolution as I never felt before that time.

On the left hand of the goddess sat the Genius of the Commonwealth, with the cap of Liberty on her head, and in her hand a wand, like that with which a Roman citizen used to give his slaves their freedom. There was something mean and vulgar, but at the same time exceeding bold and daring, in her air ; her eyes were full of fire ; but had in them such crafts of fierceness and cruelty, as made her appear to me rather dread-ful than amiable. On her shoulders she wore a mantle, on which there was wrought a great confusion of figures. As it flew in the wind, I could not discern the particular design of them, but saw wounds in the bodies of some, and agonies in the faces of others ; and over one part of it could read in letters of blood, " The Ides of March."

On the right-hand of the goddess was the Genius of

Monarchy. She was clothed in the whitest ermine, and wore a crown of the purest gold upon her head. In her hand she held a sceptre like that which is borne by the British monarchs. A couple of tame lions lay crouching at her feet. Her countenance had in it a very great majesty without any mixture of terror. Her voice was like the voice of an angel, filled with so much sweetness, accompanied with such an air of condescension, as tempered the awfulness of her appearance, and equally inspired love and veneration into the hearts of all that beheld her.

In the train of the goddess of Liberty were the several Arts and Sciences, who all of them flourished underneath her eye. One of them in particular made a greater figure than any of the rest, who held a thunderbolt in her hand which had the power of melting, piercing, or breaking, every thing that stood in its way. The name of this goddess was Eloquence.

There were two other dependent goddesses, who made a very conspicuous figure in this blissful region. The first of them was seated upon a hill, that had every plant growing out of it, which the soil was in its own nature capable of producing. The other was seated in a little island, that was covered with grooves of spices, olives and orange-trees ; and in a word, with the products of every foreign clime. The name of the first was Plenty, of the second Commerce. The first leaned her right arm upon a plough, and under her left held a huge horn, out of which she poured a *whole autumn of fruits*. The other wore a rostral crown upon her head, and kept her eyes fixed upon a compass.

I was wonderfully pleased in ranging through this delightful place, and the more so, because it was not incumbered with fences and inclosures ; until at length, methought, I sprung from the ground, and pitched upon the top a hill, that presented several objects to my sight which I had not before taken notice of. The winds that passed over this flowery plain, and through the tops of the trees which were full of blossoms, blew upon me in such a continued breeze of sweets, that I was wonderfully charmed with my situation. I here saw all the *inner declivities* of that great circuit of mountains, whose outside was covered with snow, over-grown with huge forests of fir-trees, which indeed are very frequently found in other parts of the Alps. These trees were inhabited by storks, that came thither in great flights from very distant quarters of the world. *Methought*, I was pleased in my dream to see what became of these birds, when, upon leaving the places to which they make an annual visit, they rise in great flocks so high until they are out of sight, and for that reason have been thought by some modern philosophers to take a flight to the moon. But my eyes were soon diverted from this prospect, when I observed two great gaps that led through this circuit of mountains, where guards and watches were posted day and night. Upon examination, I found that there were two formidable enemies encamped before each of these avenues, who kept the place in a perpetual alarm, and watched all opportunities of invading it.

Tyranny was at the head of one of these armies, dressed in an Eastern habit, and grasping in her hand an iron sceptre. Behind her was Barbarity, with the garb and complexion of an Ethiopian; Ignorance, with a turban upon her head; and Persecution holding up a bloody flag, embroidered with flower-de-luces. These were followed by Oppression, Poverty, Famine, Torture, and a dreadful train of appearances that made me tremble to behold them. Among the baggage of this army, I could discover racks, wheels, chains, and gibbets, with all the instruments art could invent to make human nature miserable. Before the other avenue I saw Licentiousness, dressed in a garment not unlike the Polish cassock, and leading up a whole army of monsters, such as Clamour, with a hoarse voice and an hundred tongues; Confusion, with a misshapen body, and a thousand heads; Impudence, with a forehead of brass; and Rapine, with hands of iron. The tumult, noise, and uproar in this quarter, were so very great, that they disturbed my imagination more than is consistent with sleep, and by that means awaked me.

NED SOFTLY.

No. 163.   TUESDAY, April 25, 1710.   [Addison.]

Idem inficeto est inficetior rure,
Simul poemata attigit ; neque idem unquam
Æquè est beatus, ac poema cum scribit :
Tam gaudet in se, tamque se ipse miratur.
· Nimirum idem omnes fallimur ; neque est quisquam
Quem non in aliquâ re videre Suffenum
Possis ——   Catul. de Suffeno, xx. 14.

Suffenus has no more wit than a mere clown when he attempts to write verses, and yet he is never happier than when he is scribbling ; so much does he admire himself and his compositions. And, indeed, this is the foible of every one of us, for there is no man living who is not a Suffenus in one thing or other.

I yesterday came hither* about two hours before the company generally make their appearance, with a design to read over all the newspapers ; but, upon my sitting down, I was accosted by Ned Softly, who saw me from a corner in the other end of the room, where I found he had been writing something. "Mr. Bickerstaff," says he, "I observe by a late Paper of yours, that you and I are just of a humour ; for you must know, of all impertinences, there is nothing which I so much hate as news. I never read a Gazette in my life ; and never trouble my head about our armies, whether they win or lose, or in what part of the world they lie encamped." Without giving me time to reply, he drew a paper of verses out of his pocket, telling me, "that he had something which would entertain me more agreeably ; and that he would desire my judgment upon every line, for that we had time enough before us until the company came in."

Ned Softly is a very pretty poet, and a great admirer of easy lines. Waller is his favourite : and as that admirable writer has the best and worst verses of any among our great English poets, Ned Softly, has got all the bad ones without book ; which he repeats upon occasion, to shew his reading,

* Will's Coffee-house.

and garnish his conversation.　Ned is indeed a true English reader, incapable of relishing the great and masterly strokes of this art; but wonderfully pleased with the little Gothic ornaments of epigrammatical conceits, turns, points, and quibbles, which are so frequent in the most admired of our English poets, and practised by those who want genius and strength to represent, after the manner of the ancients, simplicity in its natural beauty and perfection.

Finding myself unavoidably engaged in such a conversation, I was resolved to turn my pain into a pleasure, and to divert myself as well as I could with so very odd a fellow. "You must understand," says Ned, "that the sonnet I am going to read to you was written upon a lady, who shewed me some verses of her own making, and is, perhaps, the best poet of our age.　But you shall hear it."

Upon which he began to read as follows :

TO MIRA ON HER INCOMPARABLE POEMS.

I

When dress'd in laurel wreaths you shine,
　And tune your soft melodious notes,
You seem a sister of the Nine,
　Or Phœbus' self in petticoats.

II.

I fancy, when your song you sing,
　(Your song you sing with so much art)
Your pen was plucked from Cupid's wing ;
　For, ah ! it wounds me like his dart.

"Why," says I, "this is a little nosegay of conceits, a very lump of salt : every verse has something in it that piques ; and then the *dart* in the last line is certainly as pretty a sting in the tail of an epigram, for so I think you critics call it, as ever entered into the thought of a poet." "Dear Mr. Bickerstaff," says he, shaking me by the hand, "everybody knows you to be a judge of these things ; and to tell you truly, I read over Roscommon's translation of 'Horace's Art of Poetry' three several times, before I sat down to write the sonnet which I have shown you.　But you shall hear it again, and pray observe every line of it ; for not one of them shall pass without your approbation.

> When dress'd in laurel wreaths you shine,

"That is," says he, "when you have your garland on ; when you are writing verses." To which I replied, "I know your meaning : a metaphor !" "The same," said he, and went on.

> "And tune your soft melodious notes.

Pray observe the gliding of that verse ; there is scarce a consonant in it : I took care to make it run upon liquids. Give me your opinion of it." "Truly," said I, "I think it as good as the former." "I am very glad to hear you say so," says he ; "but mind the next."

> You seem a sister of the Nine,

"That is," says he, "you seem a sister of the Muses ; for, if you look into ancient authors, you will find it was their opinion that there were nine of them." "I remember it very well," said I ; "but pray proceed."

> "Or Phœbus' self in petticoats.

"Phœbus," says he, "was the god of poetry. These little instances, Mr. Bickerstaff, shew a gentleman's reading. Then, to take off from the air of learning, which Phœbus and the Muses had given to this first stanza, you may observe, how it falls all of a sudden into the familiar ; ' in Petticoats ' !

> "Or Phœbus' self in petticoats.

"Let us now," says I, "enter upon the second stanza ; I find the first line is still a continuation of the metaphor,

> I fancy, when your song you sing."

"It is very right," says he, "but pray observe the turn of words in those two lines. I was a whole hour in adjusting of them, and have still a doubt upon me, whether in the second line it should be 'Your song you sing; or, You sing your song?' You shall hear them both:

> I fancy, when your song you sing,
>   (Your song you sing with so much art)
>   OR
> I fancy, when your song you sing,
>   (You sing your song with so much art.) "

"Truly," said I, "the turn is so natural either way, that you have made me almost giddy with it." " Dear sir," said he, grasping me by the hand, " you have a great deal of patience; but pray what do you think of the next verse?

> Your pen was pluck'd from Cupid's wing."

"Think!" says I; "I think you have made Cupid look like a little goose." "That was my meaning," says he: " I think the ridicule is well enough hit off. But we come now to the last, which sums up the whole matter.

> For, ah! it wounds me like his dart.

"Pray how do you like that *Ah!* doth it not make a pretty figure in that place? *Ah!* ——it looks as if I felt the dart, and cried out as being pricked with it.

> For, ah! it wounds me like his dart.

"My friend Dick Easy," continued he, " assured me, he would rather have written that *Ah!* than *to* have been the author of the Æneid. He indeed objected, that I made Mira's pen like a quill in one of the lines, and like a dart in the other. But as to that——" " Oh! as to that," says I, " it is but supposing Cupid to be like a porcupine, and his quills and darts will be the same thing." He was going to embrace me for the hint; but half a dozen critics coming into the room, whose faces he did not like, he conveyed the sonnet into his pocket, and whispered me in the ear, "he would shew it me again as soon as his man had written it over fair."

THE CRITIC.

No. 165. SATURDAY, April 29, 1710. [Addison.]

It has always been my endeavour to distinguish between realities and appearances, and to separate true merit from the pretence to it. As it shall ever be my study to make discoveries of this nature in human life, and to settle the proper distinctions between the virtues and perfections of mankind, and those false colours and resemblances of them that shine alike in the eyes of the vulgar; so I shall be more particularly careful to search into the various merits and pretences of the learned world. This is the more necessary, because there seems to be a general combination among the Pedants to extol one another's labours, and cry up one another's parts; while men of sense, either through that modesty which is natural to them, or the scorn they have for such trifling commendations, enjoy their stock of knowledge, like a hidden treasure, with satisfaction and silence. Pedantry indeed in learning is like hypocrisy in religion, a form of knowledge without the power of it; that attracts the eyes of the common people; breaks out in noise and show; and finds its reward not from any inward pleasure that attends it, but from the praises and approbations which it receives from men.

Of this shallow species there is not a more importunate, empty, and conceited animal, than that which is generally known by the name of a Critic. This, in the common acceptation of the word, is one that, without entering into the sense and soul of an author, has a few general rules, which, like mechanical instruments, he applies to the works of every writer; and as they quadrate with them, pronounces the author perfect or defective. He is master of a certain set of words, as *Unity, Style, Fire, Phlegm, Easy, Natural, Turn, Sentiment,* and the like; which he varies, compounds, divides, and throws together, in every part of his discourse, without any thought o

meaning.　The marks you may know him by are, an elevated
eye, and dogmatical brow, a positive voice, and a contempt
for every thing that comes out, whether he has read it or not.
He dwells altogether in generals.　He praises or dispraises in
the lump.　He shakes his head very frequently at the
Pedantry of universities, and bursts into laughter when you
mention an author that is *not known* at Will's.　He hath
formed his judgment upon Homer, Horace, and Virgil, not
from their own works, but from those of Rapin and Bossu.
He knows his own strength so well, that he never dares praise
anything in which he has not a French author for his
voucher.

　With these extraordinary talents and accomplishments, Sir
Timothy Tittle *puts men in vogue*, or condemns them to
obscurity ; and sits as judge of life and death upon every
author that appears in public.　It is impossible to represent
the pangs, agonies, and convulsions, which Sir Timothy
expresses in every feature of his face, and muscle of his body,
upon the reading of a bad poet.

　About a week ago, I was engaged, at a friend's house of
mine, in an agreeable conversation with his wife and daughters,
when, in the height of our mirth, Sir Timothy, who makes
love to my friend's eldest daughter, came in amongst us,
puffing and blowing as if he had been very much out of breath.
He immediately called for a chair, and desired leave to sit
down without any further ceremony.　I asked him, where he
had been ? whether he was out of order ? he only replied, that
he was quite spent, and fell a cursing in soliloquy.　I could
hear him cry, " A wicked rogue——An execrable wretch——
Was there ever such a monster ! "——The young ladies upon
this began to be affrighted, and asked, whether any one had
hurt him ? he answered nothing, but still talked to himself.
" To lay the first scene," says he, " in St. James's-Park, and the
last in Northamptonshire ! " " Is that all ? " said I.　" Then I
suppose you have been at the rehearsal of a play this morning."
" Been ! " says he, " I have been at Northampton, in the Park,
in a lady's bed-chamber, in a dining-room, every where ; the

rogue has led me such a dance——" Though I could scarce
forbear laughing at his discourse, I told him I was glad it
was no worse, and that he was only metaphorically weary. "In
short, sir," says he, "the author has not observed a single
Unity in his whole play ; the scene shifts in every dialogue ;
the villain has hurried me up and down at such a rate, that I
am tired off my legs." I could not but observe with some
pleasure, that the young lady whom he made love to, conceived
a very just aversion towards him, upon seeing him so very
passionate in trifles. And as she had that natural sense, which
makes her a better judge than a thousand critics, she began to
rally him upon his foolish humour. "For my part," says she,
"I never knew a play take that was written up to your rules, as
you call them." "How, madam ! " says he, "is that your
opinion ? I am sure you have a better taste." "It is a pretty
kind of magic," says she, "the poets have, to transport an
audience from place to place without the help of a coach and
horses ; I could travel round the world at such a rate. It is
such an entertainment as an enchantress finds when she fancies
herself in a wood, or upon a mountain, at a feast, or a
solemnity ; though at the same time she has never stirred out
of her cottage." "Your simile, madam," says Sir Timothy, "is
by no means just." "Pray," says she, "let my similes pass without a criticism. I must confess," continued she, (for I found
she was resolved to exasperate him) "I laughed very heartily
at the last new comedy which you found so much fault with."
"But, madam," says he, "you ought not to have laughed ; and
I defy any one to shew me a single rule that you could laugh
by." "Ought not to laugh ! " says she ; "pray who should
hinder me ? " "Madam," says he, "there are such people in
the world as Rapin, Dacier, and several others, that ought to
have spoiled your mirth." "I have heard," says the young
lady, "that your great critics are always very bad poets ; I
fancy there is as much difference between the works of the one
and the other, as there is between the carriage of a dancing-
master and a gentleman. I must confess," continued she, "I
would not be troubled with so fine a judgment as yours is ; for

I find you feel more vexation in a bad comedy, than I do in a deep tragedy." " Madam," says Sir Timothy, " that is not my fault ; they should learn the art of writing." " For my part," says the young lady, " I should think the greatest art in your writers of comedies is to please." " To please ! " says Sir Timothy ; and immediately fell a-laughing. " Truly," says she, " that is my opinion." Upon this, he composed his countenance, looked upon his watch, and took his leave.

I hear that Sir Timothy has not been at my friend's house since this notable conference, to the great satisfaction of the young lady, who by this means has got rid of a very imperti- nent fop.

IN MEMORIAM.

No. 181. TUESDAY, June 6, 1710. [Steele.]

—— Dies, ni fallor, adest, quem semper acerbum,
Semper honoratum, sic dii voluistis habebo.
Virg. Æn. v. 49.

And now the rising day renews the year,
A day for ever sad, for ever dear.

There are those among mankind, who can enjoy no relish of their being, except the world is made acquainted with all that relates to them, and think every thing lost that passes unobserved ; but others find a solid delight in stealing by the crowd, and modelling their life after such a manner, as is as much above the approbation as the practice of the vulgar. Life being too short to give instances great enough of true friendship or good will, some sages have thought it pious to preserve a certain reverence for the *Manes* of their deceased friends ; and have withdrawn themselves from the rest of the world at certain seasons, to commemorate in their own thoughts such of their acquaintance who have gone before them out of this life. And indeed, when we are advanced in years, there is not a more pleasing entertainment, than to recollect in a

gloomy moment the many we have parted with, that have been
dear and agreeable to us, and to cast a melancholy thought or
two after those, with whom, perhaps, we have indulged ourselves in whole nights of mirth and jollity.   With such inclinations in my heart I went to my closet yesterday in the
evening, and resolved to be sorrowful ; upon which occasion I
could not but look with disdain upon myself, that though all
the reasons which I had to lament the loss of many of my
friends are now as forcible as at the moment of their departure,
yet did not my heart swell with the same sorrow which I felt
at that time ; but I could, without tears, reflect upon many
pleasing adventures I have had with some, who have long been
blended with common earth.

Though it is by the benefit of nature, that length of time thus
blots out the violence of afflictions ; yet with tempers too much
given to pleasure, it is almost necessary to revive the old places
of grief in our memory ; and ponder step by step on past life, to
lead the mind into that sobriety of thought which poises the heart,
and makes it beat with due time, without being quickened with
desire, or retarded with despair, from its proper and equal
motion.   When we wind up a clock that is out of order, to
make it go well for the future, we do not immediately set the
hand to the present instant, but we make it strike the round of
all its hours, before it can recover the regularity of its time.
Such, thought I, shall be my method this evening ; and since
it is that day of the year which I dedicate to the memory of
such in another life as I much delighted in when living, an
hour or two shall be sacred to sorrow and their memory, while
I run over all the melancholy circumstances of this kind which
have occurred to me in my whole life.   The first sense of
sorrow I ever knew was upon the death of my father at which
time I was not quite five years of age ; but was rather amazed
at what all the house meant, than possessed with a real understanding why nobody was willing to play with me. I remember
I went into the room where his body lay, and my mother sat
weeping alone by it.   I had my battledore in my hand, and
fell a-beating the coffin, and calling papa ; for, I know not

how, I had some slight idea that he was locked up there. My mother catched me in her arms, and, transported beyond all patience of the silent grief she was before in, she almost smothered me in her embraces ; and told me, in a flood of tears, " Papa could not hear me, and would play with me no more, for they were going to put him under ground, whence he could never come to us again." She was a very beautiful woman, of a noble spirit, and there was a dignity in her grief amidst all the wildness of her transport, which, methought, struck me with an instinct of sorrow, that, before I was sensible of what it was to grieve, seized my very soul, and has made pity the weakness of my heart ever since. The mind in infancy is, methinks, like the body in embryo, and receives impressions so forcible, that they are as hard to be removed by reason, as any mark, with which a child is born, is to be taken away by any future application. Hence it is, that good-nature in me is no merit ; but having been so frequently over-whelmed with her tears before I knew the cause of any affliction, or could draw defences from my own judgment. I imbibed commiseration, remorse, and an unmanly gentleness of mind, which has since insnared me into ten thousand calamities ; from whence I can reap no advantage, except it be, that, in such a humour as I am now in, I can the better indulge my-self in the softnesses of humanity, and enjoy that sweet anxiety which arises from the memory of past afflictions.

We, that are very old, are better able to remember things which befel us in our distant youth, than the passages of later days. For this reason it is, that the companions of my strong and vigorous years present themselves more immediately to me in this office of sorrow. Untimely and unhappy deaths are what we are most apt to lament ; so little are we able to make it indifferent when a thing happens, though we know it must happen. Thus we groan under life, and bewail those who are relieved from it. Every object that returns to our imagination raises different passions, according to the circumstances of their departure. Who can have lived in an army, and in a serious hour reflect upon the many gay and agreeable men that

Y

might long have flourished in the arts of peace, and not join
with the imprecations of the fatherless and widow on the
tyrant to whose ambition they fell sacrifices ? But gallant men,
who are cut off by the sword, move rather our veneration than
our pity; and we gather relief enough from their own contempt of death, to make that no evil, which was approached
with so much cheerfulness, and attended with so much honour.
But when we turn our thoughts from the great parts of life on
such occasions, and instead of lamenting those who stood ready
to give death to those from whom they had the fortune to
receive it ; I say, when we let our thoughts wander from such
noble objects, and consider the havock which is made among
the tender and the innocent, pity enters with an unmixed softness, and possesses all our souls at once.

Here (were their words to express such sentiments with
proper tenderness) I should record the beauty, innocence and
untimely death, of the first object my eyes ever beheld with
love.   The beauteous virgin ! how ignorantly did she charm,
how carelessly excel ! Oh Death ! thou hast right to the bold,
to the ambitious, to the high, and to the haughty ; but why
this cruelty to the humble, to the meek, to the undiscerning,
to the thoughtless ? Nor age, nor business, nor distress, can
erase the dear image from my imagination.   In the same
week, I saw her dressed for a ball, and in a shroud.   How ill
did the habit of death become the pretty trifler ? I still behold
the smiling earth——A large train of disasters were coming
on to my memory, when my servant knocked at my closet-door,
and interrupted me with a letter, attended with a hamper of
wine, of the same sort with that which is to be put to sale,
on Thursday next, at Garraway's coffee-house.   Upon the
receipt of it, I sent for three of my friends.   We are so intimate, that we can be company in whatever state of mind we
meet, and can entertain each other without expecting always to
rejoice.   The wine we found to be generous and warming, but
with such an heat as moved us rather to be cheerful than
frolicksome.   It revived the spirits, without firing the blood.
We commended it until two of the clock this morning ; and

having to-day met a little before dinner, we found, that though we drank two bottles a man, we had much more reason to recollect than forget what had passed the night before.

CONSTANCY.

No. 192. SATURDAY, July 1, 1710. [Addison.]

Tecum vivere amem, tecum obeam libens.
Hor. 3 Od. ix.

—— Gladly I
With thee would live, with thee would die.

SOME years since I was engaged with a coachful of friends to take a journey as far as the Land's End. We were very well pleased with one another the first day ; every one endeavouring to recommend himself by his good humour, and complaisance to the rest of the company. This good correspondence did not last long ; one of our party was soured the very first evening by a plate of butter, which had not been melted to his mind, and which spoiled his temper to such a degree, that he continued upon the fret to the end of our journey. A second fell off from his good humour the next morning, for no other reason, that I could imagine, but because I chanced to step into the coach before him, and place myself on the shady side. This, however, was but my own private guess ; for he did not mention a word of it, nor indeed of anything else, for three days following. The rest of our company held out very near half the way, when on a sudden Mr. Sprightly fell asleep ; and instead of endeavouring to divert and oblige us, as he had hitherto done, carried himself with an unconcerned, careless, drowsy behaviour, until we came to our last stage. There were three of us who still held up our heads, and did all we could to make our journey agreeable ; but, to my shame be it spoken, about three miles on this side Exeter, I was taken with an unaccountable fit of sullenness, that hung upon me for above

Y 2

threescore miles ; whether it were for want of respect, or from an accidental tread upon my foot, or from a foolish maid's calling me "The old gentleman," I cannot tell. In short, there was but one who kept his good humour to the Land's End.

There was another coach that went along with us, in which I likewise observed, that there were many secret jealousies, heart-burnings, and animosities : for when we joined companies at night, I could not but take notice that the passengers neglected their own company, and studied how to make themselves esteemed by us, who were altogether strangers to them ; until at length they grew so well acquainted with us, that they liked us as little as they did one another. When I reflect upon this journey, I often fancy it to be a picture of human life, in respect to the several friendships, contracts, and alliances, that are made and dissolved in the several periods of it. The most delightful and most lasting engagements are generally those which pass between man and woman ; and yet upon what trifles are they weakened, or entirely broken ! Sometimes the parties fly asunder even in the midst of courtship, and sometimes grow cool in the very honey-month. Some separate before the first child, and some after the fifth ; others continue good until thirty, others until forty ; while some few, whose souls are of an happier make, and better fitted to one another, travel on together to the end of their journey in a continual intercourse of kind offices, and mutual endearments.

When we therefore choose our companions for life, if we hope to keep both them and ourselves in good humour to the last stage of it, we must be extremely careful in the choice we make, as well as in the conduct on our own part. When the persons to whom we join ourselves can stand an examination, and bear the scrutiny ; when they mend upon our acquaintance with them, and discover new beauties, the more we search into their characters ; our love will naturally rise in proportion to their perfections.

But because there are very few possessed of such accomplishments of body and mind, we ought to look after those qualifications both in ourselves and others, which are indispensably necessary towards this happy union, and which are in the power of every one to acquire, or at least to cultivate and improve. These, in my opinion, are cheerfulness and constancy. A cheerful temper joined with innocence will make beauty attractive, knowledge delightful, and wit good-natured. It will lighten sickness, poverty, and affliction ; convert ignorance into an amiable simplicity ; and render deformity itself agreeable.

Constancy is natural to persons of even tempers and uniform dispositions ; and may be acquired by those of the greatest fickleness, violence, and passion, who consider seriously the terms of union upon which they come together, the mutual interest in which they are engaged, with all the motives that ought to incite their tenderness and compassion towards those, who have their dependence upon them, and are embarked with them for life in the same state of happiness or misery. Constancy, when it grows in the mind upon considerations of this nature, becomes a moral virtue, and a kind of good-nature, that is not subject to any change of health, age, fortune, or any of those accidents, which are apt to unsettle the best dispositions that are founded rather in constitution than in reason. Where such a constancy as this is wanting, the most inflamed passion may fall away into coldness and indifference, and the most melting tenderness degenerate into hatred and aversion. I shall conclude this paper with a story, that is very well known in the North of England.

About thirty years ago, a packet-boat that had several passengers on board was cast away upon a rock, and in so great danger of sinking, that all who were in it endeavoured to save themselves as well as they could ; though only those who could swim well had a bare possibility of doing it. Among the passengers there were two women of fashion, who, seeing themselves in such a disconsolate condition, begged of their husbands not to leave them. One of them chose rather to die with his wife, than to forsake her ; the other, though he was moved with the utmost compassion for his wife, told her, " that for the good of their children, it was better one of them should live than both perish." By a great piece of good luck, next to a miracle, when one of our good men had taken the last and long farewell in order to save himself, and the other held in his arms the person that was dearer to him than life, the ship was preserved. It is with a secret sorrow and vexation of mind that I must tell the sequel of the story, and let my reader know, that this faithful pair who were ready to have died in each other's arms, about three years after their escape, upon some trifling disgust grew to a coldness at first, and at length fell out to such a degree, that they left one another, and parted for ever. The other couple lived together in an uninterrupted friendship and felicity ; and what was remarkable, the husband, whom the shipwreck had like to have separated from his wife, died a few months after her, not being able to survive the loss of her.

I must confess, there is something in the changeableness and inconstancy of human nature, that very often both dejects and terrifies me. Whatever I am at present, I tremble to think what I may be. While I find this principle in me, how can I assure myself that I shall be always true to my God, my friend, or myself? In short, without constancy there is neither love, friendship, nor virtue, in the world.

PATRON AND CLIENT.

No. 196. TUESDAY, July 11, 1710. [Steele.]

> Dulcis inexperto cultura potentis amici,
> Expertus metuit.——   Hor. 1 Ep. xviii. 86.

> Untry'd, how sweet a court attendance !
> When try'd, how dreadful the dependence !

The intended course of my studies was altered this evening by a visit from an old acquaintance, who complained to me, mentioning one upon whom he had long depended, that he found his labour and perseverance in his patron's service and interests wholly ineffectual ; and he thought now, after his best years were spent in a professed adherence to him and his fortunes, he should in the end be forced to break with him, and give over all farther expectations from him.   He sighed, and ended his discourse, by saying, " You, Mr. Censor, some time ago, gave us your thoughts of the behaviour of great men to their creditors.   This sort of demand upon them, for what they invite men to expect, is a debt of honour ; which, according to custom, they ought to be most careful of paying, and would be a worthy subject for a Lucubration."

Of all men living, I think, I am the most proper to treat of this matter ; because, in the character and employment of the Censor, I have had encouragement so infinitely above my desert, that what I say cannot possibly be supposed to arise from peevishness, or any disappointment in that kind, which I myself have met with.   When we consider Patrons and their Clients, those who receive addresses, and those who are addressed to, it must not be understood that the dependents are such as are worthless in their natures, abandoned to any vice or dishonour, or such as without a call thrust themselves upon men in power ; nor when we say Patrons, do we mean such as have it not in their power, or have no obligation, to assist their friends ; but we speak of such leagues where there are power and obligation on the one part, and merit and expectation on the other. Were we to be very particular on this subject, I take it, that the division of Patron and Client may include a third part of our nation.   The want of merit and real worth will strike out about ninety-nine in the hundred of these ; and want of ability in the Patron will dispose of as many of that order.   He, who out of mere vanity to be applied to, will take up another's time and fortune in his service, where he has no prospect of returning it, is as much more unjust, as those who took up my friend the Upholder's goods without paying him for them ; I say, he is as much more unjust, as our life and time is more valuable than our goods and movables.   Among many whom you see about the great, there is a contented well-pleased set, who seem to like the attendance for its own sake, and are early at the abodes of the powerful, out of mere fashion. This sort of vanity is as well grounded, as if a man should lay aside his own plain suit, and dress himself up in a gay livery of another.

There are many of this species who exclude others of just expectations, and make those proper dependents appear impatient, because they are not so cheerful as those who expect nothing. I have made use of the penny-post for the instruction of these voluntary slaves, and informed them, that they will never be provided for; but they double their diligence upon admonition. Will Afterday has told his friends, that he was to have the next thing, these ten years; and Harry Linger has been fourteen, within a month, of a considerable office. However the fantastic complaisance which is paid to them, may blind the great from seeing themselves in a just light; they must needs, if they in the least reflect, at some times, have a sense of the injustice they do in raising in others a false expectation. But this is so common a practice in all the stages of power, that there are not more cripples come out of the wars, than from the attendance of Patrons. You see in one a settled melancholy, in another a bridled rage; a third has lost his memory, and a fourth his whole constitution and humour. In a word, when you see a particular cast of mind or body, which looks a little upon the distracted, you may be sure the poor gentleman has formerly had great friends. For this reason, I have thought it a prudent thing to take a nephew of mine out of a lady's service, where he was a page, and have bound him to a shoe-maker.

But what, of all the humours under the sun, is the most pleasant to consider is, that you see some men lay, as it were, a set of acquaintance by them, to converse with when they are out of employment, who had no effect of their power when they were in. Here Patrons and Clients both make the most fantastical figure imaginable. Friendship indeed is most manifested in adversity; but I do not know how to behave myself to a man, who thinks me his friend at no other time but that.

Dick Reptile of our club had this in his head the other night, when he said, " I am afraid of ill news, when I am visited by any of my old friends." These Patrons are a little like some fine gentlemen, who spend all their hours of gaiety with their wenches, but when they fall sick will let no one come near them but their wives. It seems, truth and honour are companions too sober for prosperity. It is certainly the most black ingratitude, to accept of a man's best endeavours to be pleasing to you, and return it with indifference.

I am so much of this mind, that Dick Eastcourt the comedian, for coming one night to our club, though he laughed at us all the time he was there, shall have our company at his play on Thursday. A man of talents is to be favoured, or never admitted. Let the ordinary world truck for money and wares; but men of spirit and conversation should in every kind do others as much pleasure as they receive from them. But men are so taken up with outward forms, that they do not consider their actions ; else how should it be, that a man should deny that to the entreaties, and almost tears of an old friend, which he shall solicit a new one to accept of ? I remember when I first came out of Staffordshire, I had an intimacy with a man of quality, in whose gift there fell a very good employment. All the town cried, " There's a thing for Mr. Bickerstaff ! " when, to my great astonishment, I found my Patron had been forced upon twenty artifices to surprise a man with it, who never thought of it : but sure, it is a degree of murder to amuse men with vain . hopes. If a man takes away another's life, where is the difference, whether he does it by taking away the minutes of his time, or the drops of his blood ? But indeed, such as have hearts barren of kindness are served accordingly by those whom they employ ; and pass their lives away with an empty show of civility for love, and an insipid intercourse of a commerce in which their affections are no way concerned. But, on the other side, how beautiful is the life of a Patron who performs his duty to his inferiors ? A worthy merchant, who employs a crowd of artificers ? A great lord, who is generous and merciful to the several necessities of his tenants ?

A courtier, who uses his credit and power for the welfare of his
friends ?   These have in their several stations a quick relish of
the exquisite pleasure of doing good.   In a word, good Patrons
are like the *Guardian Angels* of Plato, who are ever busy, though
unseen, in the care of their wards ; but ill Patrons are like the
Deities of Epicurus, supine, indolent, and unconcerned, though
they see mortals in storms and tempests, even while they are
offering incense to their power.

THE HISTORY OF CÆLIA.

No. 198.   SATURDAY, July 15, 1710.   [Steele.]

Quale sit id quod amas celeri circumspice mente,
Et tua læsuro substrahe colla jugo.
                              Ovid. Rem. Amor. i. 89.

On your choice deliberate, nor rashly yield
A willing neck to Hymen's galling yoke.

It is not necessary to look back into the first years of this
young lady, whose story is of consequence only as her life has
lately met with passages very uncommon.   She is now in the
twentieth year of her age, and owes a strict, but cheerful
education, to the care of an aunt ; to whom she was recommended by her dying father, whose decease was hastened by
an inconsolable affliction for the loss of her mother.

As Cælia is the offspring of the most generous passion that
has been known in our age, she is adorned with as much beauty
and grace as the most celebrated of her sex possess ; but her
domestic life, moderate fortune, and religious education, gave
her but little opportunity, and less inclination, to be admired
in public assemblies.   Her abode has been for some years at a
convenient distance from the cathedral of St. Paul's, where her
aunt and she chose to reside for the advantage of that rapturous
way of devotion, which gives ecstasy to the pleasures of innocence, and, in some measure, is the immediate possession of
those heavenly enjoyments for which they are addressed.

As you may trace the usual thoughts of men in their countenances, there appeared in the face of Cælia a cheerfulness, the constant companion of unaffected virtue, and a gladness, which is as inseparable from true piety.   Her every look and motion spoke the peaceful, mild, resigning, humble inhabitant, that animated her beauteous body.   Her air discovered her body a mere machine of her mind, and not that her thoughts were employed in studying graces and attractions for her person.   Such was Cælia, when she was first seen by Palamede at her usual place of worship.   Palamede is a young man of two-and-twenty, well-fashioned, learned, genteel and discreet ; the son and heir of a gentleman of a very great estate, and himself possessed of a plentiful one by the gift of an uncle. He became enamoured with Cælia ; and after having learned her habitation had address enough to communicate his passion and circumstances with such an air of good sense and integrity, as soon obtained permission to visit and profess his inclinations towards her.   Palamede's present fortune and future expectations were no way prejudicial to his addresses ; but after the lovers had passed some time in the agreeable entertainments of a successful courtship, Cælia one day took occasion to interrupt Palamede, in the midst of a very pleasing discourse of the happiness he promised himself in so accomplished a companion ; and, assuming a serious air, told him, there was another heart to be won before he gained hers, which was that of his father.   Palamede seemed much disturbed at the overture ; and lamented to her, that his father was one of those too provident parents, who only place their thoughts upon bringing riches into their families by marriages, and are wholly insensible of all other considerations.   But the strictness of Cælia's rules of life made her insist upon this demand ; and the son, at a proper hour, communicated to his father the circumstances of his love, and the merit of the object.   The next day the father made her a visit.   The beauty of her person, the fame of her virtue, and a certain irresistible charm in her whole behaviour, on so tender and delicate an occasion, wrought so much upon him, in spite of all prepossessions, that he hastened the marriage with an impatience equal to that of his son. Their nuptials were celebrated with a privacy suitable to the character and modesty of Cælia ; and from that day until a fatal one *last week,* they lived together with all the joy and happiness which attend minds entirely united.

It should have been intimated, that Palamede is a student of the Temple, and usually retired thither early in the morning ; Cælia still sleeping.

It happened, *a few days since,* that she followed him thither to communicate to him something she had omitted, in her redundant fondness, to speak of the evening before. When she came to his apartment, the servant there told her, she was coming with a letter to her. While Cælia in an inner room was reading an apology from her husband, " That he had been suddenly taken by some of his acquaintance to dine at Brentford, but that he should return in the evening," a country girl, decently clad, asked, if those were not the chambers of Mr. Palamede ? She was answered, they were ; but that he was not in town. The stranger asked, when he was expected at home ? The servant replied, she would go in and ask his wife. The young woman repeated the word *wife,* and fainted. This accident raised no less curiosity than amazement in Cælia, who caused her to be removed into the inner room. Upon proper applications to revive her, the unhappy young creature returned to herself ; and said to Cælia, with an earnest and beseeching tone, " Are you really Mr. Palamede's wife ? " Cælia replies, " I hope I do not look as if I were any other in the condition you see me." The stranger answered, " No, Madam, he is my husband." At the same instant, she threw a bundle of letters into Cælia's lap, which confirmed the truth of what she asserted. Their mutual innocence and sorrow made them look at each other as partners in distress, rather than rivals in love. The superiority of Cælia's understanding and genius gave her an authority to examine into this adventure, as if she had been offended against, and the other the delinquent. The stranger spoke in the following manner :

" MADAM,

" If if shall please you, Mr. Palamede, having an uncle of a good estate near Winchester, was bred at the school there, to gain the more his good-will by being in his sight. His uncle died, and left him the estate which my husband now has. When he was a mere youth, he set his affections on me ; but when he could not gain his ends, he married me ; making me and my mother, who is a farmer's widow, swear we would never tell it upon any account whatsoever ; for that it would not look well for him to marry such a one as me ; besides, that his father would cut him off of the estate. I was glad to have him in an honest way ; and he now and then came and stayed a night and away at our house. But very lately, he came down to see us with a fine young gentleman, his friend, who stayed behind there with us, pretending to like the place for the summer : but ever since master Palamede went, he has attempted to abuse me ; and I ran hither to acquaint him with it, and avoid the wicked intentions of his false friend."

Cælia had no more room for doubt ; but left her rival in the same agonies she felt herself. Palamede returns in the evening ; and finding his wife at his chambers, learned all that had passed, and hastened to Cælia's lodgings.

It is much easier to imagine, than express, the sentiments of either the criminal, or the injured, at this encounter.

As soon as Palamede had found way for speech, he confessed his marriage, and his placing his companion on purpose to vitiate his wife, that he might break through a marriage made in his nonage, and devote his riper and knowing years to Cælia. She made him no answer ; but retired to her closet. He returned to the Temple, where he soon after received from her the following letter :

" SIR,

" You, who this morning were the best, are now the worst of men who breathe vital air. I am at once overwhelmed with love, hatred, rage, and disdain. Can infamy and innocence live together ? I feel the weight of the one too strong for the

comfort of the other.   How bitter, Heaven ! how bitter is my
portion !   How much have I to say ! but the infant which I
bear about me stirs with my agitation.   I am, Palamede, to
live in shame, and this creature be heir to it.   Farewell for
ever ! ''

MATRIMONY.

No. 200.   THURSDAY, July 20, 1710.   [Steele.]

HAVING devoted the greater part of my time to the service
of the fair sex ; I must ask pardon of my men correspondents,
if I postpone their commands, when I have any from the
ladies which lie unanswered.   That which follows is of importance.

" SIR,

        " You cannot think it strange if I, who know little
of the world, apply to you for advice in the weighty affair of
matrimony ; since you yourself have often declared it to be
of that consequence as to require the utmost deliberation.
Without farther preface, therefore, give me leave to tell you,
that my father at his death left me a fortune sufficient to make
me a match for any gentleman.   My mother, for she is still
alive, is very pressing with me to marry ; and I am apt to
think, to gratify her, I shall venture upon one of two gentlemen, who at this time make their addresses to me.   My
request is, that you would direct me in my choice ; which that
you may the better do, I shall give you their characters ; and,
to avoid confusion, desire you to call them by the names of
Philander and Silvius.   Philander is young, and has a good
estate ; Silvius is as young, and has a better.   The former has
had a liberal education, has seen the town, is retired from
thence to his estate in the country, is a man of few words, and
much given to books.   The latter was brought up under his

father's eye, who gave him just learning enough to enable him
to keep his accounts; but made him withal very expert in
country business, such as ploughing, sowing, buying, selling,
and the like. They are both very sober men, neither of their
persons is disagreeable, nor did I know which to prefer until
I had heard them discourse; when the conversation of
Philander so much prevailed, as to give him the advantage
with me, in all other respects. My mother pleads strongly for
Silvius; and uses these arguments: that he not only has the
larger estate at present, but by his good husbandry and
management increases it daily: that his little knowledge in
other affairs will make him easy and tractable; whereas,
according to her, men of letters know too much to make good
husbands. To part of this, I imagine, I answer effectually, by
saying, Philander's estate is large enough; that they who
think two thousand pounds a year sufficient, make no
difference between that and three. I easily believe him less
conversant in those affairs, the knowledge of which she so
much commends in Silvius; but I think them neither so
necessary, or becoming a gentleman, as the accomplishments
of Philander. It is no great character of a man to say, he
rides in his coach and six, and understands as much as he who
follows the plough. Add to this, that the conversation of
these sort of men seems so disagreeable to me, that though
they make good bailiffs, I can hardly be persuaded they can
be good companions. It is possible I may seem to have odd
notions, when I say, I am not fond of a man only for being of,
what is called, a thriving temper. To conclude, I own I am
at a loss to conceive, how good sense should make a man an ill
husband, or conversant with books less complaisant.

"CÆLIA."

The resolution which this lady is going to take, she
may very well say, is founded on reason; for, after the
necessities of life are served, there is no manner of competition
between a man of a liberal education and an illiterate. Men
are not altered by their circumstances, but as they give them

opportunities of exerting what they are in themselves ; and a powerful clown is a tyrant in the most ugly form he can possibly appear. There lies a seeming objection in the thoughtful manner of Philander : but let her consider, which she shall oftener have occasion to wish, that Philander would speak, or Silvius hold his tongue.

The train of my discourse is prevented by the urgent haste of another correspondent.

"MR. BICKERSTAFF,   *July* 14.

"This comes to you from one of those virgins of twenty-five years old and upwards, that you, like a patron of the distressed, promised to provide for ; who makes it her humble request, that no *occasional stories* or subjects may, as they have for three or four of your last days, prevent your publishing the scheme you have communicated to Amanda ; for every day and hour is of the greatest consequence to damsels of so advanced an age. Be quick, then, if you intend to do any service for your admirer,

"DIANA FORECAST."

In this important affair, I have not neglected the proposals of others. Among them is the following sketch of a lottery for persons. The author of it has proposed very ample encouragement, not only to myself, but also to Charles Lillie and John Morphew. If the matter bears, I shall not be unjust to his merit : I only desire to enlarge his plan ; for which purpose I lay it before the town, as well for the improvement as the encouragement of it.

THE AMICABLE CONTRIBUTION FOR RAISING THE FORTUNES OF TEN YOUNG LADIES.

"*Imprimis,*—It is proposed to raise one hundred thousand crowns by way of lots, which will advance for each lady two thousand five hundred pounds ; which sum, together with one of the ladies, the gentleman that shall be so happy as to draw a prize, provided they both like, will be entitled to, under such restrictions hereafter mentioned. And in case they do not like, then either party that refuses shall be entitled to one thousand pounds only, and the remainder to him or her that shall be willing to marry, the man being first to declare his mind. But it is provided, that if both parties shall consent to have one another, the gentleman shall, before he receives the money thus raised, settle one thousand pounds of the same in substantial hands (who shall be as trustees for the said ladies), and shall have the whole and sole disposal of it for her use only.

" *Note*, each party shall have three months' time to consider, after an interview had, which shall be within ten days after the lots are drawn.

" *Note* also, the name and place of abode of the prize shall be placed on a proper ticket.

" *Item*, they shall be ladies that have had a liberal education, between fifteen and twenty-three ; all genteel, witty, and of unblameable characters.

" The money to be raised shall be kept in an iron box ; and when there shall be two thousand subscriptions, which amounts to five hundred pounds, it shall be taken out and put into a *goldsmith's* hand, and the note made payable to the proper lady, or her assigns, with a clause therein to hinder her from receiving it, until the fortunate person that draws her shall first sign the note, and so on until the whole sum is subscribed for : and as soon as one hundred thousand subscriptions are completed, and two hundred crowns more to pay the charges, the lottery shall be drawn at a proper place, to be appointed a fortnight before the drawing.

" *Note*, Mr. Bickerstaff objects to the marriageable years here mentioned ; and is of opinion, they should not commence until after twenty-three. But he appeals to the learned, both of Warwick Lane and Bishopsgate Street,* on this subject."

* The College of Physicians met at that time in Warwick Lane, and the Royal Society at Gresham College, in Bishopsgate Street.

Z.

AMBITION.

No. 202.   TUESDAY, July 25, 1710.   [Steele.]

—— Est hic,
Est Ulubris, animus si te non deficit æquus.
Hor. 1 Ep. xi.

True happiness is to no spot confin'd :
If you preserve a firm and equal mind,
'Tis here, 'tis there, and every where.——

This afternoon I went to visit a gentleman of my acquaintance at Mile-End ; and passing through Stepney church-yard, I could not forbear entertaining myself with the inscriptions on the tombs and graves.   Among others, I observed one with this notable memorial :

"Here lies the body of T. B."

This fanatical desire, of being remembered only by the two first letters of a name, led me into the contemplation of the vanity and imperfect attainments of ambition in general. When I run back in my imagination all the men whom I have ever known and conversed with in my whole life, there are but very few who have not used their faculties in the pursuit of what it is impossible to acquire ; or left the possession of what they might have been, at their setting out, masters, to search for it where it was out of their reach.   In this thought it was not possible to forget the instance of Pyrrhus, who proposing to himself in discourse with a philosopher, one, and another, and another conquest, was asked, what he would after all that ? " Then," says the king, " we will make merry."   He was well answered, " What hinders you doing that in the condition you are already ? "   The restless desire of exerting themselves above the common level of mankind is not to be resisted in some tempers ; and minds of this make may be observed in every condition of life.   Where such men do not make to themselves, or meet with employment, the soil of their constitution runs into tares and weeds.   An old friend of mine,

who lost a major's post forty years ago, and quitted, has ever
since studied maps, encampments, retreats, and counter-
marches ; with no other design but to feed his spleen and
ill-humour, and furnish himself with matter for arguing against
all the successful actions of others. He that, at his first
setting out in the world, was the gayest man in our regiment ;
ventured his life with alacrity, and enjoyed it with satisfaction ;
encouraged men below him, and was courted by men above
him, has been ever since the most froward creature breathing.
His warm complexion spends itself now only in a general
spirit of contradiction ; for which he watches all occasions,
and is in his conversation still *upon centry*, treats all men like
enemies, with every other impertinence of a speculative
warrior.

He, that observes in himself this natural inquietude, should
take all imaginable care to put his mind in some method of
gratification ; or he will soon find himself grow into the condition of this disappointed major. Instead of courting proper
occasions to rise above others, he will be ever studious of
pulling others down to him : it being the common refuge of
disappointed ambition, to ease themselves by detraction. It
would be no great argument against ambition, that there are
such *mortal* things in the disappointment of it ; but it certainly is a forcible exception, that there can be no solid
happiness in the success of it. If we value popular praise, it
is in the power of the meanest of the people to disturb us by
calumny. If the fame of being happy, we cannot look into a
village, but we see crowds in actual possession of what we
seek only the appearance. To this may be added, that there
is I know not what malignity in the minds of ordinary men,
to oppose you in what they see you fond of ; and it is a certain
exception against a man's receiving applause, that he visibly
courts it. However, this is not only the passion of great and
undertaking spirits ; but you see it in the lives of such as, one
would believe, were far enough removed from the ways of
ambition. The rural esquires of this nation even eat and
drink out of vanity. A vain-glorious fox-hunter shall enter-

tain half a county, for the ostentation of his beef and beer, without the least affection for any of the crowd about him. He feeds them, because he thinks it a superiority over them that he does so ; and they devour him, because they know he treats them out of insolence. This indeed is ambition in grotesque ; but may figure to us the condition of politer men, whose only pursuit is glory. When the superior acts out of a principle of vanity, the dependent will be sure to allow it him ; because he knows it destructive of the very applause which is courted by the man who favours him, and consequently makes him nearer himself.

But as every man living has more or less of this incentive, which makes men impatient of an inactive condition, and urges men to attempt what may tend to their reputation ; it is absolutely necessary they should form to themselves an ambition, which is in every man's power to gratify. This ambition would be independent, and would consist only in acting what, to a man's own mind, appears most great and laudable. It is a pursuit in the power of every man, and is only a regular prosecution of what he himself approves. It is what can be interrupted by no outward accidents ; for no man can be robbed of his good intention. One of our society of the Trumpet * therefore started last night a notion, which I thought had reason in it. "It is, methinks," said he, "an unreasonable thing, that honest virtue should, as it seems to be at present, be confined to a certain order of men, and be attainable by none but those whom fortune has elevated to the most conspicuous stations. I would have everything to be esteemed as heroic, which is great and uncommon in the circumstances of the man who performs it." Thus there would be no virtue in human life, which every one of the species would not have a pretence to arrive at, and an ardency to exert. Since fortune is not in our power, let us be as little as possible in hers. Why should it be necessary that a man should be rich, to be generous ? If we measured by the quality

---

* A tavern in Sheer Lane.

and not the quantity of things, the particulars which accompany an action is what should denominate it mean or great. The highest station of human life is to be attained by each man that pretends to it: for any man can be as valiant, as generous, as wise, and as merciful, as the faculties and opportunities which he has from heaven and fortune will permit. He that can say to himself, "I do as much good, and am as virtuous as my most earnest endeavours will allow me," whatever is his station in the world, is to himself possessed of the highest honour. If ambition is not thus turned, it is no other than a continual succession of anxiety and vexation. But when it has this cast, it invigorates the mind; and the consciousness of its own worth is a reward, which is not in the power of envy, reproach, or detraction, to take from it. Thus the seat of solid honour is in a man's own bosom; and no one can want support who is in possession of an honest conscience, but he who would suffer the reproaches of it for other greatness.

VAGARIES OF FORTUNE.

No. 203.   THURSDAY, July 27, 1710.   [Steele.]

Ut tu fortunam, sic nos te, Celse, feremus.
                    Hor. 1 Ep. viii.

As Celsus bears this change of fortune,
So will his friends bear him.

It is natural for the imaginations of men, who lead their lives in too solitary a manner, to prey upon themselves, and form from their own conceptions, beings and things which have no place in nature. This often makes an adept as much at a loss, when he comes into the world, as a mere savage. To avoid therefore that ineptitude for society, which is frequently the fault of us scholars, and has, to men of understanding and breeding, something much more shocking and untractable than rusticity itself; I take care to visit all public solemnities, and go into assemblies as often as my studies will permit. This being therefore the first day of the drawing of the lottery, I did not neglect spending a considerable time in the crowd : but as much a philosopher as I pretend to be, I could not but look with a sort of veneration upon the two boys * who received the tickets from the wheels, as the impartial and equal dispensers of the fortunes which were to be distributed among the crowd, who all stood expecting the same chance. It seems at first thought very wonderful, that one passion should so universally have the pre-eminence of another in the possession of men's minds, as that in this case all in general have a secret hope of the great ticket : and yet fear in another instance, as in going into a battle, shall have so little influence, as that, though each man believes there will be many thousands slain, each is confident he himself shall escape. This certainly proceeds from our vanity ; for every man sees abundance in himself that deserves reward, and nothing which should meet with mortification.

But of all the adventurers that filled the hall, there was one who stood by me, who I could not but fancy expected the thousand pounds *per annum*, as a mere justice to his parts and industry. He had his pencil and table-book ; and was, at the drawing of each lot, counting how much a man with seven tickets was now nearer the great prize, by the striking out another, and another competitor. This man was of the most particular constitution I had ever observed ; his passions were so active, that he worked in the utmost stretch of hope and fear. When one rival fell before him, you might see a gleam of triumph in his countenance ; which immediately vanished at the approach of another. What added to the particularity of this man was, that he every moment cast a look either upon the commissioners, the wheels, or the boys. I gently whispered him, and asked, " when he thought the thousand pounds would come up ? " " Pugh," says he, " who knows that ? " And then looks upon a little list of his own

---

* Blue-coat boys were selected to draw out the tickets.

tickets, which were pretty high in their numbers, and said it would not come this ten days. This fellow will have a good chance, though not that which he has put his heart on. The man is mechanically turned, and made for getting. The simplicity and eagerness which he is in, argues an attention to his point ; though what he is labouring at does not in the least contribute to it. Were it not for such honest fellows as these, the men who govern the rest of their species would have no tools to work with : for the outward show of the world is carried on by such as cannot find out that they are doing nothing. I left my man with great reluctance, seeing the care he took to observe the whole conduct of the persons concerned, and compute the inequality of the chances with his own hands and eyes. "Dear sir," said I, "they must rise early that cheat you." "Ay," said he, "there is nothing like a man's minding his business himself." "It is very true," said I ; "the master's eye makes the horse fat."

As much the greater number are to go without prizes, it is but very expedient to turn our lecture, to the forming just sentiments on the subjects of fortune. One said this morning, "that the chief lot, he was confident, would fall upon some puppy ;" but this gentleman is one of those wrong tempers, who approve only the unhappy, and have a natural prejudice to the fortunate. But, as it is certain that there is a great meanness in being attached to a man purely for his fortune ; there is no less a meanness in disliking him for his happiness. It is the same perverseness under different colours ; and both these resentments arise from mere pride.

True greatness of mind consists in valuing men apart from their circumstances, or according to their behaviour in them. Wealth is a distinction only in traffic ; but it must not be allowed as a recommendation in any other particular, but only just as it is applied. It was very prettily said, "That we may learn the little value of fortune by the persons on whom heaven is pleased to bestow it." However, there is not a harder part in human life, than becoming wealth and greatness. He must be very well stocked with merit, who is not willing to draw some superiority over his friends from his fortune ; for it is not every man that can entertain with the air of a guest, and do good offices with the mien of one that receives them.

I must confess, I cannot conceive how a man can place himself in a figure wherein he can so much enjoy his own soul, and, that greatest of pleasures, the just approbation of his own actions, than as an adventurer on this occasion, to sit and see the lots go off without hope and fear ; perfectly unconcerned as to himself, but taking part in the good fortune of others.

I will believe there are happy tempers in being, to whom all the good that arrives to any of their fellow-creatures gives a pleasure. These live in a course of lasting and substantial happiness, and have the satisfaction to see all men endeavour to gratify them. This state of mind not only lets a man into certain enjoyments, but relieves him from as certain anxieties. If you will not rejoice with happy men, you must repine at them. Dick Reptile alluded to this when he said, "he would hate no man, out of pure idleness." As for my own part, I look at Fortune in quite another view than the rest of the world ; and, by my knowledge in futurity, tremble at the approaching prize, which I see coming to a young lady for whom I have much tenderness ; and have therefore writ to her the following letter, to be sent by Mr. Elliot, with the notice of her ticket.

" MADAM,

"You receive, at the instant this comes to your hands, an account of your having, what you only wanted, fortune ; and to admonish you, that you may not now want every thing else. You had yesterday wit, virtue, beauty ; but you never heard of them until to-day. They say Fortune is blind ; but you will find she has opened the eyes of all your beholders. I beseech you, madam, make use of the advantages of having been educated without flattery. If you can still be Chloe, Fortune has indeed been kind to you ; if you are altered, she has it not in her power to give you an equivalent."

SOUNDS OF HONOUR.

No. 204.   SATURDAY, July 29, 1710.   [Steele.]

Gaudent prænomine molles
 Auriculæ ——   Hor. 2 Sat. v. 32.

—— He with rapture hears
A little tingling in his tender ears.

MANY are the inconveniences which happen from the improper manner of address in common speech, between persons
of the same or of different quality.   Among these errors, there
is none greater than that of the impertinent use of title, and
a paraphrastical way of saying, *You.*   I had the curiosity the
other day, to follow a crowd of people near Billingsgate, who
were conducting a passionate woman that sold fish to a
magistrate, in order to explain some words, which were ill
taken by one of her own quality and profession in the public
market.   When she came to her defence, she was so very full
of, " His Worship," and of, " If it should please his Honour,"
that we could, for some time, hardly hear any other apology
she made for herself, than that of atoning for the ill language
she had been accused of towards her neighbour, by the great
civilities she paid to her judge.   But this extravagance in
her sense of doing honour was no more to be wondered at,
than that her many rings on each finger were worn as instances
of finery and dress.   The vulgar may thus heap and huddle
terms of respect, and nothing better be expected from them ;
but for people of rank to repeat appellatives insignificantly,
is a folly not to be endured, neither with regard to our time,
or our understanding.   It is below the dignity of speech to
extend it with more words or phrases than are necessary to
explain ourselves with elegance ; and it is, methinks, an
instance of ignorance, if not of servitude, to be redundant in
such expressions.

I waited upon a man of quality some mornings ago.   He
happened to be dressing ; and his shoe-maker fitting him,

told him, "that if his Lordship would please to tread hard, or that if his Lordship would stamp a little, his Lordship would find his Lordship's shoe will fit as easy as any piece of work his Lordship should see in England." As soon as my lord was dressed, a gentleman approached him with a very good air, and told him, "he had an affair which had long depended in the lower courts; which through the inadvertency of his ancestors on the one side, and the ill arts of their adversaries on the other, could not possibly be settled according to the rules of the lower courts; that, therefore, he designed to bring his cause before the House of Lords next session, where he should be glad if his Lordship should happen to be present; for he doubted not but his cause would be approved by all men of justice and honour." In this place the word Lordship was gracefully inserted; because it was applied to him in that circumstance wherein his quality was the occasion of the discourse, and wherein it was most useful to the one, and most honourable to the other.

This way is so far from being disrespectful to the honour of nobles, that it is an expedient for using them with greater deference. I would not put Lordship to a man's hat, gloves, wig, or cane; but to desire his Lordship's favour, his Lordship's judgment, or his Lordship's patronage, is a manner of speaking, which expresses an alliance between his quality and his merit. It is this knowledge, which distinguished the discourse of the shoe-maker from that of the gentleman. The highest point of good-breeding, if any can hit it, is to shew a very nice regard to your own dignity, and, with that in your heart, express your value for the man above you.

But the silly humour to the contrary has so much prevailed, that the lavish addition of title enervates discourse, and renders the application of it almost ridiculous. We writers of Diurnals are nearer in our style to that of common talk than any other writers, by which means we use words of respect sometimes very unfortunately. The Post-man, who is one of the most celebrated of our fraternity, fell into this misfortune yesterday in his paragraph from Berlin of the twenty-sixth of July. "Count Wartembourg," says he, "great chamberlain, and chief minister of this court, who on Monday last accompanied the King of Prussia to Oranienburg, was taken so very ill, that on Wednesday his life was despaired of ; and we had a report, that his Excellency was dead."

I humbly presume that it flattens the narration, to say his Excellency in a case which is common to all men ; except you would infer what is not to be inferred, to wit, that the author designed to say, "all wherein he excelled others was departed from him."

Were distinctions used according to the rules of reason and sense, those additions to men's names would be, as they were first intended, significant of their worth, and not their persons ; so that in some cases it might be proper to say, "The man is dead ; but his Excellency will never die." It is, methinks, very unjust to laugh at a Quaker, because he has taken up a resolution to treat you with a word, the most expressive of complaisance that can be thought of, and with an air of good-nature and charity calls you Friend. I say, it is very unjust to rally him for this term to a stranger, when you yourself, in all your phrases of distinction, confound phrases of honour into no use at all.

Tom Courtly, who is the pink of courtesy, is an instance of how little moment an undistinguishing application of sounds of honour are to those who understand themselves. Tom never fails of paying his obeisance to every man he sees, who has title or office to make him conspicuous ; but his deference is wholly given to outward considerations. I, who know him, can tell him within half an acre, how much land one man has more than another by Tom's bow to him. Title is all he knows of honour, and civility of friendship for this reason, because he cares for no man living, he is religiously strict in performing, what he calls, his respects to you. To this end he is very learned in pedigree ; and will abate something in the ceremony of his approaches to a man, if he is in any doubt about the bearing of his coat of arms. What is the most pleasant of all his character is, that he acts with a

sort of integrity in these impertinences ; and though he would
not do any solid kindness, he is wonderfully just and careful
not to wrong his quality.   But as integrity is very scarce in
the world, I cannot forbear having respect for the impertinent :
it is some virtue to be bound by any thing.   Tom and I are
upon very good terms, for the respect he has for the house of
Bickerstaff.   Though one cannot but laugh at his serious
consideration of things so little essential, one must have a
value even for a frivolous good conscience.

LOVE AND ESTEEM.

No. 206.   THURSDAY, August 3, 1710.   [Steele.]

Metiri se quemque suo modulo ac pede verum est.
Hor. 1. Ep. vii.

—— All should be confin'd
Within the bounds, which nature hath assign'd.

The general purposes of men in the conduct of their lives, I
mean with relation to this life only, end in gaining either the
affection or the esteem of those with whom they converse.
Esteem makes a man powerful in business, and affection
desirable in conversation; which is certainly the reason that
very agreeable men fail of their point in the world, and those
who are by no means such arrive at it with much ease.   If it
be visible in a man's carriage that he has a strong passion to
please, no one is much at a loss how to keep measure with
him ; because there is always a balance in people's hands to
make up with him, by giving him what he still wants in
exchange for what you think fit to deny him.   Such a person
asks with diffidence, and ever leaves room for denial by that
softness of his complexion.   At the same time he himself is
capable of denying nothing, even what he is not able to
perform.   The other sort of man who courts esteem, having a
quite different view, has as different a behaviour ; and acts as

much by the dictates of his reason, as the other does by the impulse of his inclination. You must pay for every thing you have of him. He considers mankind as a people in commerce, and never gives out of himself what he is sure will not come in with interest from another. All his words and actions tend to the advancement of his reputation and his fortune, towards which he makes hourly progress, because he lavishes no part of his good-will upon such as do not make some advances to merit it. The man who values affection, sometimes becomes popular ; he who aims at esteem, seldom fails of growing rich.

Thus far we have looked at these different men, as persons who endeavoured to be valued and beloved from design or ambition ; but they appear quite in another figure, when you observe the men who are agreeable and venerable from the force of their natural inclinations. We affect the company of him who has least regard of himself in his carriage, who throws himself into unguarded gaiety, voluntary mirth, and general good humour ; who has nothing in his head but the present hour, and seems to have all his interest and passions gratified, if every man else in the room is unconcerned as himself. This man usually has no quality or character among his companions ; let him be born of whom he will, have what great qualities he please ; let him be capable of assuming for a moment what figure he pleases, he still dwells in the imagination of all who know him but as Jack Such-a-one. This makes Jack brighten up the room wherever he enters, and change the severity of the company into that gaiety and good humour, into which his conversation generally leads them. It is not unpleasant to observe even this sort of creature go out of his character, to check himself sometimes for his familiarities, and pretend so aukwardly at procuring to himself more esteem than he finds he meets with. I was the other day walking with Jack Gainly towards Lincoln's-inn-walks : we met a fellow who is a lower officer where Jack is in the direction. Jack cries to him, " So how is it, Mr. ———— ? " He answers, " Mr. Gainly, I am glad to see you well." This ex-pression of equality gave my friend a pang, which appeared in the flush of his countenance. " Pr'ythee, Jack," says I, " do not be angry at the man ; for do what you will, the man can only love you ; be contented with the image the man has of thee ; for if thou aimest at any other, it must be hatred and contempt." I went on, and told him, " Look you, Jack, I have heard thee sometimes talk like an oracle for half an hour, with the sentiments of a Roman, the closeness of a schoolman, and the integrity of a divine ; but then, Jack, while I admired thee, it was upon topics which did not concern thyself ; and where the greatness of the subject, added to thy being personally unconcerned in it, created all that was great in thy discourse." I did not mind his being a little out of humour ; but comforted him, by giving him several instances of men of our acquaintance, who had no one quality in any eminence, that were much more esteemed than he was with very many : " but the thing is, if your character is to give pleasure, men will consider you only in that light, and not in those acts which turn to esteem and veneration."

When I think of Jack Gainly, I cannot but reflect also upon his sister Gatty. She is young, witty, pleasant, innocent. This is her natural character ; but when she observes any one admired for what they call a fine woman, she is all the next day womanly, prudent, observing, and virtuous. She is every moment asked in her prudential behaviour, whether she is not well ? Upon which she as often answers in a fret, " Do people think one must be always romping, always a Jack-pudding ? " I never fail to enquire of her, if my lady such-a-one, that awful beauty, was not at the play last night ? She knows the connection between that question and her change of humour, and says, " It would be very well if some people would examine into themselves, as much as they do into others." Or, " Sure, there is nothing in the world so ridiculous as an amorous old man."

As I was saying, there is a class which every man is in by his post in nature, from which it is impossible for him to withdraw to another, and become it. Therefore it is necessary that each should be contented with it, and not endeavour at any progress out of that track. To follow nature is the only agreeable course, which is what I would fain inculcate to those jarring companions, Flavia and Lucia. They are mother and daughter. Flavia, who is the mamma, has all the charms and desires of youth still about her, and *is* not much turned of thirty. Lucia is blooming and amorous, and but a little above fifteen. The mother looks very much younger than she is, the girl very much older. If it were possible to fix the girl to her sick bed, and preserve the portion, the use of which the mother partakes, the good widow Flavia would certainly do it. But for fear of Lucia's escape, the mother is forced to be constantly attended with a rival, that explains her age, and draws off the eyes of her admirers. The jest is, they can never be together in stranger's company, but Lucia is eternally reprimanded for something very particular in her behaviour ; for which she has the malice to say, "she hopes she shall always obey her parents." She carried her passion jealously to that height the other day, that coming suddenly into the room, and surprising colonel Lofty speaking rapture on one knee to her mother, she clapped down by him and asked her blessing.

I do not know whether it is so proper to tell family occurrences of this nature ; but we every day see the same thing happen in public conversation of the world. Men cannot be contented with what is laudable, but they must have all that is laudable. This affectation is what decoys the familiar man into pretences to take state upon him, and the contrary character to the folly of aiming at being winning and complaisant. But in these cases men may easily lay aside what they are, but can never arrive at what they are not.

As to the pursuits after affection and esteem, the fair sex are happy in this particular, that with them the one is much more nearly related to the other than in men. The love of a woman is inseparable from some esteem of her ; and as she is naturally the object of affection, the woman who has your esteem has also some degree of your love. A man that dotes on a woman for a beauty will whisper his friend, " that creature has a great deal of wit when you are well acquainted with

her." And if you examine the bottom of your esteem for a
woman, you will find you have a greater opinion of her beauty
than any body else.   As to us men, I design to pass most of
my time with the facetious Harry Bickerstaff; but William
Bickerstaff, the most prudent man of our family, shall be my
executor.

THE THREE NEPHEWS.

No. 207. SATURDAY, August 5, 1710. [Steele.]

HAVING yesterday morning received a paper of Latin verses,
written with much elegance in honour of these my papers, and
being informed at the same time, that they were composed by
a youth under age, I read them with much delight, as an
instance of his improvement.   There is not a greater pleasure to
old age, than feeling young people entertain themselves in such
a manner as that we can partake of their enjoyments. On such
occasions we flatter ourselves, that we are not quite laid aside
in the world ; but that we are either used with gratitude for
what we were, or honoured for what we are.   A well-inclined
young man, and whose good breeding is founded upon the principles of nature and virtue, must needs take delight in being
agreeable to his elders, as we are truly delighted when we are
not the jest of them.   When I say this, I must confess I cannot but think it a very lamentable thing, that there should be
a necessity for making that a rule of life, which should be,
methinks, a mere instinct of nature.   If reflection upon a man
in poverty, whom we once knew in riches, is an argument of
commiseration with generous minds ; sure old age, which a
decay from that vigour which the young possess, and must certainly, if not prevented against their will, arrive at, should be
more forcibly the object of that reverence, which honest spirits
are inclined to, from a sense of being themselves liable to what
they observe has already overtaken others.

My three nephews, whom, in June last *was twelvemonth*, I

disposed of according to their several capacities and inclinations ; the first to the university, the second to a merchant, and the third to a woman of quality as her page, by my invitatation dined with me to-day.   It is my custom often, when I have a mind to give myself a more than ordinary cheerfulness, to invite a certain young gentlewoman of our neighbourhood to make one of the company.   She did me that favour this day. The presence of a beautiful woman of honour, to minds which are not trivially disposed, displays an alacrity which is not to be communicated by any other object.   It was not unpleasant to me, to look into her thoughts of the company she was in. She smiled at the party of pleasure I had thought of for her, which was composed of an old man and three boys.   My scholar, my citizen, and myself, were very soon neglected ; and the young courtier, by the bow he made to her at her entrance, engaged her observation without a rival.

I observed the Oxonian not a little discomposed at this preference, while the trader kept his eye upon his uncle. My nephew Will had a thousand secret resolutions to break in upon the discourse of his younger brother, who gave my fair companion a full account of the fashion, and what was reckoned most becoming to this complexion, and what sort of habit appeared best upon the other shape.   He proceeded to acquaint her, who of quality was well or sick within the bills of mortality, and named very familiarly all his lady's acquaintance, not forgetting her very words when he spoke of their characters.   Besides all this, he had a road of flattery ; and upon her inquiring, what sort of woman lady Lovely was in her person, " Really, Madam," says the Jackanapes, " she is exactly of your height and shape ; but as you are fair, she is a brown woman."   There was no enduring that this fop should outshine us all at this unmerciful rate ; therefore I thought fit to talk to my young scholar concerning his studies ; and because I would throw his learning into present service, I desired him to repeat to me the translation he had made of some tender verses in Theocritus.   He did so, with an air of elegance peculiar to the college to which I sent him.   I made some exceptions to the turn of the phrases ;

A A

which he defended with much modesty, as believing in that place the matter was rather to consult the softness of a swain's passion, than the strength of his expressions. It soon appeared, that Will had outstripped his brother in the opinion of our young lady. A little poetry, to one who is bred a scholar, has the same effect that a good carriage of his person has on one who is to live in courts. The favour of women is so natural a passion, that I envied both the boys their success in the approbation of my guest; and I thought the only person invulnerable was my young trader. During the whole meal, I could observe in the children a mutual contempt and scorn of each other, arising from their different way of life and education, and took that occasion to advertise them of such growing distastes ; which might mislead them in their future life, and disappoint their friends, as well as themselves, of the advantages, which might be expected from the diversity of their professions and interests.

The prejudices, which are growing up between these brothers from the different ways of education, are what create the most fatal misunderstandings in life. But all distinctions of disparagement, merely from our circumstances, are such as will not bear the examination of reason. The courtier, the trader, and the scholar, should all have an equal pretension to the denomination of a gentleman. That tradesman, who deals with me in a commodity which I do not understand, with uprightness, has much more right to that character, than the courtier that gives me false hopes, or the scholar who laughs at my ignorance.

The appellation of gentleman is never to be affixed to a man's circumstances, but to his behaviour in them. For this reason I shall ever, as far as I am able, give my nephews such impressions as shall make them value themselves rather as they are useful to others, than as they are conscious of merit in themselves. There are no qualities for which we ought to pretend to the esteem of others, but such as render us serviceable to them : for free men have no superiors but benefactors.

FLATTERY AS AN ART.

No. 208. TUESDAY, August 8, 1710. [Steele.]

Si dixeris æstuo, sudat.——   Juv. Sat. iii. 103.

—— If you complain of heat,
They rub th' unsweating brow, and swear they sweat.

An old acquaintance, who met me this morning, seemed overjoyed to see me, and told me I looked as well as he had known me do these forty years : "but," continued he, "not quite the man you were, when we visited together at lady Brightly's. Oh ! Isaac, those days are over. Do you think there are any such fine creatures now living, as we then conversed with ?" He went on with a thousand incoherent circumstances, which, in his imagination, must needs please me ; but they had the quite contrary effect. The flattery with which he began, in telling me how well I wore, was not disagreeable ; but his indiscreet mention of a set of acquaintance we had outlived, recalled ten thousand things to my memory, which made me reflect upon my present condition with regret. Had he indeed been so kind as, after a long absence, to felicitate me upon an indolent and easy old age ; and mentioned how much he and I had to thank for, who at our time of day could walk firmly, eat heartily, and converse cheerfully, he had kept up my pleasure in myself. But of all mankind, there are none so shocking as these injudicious civil people. They ordinarily begin upon something, that they know must be a satisfaction ; but then, for fear of the imputation of flattery, they follow it with the last thing in the world of which you would be reminded. It is this that perplexes civil persons. The reason that there is such a general outcry among us against flatterers is, that there are so very few good ones. It is the nicest art in this life, and is a part of eloquence which does not want the preparation that is necessary to all other parts of it, that your audience should be your well-wishers : for praise from an enemy is the most pleasing of all commendations.

A A 2

It is generally to be observed, that the person most agreeable to a man *for a constancy* is he that has no shining qualities, but is a certain degree above great imperfections; whom he can live with as his inferior, and who will either overlook, or not observe his little defects. Such an easy companion as this either now and then throws out a little flattery, or lets a man silently flatter himself in his superiority to him. If you take notice, there is hardly a rich man in the world, who has not such *a led friend* of small consideration, who is a darling for his insignificancy. It is a great ease to have one in our own shape a species below us, and who, without being lifted in our service, is by nature of our retinue. These dependents are of excellent use on a rainy day, or when a man has not a mind to dress; or to exclude solitude, when one has neither a mind to that or to company. There are of this good-natured order, who are so kind as to divide themselves, and do these good offices to many. Five or six of them visit a whole quarter of the town, and exclude the spleen, without fees, from the families they frequent. If they do not prescribe physic, they can be company when you take it. Very great benefactors to the rich, or those whom they call people at their ease, are your persons of no consequence. I have known some of them, by the help of a little cunning, make delicious flatterers. They know the course of the town, and the general characters of persons : by *this means* they will sometimes tell the most agreeable falsehoods imaginable. They will acquaint you, that such a one of a quite contrary party said, " That though you were engaged in different interests, yet he had the greatest respect for your good sense and address." When one of these has a little cunning, he passes his time in the utmost satisfaction to himself and his friends : for his position, is never to report or speak a displeasing thing to his friend. As for letting him go on in an error, he knows, advice against them is the office of persons of greater talents and less discretion.

The Latin word for a flatterer, *assentator*, implies no more than a person that barely consents ; and indeed such a one, if a man were able to purchase or maintain him, cannot be bought too dear. Such a one never contradicts you ; but gains upon you, not by a fulsome way of commending you in broad terms, but liking whatever you propose or utter ; at the same time, is ready to beg your pardon, and gainsay you, if you chance to speak ill of yourself. An old lady is very seldom without such a companion as this, who can recite the names of all her lovers, and the matches refused by her in the days when she minded such vanities, as she is pleased to call them, though she so much approves the mention of them. It is to be noted, that a woman's flatterer is generally elder than herself; her years serving at once to recommend her patroness's age, and to add weight to her complaisance in all other particulars.

We gentlemen of small fortunes are extremely necessitous in this particular. I have indeed one who smokes with me often ; but his parts are so low, that all the incense he does me is to fill his pipe with me, and to be out at just as many whiffs as I take. This is all the praise or assent that he is capable of ; yet there are more hours when I would rather be in his company, than in that of the brightest man I know. It would be an hard matter to give an account of this inclination to be flattered ; but if we go to the bottom of it, we shall find, that the pleasure in it is something like that of receiving money which lay out. Every man thinks he has an estate of reputation, and is glad to see one that will bring any of it home to him. It is no matter how dirty a bag it is conveyed to him in, or by how clownish a messenger, so the money be good. All that we want, to be pleased with flattery, is to believe that the man is sincere who gives it us. It is by this one accident, that absurd creatures often out-run the most skilful in this art. Their want of ability is here an advantage ; and their bluntness, as it is the seeming effect of sincerity, is the best cover to artifice.

Terence introduces a flatterer talking to a coxcomb, whom he cheats out of a livelihood ; and a third person on the stage makes on him this pleasant remark, " This fellow has an art of making fools madmen." The love of flattery is, indeed, sometimes the weakness of a great mind ; but you see it also in persons, who otherwise discover no manner of relish of any thing above mere sensuality. These latter it sometimes improves; but always debases the former. A fool is in himself the object of pity, until he is flattered. By the force of that, his stupidity is raised into affectation, and he becomes of dignity enough to be ridiculous. I remember a droll, that upon one's saying, " The times are so ticklish, that there must great care be taken what one says in conversation;" answered with an air of surliness and honesty, " If people will be free, let them be so in the manner that I am, who never abuse a man but to his face." He had no reputation for saying dangerous truths; therefore when it was repeated, " You abuse a man but to his face ? " " Yes," says he, " I flatter him."

It is indeed the greatest of injuries to flatter any but the unhappy, or such as are displeased with themselves for some infirmity. In this latter case we have a member of our club, who, when Sir Jeffery falls asleep, wakens him with snoring. This makes Sir Jeffery hold up for some moments the longer to see there are men younger than himself among us, who are more lethargic than he is.

When flattery is practised upon any other consideration, it is the most abject thing in nature ; nay, I cannot think of any character below the flatterer, except he that envies him. You meet with fellows, prepared to be as mean as possible in their condescensions and expressions; but they want persons and talents to rise up to such a baseness. As a coxcomb is a fool of parts, so is a flatterer a knave of parts.

The best of this order, that I know, is one who disguises it under a spirit of contradiction or reproof. He told an arrant driveller the other day, that he did not care for being in company with him, because he heard he turned his absent friends into ridicule. And upon lady Autumn's disputing with him about something that happened at the Revolution, he replied with a very angry tone, " Pray, madam, give me leave to know more of a thing in which I was actually concerned, than you who were then in your nurse's arms."

A HISTORY PIECE.

No. 209. SATURDAY, August 10, 1710. [Steele.]

A NOBLE painter, who has an ambition to draw a history piece, has desired me to give him a subject, on which he may shew the utmost force of his art and genius. For this purpose, I have pitched upon that remarkable incident between Alexander the Great and his physician. This prince, in the midst of his conquests in Persia, was seized by a violent fever ; and, according to the account we have of his vast mind, his thoughts were more employed about his recovery, as it regarded the war, than as it concerned his own life. He professed, a slow method was worse than death to him ; because it was, what he more dreaded, an interruption of his glory. He desired a dangerous, so it might be a speedy remedy. During this impatience of the king, it is well known that Darius had offered an immense sum to any one who should take away his life. But Philippus, the most esteemed and most knowing of his physicians, promised, that within three days' time he would prepare a medicine for him, which should restore him more expeditiously than could be imagined. Immediately after this engagement, Alexander receives a letter from the most considerable of his captains, with intelligence that Darius had bribed Philippus to poison him. Every circumstance imaginable favoured this suspicion ; but this monarch, who did nothing but in an extraordinary manner, concealed the letter ; and, while the medicine was preparing, spent all his thoughts upon his behaviour in this important incident. From his long soliloquy, he came to this resolution : ' Alexander must not lie here alive to be oppressed by his enemy. I will not believe my physician guilty ; or, I will perish rather by his guilt, than my own diffidence.'

At the appointed hour, Philippus enters with the potion. One cannot but form to one's self on this occasion the encounter of their eyes, the resolution in those of the patient, and the benevolence in the countenance of the physician. The hero raised himself in his bed, and, holding the letter in one hand, and the potion in the other, drank the medicine. It will exercise my friend's pencil and brain to place this action in its proper beauty. A prince observing the features of a suspected traitor, after having drunk the poison he offered him, is a circumstance so full of passion, that it will require the highest strength of his imagination to conceive it, much more to express it. But as painting is eloquence and poetry in mechanism, I shall raise his ideas, by reading with him the finest draughts of the passions concerned in this circumstance, from the most excellent poets and orators. The confidence, which Alexander assumes from the air of Philippus's face as he is reading his accusation, and the generous disdain which is to rise in the features of a falsely accused man, are principally to be regarded. In this particular he must heighten his thoughts, by reflecting, that, he is not drawing only an innocent man traduced, but a man zealously affected to his person and safety, full of resentment for being thought false. How shall we contrive to express the highest admiration, mingled with disdain ? How shall we in strokes of a pencil say, what Philippus did to his prince on this occasion ? 'Sir, my life never depended on yours more than it does now. Without knowing this secret, I prepared the potion, which you have taken as what concerned Philippus no less than Alexander ; and there is nothing new in this adventure, but that it makes me still more admire the generosity and confidence of my master.' Alexander took him by the hand, and said, 'Philippus, I am confident you had rather I had any other way to have manifested the faith I have in you, than a case which so nearly concerns me : and in gratitude I now assure you, I am anxious for the effect of your medicine, more for your sake than my own.'

My painter is employed by a man of sense and wealth to furnish him a gallery ; and I shall join with my friend in the designing part. It is the great use of pictures, to raise in our minds either agreeable ideas of our absent friends ; or high images of eminent personages. But the latter design is, methinks, carried on in a very improper way; for to fill a room full of battle-pieces, pompous histories of sieges, and a tall hero alone in a crowd of insignificant figures about him, is of no consequence to private men. But to place before our eyes great and illustrious men in those parts and circumstances of life, wherein their behaviour may have an effect upon our minds ; as being such as we partake with them merely as they were men : such as these, I say, may be just and useful ornaments of an elegant apartment. In this collection therefore that we are making, we will not have the battles, but the sentiments of Alexander. The affair we were just now speaking of has circumstances of the highest nature ; and yet their grandeur has little to do with his fortune. If, by observing such a piece, as that of his taking a bowl of poison with so much magnanimity, a man, the next time he has a fit of the spleen, is less froward to his friend or his servants ; thus far is some improvement.

I have frequently thought, that if we had many draughts which were historical of certain passions, and had the true figure of the great men we see transported by them, it would be of the most solid advantage imaginable. To consider this mighty man on one occasion, administering to the wants of a poor soldier benumbed with cold, with the greatest humanity ; at another, barbarously stabbing a faithful officer : at one time, so generously chaste and virtuous as to give his captive Statira her liberty ; at another, burning a town at the instigation of Thais. These changes in the same person are what would be more beneficial lessons of morality, than the several revolutions in a great man's fortune. There are but one or two in an age, to whom the pompous incidents of his life can be exemplary ; but I, or any man, may be as sick, as good-natured, as compassionate, and as angry, as Alexander the Great. My purpose in all this chat is, that so excellent a furniture may not for the future have so romantic a turn, but allude to incidents which come within the fortunes of the ordinary race of men. I do not know but it is by the force of this senseless custom, that people are drawn in postures they would not for half they are worth be surprised in. The unparalleled fierceness of some rural esquires drawn in red, or in armour, who never dreamed to destroy any thing above a fox, is a common and ordinary offence of this kind. But I shall give an account of our whole gallery on another occasion.

DEVOTION.

No. 211. THURSDAY, August 15, 1710. [Steele.]

—— Nequeo monstrare, et sentio tantum.
                                        Juv. Sat. vii. 56.

What I can fancy, but can ne'er express.

If there were no other consequences of it, but barely that human creatures on this day assemble themselves before their Creator, without regard to their usual employments, their minds at leisure from the cares of this life, and their bodies adorned with the best attire they can bestow upon them; I say, were this mere outward celebration of the Sabbath all that is expected from men, even that were a laudable distinction, and a purpose worthy the human nature. But when there is added to it the sublime pleasure of devotion, our being is exalted above itself; and he, who spends a seventh day in the contemplation of the next life, will not easily fall into the corruptions of this in the other six. They, who never admit thoughts of this kind into their imaginations, lose higher and sweeter satisfaction than can be raised by any other entertainment. The most illiterate man who is touched with devotion, and uses frequent exercises of it, contracts a certain greatness of mind, mingled with a noble simplicity, that raises him above those of the same condition; and there is an indelible mark of goodness in those who sincerely possess it. It is hardly possible it should be otherwise; for the fervours of a pious mind will naturally contract such an earnestness and attention towards a better being, as will make the ordinary passages of life go off with a becoming indifference. By this a man in the lowest condition will not appear mean, or in the most splendid fortune insolent.

As to all the intricacies and vicissitudes, under which men are ordinarily entangled with the utmost sorrow and passion, one who is devoted to heaven when he falls into such difficulties, is led by a clue through a labyrinth. As to this world, he does not pretend to skill in the mazes of it ; but fixes his thoughts upon one certainty, that he shall soon be out of it. And we may ask very boldly, what can be a more sure consolation than to have an hope in death ? When men are arrived at thinking of their very dissolution with pleasure, how few things are there that can be terrible to them ! Certainly, nothing can be dreadful to such spirits, but what would make death terrible to them, falsehood towards man, or impiety towards heaven. To such as these, as there are certainly many such, the gratifications of innocent pleasures are doubled, even with reflections upon their imperfection. The disappointments which naturally attend the great promises we make ourselves in expected enjoyments, strike no damp upon such men, but only quicken their hopes of soon knowing joys, which are too pure to admit of allay or satiety.

It is thought, among the politer sort of mankind, an imperfection to want a relish of any of those things which refine our lives. This is the foundation of the acceptance which eloquence, music, and poetry make in the world ; and I know not why devotion, considered merely as an exaltation of our happiness, should not at least be so far regarded as to be considered. It is possible, the very inquiry would lead men into such thoughts and gratifications, as they did not expect to meet with in this place. Many a good acquaintance has been lost from a general prepossession in his disfavour, and a severe aspect has often hid under it a very agreeable companion.

There are no distinguishing qualities among men to which there are not false pretenders ; but though none is more pretended to than that of devotion, there are, perhaps, fewer

successful impostors in this kind than any other. There is
something so natively great and good in a person that is truly
devout, that an awkward man may as well pretend to be
genteel, as an hypocrite to be pious. The constraint in words
and actions are equally visible in both cases ; and anything set
up in their room does but remove the endeavours farther off
from their pretensions. But, however, the sense of true piety
is abated, there is no other motive of action that can carry us
through all the vicissitudes of life with alacrity and resolution.
But piety, like philosophy, when it is superficial, does but make
men appear the worse for it ; and a principle that is but half
received does but distract, instead of guiding our behaviour.
When I reflect upon the unequal conduct of Lotius, I see many
things that run directly counter to his interest ; therefore I
cannot attribute his labours for the public good to ambition.
When I consider his disregard to his fortune, I cannot esteem
him covetous. How then can I reconcile his neglect of himself, and his zeal for others ? I have long suspected him to
be a "little pious :" but no man ever hid his vice with greater
caution, than he does his virtue. It was the praise of a great
Roman, " that he had rather be, than appear, good." But such
is the weakness of Lotius, that I dare say, he had rather be
esteemed irreligious than devout. By I know not what impatience of raillery, he is wonderfully fearful of being thought
too great a believer. A hundred little devices are made use of
to hide a time of private devotion ; and he will allow you any
suspicion of his being ill employed, so you do not tax him with
being well. But, alas! how mean is such a behaviour ? To
boast of virtue is a most ridiculous way of disappointing the
merit of it, but not so pitiful as that of being ashamed of it.
How unhappy is the wretch, who makes the most absolute and
independent motive of action the cause of perplexity and inconstancy ! How different a figure does Cælicolo * make with
all who know him ! His great and superior mind, frequently

* This appears to be one of Steele's political papers, in which his principal
design seems to have been to contrast the character of Harley, afterwards
Lord Oxford, the Treasurer then in office, with that of Lord Godolphin, who
was Harley's immediate predecessor.

exalted by the raptures of heavenly meditation, is to all his
friends of the same use, as if an angel were to appear at the
decision of their disputes. They very well understand, he is as
much disinterested and unbiassed as such a being. He considers all applications made to him, as those addresses will
affect his own application to heaven. All his determinations
are delivered with a beautiful humility ; and he pronounces
his decisions with the air of one who is more frequently a
supplicant than a judge.

Thus humble, and thus great, is the man who is moved by
piety, and exalted by devotion. But behold this recommended
by the masterly hand of a great divine I have heretofore made
bold with.*

"It is such a pleasure as can never cloy or overwork the
mind ; a delight that grows and improves under thought and
reflection ; and while it exercises, does also endear itself to the
mind. All pleasures that affect the body must needs weary,
because they transport ; and all transportation is a violence ;
and no violence can be lasting ; but determines upon the
falling of the spirits, which are not able to keep up that height
of motion that the pleasure of the senses raises them to. And
therefore how inevitably does an immoderate laughter end in a
sigh, which is only nature's recovering itself after a force done
to it : but the religious pleasure of a well-disposed mind moves
gently, and therefore constantly. It does not affect by rapture
and ecstasy, but is like the pleasure of health, greater and
stronger than those that call up the senses with grosser and
more affecting impressions. No man's body is as strong as
his appetites ; but Heaven has corrected the boundlessness of
his voluptuous desires by stinting his strength, and contracting
his capacities.—The pleasure of the religious man is an easy
and a portable pleasure, such an one as he carries about in his
bosom, without alarming either the eye or the envy of the
world. A man putting all his pleasures into this one, is like
a traveller putting all his goods into one jewel ; the value is
the same, and the convenience greater."

* Dr. South.

ON DRESS.

No. 212. THURSDAY, August 17, 1710. [Steele.]

I HAVE had much importunity to answer the following letter.

" MR. BICKERSTAFF,

"Reading over a volume of yours, I find the words *Simplex Munditiis* mentioned as a description of a very well-dressed woman. I beg of you, for the sake of the sex, to explain these terms. I cannot comprehend what my brother means, when he tells me, they signify my own name, which is, Sir,

"Your humble servant,

"PLAIN ENGLISH."

I think the lady's brother has given us a very good idea of that elegant expression ; it being the greatest beauty of speech to be close and intelligible. To this end, nothing is to be more carefully consulted than plainness. In a lady's attire this is the single excellence ; for to be, what some people call, fine, is the same vice in that case, as to be florid is, in writing or speaking. I have studied and writ on this important subject, until I almost despair of making a reformation in the females of this island ; where we have more beauty than in any spot in the universe, if we did not disguise it by false garniture, and detract from it by impertinent improvements. I have by me a treatise concerning *pinners*, which, I have some hopes, will contribute to the amendment of the present head-dresses, to which I have solid and unanswerable objections. But most of the errors of that, and other particulars of adorning the head, are crept into the world from the ignorance of the modern *tirewomen ;* for it is come to that pass, that an awkward creature in the first year of her apprenticeship, that can hardly stick a pin, shall take upon her to dress a woman of the first quality. However, it is certain, that there requires in a good tirewoman a perfect skill in optics ; for all the force of ornament is to contribute to the intention of the eyes. Thus she, who has a mind to look killing, must arm her face accordingly, and not leave her eyes and cheeks undressed. There is Araminta, who is so sensible of this, that she never will see even her own husband, without a *hood* * on. Can any one living bear to see Miss Gruel, lean as she is, with *her hair tied back* after the modern way ? But such is the folly of our ladies, that because one who is a beauty, out of ostentation of her being such, takes care to wear something that she knows cannot be of any consequence to her complexion ; I say, our women run on so heedlessly in the fashion, that though it is the interest of some to hide as much of their faces as possible, yet because a leading toast appeared with *a backward head-dress*, the rest shall follow the mode, without observing that the author of the fashion assumed it because it could become no one but herself.

Flavia † is ever well-dressed, and always the genteelest woman you meet, but the make of her mind very much contributes to the ornament of her body. She has the greatest simplicity of manners, of any of her sex. This makes every thing look native about her, and her clothes are so exactly fitted, that they appear, as it were, part of her person. Every one that sees her knows her to be of quality ; but her distinction is owing to her manner, and not to her habit. Her beauty is full of attraction, but not of allurement. There is such a composure in her looks, and propriety in her dress, that you would think it impossible she should change the garb you one day see her in, for any thing so becoming, until you next day see her in another. There is no other mystery in this, but

---

* Hoods of various kinds began to come into fashion in the latter part of the reign of Charles II., when the ladies wore their hair curled and frizzled with the nicest art. They frequently set it off with *heart-breakers*, artificial curls so called. Sometimes a string of pearls or an ornament of ribband was worn on the head.

† This picture of Flavia is intended for Mrs. Anne Oldfield, the favourite actress.

that however she is apparelled, she is herself the same : for there is so immediate a relation between our thoughts and gestures, that a woman must think well to look well.

A POLITICAL BAROMETER.

No. 214.   TUESDAY, August 22, 1710.   [Steele.]

—— Soles et aperta serena
Prospicere, and certis poteris cognoscere signis.
                    Virg. Georg. i. 393.

—— 'Tis easy to descry
Returning suns, and a serener sky.

In every party there are two sorts of men, the rigid and the supple. The rigid are an intractable race of mortals, who act upon principle, and will not, forsooth, fall into any measures that are not consistent with their received notions of honour. These are persons of a stubborn unpliant morality ; that sullenly adhere to their friends, when they are disgraced, and to their principles, though they are exploded. I shall therefore give up this stiff-necked generation to their own obstinacy, and turn my thoughts to the advantage of the supple, who pay their homage to places, and not persons ; and, without enslaving themselves to any particular scheme of opinions, are as ready to change their conduct in point 'of sentiment as of fashion. The well-disciplined part of a court are generally so perfect at their exercise, that you may see a whole assembly, from front to rear, face about at once to a new man of power, though at the same time they turn their backs upon him that brought them thither. The great hardship these complaisant members of society are under, seems to be the want of warning upon any approaching change or revolution ; so that they are obliged in a hurry to tack about with every wind, and stop short in the midst of a full career, to the great surprise and derision of their beholders.

When a man foresees a decaying ministry, he has leisure to

grow a malcontent, reflect upon the present conduct, and by gradual murmurs fall off from his friends into a new party, by just steps and measures. For want of such notices, I have formerly known a very well-bred person refuse to return a bow of a man whom he thought in disgrace, that was next day made secretary of state ; and another, who, after a long neglect of a minister, came to his levee, and made professions of zeal for his service the very day before he was turned out.

This produces also unavoidable confusions and mistakes in the descriptions of great men's parts and merits. That ancient lyric, Mr. D'Ursey, some years ago writ a dedication to a certain lord, in which he celebrated him for the greatest poet and critic of that age, upon a misinformation in Dyer's Letter, that his noble patron was made lord chamberlain.* In short, innumerable votes, speeches, and sermons, have been thrown away, and turned to no account, merely for want of due and timely intelligence. Nay, it has been known, that a panegyric has been half printed off, when the poet, upon the removal of the minister, has been forced to alter it into a satire.

For the conduct therefore of such useful persons, as are ready to do their country service upon all occasions, I have an engine in my study, which is a sort of a Political Barometer, or, to speak more intelligibly, a State Weather-glass, that, by the rising and falling of a certain magical liquor, presages all changes and revolutions in government, as the common glass does those of the weather. This Weather-glass is said to have been invented by Cardan, and given by him as a present to his great countryman and contemporary Machiavel ; which, by the way, may serve to rectify a received error in chronology, that places one of these some years after the other. How or

---

* This dedication was to the "Second Part of Don Quixote," which D'Ursey addressed to Charles, Earl of Dorset. In it are these lines :—

> " You have, my Lord, a patent from above,
> And can monopolize both wit and love,
> Inspir'd and blest by Heaven's peculiar care,
> Ador'd by all the wise and all the fair ;
> To whom the world united give this due,
> Best judge of men, and best of poets too."

when it came into my hands, I shall desire to be excused, if I
keep to myself ; but so it is, that I have walked by it for the
better part of a century to my safety at least, if not to my
advantage; and have among my papers a register of all the
changes that have happened in it from the middle of queen
Elizabeth's reign.

In the time of that princess it stood long at Settled Fair.
At the latter end of king James the First, it fell to Cloudy.
It held several years after at Stormy ; insomuch, that at last,
despairing of seeing any clear weather at home, I followed the
royal exile, and some time after finding my Glass rise, returned
to my native country, with the rest of the loyalists. I was
then in hopes to pass the remainder of my days in Settled
Fair : but, alas ! during the greatest part of that reign the
English nation lay in a dead calm, which, as is usual, was
followed by high winds and tempests, until of late years ; in
which, with unspeakable joy and satisfaction, I have seen our
political weather returned to Settled Fair.   I must only
observe, that for all this last summer my Glass has pointed at
Changeable. Upon the whole, I often apply to Fortune Ænea's
speech to the Sibyl :

> —— Non ulla laborum
> O virgo, nova mi facies inopinave surgit :
> Omnia præcepi, atque animo mecum ante peregi.

> —— No terror to my view,
> No frightful face of danger can be new :
> The mind foretels whatever comes to pass ;
> A thoughtful mind, is Fortune's Weather-glass.

The advantages, which have accrued to those whom I have
advised in their affairs, by virtue of this sort of prescience,
have been very considerable. A nephew of mine, who has
never put his money into the stocks, or taken it out, without
my advice, has in a few years raised five hundred pounds to
almost so many thousands. As for myself, who look upon
riches to consist rather in content than possessions, and
measure the greatness of the mind rather by its tranquillity
than its ambition, I have seldom used my Glass to make my

way in the world, but often to retire from it. This is a bye-path to happiness, which was first discovered to me by a most pleasing apophthegm of Pythagoras : " When the winds," says he, " rise, worship the echo." That great philosopher (whether to make his doctrines more venerable, or to gild his precepts with the beauty of imagination, or to awaken the curiosity of his disciples, for I will not suppose, what is usually said, that he did it to conceal his wisdom from the vulgar) has couched several admirable precepts in remote allusions and mysterious sentences. By the winds in this apophthegm, are meant state hurricanes and popular tumults. " When these rise," says he, " worship the echo ; " that is, withdraw yourself from the multitude into deserts, woods, solitudes, or the like retirements, which are the usual habitations of the echo.

LEGACY OF A VIRTUOSO.

No. 216. SATURDAY, AUGUST 26, 1710. [ADDISON.]

—— Nugis addere pondus.   HOR. 1 Ep. i. 42.

Weight and importance some to trifles give.

NATURE is full of wonders ; every atom is a standing miracle, and endowed with such qualities as could not be impressed on it by a power and wisdom less than infinite. For this reason, I would not discourage any searches that are made into the most minute and trivial parts of the creation. However, since the world abounds in the noblest fields of speculation, it is, methinks, the mark of a little genius, to be wholly conversant among insects, reptiles, animalcules, and those trifling rarities that furnish out the apartment of a virtuoso.

There are some men whose heads are so oddly turned this way, that though they are utter strangers to the common occurrences of life, they are able to discover the sex of a cockle, or describe the generation of a mite, in all its circum-

B B 2

stances.   They are so little versed in the world, that they scarce know a horse from an ox ; but, at the same time, will tell you with a great deal of gravity, that a flea is a rhinoceros, and a snail an hermaphrodite.   I have known one of these whimsical philosophers, who has set a greater value upon a collection of spiders than he would upon a flock of sheep, and has sold his coat off his back to purchase a tarantula.

I would not have a scholar wholly unacquainted with these secrets and curiosities of nature ; but certainly the mind of man, that is capable of so much higher contemplations, should not be altogether fixed upon such mean and disproportioned objects.   Observations of this kind are apt to alienate us too much from the knowledge of the world, and to make us serious upon trifles ; by which means they expose philosophy to the ridicule of the witty, and contempt of the ignorant. In short, studies of this nature should be the diversions, relaxations, and amusements ; not the care, business, and concern of life.

It is indeed wonderful to consider, that there should be a sort of learned men, who are wholly employed in gathering together the refuse of nature, if I may call it so, and hoarding up in their chests and cabinets such creatures as others industriously avoid the sight of.   One does not know how to mention some of the most precious parts of their treasure, without a kind of an apology for it.   I have been shewn a beetle valued at twenty crowns, and a toad at an hundred : but we must take this for a general rule, "That whatever appears trivial or obscene in the common notions of the world, looks grave and philosophical in the eye of a Virtuoso."

To shew this humour in its perfection, I shall present my reader with the legacy of a certain Virtuoso * who laid out a considerable estate in natural rarities and curiosities, which upon his death-bed he bequeathed to his relations and friends, in the following words:

---

* Dr. John Woodward was supposed to have been alluded to here.

THE WILL OF A VIRTUOSO.

I Nicholas Gimcrack, being in sound health of mind, but in great weakness of body, do by this my last will and testament bestow my worldly goods and chattels in manner following :

Imprimis, To my dear wife,
  One box of butterflies,
  One drawer of shells,
  A female skeleton,
  A dried cockatrice.

Item, To my daughter Elizabeth,
  My receipt for preserving dead caterpillars,
  As also my preparations of winter May-dew, and embryo-pickle.

Item, To my little daughter Fanny,
  Three crocodile's eggs.
And upon the birth of her first child, if she marries with her mother's consent,
  The nest of an humming-bird.

Item, To my eldest brother, as an acknowledgment for the lands he has vested in my son Charles, I bequeath,
  My last year's collection of grashoppers.

Item, To his daughter Susanna, being his only child, I bequeath my
  English weeds pasted on royal paper,
  With my large folio of Indian Cabbage.

Having fully provided for my nephew Isaac, by making over to him some years since,
  A horned Scarabæus,
  The skin of a rattle-snake, and
  The mummy of an Egyptian king,
I make no further provision for him in this my Will.

My eldest son John, having spoke disrespectfully of his little sister, whom I keep by me in spirits of wine, and in

many other instances behaved himself undutifully towards me
·I do disinherit, and wholly cut off from any part of this my
personal estate, by giving him a single cockle-shell.

To my second son Charles I give and bequeath all my
flowers, plants, minerals, mosses, shells, pebbles, fossils, beetles,
butterflies, caterpillars, grashoppers, and vermin, not above
specified ; as also all my monsters, both wet and dry ; making
the said Charles whole and sole executor of this my last will
and testament ; he paying, or causing to be paid, the aforesaid
legacies within the space of six months after my decease. And
I do hereby revoke all other wills whatsoever by me formerly
made.

ON SCOLDS.

No. 217. TUESDAY, August 29, 1710. [Steele.]

Atque deos atque astra vocat crudelia mater.
VIRG. Ecl. v. ver. 23.

She sigh'd, she sobb'd, and furious with despair,
Accused all the gods, and every star.

As I was passing by a neighbour's house this morning, I
overheard the wife of the family speaking things to her husband which gave me much disturbance, and put me in mind of
a character which I wonder I have so long omitted, and that is,
an outrageous species of the fair sex, which is distinguished by
the term Scolds. The generality of women are by nature
loquacious ; therefore mere volubility of speech is not to be
imputed to them, but should be considered with pleasure when
it is used to express such passions as tend to sweeten or adorn
conversation : but when through rage, females are vehement
in their eloquence, nothing in the world has so ill an effect
upon the features ; for by the force of it I have seen the most
amiable become the most deformed ; and she that appeared one
of the Graces, immediately turned into one of the Furies. I
humbly conceive, the great cause of this evil may proceed from

a false notion the ladies have of, what we call, a modest woman.
They have too narrow a conception of this lovely character ;
and believe they have not at all forfeited their pretensions to
it, provided they have no imputations on their chastity.   But,
alas ! the young fellows know they pick out better women in
the side-boxes, than many of those who pass upon the world
and themselves for modest.

Modesty never rages, never murmurs, never pouts ; when it
is ill-treated, it pines, it beseeches, it languishes.   The neighbour I mention is one of your common modest women, that is
to say, those who are ordinarily reckoned such.   Her husband
knows every pain in life with her, but jealousy.   Now, because
she is clear in this particular, the man cannot say his soul is his
own, but she cries, "No modest woman is respected now a-
days."   What adds to the comedy in this case is, that it is
very ordinary with this sort of women to talk in the language
of distress ; they will complain of the forlorn wretchedness of
their condition, and then the poor helpless creatures shall
throw the next thing they can lay their hands on at the person who offends them.   Our neighbour was only saying to his
wife "she went a little too fine," when she immediately pulled
his periwig off, and stamping it under her feet, wrung her
hands, and said, "Never modest woman was so used."   These
ladies of irresistible modesty are those, who make virtue un-
amiable ; not that they can be said to be virtuous, but as they
live without scandal ; and being under the common denomination of being such, men fear to meet their faults in those
who are as agreeable as they are innocent.

I take the Bully among men, and the Scold among women,
to draw the foundation of their actions from the same defect in
the mind.   A Bully thinks honour consists wholly in being
brave ; and therefore has regard to no one rule of life, if he
preserves himself from the accusation of cowardice.   The froward woman knows chastity to be the first merit in a woman ;
and therefore, since no one can call her one ugly name, she
calls all mankind all the rest.

These ladies, where their companions are so imprudent as to

take their speeches for any other, than exercises of their own lungs and their husbands' patience, gain by the force of being resisted, and flame with open fury, which is no way to be opposed but by being neglected; though at the same time human frailty makes it very hard, to relish the philosophy of contemning every frivolous reproach. There is a very pretty instance of this infirmity in a man of the best sense that ever was, no less a person than Adam himself. According to Milton's description of the first couple, as soon as they had fallen, and the turbulent passions of anger, hatred, and jealousy, first entered their breasts; Adam grew moody, and talked to his wife, as you may find it in the three hundred and fifty-ninth page, and ninth book, of Paradise Lost, in the octavo edition, which out of heroics, and put into domestic style, would run thus:

"Madam, if my advices had been of any authority with you, when that strange desire of gadding possessed you this morning, we had still been happy; but your cursed vanity and opinion of your own conduct, which is certainly very wavering when it seeks occasions of being proved, has ruined both yourself and me, who trusted you."

Eve had no fan in her hand to ruffle, or tucker to pull down; but with a reproachful air she answered:

"Sir, do you impute that to my desire of gadding, which might have happened to yourself, with all your wisdom and gravity? The serpent spoke so excellently, and with so good a grace, that———Besides, what harm had I ever done him, that he should design me any? Was I to have been always at your side, I might as well have continued there, and been but your rib still: but if I was so weak a creature as you thought me, why did you not interpose your sage authority more absolutely? You denied me going as faintly, as you say I resisted the serpent. Had not you been too easy, neither you nor I had now transgressed."

Adam replied, "Why, Eve, hast thou the impudence to upbraid me as the cause of thy transgression for my indulgence to thee? Thus will it ever be with him, who trusts too much to woman. At the same time that she refuses to be governed, if she suffers by her obstinacy, she will accuse the man that shall leave her to herself."

> Thus they in mutual accusation spent
> The fruitless hours, but neither self-condemning ;
> And of their contest appear'd no end.

This, to the modern, will appear but a very faint piece of conjugal enmity : but you are to consider, that they were but just begun to be angry, and they wanted new words for expressing their new passions ; but by her accusing him of letting her go, and telling him how good a speaker, and how fine a gentleman the devil was, we must reckon, allowing for the improvements of time, that she gave him the same provocation as if she had called him cuckold. The passionate and familiar terms, with which the same case repeated daily for so many thousand years has furnished the present generation, were not then in use ; but the foundation of debate has ever been the same, a contention about their merit and wisdom. Our general mother was a beauty ; and hearing there was another now in the world, could not forbear, as Adam tells her, shewing herself, though to the devil, by whom the same vanity made her liable to be betrayed.

I cannot, with all the help of science and astrology, find any other remedy for this evil, but what was the medicine in this first quarrel ; which was, as appears in the next book, that they were convinced of their being both weak, but the one weaker than the other.

If it were possible that the beauteous could but rage a little before a glass, and see their pretty countenances grow wild, it is not to be doubted but it would have a very good effect : but that would require temper : for lady Firebrand, upon observing her features swell when her maid vexed her the other day, stamped her dressing-glass under her feet. In this case, when one of this temper is moved, she is like a witch in an operation, and makes all things turn round with her. The very fabric is in a vertigo when she begins to charm. In an instant, whatever was the occasion that moved her blood, she has such intolerable servants, Betty is so awkward, Tom cannot carry a message, and her husband has so little respect for her, that she, poor woman, is weary of this life, and was born to be unhappy.

Desunt multa.

PERT PUPPIES.

No. 219. SATURDAY, September 2, 1710. [Steele.]

—— Solutos
Qui captat risus hominum, famamque dicacis—
Affectat, niger est; hunc, tu Romane, caveto.
Hor. 1 Sat. iv. 82.

Who trivial bursts of laughter strives to raise,
And courts of prating petulance the praise,
This man is vile; here, Roman, fix your mark;
His soul is black, as his complexion's dark.

Never were men so perplexed as a select company of us were this evening with a couple of professed wits, who, through our ill fortune, and their own confidence, had thought fit to pin themselves upon a gentleman who had owned to them that he was going to meet such and such persons, and named us one by one. These pert puppies immediately resolved to come with him; and from the beginning to the end of the night entertained each other with impertinences, to which we were perfect strangers. I am come home very much tired; for the affliction was so irksome to me, that it surpasses all other I ever knew, insomuch I cannot reflect upon this sorrow with pleasure, though it is past.

An easy manner of conversation is the most desirable quality a man can have; and for that reason coxcombs will take upon them to be familiar with people whom they never saw before. What adds to the vexation of it is, that they will act upon the foot of knowing you by fame; and rally with you, as they call it, by repeating what your enemies say of you; and court you, as they think, by uttering to your face, at a wrong time, all the kind things your friends speak of you in your absence.

These people are the more dreadful, the more they have of what is usually called wit: for a lively imagination, when it is not governed by a good understanding, makes such miserable havoc both in conversation and business, that it lays you defenceless, and fearful to throw the least word in its way, that may give it new matter for its farther errors.

Tom Mercet has as quick a fancy as anyone living; but there is no reasonable man can bear him half an hour. His purpose is to entertain, and it is of no consequence to him what is said, so it be what is called well said; as if a man must bear a wound with patience, because he that pushed at you came up with a good air and mien. That part of life which we spend in company is the most pleasing of all our moments; and therefore I think our behaviour in it should have its laws, as well as the part of our being which is generally esteemed the more important. From hence it is, that from long experience I have made it a maxim, that however we may pretend to take satisfaction in sprightly mirth and high jollity, there is no great pleasure in any company where the basis of the society is not mutual good-will. When this is in the room, every trifling circumstance, the most minute accident, the absurdity of a servant, the repetition of an old story, the look of a man when he is telling it, the most indifferent and the most ordinary occurrences, are matters which produce mirth and good-humour. I went to spend an hour after this manner with some friends, who enjoy it in perfection whenever they meet, when those destroyers above-mentioned came in upon us. There is not a man among them who has any notion of distinction of superiority to one another, either in their fortunes or their talents, when they are in company. Or if any reflection to the contrary occurs in their thoughts, it only strikes a delight upon their minds, that so much wisdom and power is in possession of one whom they love and esteem.

In these my Lucubrations, I have frequently dwelt upon this one topic. The above maxim would make short work for us reformers ; for it is only want of making this a position that renders some characters bad, which would otherwise be good. Tom Mercet means no man ill, but does ill to every body. His ambition is to be witty ; and to carry on that design, he breaks through all things that other people hold sacred. If he thought that wit was no way to be used but to the advantage of society, that sprightliness would have a new turn, and we should expect what he is going to say with satisfaction instead of fear. It is no excuse for being mischievous, that a man is mischievous without malice ; nor will it be thought an atonement, that the ill was done not to injure the party concerned, but to divert the indifferent.

It is, methinks, a very great error, that we should not profess honesty in conversation, as much as in commerce. If we consider, that there is no greater misfortune than to be ill received ; where we love the turning a man to ridicule among his friends, we rob him of greater enjoyments than he could have purchased by his wealth ; yet he that laughs at him would, perhaps, be the last man who would hurt him in this case of less consequence. It has been said, the history of Don Quixote utterly destroyed the spirit of gallantry in the Spanish nation ; and I believe we may say much more truly, that the humour of ridicule has done as much injury to the true relish of company in England.

Such satisfactions as arise from the secret comparisons of ourselves to others, with relation to their inferior fortunes or merit, are mean and unworthy. The true and high state of conversation is, when men communicate their thoughts to each other upon such subjects, and in such a manner, as would be pleasant if there were no such thing as folly in the world ; for it is but a low condition of wit in one man, which depends upon folly in another.

AN ECCLESIASTICAL THERMOMETER.

No. 220.   TUESDAY, SEPTEMBER 5, 1710.   [ADDISON.]

Insani sapiens nomen ferat, æquus iniqui,
Ultra quam satis est; virtutem si petat ipsam.
HOR. 1 Ep. vi. 15.

Even virtue, when pursu'd with warmth extreme,
Turns into vice, and fools the sage's fame.

HAVING received many letters filled with compliments and acknowledgments for my late useful discovery of the political barometer, I shall here communicate to the public an account of my ecclesiastical thermometer, the latter giving as manifest prognostications of the changes and revolutions in church, as the former does of those in state; and both of them being absolutely necessary for every prudent subject who is resolved to keep what he has, and get what he can.

The church-thermometer, which I am now to treat of, is supposed to have been invented in the reign of Henry the Eighth, about the time when that religious prince put some to death for owning the Pope's supremacy, and others for denying transubstantiation. I do not find, however, any great use made of this instrument, until it fell into the hands of a learned and vigilant priest or minister, for he frequently wrote himself both one and the other, who was some time Vicar of Bray. This gentleman lived in his vicarage to a good old age; and, after having seen several successions of his neighbouring clergy either burned or banished, departed this life with the satisfaction of having never deserted his flock, and died Vicar of Bray,*   As this glass was first designed to calculate the different degrees of heat in religion, as it raged in popery, or as it cooled and grew temperate in the reformation; it was marked at several distances, after the manner our

* The Rev. Symon Symonds was the Vicar of Bray, Berks, here alluded to. He was twice a Papist and twice a Protestant in four successive reigns—those of Henry VIII., Edward VI., Mary, and Elizabeth.

ordinary thermometer is to this day, *viz.* " Extreme Heat, Sultry Heat, Very Hot, Hot, Warm, Temperate, Cold, Just Freezing, Frost, Hard Frost, Great Frost, Extreme Cold."

It is well known, that Toricellius, the inventor of the common weather-glass, made the experiment in a long tube, which held thirty-two feet of water ; and that a more modern *virtuoso,* finding such a machine altogether unwieldy and useless, and considering that thirty-two inches of quicksilver weighed as much as so many feet of water in a tube of the same circumference, invented that sizable instrument which is now in use.   After this manner, that I might adapt the thermometer I am now speaking of to the present constitution of our church, as divided into high and low, I have made some necessary variations both in the tube and the fluid it contains. In the first place, I ordered a tube to be cast in a planetary hour, and took care to seal it hermetically, when the Sun was in conjunction with Saturn.   I then took the proper precautions about the fluid, which is a compound of two very different liquors ; one of them a spirit drawn out of a strong heady wine ; the other a particular sort of rock-water, colder than ice, and clearer than crystal.   The spirit is of a red fiery colour, and so very apt to ferment, that unless it be mingled with a proportion of the water, or pent up very close, it will burst the vessel that holds it, and fly up in fume and smoke. The water, on the contrary, is of such a subtle piercing cold, that, unless it be mingled with a proportion of the spirits, it will sink almost through everything that it is put into ; and seems to be of the same nature as the water mentioned by Quintus Curtius, which, says the historian, could be contained in nothing but in the hoof, or, as the Oxford manuscript has it, in the skull of an ass.   The thermometer is marked according to the following figure ; which I set down at length, not only to give my reader a clear idea of it, but also to fill up my paper.

Ignorance.
Persecution.
Wrath.

Zeal.
CHURCH.
Moderation.
Lukewarmness.
Infidelity.
Ignorance.

The reader will observe, that the Church is placed in the middle point of the glass, between Zeal and Moderation ; the situation in which she always flourishes, and in which every good Englishman wishes her, who is a friend to the constitution of this country.   However, when it mounts to Zeal, it is not amiss ; and, when it sinks to Moderation is still in a most admirable temper.   The worst of it is, that when once it begins to rise, it has still an inclination to ascend ; insomuch that it is apt to climb up from Zeal to Wrath, and from Wrath to Persecution, which alway ends in ignorance, and very often proceeds from it.   In the same manner it frequently takes its progress through the lower half of the glass ; and, when it has a tendency to fall, will gradually descend from Moderation to Lukewarmness, and from Lukewarmness to Infidelity, which very often terminates in Ignorance, and always proceeds from it.

It is a common observation, that the ordinary thermometer will be affected by the breathing of people who are in the room where it stands ; and indeed it is almost incredible to conceive, how the glass I am now describing will fall by the breath of a multitude crying " Popery ; " or, on the contrary, how it will rise when the same multitude, as it sometimes happens, cry out in the same breath, " The church is in danger."

As soon as I had finished this my glass, and adjusted it to the above-mentioned scale of religion ; that I might make proper experiments with it, I carried it under my cloak to several coffee-houses, and other places of resort about this great city.   At Saint *James's* coffee-house the liquor stood at Moderation ; but at *Will's*, to my great surprise, it subsided to the very lowest mark on the glass.   At the *Grecian* it mounted but just one point higher ; at the *Rainbow* it still ascended two degrees ; *Child's* fetched it up to Zeal ; and other adjacent coffee-houses, to Wrath.

It fell in the lower half of the glass, as I went farther into the city, until at length it settled at Moderation, where it continued all the time I staid about the Exchange, as also while I passed by the Bank. And here I cannot but take notice, that through the whole course of my remarks, I never observed my glass to rise at the same time the stocks did.

To complete the experiment, I prevailed upon a friend of mine, who works under me in the Occult Sciences, to make a progress with my glass through the whole island of Great Britain ; and after his return, to present me with a register of his observations. I guessed before-hand at the temper of several places he passed through, by the characters they have had time out of mind. Thus that facetious divine, Dr. Fuller, speaking of the town of Banbury near a hundred years ago, tells us, it was a place famous for cakes and zeal, which I find by my glass is true to this day as to the latter part of this description ; though I must confess, it is not in the same reputation for cakes that it was in the time of our learned author ; and thus of other places. In short, I have now by me, digested in an alphabetical order, all the counties, corporations, and boroughs in Great Britain, with their respective tempers, as they stand related to my thermometer. But this I shall keep to myself, because I would by no means do anything that may seem to influence any ensuing elections.

The point of doctrine which I would propagate by this my invention, is the same which was long ago advanced by that able teacher Horace, out of whom I have taken my text for this discourse. We should be careful not to over-shoot ourselves in the pursuits even of virtue. Whether Zeal or Moderation be the point we aim at, let us keep fire out of the one, and frost out of the other. But, alas ! the world is too wise to want such a precaution. The terms High-church and Low-church, as commonly used, do not so much denote a principle, as they distinguish a party. They are like words of battle, they have nothing to do with their original signification ; but are only given out to keep a body of men together, and to let them know friends from enemies.

I must confess I have considered, with some little attention, the influence which the opinions of these great national sects have upon their practice ; and do not look upon it as one of the unaccountable things of our times, that multitudes of honest gentlemen, who entirely agree in their lives, should take it in their heads to differ in their religion.

LADY GIMCRACK'S LETTER.

No. 221.   THURSDAY, September 7, 1710.   [Addison.]

—— Sicut meus est mos,
Nescio quid meditans nugarum, et totus in illis.
Hor. 1 Sat. ix. 1.

Musing, as wont, on this and that,
Such trifles, as I know not what.

As I was this morning going out of my house, a little boy in a black coat delivered me the following letter. Upon asking who he was, he told me, that he belonged to my Lady Gimcrack. I did not at first recollect the name ; but, upon inquiry, I found it to be the widow of Sir Nicholas, whose legacy I lately gave some account of to the world. The letter ran thus :

"Mr. Bickerstaff,

"I hope you will not be surprised to receive a letter from the widow Gimcrack. You know, sir, that I have lately lost a very whimsical husband, who, I find by one of your last week's papers, was not altogether a stranger to you. When I married this gentleman, he had a very handsome estate ; but upon buying a set of microscopes, he was chosen *a Fellow of the Royal Society ; from which time I do not remember ever to have heard him speak as other people did,* or talk in a manner that

c c

any of his family could understand him.   He used, however, to
pass away his time very innocently in conversation with several
members of that learned body ; for which reason, I never
advised him against their company for several years, until at
last I found his brain quite turned with their discourses.   The
first symptom which he discovered of his being a *virtuoso*, as
you call him, poor man ! was about fifteen years ago ; when he
gave me positive orders to turn off an old weeding-woman, that
had been employed in the family for some years.   He told me at
the same time, that there was no such thing in nature as a
weed, and that it was his design to let his garden produce what
it pleased ; so that, you may be sure, it makes a very pleasant
show as it now lies.   About the same time he took a humour
to ramble up and down the country, and would often bring
home with him his pockets full of moss and pebbles.   This,
you may be sure, gave me a heavy heart ; though at the same
time I must needs say, he had the character of a very honest
man, notwithstanding he was reckoned a little weak, until he
began to sell his estate, and buy those strange baubles that you
have taken notice of.   Upon Midsummer-day last, as he was
walking with me in the fields, he saw a very odd-coloured
butterfly just before us.   I observed that he immediately
changed colour, like a man that is surprised with a piece of
good luck ; and telling me, that it was what he had looked for
above these twelve years, he threw off his coat, and followed it.
I lost sight of them both in less than a quarter of an hour ;
but my husband continued the chase over hedge and ditch until
about sunset ; at which time, as I was afterwards told, he
caught the butterfly as she rested herself upon a cabbage, near
five miles from the place where he first put her up.   He was
here lifted from the ground by some passengers in a very
fainting condition, and brought home to me about midnight.
His violent exercise threw him into a fever, which grew upon
him by degrees, and at last carried him off.   In one of the
intervals of his distemper he called to me, and, after having
excused himself for running out his estate, he told me, that he
had always been more industrious to improve his mind than

his fortune ; and that his family must rather value themselves
upon his memory as he was a wise man, than a rich one.   He
then told me, that it was a custom among the Romans for a
man to give his slaves their liberty when he lay upon his
death-bed.   I could not imagine what this meant, until, after
having a little composed himself, he ordered me to bring him a
flea which he had kept for several months in a chain, with a
design, as he said, to give it its manumission.   This was done
accordingly.   He then made the will, which I have since seen
printed in your works word for word.   Only I must take
notice, that you have omitted the codicil, in which he left a
large *Concha Veneris*, as it is there called, to *a Member of the
Royal Society*, who was often with him in his sickness, and
assisted him in his will.   And now, sir, I come to the chief
business of my letter, which is to desire your friendship and
assistance in the disposal of those many rarities and curiosities
which lie upon my hands.   If you know any one that has an
occasion for a parcel of dried spiders, I will sell them a pennyworth.   I could likewise let any one have a bargain of cockle-
shells.   I would also desire your advice, whether I had best
sell my beetles in a lump, or by retail.   The gentleman above-
mentioned, who was my husband's friend, would have me make
an auction of all his goods, and is now drawing up a catalogue
of every particular for that purpose, with the two following
words over the head of them, *Auctio Gimcrackiana*.   But, upon
talking with him, I begin to suspect he is as mad as poor Sir
Nicholas was.   Your advice in all these particulars will be a
great piece of charity to, Sir,

Your most humble servant,

" ELIZABETH GIMCRACK."

I shall answer the foregoing letter, and give the widow my
best advice, as soon as I can find out chapmen for the wares
which she has to put off.   In the mean time, I shall give my
reader the sight of a letter, which I have received from another
female correspondent by the same post.

" Good Mr. Bickerstaff,

" I am convinced by a late paper of yours, that a
passionate woman, who among the common people goes under
the name of a scold, is one of the most insupportable creatures
in the world.   But, alas ! Sir, what can we do ?   I have made
a thousand vows and resolutions every morning, to guard
myself against this frailty ; but have generally broken them
before dinner, and could never in my life hold out until the
second course was set upon the table.   What most troubles me
is, that my husband is as patient and good-natured as your own
worship, or any man living, can be.   Pray give me some directions, for I would observe the strictest and severest rules you
can think of to cure myself of this distemper, which is apt to
fall into my tongue every moment.   I am, Sir,

"Your most humble servant, &c."

In answer to this most unfortunate lady, I must acquaint
her, that there is now in town an ingenious physician of my
acquaintance, who undertakes to cure all the vices and defects
of the mind by inward medicines or outward applications.   I
shall give the world an account of his patients and his cures in
other papers, when I shall be more at leisure to treat upon this
subject.   I shall only here inform my correspondent, that, for
the benefit of such ladies as are troubled with virulent tongues,
he has prepared a cold-bath, over which there is fastened, at the
end of a long pole, a very convenient chair, curiously gilt and .
carved.   When the patient is seated in this chair, the doctor
lifts up the pole, and gives her two or three total immersions
in the cold-bath, until such time as she has quite lost the use
of speech.   The operation so effectually chills the tongue, and
refrigerates the blood, that a woman, who at her entrance into
the chair is extremely passionate and sonorous, will come out
as silent and gentle as a lamb.   The doctor told me, he would
not practise this experiment upon women of fashion, had not
he seen it made upon those of meaner condition with very good
effect.

ON ADVERTISEMENTS.

No. 224. THURSDAY, September 14, 1710. [Addison.]

Materiam superabat opus.——   Ovid. Met. ii. 5.

The matter equall'd not the artist's skill.

It is my custom, in a dearth of news, to entertain myself with those collections of advertisements that appear at the end of all our public prints. These I consider as accounts of news from the little world, in the same manner that the foregoing parts of the paper are from the great. If in one we hear that a sovereign prince is fled from this capital city, in the other we hear of a tradesman who hath shut up his shop, and run away. If in one we find the victory of a general, in the other we see the desertion of a private soldier. I must confess I have a certain weakness in my temper, that is often very much affected by these little domestic occurrences, and have frequently been caught with tears in my eyes over a melancholy advertisement.

But to consider this subject in its most ridiculous lights, advertisements are of great use to the vulgar. First of all, as they are instruments of ambition. A man that is by no means big enough for the Gazette, may easily creep into the advertisements ; by which means we often see an apothecary in the same paper of news with a plenipotentiary, or a running-footman with an ambassador. An advertisement from Piccadilly goes down to posterity with an article from Madrid, and John Bartlett of Goodman's-fields * is celebrated in the same paper with the emperor of Germany. Thus the fable tells us, that the wren mounted as high as the eagle, by getting upon his back.

A second use which this sort of writings hath been turned to of late years, has been the management of controversy ; insomuch that above half the advertisements one meets with now-a-days are purely polemical. The inventors of " Strops

---

* A truss-maker.

for razors " have written against one another this way for several years, and that with great bitterness ; as the whole argument *pro* and *con* in the case of " the morning gown " is still carried on after the same manner.   I need not mention the several proprietors of Dr. Anderson's pills ; nor take notice of the many satirical works of this nature so frequently published by Dr. Clark, who has had the confidence to advertise upon that learned knight, my very worthy friend, Sir William Read : but I shall not interpose in their quarrel : Sir William can give him his own in advertisements, that, in the judgment of the impartial, are as well penned as the doctor's.

The third and last use of these writings is to inform the world, where they may be furnished with almost every thing that is necessary for life.   If a man has pains in his head, colics in his bowels, or spots in his cloaths, he may here meet with proper cures and remedies.   If a man would recover a wife or a horse that is stolen or strayed ; if he wants new sermons, electuaries, asses' milk,* or any thing else, either for his body or his mind ; this is the place to look for them in.

The great art in writing advertisements, is the finding out a proper method to catch the reader's eye, without which a good thing may pass over unobserved, or be lost among commissions of bankrupts.   Asterisks and hands were formerly of great use for this purpose.   Of late years the N. B. has been much in fashion, as also little cuts and figures, the invention of which we must ascribe to the author of spring-trusses.   I must not here omit the blind Italian character, which, being scarce legible, always fixes and detains the eye, and gives the curious reader something like the satisfaction of prying into a secret.

But the great skill in an advertiser is chiefly seen in the style which he makes use of.   He is to mention " the universal esteem, or general reputation," of things that were never heard of.   If he is a physician or astrologer, he must

* Asses' milk to be had at Richard Stout's, at the sign of the Ass, at Knightsbridge, for three shillings and sixpence *per* quart ; the ass to be brought to the buyer's door.—*Post-Boy*, Dec. 6, 1711.

change his lodgings frequently ; and, though he never saw any
body in them besides his own family, give public notice of it,
" for the information of the nobility and gentry." Since I am
thus usefully employed in writing criticisms on the works of
these diminutive authors, I must not pass over in silence an
advertisement, which has lately made its appearance, and is
written altogether in a Ciceronian manner.   It was sent to me,
with five shillings, to be inserted among my advertisements ;
but as it is a pattern of good writing in this way, I shall give
it a place in the body of my paper.

  " The highest compounded spirit of lavender, the most
glorious, *if the expression may be used*, enlivening scent and
flavour that can possibly be, which so raptures the spirits,
delights the gust, and gives such airs to the countenance, as
are not to be imagined but by those that have tried it.   The
meanest sort of the thing is admired by most gentlemen and
ladies ; but this far more, as by far it exceeds it, to the gaining
among all a more than common esteem.   It is sold, in neat
flint bottles fit for the pocket, only at the golden Key in
Wharton's court, near Holbourn-bars, for three shillings and
six-pence, with directions."

  At the same time that I recommend the several flowers in
which this spirit of lavender is wrapped up, *if the expression
may be used,* I cannot excuse my fellow-labourers for admitting
into their papers several uncleanly advertisements, not at all
proper to appear in the works of polite writers.   Among these
I must reckon the " Carminative Wind-expelling Pills."   If
the doctor had called them only his Carminative Pills, he had
been as cleanly as one could have wished ; but the second word
entirely destroys the decency of the first.   There are other
absurdities of this nature so very gross, that I dare not mention them ; and shall therefore dismiss this subject with a
public admonition to Michael Parrot,* That he do not presume

---

  * " Whereas I, Michael Parot, have had brought away a worm of sixteen
feet long, by taking the medicines of J. More, apothecary, in Abchurch Lane,
London.   Witness my hand, Michael Parot.   Witness, Anth. Spyer."—*Post-
Boy,* April 29, 1710.

any more to mention a certain worm he knows of, which, by the way, has grown seven feet in my memory ; for, if I am not much mistaken, it is the same that was but nine feet long about six months ago.

By the remarks I have here made, it plainly appears that a collection of advertisements is a kind of miscellany ; the writers of which, contrary to all authors, except men of quality, give money to the booksellers who publish their copies. The genius of the bookseller is chiefly shewn in his method of ranging and digesting these little tracts. The last paper I took up in my hand places them in the following order :—

The true Spanish blacking for shoes, &c.

The beautifying cream for the face, &c.

Pease and plaisters, &c.

Nectar and Ambrosia, &c.

Four freehold tenements of fifteen pounds *per annum*, &c.

Annotations upon the Tatler, &c.

The present state of England,* &c.

A commission of bankruptcy being awarded against B. L., bookseller, &c.

DETRACTORS OF THE TATLER.

No. 229.　TUESDAY, September 26, 1710.　[Addison.]

Quæsitam meritis sume superbiam.
Hor. 3 Od. xxx.
With conscious pride -——
Assume the honours justly thine.

The whole creation preys upon itself. Every living creature is inhabited. A flea has a thousand invisible insects that teaze him as he jumps from place to place, and revenge our quarrels upon him. A very ordinary microscope shews us, that a louse

---

* A book entitled "Angliæ Notitia ; or, The Present State of England," &c., was originally compiled by Edward Chamberlayne, LL.D., in 1669, and passed through three impressions in that year. A second part was added in 1671.

is itself a very lousy creature. A whale, besides those seas and oceans in the several vessels of his body, which are filled with innumerable shoals of little animals, carries about him a whole world of inhabitants ; insomuch that, if we believe the calculations some have made, there are more living creatures, which are too small for the naked eye to behold, about the Leviathan, than there are of visible creatures upon the face of the whole earth. Thus every noble creature is, as it were, the basis and support of multitudes that are his inferiors.

This consideration very much comforts me, when I think of those numberless vermin that feed upon this paper, and find their sustenance out of it ; I mean the small wits and scribblers, that every day turn a penny by nibbling at my Lucubrations. This has been so advantageous to this little species of writers, that, if they do me justice, I may expect to have my statue erected in Grub Street, as being a common benefactor to that quarter.

They say, when a fox is very much troubled with fleas, he goes into the next pool with a little lock of wool in his mouth, and keeps his body under water until the vermin get into it; after which he quits the wool, and diving, leaves his tormentors to shift for themselves, and get their livelihood where they can. I would have these gentlemen take care that I do not serve them after the same manner ; for though I have hitherto kept my temper pretty well, it is not impossible but I may some time or other disappear ; and what will then become of them ? Should I lay down my paper, what a famine would there be among the hawkers, printers, booksellers, and authors ! It would be like Doctor Burgess's * dropping his cloak, with the whole congregation hanging upon the skirts of it. To enumerate some of these my doughty antagonists ; I was threatened to be answered weekly *Tit for Tat;* I was undermined by the *Whisperer ;* haunted by *Tom Brown's Ghost ;* scolded at by a *Female Tatler ;* and slandered by another of the

* Daniel Burgess, the doctor here alluded to, resided at the court of Hanover as secretary and reader to the Princess Sophia.

same character, under the title of *Atalantis*. I have been
annotated, retattled, examined, and *condoled :* but it being my
standing maxim never to speak ill of the dead, I shall let these
authors rest in peace ; and take great pleasure in thinking,
that I have sometimes been the means of their getting a belly-
full. When I see myself thus surrounded by such formidable
enemies, I often think of the knight of the Red Cross in
Spenser's "Men of Error," who, after he has cut off the dragon's
head, and left it wallowing in a flood of ink, sees a thousand
monstrous reptiles making their attempts upon him, one with
many heads, another with none, and all of them without eyes.

> The same so sore annoyed has the Knight,
> That, well nigh choaked with the deadly stink,
> His forces fail, he can no longer fight ;
> Whose courage when the fiend perceiv'd to shrink,
> She poured forth out of her hellish sink
> Her fruitful cursed spawn of serpents small,
> Deformed monsters, foul, and black as ink ;
> Which swarming all about his legs did crawl,
> And him encumbred sore, but could not hurt at all.
>
> As gentle shepherd in sweet even tide,
> When ruddy Phœbus 'gins to welk in west,
> High on an hill, his flock to viewen wide,
> Marks which do bite their hasty supper best ;
> A cloud of cumbrous gnats do him molest,
> All striving to infix their feeble stings,
> That from their noyance he no where can rest ;
> But with his clownish hands their tender wings
> He brusheth oft, and oft doth mar their murmurings.[*]

If ever I should want such a fry of little authors to attend
me, I shall think my paper in a very decaying condition.
They are like ivy about an oak, which adorns the tree at the
same time that it eats into it ; or like a great man's equipage,
that do honour to the person on whom they feed. For my part,
when I see myself thus attacked, I do not consider my
antagonists as malicious, but hungry ; and therefore am resolved
never to take any notice of them.

As for those who detract from my labours, without being
prompted to it by an empty stomach ; in return to their

---

[*] Spenser's "Fairy Queen, b. i. canto i. 22 and 23.

censures, I shall take pains to excel, and never fail to persuade myself, that their enmity is nothing but their envy or ignorance.

Give me leave to conclude, like an old man, and a moralist, with a fable.

The owls, bats, and several other birds of the night, were one day got together in a thick shade, where they abused their neighbours in a very sociable manner. Their satire at last fell upon the sun, whom they all agreed to be very troublesome, impertinent and inquisitive. Upon which, the sun, who over-heard them, spoke to them after this manner : " Gentlemen, I wonder how you dare abuse one that, you know, could in an instant scorch you up, and burn every mother's son of you : but the only answer I shall give you, or the revenge I shall take of you, is, to ' shine on.' "

THE UPHOLSTERER'S LETTER.

No. 232.   TUESDAY, OCTOBER 3, 1710.   [STEELE.]

I HAVE received the following letter from my unfortunate old acquaintance the upholsterer, who, I observed, had long absented himself from the bench at the upper end of the Mall. Having not seen him for some time, I was in fear I should soon hear of his death ; especially since he never appeared, though the noons have been of late pretty warm, and the councils at that place very full from the hour of twelve to three, which the sages of. that board employ in conference, while the unthinking part of mankind are eating and drinking for the support of their own private persons, without any regard to the public.

" SIR,

" I should have waited on you very frequently, to have discoursed you upon some matters of moment, but that I love

to be well informed in the subject upon which I consult my
friends, before I enter into debate with them. I have therefore, with the utmost care and pains, applied myself to the
reading all the writings and pamphlets which have come out
since the trial, and have studied night and day in order to
be master of the whole controversy : but the authors are so
numerous, and the state of affairs alters so very fast, that I
am now a fortnight behind-hand in my reading, and know
only how things stood twelve days ago. I wish you would
enter into those useful subjects ; for, if I may be allowed to
say so, these are not times to jest in. As for my own part,
you know very well that I am of a public spirit, and never
regarded my own interest, but looked farther ; and let me
tell you, that while some people are minding only themselves
and families, and others are thinking only of their own
country, things go on strangely in the North. I foresee very
great evils arising from the neglect of transactions at a distance ; for which reason I am now writing a letter to a friend
in the country, which I design as an answer to the Czar of
Muscovy's letter to the Grand Seignior concerning his Majesty
of Sweden. I have endeavoured to prove, that it is not
reasonable to expect that his Swedish Majesty should leave
Bender without forty thousand men ; and I have added to
this an apology for the Cossacks. But the matter multiplies
upon me, and I grow dim with much writing ; therefore
desire, if you have an old green pair of spectacles, such as
you used about your fiftieth year, that you would send them
to me ; as also, that you would please to desire Mr. Morphew
to send me in a bushel of coals on the credit of my answer to
his Czarian Majesty ; for I design it shall be printed for
Morphew, and the weather grows sharp. I should take it
kindly if you would order him also to send me the papers as
they come out. If there are no fresh pamphlets published,
I compute that I shall know before the end of next month
what has been done in town to this day. If it were not for
an ill custom lately introduced by a certain author, of talking
Latin at the beginning of papers, matters would be in a much

clearer light than they are : but, to our comfort, there are solid writers who are not guilty of this pedantry. The Post-man writes like an angel. The Moderator is fine reading. It would do you no harm to read the Post-Boy with attention ; he is very deep of late. He is instructive ; but I confess a little satirical : a sharp pen ! he cares not what he says. The Examiner is admirable, and is become a grave and substantial author.*   But, above all, I am at a loss how to govern myself in my judgment of those whose whole writings consist in interrogatories ; and then the way of answering, by proposing questions as hard to them, is quite as extraordinary.   As for my part, I tremble at these novelties ; we expose, in my opinion, our affairs too much by it.   You may be sure the French king will spare no cost to come at the reading of them. I dread to think if the fable of the Blackbirds should fall into his hands.   But I shall not venture to say more until I see you.   In the mean time,   I am, &c."

This unhappy correspondent, whose fantastical loyalty to the King of Sweden has reduced him to this low condition of reason and fortune, would appear much more monstrous in his madness, did we not see crowds very little above his circumstances from the same cause, a passion to politics.

It is no unpleasant entertainment to consider the commerce even of the sexes interrupted by difference in state affairs. A wench and her gallant parted last week upon the words *unlimited* and *passive :* and there is such a jargon of terms got into the mouths of the very silliest of the women, that you cannot come into a room even among them, but you find them divided into Whig and Tory.   What heightens the humour is, that all the hard words they know, they certainly suppose to be terms useful in the disputes of the parties.   I came in this day where two were in very hot debate ; and

---

* "I hoped, as you did, that your friend, the Upholsterer had been dead. He was of a very low character at first, but after we had had his company so often, a long letter from him was extremely insipid."—*Examiner*, October 12, 1710.

one of them proposed to me to explain to them what was the difference between *circumcision* and *predestination*. You may be sure I was at a loss; but they were too angry at each other to wait for my explanation, and proceeded to lay open the whole state of affairs, instead of the usual topics of dress, gallantry, and scandal.

I have often wondered how it should be possible that this turn to politics should so universally prevail, to the exclusion of every other subject out of conversation; and upon mature consideration, find it is for want of discourse. Look round you among all the young fellows you meet, and you see those who have the least relish for books, company, or pleasure, though they have no manner of qualities to make them succeed in those pursuits, shall make very passable politicians. Thus the most barren invention shall find enough to say to make one appear an able man in the top coffee-houses. It is but adding a certain vehemence in uttering yourself, let the thing you say be never so flat, and you shall be thought a very sensible man, if you were not too hot. As love and honour are the noblest motives of life; so the pretenders to them, without being animated by them, are the most contemptible of all sorts of pretenders. The unjust affectation of any thing that is laudable is ignominious in proportion to the worth of the thing we affect: thus, as love of one's country is the most glorious of all passions, to see the most ordinary tools in a nation give themselves airs that way, without any one good quality in their own life, has something in it romantic, yet not so ridiculous as odious.

ON PARENTAL LOVE.

No. 235. TUESDAY, October 10, 1710. [Steele.]

Scit Genius, natale comes qui temperat astrum.
HOR. 2 Ep. ii. 187.

But whence these turns of inclination rose,
The Genius this, the God of Nature, knows :
That mystic Power, which our actions guides,
Attends our stars, and o'er our lives presides.

AMONG those inclinations which are common to all men, there is none more unaccountable than that *unequal* love by which parents distinguish their children from each other. Sometimes vanity and self-love appear to have a share towards this effect ; and in other instances I have been apt to attribute it to mere instinct : but, however that is, we frequently see the child, that has been beholden to neither of these impulses in his parents, in spite of being neglected, snubbed, and thwarted at home, acquire a behaviour which makes him as agreeable to all the rest of the world, as that of every one else of their family is to each other. I fell into this way of thinking from an intimacy which I have with a very good house in our neighbourhood, where there are three daughters of a very different character and genius. The eldest has a great deal of wit and cunning ; the second has good sense, but no artifice ; the third has much vivacity, but little understanding. The first is a fine, but scornful woman ; the second is not charming, but very winning ; the third is no way commendable, but very desirable. The father of these young creatures was ever a great pretender to wit, the mother a woman of as much coquetry. This turn in the parents has biassed their affections towards their children. The old man supposes the eldest of his own genius ; and the mother looks upon the youngest as herself renewed. By this means, all the lovers that approach the house are discarded by the father, for not observing Mrs. Mary's wit and beauty ; and by the mother, for being blind to the mien and air of Mrs. Biddy. Come never so many pretenders, they are not suspected to have the least thought of Mrs. Betty, the middle daughter. Betty, therefore, is mortified into a woman of a great deal of merit, and knows she must depend on that only for her advancement. The middlemost is thus the favourite of all her acquaintance, as well as mine; while the other two carry a certain insolence about them in all conversations, and expect the partiality which they meet with at home to attend them wherever they appear. So little do parents understand that they are, of all people, the least judges of their children's merit, that what they reckon such is seldon any thing else but a repetition of their own faults and infirmities.

There is, methinks, some excuse for being particular, when one of the offspring has any defect in nature. In this case, the child, if we may so speak, is so much the longer the child of its parents, and calls for the continuance of their care and indulgence from the slowness of its capacity, or the weakness of its body. But there is no enduring to see men enamoured only at the sight of their own impertinences repeated, and to observe, as we may sometimes, that they have a secret dislike of their children for a degeneracy from their very crimes. Commend me to lady Goodly; she is equal to all her own children, but prefers them to those of all the world beside. My lady is a perfect hen in the care of her brood; she fights and squabbles with all that appear where they come, but is wholly unbiassed in dispensing her favours among them. It is no small pains she is at to defame all the young women in her neighbourhood, by visits, whispers, intimations, and hearsays; all which she ends with thanking heaven, "that no one living is so blessed with such obedient and well-inclined children as herself. Perhaps," says she, "Betty cannot dance like Mrs. Frontinet, and it is no great matter whether she does or not; but she comes into a room with a good grace; though she says it that should not, she looks like a gentlewoman. Then, if Mrs. Rebecca is not so talkative as the mighty wit Mrs. Clapper, yet she is discreet, she knows better what she says when she does speak. If her wit be slow her tongue never runs before it." This kind parent lifts up her eyes and hands in congratulation of her own good fortune, and is maliciously thankful that none of her girls are like any of her neighbours : but this preference of her own to all others is grounded upon an impulse of nature ; while those, who like one before another of their own, are so unpardonably unjust, that it could hardly be equalled in the children, though they preferred all the rest of the world to such parents. It is no unpleasant entertainment to see a ball at a dancing school, and observe the joy of relations when the young ones, for whom they are concerned, are in motion. You need not be told whom the dancers belong to. At their first appearance, the passions of their parents are in their faces, and there is always a nod of approbation stolen at a good step, or a graceful turn.

I remember, among all my acquaintance, but one man whom I have thought to live with his children with equanimity and a good grace. He had three sons and one daughter, whom he bred with all the care imaginable in a liberal and ingenuous way. I have often heard him say, " he had the weakness to love one much better than the other, but that he took as much pains to correct that as any other criminal passion that could arise in his mind." His method was, to make it the only pretension in his children to his favour, to be kind to each other ; and he would tell them, " that he who was the best brother, he would reckon the best son." This turned their thoughts into an emulation for the superiority in kind and tender affection towards each other. The boys behaved themselves very early with a manly friendship ; and their sister, instead of the gross familiarities, and impertinent freedoms in behaviour, usual in other houses, was always treated by them with as much complaisance as any other young lady of their acquaintance. It was an unspeakable pleasure to visit, or sit at a meal, in that family. I have often seen the old man's heart flow at his eyes with joy, upon occasions which would appear indifferent to such as were strangers to the turn of his mind ; but a very slight accident, wherein he saw his children's good-will to one another, created in him the god-like pleasure of loving them because they loved each other. This great command of himself, in hiding his first impulse to partiality, at last improved to a steady justice towards them ; and that, which at first was but an expedient to correct his weakness, was afterwards the measure of his virtue.

The truth of it is, those parents who are interested in the care of one child more than that of another, no longer deserve the name of parents, but are, in effect, as childish as their children, in having such unreasonable and ungoverned inclinations. A father of this sort has degraded himself into one of his own offspring ; for none but a child would take part in the passions of children.

ITHURIEL'S SPEAR.

No. 237. SATURDAY, October 14, 1710. [Addison.]

In nova fert animus mutatas dicere formas
Corpora. Ovid.

Of bodies chang'd to various forms I sing.

Coming home last night before my usual hour, I took a book into my hand, in order to divert myself with it until bedtime. Milton chanced to be my author, whose admirable poem of "Paradise Lost" serves at once to fill the mind with pleasing ideas, and with good thoughts, and was therefore the most proper book for my purpose. I was amusing myself with that beautiful passage in which the poet represents Eve sleeping by Adam's side, with the devil sitting at her ear, and inspiring evil thoughts, under the shape of a toad. Ithuriel, one of the guardian angels of the place, walking his nightly rounds, saw the great enemy of mankind hid in this loathsome animal, which he touched with his spear. This spear being of a celestial temper, had such a secret virtue in it, that whatever it was applied to, immediately flung off all disguise, and appeared in its natural figure. I am afraid the reader will not pardon me, if I content myself with explaining the passage in prose, without giving it in the author's own inimitable words :

> —— On he led his radiant files,
> Dazzling the morn. These to the bower direct,
> In search of whom they sought. Him there they found,
> Squat like a toad, close at the ear of Eve ;
> Essaying by his devilish art to reach
> The organs of her fancy, and with them forge
> Illusions as he list, phantasms and dreams ;
> Or if, inspiring venom, he might taint
> The animal spirits (that from pure blood arise
> Like gentle breaths from rivers pure), thence raise
> At least distemper'd, discontented thoughts,
> Vain hopes, vain aims, inordinate desires,
> Blown up with high conceits, ingend'ring pride,
> Him, thus intent, Ithuriel with his spear
> Touch'd lightly ; for no falsehood can endure
> Touch of celestial temper, but returns
> Of force to his own likeness. Up he starts
> Discover'd and surpris'd. As when a spark
> Lights on a heap of nitrous powder, laid
> Fit for the tun, some magazine to store
> Against a rumour'd war, the smutty grain,
> With sudden blaze diffus'd, inflames the air ;
> So started up in his own shape the fiend.

I could not forbear thinking how happy a man would be in the possession of this spear ; or what an advantage it would be to a minister of state were he master of such a white staff. It would help him to discover his friends from his enemies, men of abilities from pretenders : it would hinder him from being imposed upon by appearances and professions ; and might be made use of as a kind of state-test, which no artifice could elude.

These thoughts made very lively impressions on my imagination, which were improved, instead of being defaced, by sleep, and produced in me the following dream : I was no sooner fallen asleep, but methought the angel Ithuriel appeared to me, and, with a smile that still added to his celestial beauty, made me a present of the spear which he held in his hand ; and disappeared. To make trials of it, I went into a place of public resort.

The first person that passed by me, was a lady that had a particular shyness in the cast of her eye, and a more than ordinary reservedness in all the parts of her behaviour. She seemed to look upon man as an obscene creature, with a certain scorn and fear of him. In the height of her airs I touched her gently with my wand, when, to my unspeakable surprise, she fell in such a manner as made me blush in my sleep. As I was hasting away from this undisguised prude, I saw a lady in earnest discourse with another, and over-heard her say, with some vehemence, " Never tell me of him, for I am resolved to die a virgin ! " I had a curiosity to try her ; but, as soon as I laid my wand upon her head, she immediately fell in labour. My eyes were diverted from her by a man and his wife, who walked near me hand in hand after a very loving manner. I gave each of them a gentle tap, and the next instant saw the woman in breeches, and the man with a fan in his hand. It would be tedious to describe the long series of metamorphoses that I entertained myself with in my night's adventure, of Whigs disguised in Tories, and Tories in Whigs ; men in red coats, that denounced terror in their countenances, trembling at the touch of my spear ; others in black, with peace in their mouths, but swords in their hands. I could tell stories of noblemen turned into usurers, and magistrates into beadles ; of free-thinkers into penitents, and reformers into whore-masters. I must not, however, omit the mention of a grave citizen who passed by me with an huge clasped Bible under his arm, and a band of a most immoderate breadth ; but, upon a touch on the shoulder, he let drop his book, and fell a-picking my pocket.

In the general I observed, that those who appeared good, often disappointed my expectations ; but that, on the contrary, those who appeared very bad, still grew worse upon the experiment ; as the toad in Milton, which one would have thought the most deformed part of the creation, at Ithuriel's stroke became more deformed, and started up into a devil.

Among all the persons that I touched, there was but one who stood the test of my wand ; and, after many repetitions of the stroke, stuck to his form, and remained steady and fixed in his first appearance. This was a young man, who boasted of foul distempers, wild debauches, insults upon holy men, and affronts to religion.

My heart was extremely troubled at this vision. The contemplation of the whole species, so entirely sunk in corruption, filled my mind with a melancholy that is inexpressible, and my discoveries still added to my affliction.

In the midst of these sorrows which I had in my heart, methought there passed before me a couple of coaches with purple liveries. There sat in each of them a person with a very venerable aspect. At the appearance of them the people, who were gathered round me in great multitudes, divided into parties, as they were disposed to favour either of those reverend persons. The enemies of one of them begged me to touch him with my wand, and assured me I should see his lawn converted into a cloke. The opposite party told me with as much assurance, that if I laid my wand upon the other, I should see his garments embroidered with flower-deluces, and his head covered with a cardinal's hat. I made the experiment, and, to my great joy, saw them both without any change, distributing their blessings to the people, and praying for those who had reviled them. Is it possible, thought I, that good men, who are so few in number, should be divided among themselves, and give better quarter to the vicious that are in their party, than the most strictly virtuous who are out of it? Are the ties of faction above those of religion?—I was going on in my soliloquies, but some sudden accident awakened me, when I found my hand grasped, but my spear gone. The reflection on so very odd a dream made me figure to myself, what a strange face the world would bear, should all mankind appear in their proper shapes and characters, without hypocrisy and disguise? I am afraid the earth we live upon would appear to other intellectual beings no better than a planet peopled with monsters. This should, methinks, inspire us with an honest ambition of recommending ourselves to those invisible spies, and of being what we would appear. There was one circumstance in my foregoing dream, which I at first intended to conceal; but, upon second thoughts, I cannot look upon myself as a candid and impartial historian, if I do not acquaint my reader, that upon taking Ithuriel's spear into my hand, though I was before an old decrepit fellow, I appeared a very handsome, jolly, black man. But I know my enemies will say this is praising my own beauty, for which reason I will speak no more of it.

A GENTLE CHASTISEMENT.

No. 239. THURSDAY, October 19, 1710. [Addison.]

——Mecum certâsse feretur ?   Ovid. Met. xiii. 20.

Shall he contend with me to get a name ?

It is ridiculous for any man to criticise on the works of another, who has not distinguished himself by his own performances. A judge would make but an indifferent figure who had never been known at the bar. Cicero was reputed the greatest orator of his age and country, before he wrote a book "De Oratore;" and Horace the greatest poet, before he published his "Art of Poetry." This observation arises naturally in any one who casts his eye upon this last-mentioned author, where he will find the criticisms placed in the latter end of his book, that is, after the finest odes and satires in the Latin tongue.

A modern, whose name I shall not mention, because I would not make a silly paper sell, was born a *Critic* and an *Examiner*, and, like one of the race of the serpent's teeth, came into the world with a sword in his hand. His works put me in mind of the story that is told of the German monk, who was taking a catalogue of a friend's library, and meeting with a Hebrew book in it, entered it under the title of, "A book that has the beginning where the end should be." This author, in the last of his crudities, has amassed together a heap of quotations, to prove that Horace and Virgil were both of them modester men than myself; and if his works were to live as long as mine, they may possibly give posterity a notion, that Isaac Bickerstaff was a very conceited old fellow, and as vain a man as either Tully or Sir Francis Bacon. Had this serious writer fallen upon me only, I could have overlooked it ; but to see Cicero abused is, I must confess, what I cannot bear. The censure he passes upon this great man runs thus : " The itch of being very abusive is almost inseparable from vain-glory. Tully has these two faults in so high a degree, that nothing but his being the best writer in the world can make amends for them." The scurrilous wretch goes on to say that I am as bad as Tully. His words are these : " And yet the Tatler, in his paper of September the twenty-sixth has outdone him in both. He speaks of himself with more arrogance, and with more insolence of others." I am afraid, by his discourse, this gentleman has no more read Plutarch than he has Tully. If he had, he would have observed a passage in that historian, wherein he has, with great delicacy, distinguished between two passions which are usually complicated in human nature, and which an ordinary writer would not have thought of separating. Not having my Greek spectacles by me, I shall quote the passage word for word as I find it translated to my hand. " Nevertheless, tho' he was intemperately fond of his own praise, yet he was very free from envying others, and most liberally profuse in commending both the ancients and his contemporaries, as is to be understood by his writings ; and many of those sayings are still recorded, as that concerning Aristotle, 'that he was a river of flowing gold :' of Plato's dialogue, ' that if Jupiter were to speak, he would discourse as he did.' Theophrastus he was wont to call his peculiar delight ; and being asked, ' which of Demosthenes his orations he liked best ?' He answered, 'The longest.'"

" And as for the eminent men of his own time either for eloquence or philosophy, there was not one of them which he did not, by writing or speaking favourably of, render more illustrious."

Thus the critic tells us, that Cicero was excessively vain-glorious and abusive ; Plutarch, that he was vain, but not abusive.   Let the reader believe which of them he pleases.

After this he complains to the world, that I call him names, and that, in my passion, I said he was a flea, a louse, an owl, a bat, a small wit, a scribbler, and a nibbler.   When he has thus bespoken his reader's pity, he falls into that admirable vein of mirth, which I shall set down at length, it being an exquisite piece of raillery, and written in great gaiety of heart. "After this list of names," *viz.* flea, louse, owl, bat, &c.   " I was surprised to hear him say, that he has hitherto kept his temper pretty well ; I wonder how he will write when he has lost his temper !   I suppose, as he is now very angry and unmannerly, he will then be exceedingly courteous and good-humoured." If I can outlive this raillery, I shall be able to bear anything.

There is a method of criticism made use of by this author, for I shall take care how I call him a scribbler again, which may turn into ridicule any work that was ever written, wherein there is a variety of thoughts.   This the reader will observe in the following words :   " He," meaning me, " is so intent upon being something extraordinary, that he scarce knows what he would be ; and is as fruitful in his similes as a brother of his* whom I lately took notice of.   In the compass of a few lines he compares himself to a fox, to Daniel Burgess, to the knight of the Red Cross, to an oak with ivy about it, and to a great man with an equipage."   I think myself as much honoured by being joined in this part of his paper with the gentleman whom he here calls my brother, as I am in the beginning of it, by being mentioned with Horace and Virgil.

It is very hard that a man cannot publish ten papers without stealing from himself ; but to show you that this is only a

* Dr. Samuel Garth.

knack of writing, and that the author is got into a certain road of criticism, I shall set down his remarks on the works of the gentleman whom he here glances upon, as they stand in his sixth paper, and desire the reader to compare them with the foregoing passage upon mine.

"In thirty lines his patron is a river, the *primum mobile*, a pilot, a victim, the sun, any thing, and nothing. He bestows increase, conceals his source, makes the machine move, teaches to steer, expiates our offences, raises vapours, and looks larger as he sets."

What poem can be safe from this sort of criticism ? I think I was never in my life so much offended, as at a wag whom I once met with in a coffee-house. He had in his hand one of the "Miscellanies," and was reading the following short copy of verses, which, without flattery to the author, is, I think, as beautiful in its kind as any one in the English tongue ; *

> Flavia the least and slightest toy
> Can with resistless art employ.
> This fan in meaner hands would prove
> An engine of small force in love ;
> But she, with such an air and mien,
> Not to be told, or safety seen,
> Directs its wanton motions so,
> That it wounds more than Cupid's bow :
> Gives coolness to the matchless dame,
> To every other breast a flame.

When this coxcomb had done reading them, "Hey-day !" says he, "what instrument is this that Flavia employs in such a manner as is not to be told, nor safely seen ? In ten lines it is a toy, a Cupid's bow, a fan, and an engine in love. It has wanton motions, it wounds, it cools, and inflames"

Such criticisms make a man of sense sick, and a fool merry.

The next paragraph of the paper we are talking of, falls upon somebody whom I am at a loss to guess at : but I find the whole invective turns upon a man who, it seems, has been imprisoned for debt. Whoever he was, I most heartily pity

* Dr. Atterbury was the author of this copy of verses ; and it is generally believed, that Mrs. Anne Oldfield was the lady here celebrated.

him ; but at the same time must put the *Examiner* in mind, that nothwithstanding he is a Critic, he still ought to remember he is a Christian.   Poverty was never thought a proper subject for ridicule ; and I do not remember that I ever met with a satire upon a beggar.

As for those little retortings of my own expressions, of "being dull by design, witty in October, shining, excelling," and so forth ; they are the common cavils of every witling, who has no other method of shewing his parts, but by little variations and repetitions of the man's words whom he attacks.

But the truth of it is, the paper before me, not only in this particular, but in its very essence, is like Ovid's Echo,

> ——Quæ nec reticere loquenti,
> Nec prior ipsa loqui didicit——

> She who in other's words her silence breaks,
> Nor speaks herself but when another speaks.

I should not have deserved the character of a Censor, had I not animadverted upon the above-mentioned author, by a gentle chastisement : but I know my reader will not pardon me, unless I declare, that nothing of this nature for the future, unless it be written with some wit, shall divert me from my care of the public.

THE POWER OF WINE.

No. 241.   TUESDAY, October 24, 1710.   [Steele.]

A method of spending one's time agreeably is a thing so little studied, that the common amusement of our young gentlemen, especially of such as are at a distance from those of the first breeding, is drinking.   This way of entertainment has custom on its side ; but, as much as it has prevailed, I believe there have been very few companies that have been guilty of excess this way, where there have not happened more accidents which make against than for the continuance of it.   It is very common that events arise from a debauch which are fatal, and always such as are disagreeable. With all a man's reason and good sense about him, his tongue is apt to utter things out of mere gaiety of heart, which may displease his best friends. Who then would trust himself to the power of wine, without saying more against it, than that it raises the imagination, and depresses the judgment ? Were there only this single consideration, that we are less masters of ourselves, when we drink in the least proportion above the exigencies of thirst ; I say, were this all that could be objected, it were sufficient to make us abhor this vice. But we may go on to say, that as he who drinks but a little is not master of himself, so he who drinks much is a slave to himself. As for my part, I ever esteemed a drunkard of all vicious persons the most vicious : for if our actions are to be weighed and considered according to the intention of them, what can we think of him, who puts himself into a circumstance wherein he can have no intention at all, but incapacitates himself for the duties and offices of life, by a suspension of all his faculties ? If a man considers that he cannot, under the oppression of drink, be a friend, a gentleman, a master, or a subject ; that he has so long banished himself from all that is dear, and given up all that is sacred to him ; he would even then think of a debauch with horror. But when he looks still farther, and acknowledges, that he is not only expelled out of all the relations of life, but also liable to offend against them all ; what words can express the terror and detestation he would have of such a condition ? And yet he owns all this of himself, who says he was drunk last night.

As I have all along persisted in it, that all the vicious in general are in a state of death ; so I think I may add to the non-existence of drunkards, that they died by their own hands. He is certainly as guilty of suicide who perishes by a slow, as he that is despatched by an immediate poison. In my last Lucubration I proposed the general use of water-gruel, and hinted that it might not be amiss at this very season. But as there are some whose cases, in regard to their families, will not admit of delay ; I have used my interest in several wards of the city, that the wholesome restorative above mentioned may be given in tavern-kitchens to all the morning-draughts-men, within the walls, when they call for wine before noon. For a farther restraint and mark upon such persons, I have given orders, that in all the offices where policies are drawn upon lives, it shall be added to the article which prohibits that the nominee should cross the sea, the words, " Provided also, that the above-mentioned A. B. shall not drink before dinner during the term mentioned in this indenture."

I am not without hopes, that by this method I shall bring some unsizeable friends of mine into shape and breadth, as well as others, who are languid and consumptive, into health and vigour. Most of the self-murderers whom I yet hinted at, are such as preserve a certain regularity in taking their poison, and make it mix pretty well with their food. But the most conspicuous of those who destroy themselves, are such as in their youth fall into this sort of debauchery; and contract a certain uneasiness of spirit, which is not to be diverted but by tippling as often as they can fall into company in the day, and conclude with downright drunkenness at night. These gentlemen never know the satisfaction of youth ; but skip the years of manhood, and are decrepit soon after they are of age. I was godfather to one of these old fellows. He is now three-and-thirty, which is the grand climacteric of a young drunkard. I went to visit the crazy wretch this morning, with no other purpose but to rally him under the pain and uneasiness of being sober.

But as our faults are double when they affect others besides ourselves, so this vice is still more odious in a married than a single man. He that is the husband of a woman of honour, and comes home over-loaded with wine, is still more contemptible in proportion to the regard we have to the unhappy consort of his bestiality. The imagination cannot shape to itself any thing more monstrous and unnatural than the familiarities between drunkenness and chastity. The wretched Astræa, who is the perfection of beauty and innocence, has long been thus condemned for life. The romantic tales of virgins devoted to the jaws of monsters, have nothing in them so terrible as the gift of Astræa to that Bacchanal.

The reflection of such a match as spotless innocence with abandoned lewdness, is what puts this vice in the worst figure it can bear with regard to others ; but when it is looked upon with respect only to the drunkard himself, it has deformities enough to make it disagreeable, which may be summed up in a word, by allowing, that he who resigns his reason, is actually guilty of all that he is liable to from the want of reason.

TRUE RAILLERY.

No. 242.   THURSDAY, October 26, 1710.   [Steele.]

—— Quis iniquæ
Tam patiens urbis, tam ferreus ut teneat se?
Juv. Sat. i. 30.

To view so lewd a town, and to refrain,
What hoops of iron could my spleen contain ?

It was with very great displeasure I heard this day a man say of a companion of his, with an air of approbation, " You know Tom never fails of saying a spiteful thing. He has a great deal of wit, but satire is his particular talent. Did you mind how he put the young fellow out of countenance that pretended to talk to him ? " Such impertinent applauses, which one meets with every day, put me upon considering, what true raillery and satire were in themselves; and this, methought, occurred to me from reflection upon the great and excellent persons that were admired for talents this way. When I had run over several such in my thoughts, I concluded, however unaccountable the assertion might appear at first sight, that good-nature was an essential quality in a satirist, and that all the sentiments which are beautiful in this way of writing, must proceed from that quality in the author. Good-nature produces a disdain for all baseness, vice, and folly ; which prompts them to express themselves with

smartness against the errors of men, without bitterness
towards their persons. This quality keeps the mind in
equanimity and never lets an offence unseasonably throw a
man out of his character. When Virgil said, "he that did not
hate Bavius might love Mævius," he was in perfect good humour;
and was not so much moved at their absurdities, as passionately to call them sots or blockheads in a direct invective,
but laughed at them with a delicacy of scorn, without any
mixture of anger.

The best good man, with the worst natur'd muse, was the
character among us of a gentleman as famous for his humanity
as his wit. *

The ordinary subjects for satire are such as incite the
greatest indignation in the best tempers, and consequently
men of such a make are the best qualified for speaking of the
offences in human life. These men can behold vice and folly,
when they injure persons to whom they are wholly unacquainted, with the same severity as others resent the ills
they do to themselves. A good-natured man cannot seé an
overbearing fellow put a bashful man of merit out of countenance, or out-strip him in the pursuit of any advantage, but
he is on fire to succour the oppressed, to produce the merit of
the one, and confront the impudence of the other.

The men of the greatest character in this kind were Horace
and Juvenal. There is not, that I remember, one ill-natured
expression in all their writings, nor one sentence of severity,
which does not apparently proceed from the contrary disposition. Whoever reads them, will, I believe, be of this mind ;
and if they were read with this view, it might possibly persuade
our young fellows, that they may be very witty men without
speaking ill of any but those who deserve it. But, in the
perusal of these writers, it may not be unnecessary to consider
that they lived in very different times. Horace was intimate
with a prince of the greatest goodness and humanity

---

* This was said, by the Earl of Rochester, of the celebrated Lord Buck-
hurst, afterwards Earl of Dorset. It is said likewise of Dr. Arbuthnot, "that
he liked an ill-natured jest the best of any good-natured man in the kingdom."

imaginable, and his court was formed after his example : therefore the faults that poet falls upon were' little inconsistencies in behaviour, false pretences to politeness, or impertinent affectations of what men were not fit for. Vices of a coarser sort could not come under his consideration, or enter the palace of Augustus. Juvenal, on the other hand, lived under Domitian, in whose reign every thing that was great and noble was banished the habitations of the men in power. Therefore he attacks vice as it passes by in triumph, not as it breaks into a conversation. The fall of empire, contempt of glory, and a general degeneracy of manners are before his eyes in all his writings. In the days of Augustus, to have talked like Juvenal had been madness ; or in those of Domitian, like Horace. Morality and virtue are every where recommended in Horace, as became a man in a polite court, from the beauty, the propriety, the convenience of pursuing them. Vice and corruption are attacked by Juvenal in a style which denotes, he fears he shall not be heard without he calls to them in their own language, with a barefaced mention of the villanies and obscenities of his contemporaries.

This accidental talk of these two great men carries me from my design, which was to tell some coxcombs that run about this town with the name of smart satirical fellows, that they are by no means qualified for the characters they pretend to, of being severe upon other men ; for they want good-nature. There is no foundation in them for arriving at what they aim at ; and they may as well pretend to flatter and rally agreeably, without being good-natured.

There is a certain impartiality necessary to make what a man says bear any weight with those he speaks to. This quality, with respect to men's errors and vices, is never seen but in good-natured men. They have ever such a frankness of mind, and benevolence to all men, that they cannot receive impressions of unkindness without mature deliberation ; and writing or speaking ill of a man upon personal considerations, is so irreparable and mean an injury, that no one possessed of this quality is capable of doing it : but in all ages there have been interpreters to authors when living, of the same genius with the commentators into whose hands they fall when dead. I dare say it is impossible for any man of more wit than one of these to take any of the four-and-twenty letters, and form out of them a name to describe the character of a vicious man with greater life, but one of these would immediately cry, " Mr. Such-a-one is meant in that place." But the truth of it is, satirists describe the age, and backbiters assign their descriptions to private men.

In all terms of reproof, when the sentence appears to arise from personal hatred or passion, it is not then made the cause of mankind, but a misunderstanding between two persons. For this reason the representations of a good-natured man bear a pleasantry in them, which shews there is no malignity at heart, and by consequence they are attended to by his hearers or readers, because they are unprejudiced. This deference is only what is due to him ; for no man thoroughly nettled can say a thing general enough, to pass off with the air of an opinion declared, and not a passion gratified. I remember a humorous fellow at Oxford, when he heard any one had spoken ill of him, used to say, " I will not take my revenge of him until I have forgiven him." What he meant by this was, that he would not enter upon this subject until it was grown as indifferent to him as any other : and I have, by this rule, seen him more than once triumph over his adversary with an inimitable spirit and humour ; for he came to the assault against a man full of sore places, and he himself invulnerable.

There is no possibility of succeeding in a satirical way of writing or speaking, except a man throws *himself* quite out of the question. It is great vanity to think any one will attend to a thing, because it is your quarrel. You must make your satire the concern of society in general, if you would have it regarded. When it is so, the good nature of a man of wit, will prompt him to many brisk and disdainful sentiments and replies, to which all the malice in the world will not be able to repartee.

THE RING OF GYGES.

No. 243.   SATURDAY, October 28, 1710.   [Addison.]

Infert se septus nebulâ, mirabile dictu !
Per medios, miscètque viris, neque cernitur ulli.
VIRG. Æn. i. 443.

Conceal'd in clouds, prodigious to relate !
He mix'd, unmark'd, among the busy throng,
—— and pass'd unseen along.

I HAVE somewhere made mention of Gyges's ring ; and intimated to my reader, that it was at present in my possession, though I have not since made any use of it.   The tradition concerning this ring is very romantic, and taken notice of both by Plato and Tully, who each of them make an admirable use of it for the advancement of morality.   This Gyges was the master shepherd to king Candaules.   As he was wandering over the plains of Lydia, he saw a great chasm in the earth and had the curiosity to enter it.   After having pretty far descended into it, he found the statue of a horse in brass, with doors in the sides of it.   Upon opening them, he found the body of a dead man, bigger than ordinary, with a ring upon his finger, which he took off, and put it upon his own.   The virtues of it were much greater than he at first imagined ; for, upon his going into the assembly of shepherds, he observed, that he was invisible when he turned the stone of the ring within the palm of his hand, and visible when he turned it towards his company.   Had Plato and Cicero been as well versed in the occult sciences as I am, they would have found a great deal of mystic learning in this tradition : but it is impossible for an adept to be understood by one who is not an adept.

As for myself, I have, with much study and application, arrived at this great secret of making myself invisible, and by that means conveying myself where I please ; or, to speak in Rosicrucian lore, I have entered into the clefts of the earth, discovered the brazen horse, and robbed the dead giant of his ring.   The tradition says farther of Gyges, that by the means

K F

of this ring he gained admission into the most retired parts of the court, and made such use of those opportunities, that he at length became king of Lydia. For my own part, I, who have always rather endeavoured to improve my mind than my fortune, have turned this ring to no other advantage, than to get a thorough insight into the ways of men, and to make such observations upon the errors of others as may be useful to the public, whatever effect they may have upon myself.

About a week ago, not being able to sleep, I got up, and put on my magical ring ; and, with a thought, transported myself into a chamber where I saw a light. I found it inhabited by a celebrated beauty, though she is of that species of women which we call a slattern. Her head-dress and one of her shoes lay upon a chair, her petticoat in one corner of the room, and her girdle, that had a copy of verses made upon it but the day before, with her thread stockings, in the middle of the floor. I was so foolishly officious, that I could not forbear gathering up her cloaths together, to lay them upon the chair that stood by her bed-side ; when, to my great surprise, after a little muttering, she cried out, "What do you do? Let my petticoat alone." I was startled at first, but soon found that she was in a dream ; being one of those who, to use Shakespeare's expression, "are too loose of thought," that they utter in their sleep every thing that passes in their imagination. I left the apartment of this female rake, and went into her neighbour's, where there lay a male coquette. He had a bottle of salts hanging over his head, and upon the table by his bed-side Suckling's poems, with a little heap of black patches on it. His snuff-box was within reach on a chair : but while I was admiring the disposition which he made of the several parts of his dress, his slumber seemed interrupted by a pang that was accompanied by a sudden oath, as he turned himself over hastily in his bed. I did not care for seeing him in his nocturnal pains, and left the room.

I was no sooner got into another bed-chamber, but I heard very harsh words uttered in a smooth uniform tone. I was amazed to hear so great a volubility in reproach, and thought it too coherent to be spoken by one asleep : but, upon looking nearer, I saw the head-dress of the person who spoke, which shewed her to be a female, with a man lying by her side broad awake, and as quiet as a lamb.   I could not but admire his exemplary patience, and discovered by his whole behaviour, that he was then lying under the discipline of a curtain-lecture.

I was entertained in many other places with this kind of nocturnal eloquence ; but observed, that most of those whom I found awake, were kept so either by envy or by love.   Some of these were fighting, and others cursing, in soliloquy ; some hugged their pillows. and others gnashed their teeth.

The covetous I likewise found to be very wakeful people.   I happened to come into a room where one of them lay sick. His physician and his wife were in close whisper near his bed-side.   I overheard the doctor say to the poor gentlewoman, " he cannot possibly live until five in the morning." She received it like the mistress of a family, prepared for all events. At the same instant in came a servant-maid, who said, " Madam, the undertaker is below, according to your order." The words were scarce out of her mouth, when the sick man cried out with a feeble voice, " Pray, doctor, how went Bank-stock to-day at 'Change ? "   This melancholy subject made me too serious for diverting myself farther this way.   As I was going home, I saw a light in a garret, and entering into it, heard a voice crying, ' and, hand, stand, band, fanned, tanned." I concluded him by this, and the furniture of his room, to be a lunatic ; but, upon listening a little longer, perceived it was a poet, writing an heroic upon the ensuing peace.*

It was now towards morning, an hour when spirits, witches, and conjurers, are obliged to retire to their own apartments, and, feeling the influence of it, I was hastening home, when I saw a man had got half way into a neighbour's house.   I immediately called to him, and turning my ring, appeared in my proper person.   There is something magisterial in the

---

* The person alluded to here was perhaps Thomas Tickell, who lived at this time under Addison's roof, and is supposed to have been mentioned before, under the name of Tom Spindle.

aspect of the Bickerstaffs, which made him run away in confusion.

As I took a turn or two in my own lodging, I was thinking that, old as I was, I need not go to bed alone, but that it was in my power to marry the finest lady in this kingdom, if I would wed her with this ring. For what a figure would she that should have it make at a visit, with so perfect a knowledge as this would give her of all the scandal in the town? But, instead of endeavouring to dispose of myself and it in matrimony, I resolved to lend it to my loving friend, the author of the " Atalantis, " * to furnish a new " Secret History of Secret Memoirs.

BRIDGET HOWD'YE.

No. 245. THURSDAY, November 2, 1710. [Steele.]

The lady hereafter-mentioned, having come to me in very great haste, and paid me much above the usual fee, as a cunning-man, to find her stolen goods, and also having approved my late discourse of advertisements obliged me to draw up this, and insert it in the body of my paper.

ADVERTISEMENT.

Whereas Bridget Howd'ye, late servant to the lady Fardingale, a short, thick, lively, hard-favoured wench of about twenty-nine years of age, her eyes small and bleared, and nose very broad at bottom, and turning up at the end, her mouth wide, and lips of an unusual thickness, two teeth out before, the rest black and uneven, the tip of her left ear being of a mouse colour, her voice loud and shrill, quick of speech, and something of a Welsh accent, withdrew herself on Wednesday last from her ladyship's dwelling-house, and, with the help of her consorts, carried off the following goods of her said lady,

---

* Mrs. De la Riviere Manley.

viz. a thick wadded callico wrapper, a musk-coloured velvet mantle lined with squirrel skins, eight night-shifts, four pair of silk stockings curiously darned, six pair of laced shoes, new and old, with the heels of half two inches higher than their fellows ; a quilted petticoat of the largest size, and one of canvas and whale-bone hoops ; three pair of stays, bolstered below the left shoulder, two pair of hips of the newest fashion, six round-about aprons with pockets, and four striped muslin night-rails very little frayed ; a silver pot for coffee or chocolate, the lid much bruised ; a broad brimmed flat silver plate for sugar with Rhenish wine * ; a silver ladle for plumb-porridge ; a silver cheese-toaster with three tongues, an ebony handle, and silvering at the end ; a silver posnet to butter eggs ; one caudle and two cordial-water cups, two cocoa-cups, and an ostrich's egg, with rims and feet of silver, a marrow-spoon with a scoop at the other end, a silver orange-strainer, eight sweet-meat spoons made with forks at the end, an agate-handle knife and fork in a sheath, a silver tongue-scraper, a silver tobacco-box, with a tulip graved on the top ; and a Bible bound in shagreen, with gilt leaves and clasps, never opened but once.   Also a small cabinet, with six drawers inlaid with red tortoise-shell, and brass gilt ornaments at the four corners, in which were two leather forehead-cloaths, three pair of oiled dog-skin gloves, seven cakes of superfine Spanish wool, half-a-dozen of Portugal dishes, and a quire of paper from thence ; two pair of bran-new plumpers, four black-lead combs, three pair of fashionable eye-brows, two sets of ivory teeth, little the worse for wearing, and one pair of box for common use ; Adam and Eve in bugle-work, without fig-leaves, upon canvas, curi-ously wrought with her ladyship's own hand ; several filli-grane curiosities ; a crotchet of one hundred and twenty-two diamonds, set strong and deep in silver, with a rump-jewel after the same fashion ; bracelets of braided hair, pomander and seed-pearl ; a large old purple velvet purse embroidered, and shutting with a spring, containing two pictures in minia-

---

* This was the wine denoted by the name of Sack.   It was so called from its being imported in sacks, or borachios, and it was used with sugar.

ture, the features visible ; a broad thick gold ring with a hand-in-hand engraved upon it, and within this poesy, " While life does last, I'll hold thee fast ; " another set round with small rubies and sparks, six wanting ; another of Turkey stone, cracked through the middle ; an Elizabeth and four Jacobus's, one guinea, the first of the coin, an angel with a hole bored through, a broken half of a Spanish piece of gold, a crown-piece with the breeches, an old nine-pence bent both ways by Lilly the almanack maker for luck at langteraloo, and twelve of the shells called blackmoor's teeth ; one small amber box with apoplectic balsam, and one silver gilt of a larger size for cashu and carraway comfits, to be taken at long sermons, the lid enamelled, representing a Cupid fishing for hearts, with a piece of gold on his hook ; over his head this rhyme, " Only with gold, You me shall hold." In the lower drawer was a large new gold repeating watch made by a Frenchman ; a gold chain, and all the proper appurtenances hung upon steel swivels, to wit, lockets with the hair of dead and living lovers, seals with arms, emblems and devices cut in cornelian, agate, and onyx, with cupids, hearts, darts, altars, flames, rocks, pickaxes, roses, thorns, and sun-flowers; as also variety of in-genious French mottos ; together with gold etuys for quills, scissars, needles, thimbles, and a spunge dipped in Hungary water, left but the night before by a young lady going upon a frolic *incog.* There was also a bundles of letters, dated between the years one thousand six hundred and seventy and one thousand six hundred and eighty two, most of them signed Philander, the rest Strephon, Amyntas, Corydon, and Adonis ; together with a collection of receipts to make pastes for the hands, pomatums, lip-salves, white-pots, beautifying cream, water of talc * and frog spawn water; decoctions for clearing the complexion, and an approved medicine to procure abor-tion.

Whoever can discover the aforesaid goods, so that they

---

* Water of talc was in repute as a cosmetic among the ladies of Ben Jonson's age. It had its name from curing a malady incident to sheep, which was so called.

may be had again, shall have fifty guineas for the whole, or proportionable for any part.

N.B. Her ladyship is pleased to promise ten pounds for the packet of letters over and above, or five for Philander's only, being her first love. " My lady bestows those of Strephon to the finder, being so written, that they may serve to any woman who reads them."

P.S. As I am a patron of persons who have no other friend to apply to, I cannot suppress the following complaint :

" SIR,

" I am a blackmoor boy, and have, by my lady's order, been christened by the chaplain. The good man has gone farther with me, and told me a great deal of good news ; as, that I am as good as my lady herself as I am a Christian, and many other things : but for all this, the parrot, who came over with me from our country, is as much esteemed by her as I am. Besides this, the shock-dog has a collar that cost almost as much as mine. I desire also to know, whether now I am a Christian, I am obliged to dress like a Turk, and wear a turban. I am, sir,

" Your most humble servant,
POMPEY. *

* Blackamoor boys were at this date in much request as pages to ladies of fashion. They were generally named Pompey, and wore a silver collar round their neck.

ADVICE TO A NORTHERN LASS.

No. 247.   TUESDAY, November 7, 1710.   [Steele.]

Edepol, næ nos æquè sumus omnes invisæ viris
Propter paucas, quæ omnes faciunt dignæ ut videamur malo.
                                    Ter. Hecyr. II. iii. 1.

How unjustly
Do husbands stretch their censure to all wives
For the offences of a few, whose vices
Reflect dishonour on the rest !

By Mrs. Jenny Distaff, Half-sister to Mr. Bickerstaff.

My brother having written the above piece of Latin,
desired me to take care of the rest of the ensuing paper.
Towards this he bid me answer the following letter, and said,
nothing I could write properly on the subject of it would be
disagreeable to the motto. It is the cause of my sex, and I
therefore enter upon it with great alacrity. The epistle is
literally thus :

 "Mr. Bickerstaff, *Edenburgh, Oct.* 23.

   " I presume to lay before you an affair of mine, and
begs you'le be very sinceir in giving me your judgment and
advice in this matter, which is as follows :

"A very agreeable young gentleman, who is endowed with
all the good qualities that can make a man complete, has
this long time maid love to me in the most passionat manner
that was posable. He has left nothing unsaid to make me
believe his affections real ; and, in his letters, expressed himself so hansomly and so tenderly, that I had all the reason
imaginable to believe him sincere. In short, he positively
has promised me he would marry me : but I find all he said
nothing ; for when the question was put to him, he would
not ; but still would continue my humble servant, and would
go on at the ould rate, repeating the assurences of his fidelity,
and at the same time has none in him. He now writs to me

in the same endearing style he ust to do, would have me spake to no man but himself. His estate is in his own hand, his father being dead. My fortune at my own disposal, mine being also dead, and to the full answers his estate. Pray, sir, be ingeinous, and tell me cordially, if you dout think I shall do myself an injury if I keep company, or a corospondance any longer with this gentleman. I hope you will faver an honest North-Britain, as I am, with your advice in this amour; for I am resolved just to follow your directions. Sir, you will do me a sensable pleasure, and very great honour, if you will please to insirt this poor scrole, with your answer to it, in your Tatler. Pray fail not to give me your answer; for on it depends the happiness of

" Disconsolat ALMEIRA."

" MADAM,

" I have frequently read over your letter, and am of opinion, that, as lamentable as it is, it is the most common of any evil that attends our sex. I am very much troubled for the tenderness you express towards your lover, but rejoice at the same time that you can so far surmount your inclination for him, as to resolve to dismiss him when you have my brother's opinion for it. His sense of the matter he desired me to communicate to you. Oh Almeira! the common failing of our sex is to value the merit of our lovers rather from the grace of their address, than the sincerity of their hearts. He has expressed himself so handsomely ! Can you say that, after you have reason to doubt his truth ? It is a melancholy thing, that in this circumstance of love, which is the most important of all others in female life, we women who are, they say, always weak, are still weakest. The true way of valuing a man, is to consider his reputation among the men. For want of this necessary rule towards our conduct, when it is too late, we find ourselves married to the outcasts of that sex ; and it is generally from being disagreeable among men, that fellows endeavour to make themselves pleasing to us. The little accomplishments of coming into a room with a good

air, and telling, while they are with us, what we cannot hear
among ourselves, usually make up the whole of a woman's
man's merit. But if we, when we began to reflect upon our
lovers, in the first place, considered what figures they make in
the camp, at the bar, on the exchange, in their country, or at
court, we should behold them in quite another view than at
present.

"Were we to behave ourselves according to this rule, we
should not have the just imputation of favouring the silliest
of mortals, to the great scandal of the wisest, who value our
favour as it advances their pleasure, not their reputation. In
a word, madam, if you would judge aright in love, you must
look upon it as in a case of friendship. Were this gentleman
treating with you for any thing but yourself, when you had
consented to his offer, if he fell off, you would call him a cheat
and an impostor. There is, therefore, nothing left for you to
do but to despise him, and yourself for doing it with regret.

I am, Madam, &c."

I have heard it often argued in conversation, that this evil
practice is owing to the perverted taste of the wits in the last
generation. A libertine on the throne could very easily make
the language and the fashion turn his own way. Hence it
is that woman is treated as a mistress, and not a wife. It is
from the writings of those times, and the traditional accounts
of the debauches of their men of pleasure, that the coxcombs
now-a-days take upon them, forsooth, to be false swains, and
perjured lovers. Methinks I feel all the woman rise in me,
when I reflect upon the nauseous rogues that pretend to
deceive us. Wretches that can never have it in their power
to over-reach any thing living but their mistresses! In the
name of goodness, if we are designed by nature as suitable
companions to the other sex, why are we not treated accordingly? If we have merit, as some allow, why is it not as
base in men to injure, as one another? If we are the
insignificants that others call us, where is the triumph in
deceiving us? But when I look at the bottom of this disaster,

and recollect the many of my acquaintance whom I have known in the same condition with the "Northern Lass" that occasions this discourse, I must own I have ever found the perfidiousness of men has been generally owing to ourselves, and we have contributed to our own deceit. The truth is, we do not conduct ourselves, as we are courted, but as we are inclined. When we let our imaginations take this un-bridled swing, it is not he that acts best is most lovely, but he that is most lovely acts best. When our humble servants make their addresses, we do not keep ourselves enough dis-engaged to be judges of their merit ; and we seldom give our judgment of our lover, until we have lost our judgment for him.

While Clarinda was passionately attended and addressed to by Strephon, who is a man of sense and knowledge in the world, and Cassio, who has a plentiful fortune, and an excel-lent understanding, she fell in love with Damon at a ball. From that moment, she that was before the most reasonable creature of all my acquaintance, cannot hear Strephon speak, but it is something "so out of the way of ladies' conversation :" and Cassio has never since opened his mouth before us, but she whispers me, "How seldom do riches and sense go together!" The issue of all this is, that for the love of Damon, who has neither experience, understanding, nor wealth, she despises those advantages in the other two which she finds wanting in her lover ; or else thinks he has them for no other reason but because he is her lover. This, and many other instances, may be given in this town ; but I hope thus much may suffice to prevent the growth of such evils at Edinburgh.

ADVENTURES OF A SHILLING.

No. 249. SATURDAY, November 11, 1710. [Addison.]

Per varios casus, per tot discrimina rerum,
Tendimus.——   Virg. Æn. i. 208.

Through various hazards, and events, we move.

I WAS last night visited by a friend of mine, who has an inexhaustible fund of discourse, and never fails to entertain his company with a variety of thoughts and hints that are altogether new and uncommon. Whether it were in complaisance to my way of living, or his real opinion, he advanced the following paradox : that it required much greater talents to fill up and become a retired life than a life of business. Upon this occasion he rallied very agreeably the busy men of the age, who only value themselves for being in motion, and passing through a series of trifling and insignificant actions. In the heat of his discourse, seeing a piece of money lying on my table, " I defy," says he, " any of these active persons to produce half the adventures that this twelve-penny piece has been engaged in, were it possible for him to give us an account of his life."

My friend's talk made so odd an impression upon my mind, that soon after I was a-bed I fell insensibly into an unaccountable reverie, that had neither moral nor design in it, and cannot be so properly called a dream as a delirium.

Methought the shilling that lay upon the table reared itself upon its edge, and, turning the face towards me, opened its mouth, and in a soft silver sound, gave me the following account of his life and adventures :

"I was born," says he, "on the side of a mountain, near a little village of Peru, and made a voyage to England in an ingot under the convoy of sir Francis Drake. I was, soon after my arrival, taken out of my Indian habit, refined, naturalized, and put into the British mode, with the face of queen Elizabeth on one side, and the arms of the country on the other. Being thus equipped, I found in me a wonderful inclination to ramble, and visit all the parts of the new world into which I was brought. The people very much favoured my natural disposition, and shifted me so fast from hand to hand, that, before I was five years old, I had travelled into almost every corner of the nation. But in the beginning of my sixth year, to my unspeakable grief, I fell into the hands of a miserable old fellow, who clapped me into an iron chest, where I found five hundred more of my own quality who lay under the same confinement. The only relief we had, was to be taken out and counted over in the fresh air every morning and evening. After an imprisonment of several years, we heard somebody knocking at our chest, and breaking it open with an hammer. This we found was the old man's heir, who, as his father lay dying, was so good as to come to our release. He separated us that very day. What was the fate of my companions I know not : as for myself, I was sent to the apothecary's shop for a pint of sack. The apothecary gave me to an herb-woman, the herb-woman to a butcher, the butcher to a brewer, and the brewer to his wife, who made a present of me to a nonconformist preacher. After this manner I made my way merrily through the world ; for, as I told you before, we shillings love nothing so much as travelling. I sometimes fetched in a shoulder of mutton, sometimes a play-book, and often had the satisfaction to treat a templer at a twelve-penny ordinary, or carry him with three friends to Westminster-hall.

" In the midst of this pleasant progress which I made from place to place, I was arrested by a superstitious old woman, who shut me up in a greasy purse, in pursuance of a foolish saying, 'that while she kept a queen Elizabeth's shilling about her, she would never be without money.' I continued here a close prisoner for many months, until at last I was exchanged for eight-and-forty farthings.

" I thus rambled from pocket to pocket until the beginning of the civil wars, when, to my shame be it spoken, I was employed in raising soldiers against the king : for, being of a very tempting breadth, a serjeant made use of me to inveigle country fellows, and lift them into the service of the Parliament.

"As soon as he had made one man sure, his way was, to oblige him to take a shilling of a more homely figure, and then practice the same trick upon another. Thus I continued doing great mischief to the crown, until my officer chancing one morning to walk abroad earlier than ordinary, sacrificed me to his pleasures, and made use of me to seduce a milk-maid. This wench bent me, and gave me to her sweetheart, applying more properly than she intended the usual form of, 'to my love and from my love.' This ungenerous gallant marrying her within a few days after, pawned me for a dram of brandy; and drinking me out next day, I was beaten flat with an hammer, and again set a-running.

"After many adventures, which it would be tedious to relate, I was sent to a young spendthrift, in company with the will of his deceased father. The young fellow, who I found was very extravagant, gave great demonstrations of joy at receiving the will; but opening it, he found himself disinherited, and cut off from the possession of a fair estate by virtue of my being made a present to him. This put him into such a passion, that, after having taken me in his hand, and cursed me, he squirred me away from him as far as he could fling me. I chanced to light in an unfrequented place under a dead wall, where I lay undiscovered and useless during the usurpation of Oliver Cromwell.

"About a year after the King's return, a poor cavalier, that was walking there about dinner-time, fortunately cast his eye upon me, and, to the great joy of us both, carried me to a cook's shop, where he dined upon me, and drank the King's health. When I came again into the world, I found that I had been happier in my retirement than I thought, having probably by that means escaped wearing a monstrous pair of breeches.*

"Being now of great credit and antiquity, I was rather looked

* The two shields on Oliver's Shilling, vulgarly called Breeches, somewhat resemble the vast trunk hose with which, and a monstrous ruff, James I. went out hunting.

upon as a medal than an ordinary coin ; for which reason a
gamester laid hold of me, and converted me to a counter,
having got together some dozens of us for that use.   We led a
melancholy life in his possession, being busy at those hours
wherein current coin is at rest, and partaking the fate of our
master ; being in a few moments valued at a crown, a pound, or
sixpence, according to the situation in which the fortune of the
cards placed us.   I had at length the good luck to see my
master break, by which means I was again sent abroad under
my primitive denomination of a shilling.

" I shall pass over many other accidents of less moment, and
hasten to that fatal catastrophe when I fell into the hands of
an artist, who conveyed me under ground, and, with an unmerciful pair of sheers, cut off my titles, clipped my brims,
retrenched my shape, rubbed me to my inmost ring ; and, in
short, so spoiled and pillaged me, that he did not leave me
worth a groat.   You may think what confusion I was in to see
myself thus curtailed and disfigured.   I should have been
ashamed to have shewn my head, had not all my old acquaintance been reduced to the same shameful figure, excepting some
few that were punched through the belly.   In the midst of
this general calamity, when every body thought our misfortune
irretrievable, and our case desperate, we were thrown into the
furnace together, and, as it often happens with cities rising out
of a fire, appeared with greater beauty and lustre than we
could ever boast of before.   What has happened to me since
this change of sex which you now see, I shall take some other
opportunity to relate.   In the mean time, I shall only repeat
two adventures, as being very extraordinary, and neither of
them having ever happened to me above once in my life.   The
first was, my being in a poet's pocket, who was so taken with the
brightness and novelty of my appearance, that it gave occasion
to the finest burlesque poem in the British language, entituled,
from me, ' The Splendid Shilling.' *   The second adventure,
which I must not omit, happened to me in the year 1703, when

* By John Philips, a poet of considerable eminence.

I was given away in charity to a blind man ; but indeed this was by mistake, the person who gave me having thrown me heedlessly into the hat * among a pennyworth of farthings."

ESTABLISHMENT OF THE COURT OF HONOUR.

No. 250. TUESDAY, November 14, 1710. [Addison.]

Scis enim justum geminâ suspenaere lance
Ancipitis libræ? PERS. Sat. iv. 10.

Know'st thou, with equal hand, to hold the scale !

I LAST winter erected a court of justice for the correcting of several enormities in dress and behaviour, which are not cognizable in any other courts of this realm. The vintner's case, which I there tried, is still fresh in every man's memory. That of the petticoat gave also a general satisfaction : not to mention the more important points of the cane and perspective ; in which, if I did not give judgments and decrees according to the strictest rules of equity and justice, I can safely say, I acted according to the best of my understanding. But as for the proceedings of that court, I shall refer my reader to an account of them, written by my secretary; which is now in the press, and will shortly be published under the title of Lillie's " Reports."

As I last year presided over a court of justice, it is my intention this year to set myself at the head of a court of honour. There is no court of this nature any where at present, except in France ; where, according to the best of my intelligence, it consists of such only as are marshals of that kingdom. I am likewise informed, that there is not one of that honourable board at present, who has not been driven out of the field by

---

* The hat and this Shilling were, it seems, nearly co-eval ; for Granger says, that " the first English portrait he remembered to have seen with a hat, was one of a Mr. Brightman, in the reign of queen Elizabeth."

the duke of Marlborough : but whether this be only an accidental or a necessary qualification, I must confess, I am not
able to determine.

As for the court of honour of which I am here speaking, I
intend to sit myself in it as president, with several men of
honour on my right-hand, and women of virtue on my left, as
my assistants. The first place on the bench I have given to
an old Tangereen captain with a wooden leg. The second is a
gentleman of a long twisted periwig without a curl in it, a
muff with very little hair upon it, and a threadbare coat with
new buttons ; being a person of great worth, and second
brother to a man of quality. The third is a gentleman-usher,
extremely well read in romances, and grandson to one of the
greatest wits in Germany, who was some time master of the
ceremonies to the duke of Wolfembuttle.

As for those who sit farther on my right-hand, as it is usual
in public courts,* they are such as will fill up the number of
faces upon the bench, and serve rather for ornament than use.

The chief upon my left-hand are—

An old maiden lady, that preserves some of the best blood of
England in her veins.

A Welsh woman of a little stature, but high spirit.

An old prude, that has censured every marriage for these
thirty years, and is lately wedded to a young rake.

Having thus furnished my bench, I shall establish corres-
pondences with the horse-guards, and the veterans of Chelsea
College ; the former to furnish me with twelve men of honour
as often as I shall have occasion for a grand jury ; and the
latter, with as many good men and true, for a petty jury.

As for the women of virtue, it will not be difficult for me to
find them about midnight at crimp and basset.

Having given this public notice of my court, I must farther
add, that I intend to open it on this day sevennight, being
Monday the twentieth instant ; and do hereby invite all such
as have suffered injuries and affronts, that are not to be re-

* This alludes to the Masters in Chancery, who sat on the Bench with the
Lord Chancellor.

F F

dressed by the common laws of this land, whether they be
short bows, cold salutations, supercilious looks, unreturned
smiles, distant behaviour, or forced familiarity ; as also all
such as have been aggrieved by any ambiguous expression,
accidental justle, or unkind repartee ; likewise all such as have
been defrauded of their right to the wall, tricked out of the
upper end of the table, or have been suffered to place themselves, in their own wrong, on the back-seat of the coach.
These, and all of these, I do, as I above said, invite to bring
in their several cases and complaints, in which they shall be
relieved with all imaginable expedition.

I am very sensible, that the office I have now taken upon
me will engage me in the disquisition of many weighty points,
that daily perplex the youth of the British nation ; and, therefore, I have already discussed several of them for my future
use : as, " how far a man may brandish his cane in telling a
story, without insulting his hearer ; " " what degree of contradiction amounts to the lie ; " " how a man shall resent
another's staring and cocking a hat in his face ; " " if asking
pardon is an atonement for treading upon one's toes ; "
" whether a man may put up with a box on the ear, received
from a stranger in the dark ; " or, " whether a man of honour
may take a blow of his wife ; " with several other subtilties of
the like nature.

For my direction in the duties of my office, I have furnished
myself with a certain astrological pair of scales, which I have
contrived for this purpose. In one of them I lay the injuries,
in the other the reparations. The first are represented by
little weights made of a metal resembling iron, and the other
of gold. These are not only lighter than the weights made
use of in avoirdupois, but also such as are used in Troy weight.
The heaviest of those that represent the injuries amount but to
a scruple ; and decrease by so many sub-divisions, that there
are several imperceptible weights which cannot be seen without
the help of a very fine microscope. I might acquaint my
reader, that these scales were made under the influence of the
sun when he was in Libra, and describe many signatures on the

weights both of injury and reparation : but as this would look rather to proceed from an ostentation of my own art, than any care for the public, I shall pass it over in silence.

THE GRAPE IN MODERATION.

No. 252. SATURDAY, November 18, 1710. [Steele.]

> Narratur et prisci Catonis
> Sæpe mero caluisse virtus.   Hor. 3 Od. xxi. 11.
>
> Of old
> Cato's virtue, we are told,
> Often with a bumper glow'd,
> And with social raptures flow'd.

The following letter, and several others to the same purpose, accuse me of a rigour of which I am far from being guilty, to wit, the disallowing the cheerful use of wine.

" From my Country-house, October 25.

" Mr. Bickerstaff,

" Your discourse against drinking, in Tuesday's Tatler, I like well enough in the main ; but, in my humble opinion, you are become too rigid, where you say to this effect : Were there only this single consideration, that we are the less masters of ourselves if we drink the least proportion beyond the exigence of thirst. I hope no one drinks wine to allay this appetite. This seems to be designed for a loftier indulgence of nature ; for it were hard to suppose that the Author of Nature, who imposed upon her her necessities and pains, does not allow her her proper pleasures ; and we may reckon among the latter the moderate use of the grape. Though I am as much against excess, or whatever approaches it, as yourself ; yet I conceive one may safely go farther than the bounds you there prescribe, not only without forfeiting the title of being one's own master, but also to possess it in a much greater

degree.   If a man's expressing himself upon any subject with
more life and vivacity, more variety of ideas, more copiously,
more fluently, and more to the purpose, argues it; he thinks
clearer, speaks more ready, and with greater choice of comprehensive and significant terms.   I have the good fortune now
to be intimate with a gentleman* remarkable for this temper,
who has an inexhaustible source of wit to entertain the curious,
the grave, the humorous, and the *frolic*.   He can transform
himself into different shapes, and adapt himself to every
company; yet in a coffee-house, or in the ordinary course of
affairs, he appears rather dull than sprightly.   You can seldom
get him to the tavern; but when once he is arrived to his
pint, and begins to look about and like his company, you
admire a thousand things in him, which before lay buried.
Then you discover the brightness of his mind, and the strength
of his judgment, accompanied with the most graceful mirth.
In a word, by this enlivening aid, he is whatever is polite,
instructive, and diverting.   What makes him still more agreeable is, that he tells a story, serious or comical, with as much
delicacy of humour as Cervantes himself.   And for all this, at
other times, even after a long knowledge of him, you shall
scarce discern in this incomparable person a whit more, than
what might be expected from one of a common capacity.
Doubtless, there are men of great parts that are guilty of downright bashfulness, that, by a strange hesitation and reluctance
to speak, murder the finest and most elegant thoughts, and
render the most lively conceptions flat and heavy.

   " In this case, a certain quantity of my white or red cordial,
which you will, is an easy, but an infallible remedy.   It
awakens the judgment, quickens the memory, ripens the
understanding, disperses melancholy, cheers the heart; in a
word, restores the whole man to himself and his friends, without the least pain or indisposition to the patient.   To be taken
only in the evening, in a reasonable quantity, before going to
bed.   Note; My bottles are sealed with three flower-de-luces

* Addison.   Until wine had made pleasant summer in his veins, Addison
was too shy in giving full rein to his brilliant powers of conversation.

and a bunch of grapes. Beware of counterfeits. I am your most humble servant, &c."

Whatever has been said against the use of wine, upon the supposition that it enfeebles the mind, and renders it unfit for the duties of life, bears forcibly to the advantage of that delicious juice in cases where it only heightens conversation, and brings to light agreeable talents, which otherwise would have lain concealed under the oppression of an unjust modesty. I must acknowledge I have seen many of the temper mentioned by this correspondent, and own wine may very allowably be used, in a degree above the supply of mere necessity, by such as labour under melancholy, or are tongue-tied by modesty. It is certainly a very agreeable change, when we see a glass raise a lifeless conversation into all the pleasures of wit and good-humour. But when Caska adds to his natural impudence the fluster of a bottle, that which fools called fire when he was sober, all men abhor as outrage when he is drunk. Thus he, that in the morning was only saucy, is in the evening tumultuous. It makes one sick to hear one of these fellows say, "they love a friend and a bottle." Noisy mirth has something too rustic in it to be considered without terror by men of politeness : but while the discourse improves in a well-chosen company, from the addition of spirits which flow from moderate cups, it must be acknowledged, that leisure time cannot be more agreeably, or perhaps more usefully, employed, than at such meetings. There is a certain prudence in this, and all other circumstances, which makes right or wrong in the conduct of ordinary life.

CHARGE OF THE CENSOR.

No. 253.   TUESDAY, November 21, 1710.

[Addison and Steele.]

—— Pietate gravem ac meritis si fortè virum quem
Conspexere, silent, arrectisque auribus astant.
Virg. Æn. i. 115.

If then some grave and pious man appear,
They hush their noise, and lend a listening ear.

Extract of the Journal of the Court of Honour, 1710.

Die Lunæ, vicesimo Novembris, horâ nonâ antemeridianâ.

THE court being *sat*, an oath prepared by the Censor was administered to the assistants on his right-hand, who were all sworn upon their honour. The women on his left-hand took the same oath upon their reputation. Twelve gentlemen of the horse-guards were impanelled, having unanimously chosen Mr. Alexander Truncheon, who is their right-hand man in the troop, for their foreman in the jury. Mr. Truncheon immediately drew his sword, and, holding it with the point towards his own body, presented it to the Censor. Mr. Bickerstaff received it; and, after having surveyed the breadth of the blade, and sharpness of the point, with more than ordinary attention, returned it to the foreman in a very graceful manner. The rest of the jury, upon the delivery of the sword to their foreman, drew all of them together as one man, and saluted the bench with such an air, as signified the most resigned submission to those who commanded them, and the greatest magnanimity to execute what they should command.

Mr. Bickerstaff, after having received the compliments on his right-hand, cast his eye upon the left, where the whole female jury paid their respects by a low courtesy, and by laying their hands upon their mouths. Their forewoman was a professed Platonist, that had spent much of her time in exhorting the sex to set a just value upon their persons, and to make the men know themselves.

There followed a profound silence, when at length, after some recollection, the Censor, who continued hitherto un-covered, put on his hat with great dignity ; and, after having composed the brims of it in a manner suitable to the gravity of his character, he gave the following charge ; which was received with silence and attention, that being the only applause which he admits of, or is ever given in his presence.

"The nature of my office, and the solemnity of this occa-sion, requiring that I should open my first session with a speech, I shall cast what I have to say under two principal heads.

"Under the first, I shall endeavour to shew the necessity and usefulness of this new-erected court ; and, under the second, I shall give a word of advice and instruction to every constituent part of it.

"As for the first, it is well observed by Phædrus, an heathen poet :

> Nisi utile est quod facimus, frustra est gloria.

which is the same, ladies, as if I should say, it would be of no reputation for me to be president of a court which is of no benefit to the publick. Now the advantages that may arise to the *weal public* from this institution will more plainly appear, if we consider what it suffers for the want of it. Are not our streets daily filled with wild pieces of justice, and random penalties ? Are not crimes undetermined, and reparations disproportioned ? How often have we seen the lie punished by death, and the liar himself deciding his own cause ! nay, not only acting the judge, but the executioner ! Have we not known a box on the ear more severely accounted for than manslaughter ? In these extra-judicial proceedings of man-kind, an unmannerly jest is frequently as capital as a premedi-tated murder.

"But the most pernicious circumstance in this case is, that

the man who suffers the injury must put himself upon the same foot of danger with him that gave it, before he can have his just revenge ; so that the punishment is altogether accidental, and may fall as well upon the innocent as the guilty.

" I shall only mention a case which happens frequently among the more polite nations of the world, and which I the rather mention, because both sexes are concerned in it, and which therefore you gentlemen, and you ladies of the jury, will the rather take notice of ; I mean, that great and known case of cuckoldom. Supposing the person who has suffered insults in his dearer and better half ; supposing, I say, this person should resent the injuries done to his tender wife ; what is the reparation he may expect ? Why, to be used worse than his poor lady, run through the body, and left breathless upon the bed of honour. What then, will you on my right-hand say, must the man do that is affronted ? Must our sides be elbowed, our shins broken ? Must the wall, or perhaps our mistress, be taken from us ? May a man knit his forehead into a frown, toss up his arm, or pish at what we say, and must the villain live after it ? Is there no redress for injured honour ? Yes, gentlemen, that is the design of the judicature we have here established.

" A court of conscience, we very well know, was first instituted for the determining of several points of property, that were too little and trivial for the cognizance of higher courts of justice. In the same manner, our court of honour is appointed for the examination of several niceties and punctilios, that do not pass for wrongs in the eye of our common laws. But notwithstanding no legislators of any nation have taken into consideration these little circumstances, they are such as often lead to crimes big enough for their inspection, though they come before them too late for their redress.

" Besides, I appeal to you, ladies (*here Mr. Bickerstaff turned to his left-hand*), if these are not the little stings and thorns in life, that make it more uneasy than its most substantial evils ? Confess ingenuously, did you never lose a morning's devotions because you could not offer them up from the highest place of the pew ? Have you not been in pain, even at a ball, because another has been taken out to dance before you ? Do you love any of your friends so much as those that are below you ? Or, have you any favourites that walk on your right-hand ? You have answered me in your looks ; I ask no more.

"I come now to the second part of my discourse, which obliges me to address myself in particular to the respective members of the court, in which I shall be very brief.

"As for you gentlemen and ladies, my assistants and grand juries, I have made choice of you on my right-hand, because I know you very jealous of your honour ; and you on my left, because I know you very much concerned for the reputation of others ; for which reason I expect great exactness and impartiality in your verdicts and judgments.

"I must, in the next place, address myself to you, gentlemen of the council : you all know that I have not chosen you for your knowledge in the litigious parts of the law; but because you have all of you formerly fought duels, of which I have reason to think you have repented, as being now settled in the peaceable state of benchers. My advice to you is, only that in your pleadings you will be short and expressive. To which end, you are to banish out of your discourses all synonymous terms, and unnecessary multiplication of verbs and nouns. I do moreover forbid you the use of the words *also* and *likewise;* and must farther declare, that if I catch any one among you, upon any pretence whatsoever, using the particle *or*, I shall instantly order him to be stripped of his gown, and thrown over the bar."

FROZEN WORDS.

No. 254. THURSDAY, November 23, 1710. [Addison.]

Splendidè mendax ——.   Hor. 2 Od. iii. 35.
Gloriously false ——.

There are no books which I more delight in than in travels, especially those that describe remote countries, and give the writer an opportunity of shewing his parts without incurring any danger of being examined or contradicted. Among all the authors of this kind, our renowned countryman, Sir John Mandevile has distinguished himself, by the copiousness of his invention, and the greatness of his genius. The second to Sir John I take to have been, Ferdinand Mendez Pinto, a person of infinite adventure, and unbounded imagination. One reads the voyages of these two great wits, with as much astonishment as the travels of Ulysses in Homer, or of the Red-Cross Knight in Spenser. All is enchanted ground, and fairy-land.

I have got into my hands, by great chance, several *manuscripts* of these two eminent authors, which are filled with greater wonders than any of those they have communicated to the public ; and indeed, were they not so well attested, they would appear altogether improbable. I am apt to think the ingenious authors did not publish them with the rest of their works, lest they should pass for fictions and fables : a caution not unnecessary, when the reputation of their veracity was not yet established in the world. But as this reason has now no farther weight, I shall make the publick a present of these curious pieces, at such times as I shall find myself unprovided with other subjects.

The present paper I intend to fill with an *extract* from Sir John's Journal, in which that learned and worthy knight gives an account of the freezing and thawing of several short speeches, which he made in the territories of *Nova Zembla*. I need not inform my reader, that the author of Hudibras alludes to this strange quality in that cold climate, when, speaking of abstracted notions cloathed in a visible shape, he adds that apt similè,

> " Like words congeal'd in northern air."

Not to keep my reader any longer in suspense, the relation put into modern language, is as follows :

" We were separated by a storm in the latitude of *seventy-three,* insomuch, that only the ship which I was in, with a Dutch and French vessel, got safe into a creek of *Nova Zembla.* We landed, in order to refit our vessels, and store ourselves with provisions. The crew of each vessel made themselves a cabin of turf and wood, at some distance from each other, to fence themselves against the inclemencies of the weather, which was severe beyond imagination. We soon observed, that in talking to one another we lost several of our words, and could not hear one another at above two yards distance, and that too when we sat very near the fire. After much perplexity, I found that our words froze in the air, before they could reach the ears of the persons to whom they were spoken. I was soon confirmed in this conjecture, when, upon the increase of the cold, the whole company grew dumb, or rather deaf ; for every man was sensible, as we afterwards found, that he spoke as well as ever ; but the sounds no sooner took air than they were condensed and lost. It was now a miserable spectacle to see us nodding and gaping at one another, every man talking, and no man heard. One might observe a seaman that could hail a ship at a league's distance, beckoning with his hand, straining his lungs, and tearing his throat ; but all in vain :

> " —— Nec vox nec verba sequuntur.
>
> " Nor voice, nor words ensued.

" We continued here three weeks in this dismal plight. At length, upon a turn of wind, the air about us began to thaw. Our cabin was immediately filled with a dry clattering sound, which I afterwards found to be the crackling of consonants that broke above our heads, and were often mixed with a gentle hissing, which I imputed to the letter *s,* that occurs so frequently in the English tongue. I soon after felt a breeze of whispers rushing by my ear ; for those, being of a soft and gentle substance, immediately liquefied in the warm wind that blew across our cabin. These were soon followed by syllables and short words, and at length by entire sentences, that melted sooner or later, as they were more or less congealed ; so that we now heard every thing that had been *spoken* during the whole three weeks that we had been *silent*, if I may use that expression. It was now very early in the morning, and yet, to my surprise, I heard somebody say, ' Sir John, it is midnight, and time for the ship's crew to go to-bed.' This I knew to be the pilot's voice ; and, upon recollecting myself, I concluded that he had spoken these words to me some days before, though I could not hear them until the present thaw. My reader will easily imagine how the whole crew was amazed to hear every man talking, and see no man opening his mouth. In the midst of this great surprise we were all in, we heard a volley of oaths and curses, lasting for a long while, and uttered in a very hoarse voice, which I knew belonged to the boat-swain, who was a very choleric fellow, and had taken his opportunity of cursing and swearing at me, when he thought I could not hear him ; for I had several times given him the strappado on that account, as I did not fail to repeat it for these his pious soliloquies, when I got him on ship-board.

" I must not omit the names of several beauties in Wapping, which were heard every now and then, in the midst of a long sigh that accompanied them ; as, ' Dear Kate ! ' ' Pretty Mrs. Peggy ! ' ' When shall I see my Sue again ! ' This betrayed several amours which had been concealed until that time, and furnished us with a great deal of mirth in our return to England.

" When this confusion of voices was pretty well over, though I was afraid to offer at speaking, as fearing I should not be heard, I proposed a visit to the Dutch cabin, which lay about a mile farther up in the country. My crew were extremely rejoiced to find they had again recovered their hearing ; though every man uttered his voice with the same apprehensions that I had done,

> " —— Et timidè verba intermissa retentat.
> " And try'd his tongue, his silence softly broke.

" At about half-a-mile's distance from our cabin we heard the groanings of a bear, which at first startled us ; but, upon enquiry, we were informed by some of our company, that he was dead, and now lay in salt, having been killed upon that very spot about a fortnight before, in the time of the frost. Not far from the same place, we were likewise entertained with some posthumous snarls, and barkings of a fox.

" We at length arrived at the little Dutch settlement ; and, upon entering the room, found it filled with sighs that smelt of brandy, and several other unsavoury sounds, that were altogether inarticulate.   My valet, who was an Irishman, fell into so great a rage at what he heard, that he drew his sword ; but not knowing where to lay the blame, he put it up again. We were stunned with these confused noises, but did not hear a single word until about half-an-hour after ; which I ascribed to the harsh and obdurate sounds of that language, which wanted more time than ours to melt, and become audible.

"After having here met with a very hearty welcome, we went to the cabin of the French, who, to make amends for their three weeks silence, were talking and disputing with greater rapidity and confusion than I ever heard in an assembly, even of that nation.   Their language, as I found, upon the first giving of the weather, fell asunder and dissolved. I was here convinced of an error, into which I had before fallen ; for I fancied, that for the freezing of the sound, it was necessary for it to be wrapped up, and, as it were, preserved in breath : but I found my mistake when I heard the sound of a kit playing a minuet over our heads.   I asked the occasion of it ; upon which one of the company told me that it would play there above a week longer ; ' for,' says he, ' finding ourselves bereft of speech, we prevailed upon one of the company, who had his musical instrument about him, to play to us from morning to night ; all which time was employed in dancing in order to dissipate our chagrin, *& tuer le temps*."

Here Sir John gives very good philosophical reason, why the kit could not be heard during the frost ; but, as they are something prolix, I pass them over in silence, and shall only observe, that the honourable author seems, by his quotations, to have been well versed in the antient poets, which perhaps raised his fancy above the ordinary pitch of historians, and very much contributed to the embellishment of his writings.

THE CHAPLAIN.

No. 255. SATURDAY, NOVEMBER 25, 1710. [ADDISON.]

—— Nec te tua plurima, Pantheu,
Labentem pietas, nec Apollinis insula texit.
VIRG. Æn. ii. 429.

Comes course the last, the red'ning doctor now
Slides off reluctant, with his meaning bow ;
Drers, letters, wit, and merit, plead in vain,
For bear he must, indignity and pain.

" To the CENSOR of Great Britain.

" SIR,

" I AM at present under very great difficulties, which it is not in the power of any one, besides yourself, to redress. Whether or no you shall think it a proper case to come before your court of honour, I cannot tell ; but thus it is. I am chaplain to an honourable family, very regular at the hours of devotion, and, I hope, of an unblameable life ; but for not offering to rise at the second course, I found my patron and his lady very sullen and out of humour, though at first I did not know the reason of it. At length, when I happened to help myself to a jelly, the lady of the house, otherwise a devout woman, told me, that it did not become a man of my cloth to delight in such frivolous food : but as I still continued to sit out the last course, I was yesterday informed by the butler that his lordship had no farther occasion for my service. All which is humbly submitted to your consideration by, sir, your most humble servant, &c."

The case of this gentleman deserves pity; especially if he loves sweetmeats, to which, if I may guess by his letter, he is no enemy. In the meantime, I have often wondered at the indecency of discharging the holiest man from the table as soon as the most delicious parts of the entertainment are served up, and could never conceive a reason for so absurd a custom. Is it because a liquorish palate, or a sweet tooth, as they call it, is not consistent with the sanctity of his character? This is but a trifling pretence. No man, of the most rigid virtue, gives offence by any excesses in plum-pudding or plum-porridge, and that because they are *the first parts of the dinner*. Is there anything that tends to incitation in sweetmeats more than in ordinary dishes? Certainly not. Sugar-plums are a very innocent diet, and conserves of a much colder nature than your common pickles. I have sometimes thought that the ceremony of the chaplain's flying away from the desert was typical and figurative, to mark out to the company how they ought to retire from all the luscious baits of temptation, and deny their appetites the gratifications that are most pleasing to them; or, at least, to signify that we ought to stint ourselves in our most lawful satisfactions, and not make our pleasure, but our support, the end of eating. But most certainly, if such a lesson of temperance had been necessary at a table, our clergy would have recommended it to all the lay masters of families, and not have disturbed other men's tables with such unseasonable examples of abstinence. The original, therefore, of this barbarous custom, I take to have been merely accidental. The chaplain retired, out of pure complaisance, to make room for the removal of the dishes, or possibly for the ranging of the desert. This by degrees grew into a duty, until at length, as the fashion improved, the good man found himself cut off from the third part of the entertainment; and, if the arrogance of the patron goes on, it is not impossible but, in the next generation, he may see himself reduced to the tythe, or tenth dish of the table ; a sufficient caution not to part with any privilege we are once possessed of.   It was usual for the priest in old times to feast upon the sacrifice, nay the honey-cake, while the hungry laity looked upon him with great devotion ; or, as the late lord Rochester describes it in a very lively manner,

> And while the priest did eat, the people star'd.

At present the custom is inverted; the laity feast, while the priest stands by as an humble spectator. This necessarily puts a good man upon making great ravages on all the dishes that stand near him ; and distinguishing himself by voracious- ness of appetite, as knowing that his time is short. I would fain ask these stiff-necked patrons, whether they would not take it ill of a chaplain, that in his grace after meat should return thanks for the whole entertainment with an exception to the desert ?   And yet I cannot but think that, in such a proceeding, he would but deal with them as they deserved. What would a Roman Catholic priest think, who is always helped first, and placed next the ladies, should he see a clergy- man giving his company the slip at the first appearance of the tarts or sweetmeats ?   Would not he believe that he had the same antipathy to a candied orange, or a piece of puff-paste, as some have to a Cheshire cheese, or a breast of mutton ?   Yet, to so ridiculous a height is this foolish custom grown, that even the Christmas pie, which in its very nature is a kind of consecrated cake, and a badge of distinction, is often forbidden to the Druid of the family. Strange ! that a surloin of beef, whether boiled or roasted, when entire, is exposed to his utmost depredations and incisions ; but if minced into small pieces, and tossed up with plums and sugar, changes its property, and, forsooth, is meat for his master.

In this case I know not which to censure, the patron, or the chaplain, the insolence of power, or the abjectness of depend- ence. For my own part, I have often blushed to see a gentleman, whom I knew to have much more wit and learning than myself, and who was bred up with me at the university upon the same foot of a liberal education, treated in such an ignominious manner, and sunk beneath those of his own rank, by reason of that character which ought to bring him honour. This deters men of generous minds from placing themselves in such a station of life, and by that means frequently excludes persons of quality from the improving and agreeable conversation of a learned and obsequious friend.

Mr. Oldham* lets us know, that he was affrighted from the thought of such an employment, by the scandalous sort of treatment which often accompanies it :

> Some think themselves exalted to the sky,
> If they light in some noble family :
> Diet, an horse, and thirty pounds a-year,
> Besides th' advantage of his lordship's ear,
> The credit of the business, and the state,
> Are things that in a youngster's sense sound great.
> Little the unexperienc'd wretch does know
> What slavery he oft must undergo,
> Who, though in silken scarf and cassock drest,
> Wears but a gayer livery at best.
> When dinner calls, the implement must wait
> With holy words to consecrate the meat,
> But hold it for a favour seldom known,
> If he be deign'd the honour to sit down.
> Soon as the tarts appear ; " Sir Crape, withdraw,
> Those dainties are not for a spiritual maw.
> Observe your distance, and be sure to stand
> Hard by the cistern with your cap in hand :
> There for diversion you may pick your teeth,
> Till the kind voider comes for your relief."
> Let others, who such meannesses can brook,
> Strike countenance to every great man's look ;
> I rate my freedom higher.

This author's raillery is the raillery of a friend, and does not turn the sacred order into ridicule ; but is a just censure on such persons as take advantage, from the necessities of a man of merit, to impose on him hardships that are by no means suitable to the dignity of his profession.

* In "A Satire, addressed to a Friend that is about to leave the University," &c.   Oldham's Works, 1703, 8vo, p. 391.

PROCEEDINGS OF THE COURT OF HONOUR.

No. 256. TUESDAY, November 28, 1710. [Addison.]*

—— Nostrûm est tantas componere lites.
VIRG. Ecl. iii. 108.
'Tis ours such warm contentions to decide.

PETER PLUMB of London, merchant, was indicted by the honourable Mr. Thomas Gules, of Gule Hall in the county of Salop, for that the said Peter Plumb did, in Lombard Street, London, between the hours of two and three in the afternoon, meet the said Mr. Thomas Gules, and, after a short salutation, put on his hat, value *five-pence*, while the honourable Mr. Gules stood bare-headed for the space of two seconds. It was further urged against the criminal, that, during his discourse with the prosecutor, he feloniously stole the wall of him, having clapped his back against it in such a manner, that it was impossible for Mr. Gules to recover it again at his taking leave of him. The prosecutor alleged, that he was the cadet of a very ancient family ; and that, according to the principles of all the younger brothers of the said family, he had never sullied himself with business, but had chosen rather to starve, like a man of honour, than do anything beneath his quality. He produced several witnesses, that he had never employed himself beyond the twisting of a whip, or the making of a pair of nut-crackers, in which he only worked for his diversion, in order to make a present now and then to his friends. The prisoner being asked, " what he could say for himself," cast several reflections upon the honourable Mr. Gules ; as, " that he was not worth a groat ; that nobody in the city would trust him for a halfpenny ; that he owed him money, which he had promised to pay him several times, but never kept his word ; and, in short, that he was an idle beggarly fellow, and of no

* In these Papers on the "Court of Honour," Addison was assisted by Steele.

use to the public." This sort of language was very severely reprimanded by the Censor, who told the criminal, "that he spoke in contempt of the Court, and that he should be proceeded against for contumacy, if he did not change his style." The prisoner, therefore, desired to be heard by his counsel, who urged for his defence, "that he put on his hat through ignorance, and took the wall by accident." They likewise produced several witnesses, that he made several motions with his hat in his hand, which are generally understood as an invitation to the person we talk with to be covered ; and that, the gentleman not taking the hint, he was forced to put on his hat, as being troubled with a cold. There was likewise an Irishman, who deposed, "that he had heard him cough three-and-twenty times that morning." And as for the wall, it was alleged, that he had taken it inadvertently, to save himself from a shower of rain which was then falling. The Censor, having consulted the men of honour who sat at his right hand on the bench, found they were all of opinion, that the defence made by the prisoner's counsel did rather aggravate than extenuate his crime ; that the motions and intimations of the hat were a token of superiority in conversation, and therefore not to be used by the criminal to a man of the prosecutor's quality, who was likewise vested with a double title to the wall at the time of their conversation, both as it was the upper hand, and as it was a shelter from the weather. The evidence being very full and clear, the jury, without going out of court, declared their opinion unanimously, by the mouth of their foreman, "that the prosecutor was bound in honour to make the sun shine through the criminal," or, as they afterwards explained themselves, " to whip him through the lungs."

The Censor, knitting his brows into a frown, and looking very sternly upon the jury, after a little pause, gave them to know, "that this court was erected for the finding out of penalties suitable to offences, and to restrain the outrages of private justice ; and that he expected they should moderate their verdict." The jury therefore retired, and being willing to comply with the advices of the Censor, after an hour's conversation, delivered their opinion as follows :

" That, in consideration this was Peter Plumb's first offence, and that there did not appear any malice prepense in it, as also that he lived in good reputation among his neighbours, and that his taking the wall was only *se defendendo*, the prosecutor should let him escape with life, and content himself with the slitting of his nose, and the cutting off both his ears." Mr. Bickerstaff, smiling upon the court, told them, " that he thought the punishment, even under its present mitigation, too severe ; and that such penalties might be of ill consequence in a trading nation." He therefore pronounced sentence against the criminal in the following manner : " that his hat, which was the instrument of offence, should be forfeited to the court ; that the criminal should go to the warehouse from whence he came, and thence, as occasion should require, proceed to the Exchange, or Garraway's coffee-house, in what manner he pleased ; but that neither he, nor any of the family of the Plumbs, should hereafter appear in the streets of London out of their coaches, that so the foot-way might be left open and undisturbed for their betters."

Dathan, a peddling Jew, and T. R——, a Welshman, were indicted by the keeper of an alehouse in Westminster, for breaking the peace and two earthen mugs, in a dispute about the antiquity of their families, to the great detriment of the house, and disturbance of the whole neighbourhood. Dathan said for himself, that he was provoked to it by the Welshman, who pretended that the Welsh were an antienter people than the Jews ; " whereas," says he, " I can shew by this genealogy in my hand, that I am the son of Mesheck, that was the son of Naboth, that was the son of Shalem, that was the son of ——." The Welshman here interrupted him, and told him, "that he could produce *shennalogy* as well as himself ; " for " that he was John ap Rice, ap Shenken, ap Shones." He then turned himself to the Censor, and told him in the same broken accent, and with much warmth, " that the Jew would needs uphold, that king Cadwallader was younger than Issachar." Mr.

Bickerstaff seemed very much inclined to give sentence against Dathan, as being a Jew ; but finding reasons, by some expressions which the Welshman let fall in asserting the antiquity of his family, to suspect that the said Welshman was a *Præ-Adamite*, he suffered the jury to go out, without any previous admonition. After some time they returned, and gave their verdict, "that it appearing the persons at the bar did neither of them wear a sword, and that consequently they had no right to quarrel upon a point of honour ; to prevent such frivolous appeals for the future, they should both of them be tossed in the same blanket, and there adjust the superiority as they could agree on it between themselves." The Censor confirmed the verdict.

Richard Newman was indicted by major Punto, for having used the words, "perhaps it may be so," in a dispute with the said Major. The Major urged, "that the word *perhaps* was questioning his veracity, and that it was an indirect manner of giving him the lie." Richard Newman had nothing more to say for himself, than that "he intended no such thing ; " and threw himself upon the mercy of the court. The jury brought in their verdict special.

Mr. Bickerstaff stood up, and, after having cast his eyes over the whole assembly, hemmed thrice. He then acquainted them, "that he had laid down a rule to himself, which he was resolved never to depart from, and which, as he conceived, would very much conduce to the shortening the business of the court : I mean," says he, " never to allow of the lie being given by construction, implication, or induction, but by the sole use of the word itself." He then proceeded to shew the great mischiefs that had arisen to the English nation from that pernicious monosyllable ; that it had bred the most fatal quarrels between the dearest friends ; that it had frequently thinned the guards, and made great havock in the army ; that it had sometimes weakened the city trained-bands ; and, in a word, had destroyed many of the bravest men in the isle of Great-Britain. For the prevention of which evils for the future, he instructed the jury to present the word itself as a nuisance in the English tongue; and farther promised them, that he would, upon such their preferment, publish an edict of the court, for the entire banishment and exclusion of it out of the discourses and conversation of all civil societies.

VARIETY OF SECTS.

No. 257.   THURSDAY, November 30, 1710.

[Addison and Steele.]

In nova fert animus mutatas dicere formas
Corpora : Dii, cœptis, nam vos mutâstis et illas,
Aspirate meis !——   Ovid, Met. i. 1.

Of bodies chang'd to various forms I sing ;
Ye gods, from whom these miracles did spring,
Assist me in this arduous task !——

Every nation is distinguished by productions that are peculiar to it. Great Britain is particularly fruitful in religions, that shoot up and flourish in this climate more than any other. We are so famous abroad for our great variety of sects and opinions, that an ingenious friend of mine, who is lately returned from his travels, assures me, there is a show at this time carried up and down in Germany, which represents all the religions of Great-Britain in wax-work. Notwithstanding that the pliancy of the matter, in which the images are wrought, makes it capable of being moulded into all shapes and figures ; my friend tells me, that he did not think it possible for it to be twisted and tortured into so many screwed faces, and wry features, as appeared in several of the figures that composed the show. I was indeed so pleased with the design of the German artist, that I begged my friend to give me an account of it in all its particulars, which he did after the following manner :

"I have often," says he, "been present at a show of elephants, camels, dromedaries, and other strange creatures, but I never saw so great an assembly of spectators as were met together at the opening of this great piece of wax-work. We were all placed in a large hall, according to the price that we had paid for our seats. The curtain that hung before the show was made by a master of tapestry, who had woven it in the figure of a monstrous Hydra that had several heads, which brandished out their tongues, and seemed to hiss at each other. Some of these heads were large and entire; and where any of them had been lopped away, there sprouted up several in the room of them; insomuch, that for one head cut off, a man might see ten, twenty, or an hundred, of a smaller size, creeping thro' the wound. In short, the whole picture was nothing but confusion and blood-shed. On a sudden," says my friend, "I was startled with a flourish of many musical instruments that I had never heard before, which was followed by a short tune, if it might be so called, wholly made up of jars and discords. Among the rest, there was an organ, a bagpipe, a groaning board, a stentorophontic trumpet, with several wind instruments of a most disagreeable sound, which I do not so much as know the names of. After a short flourish, the curtain was drawn up, and we were presented with the most extraordinary assembly of figures that ever entered into a man's imagination. The design of the workman was so well expressed in the dumb show before us, that it was not hard for an Englishman to comprehend the meaning of it.

" The principal figures were placed in a row, consisting of seven persons. The middle figure, which immediately attracted the eyes of the whole company, and was much bigger than the rest, was formed like a matron, dressed in the habit of an elderly woman of quality in queen Elizabeth's days. The most remarkable parts of her dress were, the beaver with the steeple crown, the scarf that was darker than sable, and the lawn apron that was whiter than ermin. Her gown was of the richest black velvet; and just upon her heart studded with large diamonds of an inestimable value, disposed in the form of a cross. She bore an inexpressible cheerfulness and dignity in her aspect; and, though she seemed in years, approached

with so much spirit and vivacity, as gave her at the same time
an air of old age and immortality. I found my heart touched
with so much love and reverence at the sight of her, that the
tears ran down my face as I looked upon her ; and still the
more I looked upon her, the more my heart was melted with
the sentiments of filial tenderness and duty. I discovered
every moment something so charming in this figure, that I
could scarce take my eyes off it. On its right-hand there sat
the figure of a woman so covered with ornaments, that her
face, her body, and her hands, were almost entirely hid
under them. The little you could see of her face was painted ;
and, what I thought very odd, had something in it like
artificial wrinkles ; but I was the less surprized at it, when I
saw upon her forehead an old-fashioned tower of gray-hairs.
Her head-dress rose very high by three several stories or
degrees ; her garments had a thousand colours in them, and
were embroidered with crosses in gold, silver, and silk. She
had nothing on, so much as a glove or a slipper, which was
not marked with this figure ; nay, so superstitiously fond did
she appear of it, that she sat cross-legged. I was quickly sick
of this tawdry composition of ribbands, silks, and jewels, and
therefore cast my eye on a dame which was just the reverse of
it. I need not tell my reader, that the lady before described
was Popery, or that she I am going to describe is Presbytery.
She sat on the left hand of the venerable matron, and so much
resembled her in the features of her countenance, that she
seemed her sister; but at the same time that one observed a
likeness in her beauty, one could not but take notice, that
there was something in it sickly and splenetic. Her face had
enough to discover the relation ; but it was drawn up into a
peevish figure, soured with discontent, and overcast with
melancholy. She seemed offended at the matron for the shape
of her hat, as too much resembling the triple coronet of the
person who sat by her. One might see likewise, that she dis-
sented from the white apron and the cross ; for which reasons
she had made herself a plain homely dowdy, and turned her
face towards the sectaries that sat on her left-hand, as being

afraid of looking upon the matron, lest she should see the harlot by her.

"On the right hand of Popery sat Judaism, represented by an old man embroidered with phylacteries, and distinguished by many typical figures, which I had not skill enough to unriddle. He was placed among the rubbish of a temple; but, instead of weeping over it, which I should have expected from him, he was counting out a bag of money upon the ruins of it.

"On his right hand was Deism, or Natural Religion. This was a figure of a half-naked awkward country wench, who, with proper ornaments and education, would have made an agreeable and beautiful appearance; but for want of those advantages, was such a spectacle as a man would blush to look upon.

"I have now," continued my friend, "given you an account of those who were placed on the right hand of the matron, and who, according to the order in which they sat, were Deism, Judaism, and Popery. On the left-hand, as I told you, appeared Presbytery. The next to her was a figure which somewhat puzzled me: it was that of a man looking, with horror in his eyes, upon a silver bason filled with water. Observing something in his countenance that looked like lunacy, I fancied at first, that he was to express that kind of distraction which the physicians call the *hydro-phobia*; but considering what the intention of the show was, I immediately recollected myself, and concluded it to be Anabaptism.

"The next figure was a man that sat under a most profound composure of mind. He wore a hat whose brims were exactly parallel with the horizon. His garment had neither sleeve nor skirt, nor so much as a superfluous button. What they called his cravat, was a little piece of white linen quilled with great exactness, and hanging below his chin about two inches. Seeing a book in his hand, I asked our artist what it was; who told me it was "The Quaker's Religion;" upon which I desired a sight of it. Upon perusal, I found it to be nothing but a new-fashioned grammar, or an art of abridging

ordinary discourse. The nouns were reduced to a very small
number, as *the Light, Friend, Babylon.* The principal of his
pronouns was *thou* ; and as for *you, ye* and *yours*, I found they
were not looked upon as parts of speech in this grammar. All
the verbs wanted the second person plural ; the participles
ended all in *ing* or *ed*, which were marked with a particular
accent. There were no adverbs besides *nay* and *yea*. The
same thrift was observed in the prepositions. The conjunc-
tions were only *hem !* and *ha !* and the interjections brought
under the three heads of *fighting, sobbing*, and *groaning.*

"There was at the end of the grammar a little nomenclature,
called, ' The Christian Man's Vocabulary,' which gave new
appellations, or, if you will, Christian names, to almost every
thing in life. I replaced the book in the hand of the figure,
not without admiring the simplicity of its garb, speech, and
behaviour.

"Just opposite to this row of religions, there was a statue
dressed in a fool's coat, with a cap of bells upon his head,
laughing and pointing at the figures that stood before him.
This idiot is supposed to say in his heart what David's fool
did some thousands of years ago, and was therefore designed
as a proper representative of those among us, who are
called Atheists and Infidels by others, and Freethinkers by
themselves.

" There are many other groups of figures which I did not
know the meaning of ; but seeing a collection of both sexes
turning their backs upon the company, and laying their heads
very close together, I inquired after their religion, and found
that they called themselves the Philadelphians, or the family
of love.

" In the opposite corner there sat another little congregation
of strange figures, opening their mouths as wide as they could
gape, and distinguished by the title of the Sweet Singers
of Israel.

" I must not omit, that in this assembly of wax there were
several pieces that moved by clock-work, and gave great
satisfaction to the spectators. Behind the matron there stood

one of these figures, and behind Popery another, which, as the artist told us, were each of them the genius of the person they attended. That behind Popery represented Persecution, and the other Moderation. The first of these moved by secret springs towards a great heap of dead bodies, that lay piled upon one another at a considerable distance behind the principal figures. There were written on the foreheads of these dead men several words, as, *Præ-Adamites, Sabbatarians, Camaronians, Muggletonians, Brownists, Independents, Masonites, Camissars,* and the like. At the approach of Persecution, it was so contrived, that, as she held up her bloody flag, the whole assembly of dead men, like those in the " Rehearsal," started up and drew their swords. This was followed by great clashings and noise, when, in the midst of the tumult, the figure of Moderation moved gently towards this new army, which, upon her holding up a paper in her hand, inscribed ' Liberty of Conscience,' immediately fell into a heap of carcasses, remaining in the same quiet posture in which they lay at first."

PROCEEDINGS OF THE COURT OF HONOUR.—Continued.

No. 259. TUESDAY, December 5, 1710. [Addison.]

—— Vexat censura columbas.   Juv. Sat. ii. 63.
Censure acquits the crow, condemns the dove.

Elizabeth Makebate, of the parish of St. Catharine's, spinster, was indicted for surreptitiously taking away the hassock from under the lady Grave-Airs, between the hours of four and five, on Sunday the 26th of November. The prosecutor deposed, " that as she stood up to make a courtesy to a person of quality in a neighbouring pew, the criminal conveyed away the hassock by stealth; insomuch, that the prosecutor was obliged to sit all the while she was at church, or to say her prayers in a posture that did not become a woman of her quality." The prisoner pleaded inadvertency ; and the jury were going to bring it in chance-medley, had not several witnesses been produced against the said Elizabeth Makebate, that she was an old offender, and a woman of a bad reputation. It appeared in particular, that, on the Sunday before, she had detracted from a new petticoat of Mrs. Mary Doelittle, having said, in the hearing of several credible witnesses, "that the said petticoat was scoured," to the great grief and detriment of the said Mary Doelittle. There were likewise many evidences produced against the criminal, that though she never failed to come to Church on Sunday, she was a most notorious sabbath-breaker ; and that she spent her whole time, during divine service, in disparaging other people's cloaths, and whispering to those who sat next her. Upon the whole, she was found guilty of the indictment, and received sentence "to ask pardon of the prosecutor upon her bare knees, without either cushion or hassock under her, in the face of the court."

N.B. As soon as the sentence was executed on the criminal, which was done in open court with the utmost severity, the first lady of the bench on Mr. Bickerstaff's right-hand stood up, and made a motion to the court, " that whereas it was impossible for women of fashion to dress themselves before the church was half done ; and whereas many confusions and inconveniences did arise thereupon ; it might be lawful for them to send a footman in order to keep their places, as was usual in other polite and well-regulated assemblies." The motion was ordered to be entered in the books, and considered at a more convenient time.

Charles Cambrick, linen-draper, in the city of Westminster, was indicted for speaking obscenely to the Lady Penelope Touchwood. It appeared, that the prosecutor and her woman going in a stage-coach from London to Brentford, where they were to be met by the lady's own chariot, the criminal and another of his acquaintance travelled with them in the same coach, at which time the prisoner talked bawdy for the space of three miles and a half. The prosecutor alleged, "that over-against the Old Fox at Knightsbridge he mentioned the word linen; that at the farther end of Kensington he made use of the term smock; and that, before he came to Hammersmith, he talked almost a quarter of an hour upon weddingshifts." The prosecutor's woman confirmed what her lady had said, and added farther that she had never seen her lady in so great a confusion, and in such a taking, as she was during the whole discourse of the criminal. The prisoner had little to say for himself, but, "that he talked only in his own trade, and meant no hurt by what he said." The jury, however, found him guilty, and represented by their forewoman, that such discourses were apt to sully the imagination; and that, by a concatenation of ideas, the word linen implied many things, that were not proper to be stirred up in the mind of a woman who was of the prosecutor's quality, and therefore gave it as their verdict, "that the linendraper should lose his tongue." Mr. Bickerstaff said, he thought the prosecutor's ears were as much to blame as the prisoner's tongue, and therefore gave sentence as follows: "that they should both be placed over-against one another in the midst of the court, there to remain for the space of one quarter of an hour, during which time the linen-draper was to be gagged, and the lady to hold her hands close upon both her ears;" which was executed accordingly.

Edward Callicoat was indicted as an accomplice to Charles Cambrick, for that he the said Edward Callicoat did, by his silence and smiles, seem to approve and abet the said Charles Cambrick in every thing he said. It appeared, that the prisoner was foreman of the shop to the aforesaid Charles Cambrick, and, by his post, obliged to smile at every thing that the other should be pleased to say: upon which he was acquitted.

Josiah Shallow was indicted in the name of Dame Winifred, sole relict of Richard Dainty, esquire, for having said several times in company, and in the hearing of several persons there present, " that he was extremely obliged to the widow Dainty, and that he should never be able sufficiently to express his gratitude." The prosecutor urged, that this might blast her reputation, and that it was in effect a boasting of favours which he had never received. The prisoner seemed to be much astonished at the construction which was put upon his words, and said, "that he meant nothing by them, but that the widow had befriended him a lease, and was very kind to his younger sister." The jury finding him a little weak in his understanding, without going out of the court, brought in their verdict *ignoramus*.

Ursula Goodenough was accused by the Lady Betty Wou'dbe, for having said, that she, the Lady Betty Wou'dbe, was painted. The prisoner brought several persons of good credit to witness to her reputation, and proved, by undeniable evidences, that she was never at the place where the words were said to have been uttered. The Censor, observing the behaviour of the prosecutor, found reason to believe, that she had indicted the prisoner for no other reason, but to make her complexion be taken notice of; which indeed was very fresh and beautiful : he therefore asked the offender, with a very stern voice, how she could presume to spread so groundless a report ? and whether she saw any colours in the Lady Wou'dbe's face that could procure credit by such a falsehood ? "Do you see," says he, " any lilies or roses in her cheeks, any bloom, any probability ? " The prosecutor, not able to bear such language any longer, told him, " that he talked like a blind old fool, and she was ashamed to have entertained any opinion of his wisdom :" but she was put to silence, and sentenced "to wear her mask for five months, and not to presume to shew her face until the town should be empty."

Benjamin Buzzard, esquire, was indicted for having told the Lady Everbloom at a public ball, that she looked very well for a woman of her years. The prisoner not denying the fact, and persisting before the court that he looked upon it as a compliment, the jury brought him in *non compos mentis*.

PROCEEDINGS OF THE COURT OF HONOUR.—Continued.

No. 262. TUESDAY, December 12, 1710. [Addison.]

> Verba togæ sequeris, juncturâ callidus acri,
> Ore teres modico, pallentes radere mores
> Doctus, et ingenuo culpam desigere ludo.
>
> PERS. Sat. v. 14.

> Soft elocution does thy style renown,
> And the sweet accents of the peaceful gown ;
> Gentle or sharp, according to thy choice,
> To laugh at follies, or to lash at vice.

TIMOTHY TREATALL, gentleman, was indicted by several ladies of his sister's acquaintance for a very rude affront offered to them at an entertainment, to which he had invited them on Tuesday the seventh of November last past, between the hours of eight and nine in the evening. The indictment set forth, " that the said Mr. Treatall, upon the serving up of the supper, desired the ladies to take their places according to their different age and seniority ; for that it was the way always at his table to pay respect to years." The indictment added, "that this produced an unspeakable confusion in the company ; for that the ladies, who before had pressed together for a place at the upper end of the table, immediately crowded with the same disorder towards the end that was quite opposite ; that Mrs. Frontley had the insolence to clap herself down at the very lowest place of the table ; that the widow Partlet seated herself on the right-hand of Mrs. Frontley, alleging for her excuse, that no ceremony was to be used at a round table ; that Mrs. Fidget and Mrs. Fescue, disputed above half-an-hour for the same chair, and that the latter would not give up the cause until it was decided by the parish register, which happened to be kept hard by." The indictment farther saith, " that the rest of the company who sat down did it with a reserve to their right, which they were at liberty to assert on another occasion ; and that Mrs. Mary

Pippe, an old maid, was placed by the unanimous vote of the whole company at the upper end of the table, from whence she had the confusion to behold several mothers of families among her inferiors." The criminal alleged in his defence, "that what he had done was to raise mirth, and avoid ceremony ; and that the ladies did not complain of his rudeness until the next morning, having eaten up what he had provided for them with great readiness and alacrity." The Censor, frowning upon him, told him, "that he ought not to discover so much levity in matters of a serious nature ; " and, upon the jury's bringing him in guilty, sentenced him "to treat the whole assembly of ladies over again," and to take care that he did it with the decorum which was due to persons of their quality.

Rebecca Shapely, spinster, was indicted by Mrs. Sarah Smack, for speaking many words reflecting upon her reputation, and the heels of her silk slippers, which the prisoner had maliciously suggested to be two inches higher than they really were. The prosecutor urged, as an aggravation of her guilt, that the prisoner was "herself guilty of the same kind of forgery which she had laid to the prosecutor's charge ; for that she, the said Rebecca Shapely, did always wear a pair of steel boddice, and a false rump." The Censor ordered the slippers to be produced in open court, where the heels were adjudged to be of the statutable size. He then ordered the grand jury to search the criminal, who, after some time spent therein, acquitted her of the bodice, but found her guilty of the rump : upon which she received sentence as is usual in such cases.

William Trippet, esquire, of the Middle Temple, brought his action against the lady Elizabeth Prudely, for having refused him her hand as he offered to lead her to her coach from the opera. The plaintiff set forth, that he had entered himself into the list of those volunteers, who officiate every night behind the boxes as gentlemen-ushers of the play-house : that he had been at a considerable charge in white gloves, periwigs, and snuff-boxes, in order to quality himself for that employment, and in hopes of making his fortune by it. The counsel for the defendant replied, that the plaintiff had given out that he was within a month of wedding their client, and that she had refused her hand to him in ceremony, lest he should interpret it as a promise that she would give it him in marriage. As soon as the pleadings on both sides were finished, the Censor ordered the plaintiff to be cashiered from his office of gentleman-usher to the play-house, since it was too plain that he had undertaken it with an ill design ; and at the same time ordered the defendant either to marry the said plaintiff, or to pay him half-a-crown for the new pair of gloves and coach-hire that he was at the expence of in her service.

The lady Townly brought an action of debt against Mrs. Flambeau, for that the said Mrs. Flambeau had not been to see the lady Townly, and wish her joy, since her marriage with Sir Ralph, notwithstanding she, the said lady Townly, had paid Mrs. Flambeau a visit upon her first coming to town. It was urged in the behalf of the defendant that the plaintiff had never given her any regular notice of her being in town ; that the visit she alledged had been made on Monday, which she knew was a day on which Mrs. Flambeau was always abroad, having set aside that *only* day in the week to mind the affairs of her family : that the servant, who enquired whether she was at home, did not give the visiting knock : that it was not between the hours of five and eight in the evening : that there were *no candles lighted up :* that it was not on Mrs. Flambeau's day : and, in short, that there was not one of the essential points observed that constitute a visit. She farther proved by her porter's book, which was produced in court, that she had paid the lady Townly a visit on the twenty-fourth day of March, just before her leaving the town, in the year seventeen hundred and *nine-ten* for which she was still creditor to the said lady Townly. To this the plaintiff only replied, that she was now under covert, and not liable to any debts contracted when she was a single woman. Mr. Bickerstaff finding the cause to be very intricate, and that several points of honour were likely to arise in it, he deferred giving judgment upon it until the next session day, at which time he ordered the ladies on his left-hand to present to the court a table of all the laws relating to visits.

Winifred Leer brought an action against Richard Sly for having broken a marriage contract, and wedded another woman, after he had engaged himself to marry the said Winifred Leer. She alledged, that he had ogled her twice at an opera, thrice in St. James's church, and once at Powel's puppet-show, at which time he promised her marriage by a side-glance, as her friend could testify that sat by her. Mr. Bickerstaff finding that the defendant had made no farther overture of love or marriage, but by looks and ocular engagement; yet at the same time considering how very apt such impudent seducers are to lead the ladies' hearts astray, ordered the criminal " to stand upon the stage in the Hay-market, between each act of the new opera, there to be exposed to public view as a false ogler."

Upon the rising of the court, Mr. Bickerstaff having taken one of these counterfeits in the very fact, as he was ogling a lady of the grand jury, ordered him to be seized, and prosecuted upon the statute of ogling. He likewise directed the clerk of the court to draw up an edict against these common cheats, that make women believe they are distracted for them, by staring them out of countenance, and often blast a lady's reputation, whom they never spoke to, by saucy looks and distant familiarities.

LATE HOURS.

No. 263.   THURSDAY, December 14, 1710.   [Steele.]

Minimâ contentos nocte Britannos.   Juv. Sat. ii. 161.

Britons contented with the shortest night.

An old friend of mine being lately come to town, I went to see him on Tuesday last about eight o'clock in the evening, with a design to sit with him an hour or two, and talk over old stories ; but, upon enquiry after him, I found he was gone to-bed. The next morning, as soon as I was up and dressed, and had dispatched a little business, I came again to my friend's house about eleven o'clock, with a design to renew my visit ; but, upon asking for him, his servant told me he was just *sat* down to dinner. In short, I found that my old-fashioned friend religiously adhered to the example of his fore-fathers, and observed the same hours that had been kept in the family ever since the Conquest.

It is very plain, that the night was much longer formerly in this island than it is at present. By the night, I mean that portion of time which nature has thrown into darkness, and which the wisdom of mankind had formerly dedicated to rest and silence. This used to begin at eight o'clock in the evening, and conclude at six in the morning. The curfeu, or eight o'clock bell, was the signal throughout the nation for putting out their candles and going to-bed.

Our grandmothers, though they were wont to sit up the last in the family, were all of them fast asleep at the same hours that their daughters are busy at crimp and basset. Modern statesmen are concerting schemes, and engaged in the depth of politics at the time when their forefathers were laid down quietly to rest, and had nothing in their heads but dreams. As we have thus thrown business and pleasure into the hours of rest, and by that means made the natural night but half as long as it should be, we are forced to piece it out with a great part of the morning ; so that near two-thirds of the nation lie fast asleep for several hours in broad daylight. This irregularity is grown so very fashionable at present, that there is scarce a lady of quality in Great Britain that ever saw the sun rise. And, if the humour increases in proportion to what it has done of late years, it is not impossible but our children may hear the bell-man going about the streets at nine o'clock in the morning, and the watch making their rounds until eleven. This unaccountable disposition in mankind to continue awake in the night, and sleep in the sunshine, has made me enquire, whether the same change of inclination has happened to any other animals ?

For this reason, I desired a friend of mine in the country to let me know, whether the lark rises as early as he did formerly ; and whether the cock begins to crow at his usual hour. My friend has answered me, "that his poultry are as regular as ever, and that all the birds and beasts of his neighbourhood keep the same hours that they have observed in the memory of man ; and the same which, in all probability, they have kept for these five thousand years."

If you would see the innovations that have been made among us in this particular, you may only look into the hours of colleges, where they still *dine at eleven*, and *sup at six*, which were doubtless the hours of the whole nation at the time when those places were founded. But at present, the courts of justice are scarce opened in Westminster-hall at the time when William Rufus used to go to dinner in it. All business is driven forward. The land-marks of our fathers, if I may so call them, are removed, and planted farther up into the day ; insomuch, that I am afraid our clergy will be obliged, if they expect full congregations, not to look any more upon ten o'clock in the morning as a canonical hour. In my own memory, the dinner has crept by degrees from *twelve* o'clock to *three*, and where it will fix nobody knows.

I have sometimes thought to draw up a memorial in the behalf of supper against dinner, setting forth, that the said dinner has made several encroachments upon the said supper, and entered very far upon his frontiers ; that he has banished him out of several families, and in all has driven him from his head quarters, and forced him to make his retreat into the hours of midnight : and, in short, that he is now in danger of being entirely confounded and lost in a breakfast. Those who have read Lucian, and seen the complaints of the letter *T* against *S*, upon account of many injuries and usurpations of the same nature, will not, I believe, think such a memorial forced and unnatural. If dinner has been thus postponed, or, if you please, kept back from time to time, you may be sure that it has been in compliance with the other business of the day, and that supper has still observed a proportionable distance. There is a venerable proverb, which we have all of us heard in our infancy, of "putting the children to-bed, and laying the goose to the fire." This was one of the jocular sayings of our forefathers, but may be properly used in the literal sense at present. Who would not wonder at this perverted relish of those who are reckoned the most polite part of mankind, that prefer sea-coals and candles to the sun, and exchange so many cheerful morning hours, for the pleasures of midnight revels and debauches? If a man was only to consult his health, he would choose to live his whole time, if possible, in day-light; and to retire out of the world into silence and sleep, while the raw damps and unwholesome vapours fly abroad, without a sun to disperse, moderate, or controul them. For my own part, I value an hour in the morning as much as common libertines do an hour at midnight. When I find myself awakened into being, and perceive my life renewed within me, and at the same time see the whole face of nature recovered out of the dark uncomfortable state in which it lay for several hours, my heart overflows with such secret sentiments of joy and gratitude, as are a kind of implicit praise to the great author of nature. The mind, in these early seasons of the day, is so refreshed in all its faculties, and borne up with such new supplies of animal spirits, that she finds herself in a state of youth, especially when she is entertained with the breath of flowers, the melody of birds, the dews that hang upon the plants, and all those other sweets of nature that are peculiar to the morning.

It is impossible for a man to have this relish of being, this exquisite taste of life, who does not come into the world before it is in all its noise and hurry; who loses the rising of the sun, the still hours of the day, and, immediately upon his first getting up, plunges himself into the ordinary cares or follies of the world.

JOURNAL OF THE COURT OF HONOUR.
CONTINUED.

No. 265.   TUESDAY, December 19, 1710.   [Addison.]

Arbiter hic igitur factus de lite jocosâ.
OVID. Met. iii. 331.

—— Him therefore they create
The sov'reign umpire of their droll debate.

As soon as the Court was *sat*, the ladies of the bench presented, according to order, a table of all the laws now in force relating to visits and visiting-days, methodically digested under their respective heads, which the Censor ordered to be laid upon the table, and afterwards proceeded upon the business of the day.

Henry Heedless, esquire, was indicted by colonel Touchy of her majesty's trained-bands, upon an action of assault and battery; for that he, the said Mr. Heedless, having espied a feather upon the shoulder of the said colonel, struck it off gently with the end of a walking-staff, value three-pence. It appeared, that the prosecutor did not think himself injured until a few days after the aforesaid blow was given him; but that having ruminated with himself for several days, and conferred upon it with other officers of the militia, he concluded, that he had in effect been cudgelled by Mr. Heedless, and that he ought to resent it accordingly. The counsel for the prosecutor alleged, that the shoulder was the tenderest part in a man of honour; that it had a natural antipathy to a stick; and that every touch of it, with any thing made in the fashion of a cane, was to be interpreted as a wound in that part, and a violation of the person's honour who received it. Mr. Heedless replied, "that what he had done was out of kindness to the prosecutor, as not thinking it proper for him to appear at the head of the trained-bands with a feather upon his shoulder;" and farther added, "that the stick he made use of on this occasion was so very small, that the prosecutor could not have felt it had he broken it on his shoulders." The

Censor hereupon directed the jury to examine into the nature of the staff, for that a great deal would depend upon that particular. Upon which he explained to them the different degrees of offence that might be given by the touch of the crab-tree from that of cane, and by the touch of cane from that of a plain hazle stick. The jury, after a short perusal of the staff, declared their opinion by the mouth of their foreman, " that the substance of the staff was British oak." The Censor then observing that there was some dust on the skirts of the criminal's coat, ordered the prosecutor to beat it off with the aforesaid oaken plant ; " and thus," said the Censor, " I shall decide this cause by the law of retaliation. If Mr. Heedless did the colonel a good office, the colonel will by this means return it in kind ; but if Mr. Heedless should at any time boast that he had cudgelled the colonel, or laid his staff over his shoulders, the colonel might boast, in his turn, that he has brushed Mr. Heedless's jacket, or, to use the phrase of an ingenious author, that he has rubbed him down with an oaken towel."

Benjamin Busy of London, merchant, was indicted by Jasper Tattle, esquire, for having pulled out his watch, and looked upon it thrice, while the said esquire Tattle was giving him an account of the funeral of the said esquire Tattle's first wife. The prisoner alleged in his defence, that he was going to buy stocks at the time when he met the prosecutor ; and that, during the story of the prosecutor, the said stocks rose above two *per cent.* to the great detriment of the prisoner. The prisoner farther brought several witnesses to prove, that the said Jasper Tattle, esquire, was a most notorious story-teller ; that, before he met the prisoner, he had hindered one of the prisoner's acquaintance from the pursuit of his lawful business, with the account of his second marriage ; and that he had detained another by the button of his coat, that very morning until he had heard several witty sayings and contrivances of the prosecutor's eldest son, who was a boy of about five years of age. Upon the whole matter, Mr. Bickerstaff dismissed the accusation as frivolous, and sentenced the prosecutor " to

pay damages to the prisoner, for what the prisoner had lost by
giving him so long and patient a hearing." He farther
reprimanded the prosecutor very severely, and told him, " that
if he proceeded in his usual manner to interrupt the business
of mankind, he would set a fine upon him for every quarter of
an hour's impertinence, and regulate the said fine according as
the time of the person so injured should appear to be more or
less precious."

Sir Paul Swash, knight, was indicted by Peter Double,
gentleman, for not returning the bow which he received of the
said Peter Double, on Wednesday the sixth instant, at the
play-house in the Haymarket. The prisoner denied the
receipt of any such bow, and alleged in his defence, that the
prosecutor would oftentimes look full in his face, but that
when he bowed to the said prosecutor, he would take no
notice of it, or bow to somebody else that sat quite on the
other side of him. He likewise alledged, that several ladies
had complained of the prosecutor, who, after ogling them a
quarter of an hour, upon their making a courtesy to him,
would not return the civility of a bow. The Censor observing
several glances of the prosecutor's eye, and perceiving that
when he talked to the court he looked upon the jury, found
reason to suspect there was a wrong cast in his sight, which,
upon examination, proved true. The Censor therefore ordered
the prisoner, that he might not produce any more confusions
in public assemblies, "never to bow to any body whom he did
not at the same time call to by name."

Oliver Bluff and Benjamin Browbeat were indicted for
going to fight a duel since the erection of "The Court of
Honour." It appeared, that they were both taken up in the
street as they passed by the Court in their way to the fields
behind Montague-house. The criminals would answer
nothing for themselves, but that they were going to execute
a challenge which had been made a week before the "Court
of Honour" was erected. The Censor finding some reason to
suspect, by the sturdiness of their behaviour, that they were
not so very brave as they would have the court believe them,

ordered them both to be searched by the grand jury, who found a breast-plate upon the one, and two quires of paper upon the other. The breast-plate was immediately ordered to be hung upon a peg over Mr. Bickerstaff's tribunal, and the paper to be laid upon the table for the use of his clerk. He then ordered the criminals to button up their bosoms, and, if they pleased, proceed to their duel.. Upon which they both went very quietly out of the court, and retired to their respective lodgings.

ON GROWING OLD.

No. 266.   THURSDAY, December 21, 1710.   [Steele.]

Rideat et pulset lasciva decentiùs ætas.
Hor. 2 Ep. ii. ult.

Let youth, more decent in their follies, scoff
The nauseous scene, and hiss thee reeling off.

It would be a good appendix to " The art of Living and Dying," if any one would write " The Art of growing Old," and teach men to resign their pretensions to the pleasures and gallantries of youth, in proportion to the alteration they find in themselves by the approach of age and infirmities. The infirmities of this stage of life would be much fewer, if we did not affect those which attend the more vigorous and active part of our days ; but instead of studying to be wiser, or being contented with our present follies, the ambition of many of us is also to be the same sort of fools we formerly have been. I have often argued, as I am a professed lover of women, that our sex grows old with a much worse grace than the other does ; and have ever been of opinion, that there are more well-pleased old women, than old men. I thought it a good reason for this, that the ambition of the fair sex being confined to advantageous marriages, or shining in the eyes of men, their parts were over sooner, and consequently the errors in the performance of them.

The conversation of this evening has not convinced me of the contrary ; for one or two fop-women shall not make a balance for the crowds of coxcombs among ourselves, diversified according to the different pursuits of pleasure and business.

Returning home this evening a little before my usual hour, I scarce had seated myself in my easy chair, stirred the fire, and stroked my cat, but I heard somebody come rumbling up stairs. I saw my door opened, and a human figure advancing towards me, so fantastically put together, that it was some minutes before I discovered it to be my old and intimate friend Sam Trusty. Immediately I rose up, and placed him in my own seat ; a compliment I pay to few. The first thing he uttered was, " Isaac, fetch me a cup of your cherry-brandy before you offer to ask any question." He drank a lusty draught, sat silent for some time, and at last broke out ; " I am come," quoth he, " to insult thee for an old fantastic dotard, as thou art, in ever defending the women. I have this evening visited two widows, who are now in that state I have often heard you call an *after-life ;* I suppose you mean by it, an existence which grows out of past entertainments, and is an untimely delight in the satisfactions which they once set their hearts upon too much to be ever able to relinquish. Have but patience," continued he, " until I give you a succinct account of my ladies, and of this night's adventure. They are much of an age, but very different in their characters. The one of them, with all the advances which years have made upon her, goes on in a certain romantic road of love and friendship which she fell into in her teens ; the other has transferred the amorous passions of her first years to the love of cronies, petts, and favourites, with which she is always surrounded ; but the genius of each of them will best appear by the account of what happened to me at their houses. About five this afternoon, being tired with study, the weather inviting, and time lying a little upon my hands, I resolved at the instigation of my evil genius, to visit them ; their husbands having been our contemporaries. This I thought I could do without much trouble ; for both live in the very next street. I went first to my lady

Camomile; and the butler, who had lived long in the family, and seen me often in his master's time, ushered me very civilly into the parlour, and told me, though my lady had given strict orders to be denied, he was sure I might be admitted, and bid the black boy acquaint his lady, that I was come to wait upon her. In the window lay two letters, one broke open, the other fresh sealed with a wafer : the first directed to the divine Cosmelia, the second to the charming Lucinda ; but both by the indented characters, appeared to have been writ by very unsteady hands. Such uncommon addresses increased my curiosity, and put me upon asking my old friend the butler, if he knew who those persons were ? " Very well," says he, "this is from Mrs. Furbish to my lady, an old school-fellow and a great crony of her ladyship's ; and this the answer." I enquired in what country she lived. " Oh dear !" says he, " but just by, in the neighbourhood. Why, she was here all this morning, and that letter came and was answered within these two hours. They have taken an odd fancy, you must know, to call one another hard names ; but, for all that, they love one another hugely." By this time the boy returned with his lady's humble service to me, desiring I would excuse her ; for she could not possibly see me, nor any body else, for it was opera-night."

"Methinks," says I, "such innocent folly as two old women's courtship to each other, should rather make you merry than put you out of humour." " Peace, good Isaac," says he, " no interruption, I beseech you. I got soon to Mrs. Feeble's, she that was formerly Betty Frisk ; you must needs remember her ; Tom Feeble of Brazen Nose fell in love with her for her fine dancing. Well, Mrs. Ursula, without farther ceremony, carries me directly up to her mistress's chamber, where I found her environed by four of the most mischievous animals that can ever infest a family ; an old shock dog with one eye, a monkey chained to one side of the chimney, a great grey squirrel to the other, and a parrot waddling in the middle of the room. However, for a while, all was in a profound tranquillity. Upon the mantle-tree, for I am a pretty curious

observer, stood a pot of lambetive clectuary, with a stick of
liquorice, and near it a phial of rose-water, and powder of
tutty. Upon the table lay a pipe filled with betony and
colt's foot, a roll of wax-candle, a silver spitting-pot, and a
Seville orange. The lady was placed in a large wicker-chair,
and her feet wrapped up in flannel, supported by cushions ; and
in this attitude, would you believe it, Isaac, was she reading a
romance with spectacles on. The first compliments over, as she
was industriously endeavouring to enter upon conversation, a
violent fit of coughing seized her. This awaked Shock, and in
a trice the whole room was in an uproar ; for the dog barked, the
squirrel squealed, the monkey chattered, the parrot screamed,
and Ursula, to appease them, was more clamorous than all
the rest. You, Isaac, who know how any harsh noise affects
my head, may guess what I suffered from the hideous din of
these discordant sounds. At length all was appeased, and
quiet restored : a chair was drawn for me ; where I was no
sooner seated, but the parrot fixed his horny beak, as sharp as
a pair of sheers, in one of my heels, just above the shoe. I
sprung from the place with an unusual agility, and so, being
within the monkey's reach, he snatches off my new bob-wig,
and throws it upon two apples that were roasting by a sullen
sea-coal fire. I was nimble enough to save it from any farther
damage than singing the foretop. I put it on ; and composing
myself as well as I could, I drew my chair towards the other
side of the chimney. The good lady, as soon as she had recovered breath, employed it in making a thousand apologies,
and, with great eloquence, and a numerous train of words,
lamented my misfortune. In the middle of her harangue, I
felt something scratching near my knee, and feeling what it
should be, found the squirrel had got into my coat-pocket As
I endeavoured to remove him from his burrow, he made his
teeth meet through the fleshy part of my forefinger. This
gave me an unexpressible pain. The Hungary water was
immediately brought to bathe it, and gold-beaters' skin applied
to stop the blood. The lady renewed her excuses ; but being
now out of all patience, I abruptly took my leave, and hobbling

down stairs with heedless haste, I set my foot full in a pail of water, and down we came to the bottom together." Here my friend concluded his narrative, and, with a composed countenance, I began to make him compliments of condolence ; but he started from his chair, and said, "Isaac, you may spare your speeches, I expect no reply. When I told you this, I knew you would laugh at me ; but the next woman that makes me ridiculous shall be a young one."

LORD VERULAM'S PRAYER.

No. 267.   SATURDAY, December 23, 1710.   [Addison.]

Qui genus humanum ingenio superavit, et omnes
Restinxit stellas, exortus uti aërius sol.   Lucr. iii. 1056.

His genius quite obscur'd the brightest ray
Of human thought ; as Sol's effulgent beams,
At morn's approach, extinguish all the stars.

I have heard that it is a rule among the conventuals of several orders in the Romish church to shut themselves up at a certain time of the year, not only from the world in general, but from the members of their own fraternity ; and to pass away several days by themselves in settling accounts between their Maker and their own souls, in canceling unrepented crimes, and renewing their contracts of obedience for the future. Such stated times for particular acts of devotion, or the exercise of certain religious duties, have been enjoined in all civil governments, whatever deity they worshipped, or whatever religion they professed. That which may be done at all times, is often totally neglected and forgotten, unless fixed and determined to some time more than another ; and, therefore, though several duties may be suitable to every day of our lives, they are most likely to be performed, if some days are more particularly set apart for the practice of them. Our church has accordingly instituted several features of devotion, when time, custom, prescription, and, if I may so say, the fashion itself, call upon a man to be serious, and attentive to the great end of his being.

I have hinted in some former papers, that the greatest and wisest of men in all ages and countries, particularly in Rome and Greece, were renowned for their piety and virtue. It is now my intention to shew, how those in our own nation, that have been unquestionably the most eminent for learning and knowledge, were likewise the most eminent for their adherence to the religion of their country.

I might produce very shining examples from among the clergy ; but because priest-craft is the common cry of every cavilling, empty scribbler, I shall shew that all the laymen who have exerted a more than ordinary genius in their writings, and were the glory of their times, were men whose hopes were filled with immortality, and the prospect of future rewards, and men who lived in a dutiful submission to all the doctrines of revealed religion.

I shall, in this paper, only instance sir Francis Bacon, a man who, for greatness of genius, and compass of knowledge, did honour to his age and country ; I could almost say to human nature itself. He possessed at once all those extraordinary talents, which were divided amongst the greatest authors of antiquity. He had the sound, distinct, comprehensive knowledge of Aristotle, with all the beautiful lights, graces, and embellishments of Cicero. One does not know which to admire most in his writings, the strength of reason, force of style, or brightness of imagination.

The author has remarked in several parts of his works, that a thorough insight into philosophy makes a good believer, and that a smattering in it naturally produces such a race of despicable infidels as the little profligate writers of the present age, whom, I must confess, I have always accused to myself, not so much for their want of faith as their want of learning.

I was infinitely pleased to find, among the works of this extraordinary man, a prayer of his own composing, which, for the elevation of thought, and greatness of expression, seems rather the devotion of an angel than a man. His principal fault seems to have been the excess of that virtue which covers a multitude of faults. This betrayed him to so great an indulgence towards his servants, who made a corrupt use of it, that it stripped him of all those riches and honours which a long series of merits had heaped upon him. But in this prayer, at the same time that we find him prostrating himself before the great mercy-seat, and humbled under afflictions, which at that time lay heavy upon him, we see him supported by the sense of his integrity, his zeal, his devotion, and his love to mankind; which give him a much higher figure in the minds of thinking men, than that greatness had done from which he was fallen. I shall beg leave to write down the prayer itself, with the title with it, as it was found amongst his lordship's papers, written in his own hand; not being able to furnish my readers with an entertainment more suitable to this solemn time.

" A Prayer, or Psalm, made by my Lord Bacon, Chancellor of England.

"Most gracious Lord God, my merciful Father; from my youth up my Creator, my Redeemer, my Comforter. Thou, O Lord, soundest and searchest the depths and secrets of all hearts; thou acknowledgest the upright of heart; thou judgest the hypocrite; thou ponderest men's thoughts and doings as in a balance; thou measurest their intentions as with a line; vanity and crooked ways cannot be hid from thee.

"Remember, O Lord! how thy servant hath walked before thee; remember what I have first sought, and what hath been principal in my intentions. I have loved thy assemblies, I have mourned for the divisions of thy church, I have delighted in the brightness of thy sanctuary. This vine, which thy right-hand hath planted in this nation, I have ever prayed unto thee that it might have the first and the latter rain, and that it might stretch her branches to the seas, and to the floods. The state and bread of the poor and oppressed have been precious in mine eyes; I have hated all cruelty and hardness of heart; I have, though in a despised weed, procured the good of all men. If any have been my enemies, I thought not of them, neither hath the sun almost set upon my displeasure; but I have been, as a dove, free from superfluity of maliciousness. Thy creatures have been my books, but thy scriptures much more. I have sought thee in the courts, fields, and gardens; but I have found thee in thy temples.

"Thousands have been my sins, and ten thousands my transgressions, but thy sanctifications have remained with me, and my heart, through thy grace, hath been an unquenched coal upon thine altar.

" O Lord, my strength ! I have since my youth met with thee in all my ways, by thy fatherly compassions, by thy comfortable chastisements, and by thy most visible providence. As thy favours have increased upon me, so have thy corrections; so as thou hast been always near me, O Lord ! and ever as my worldly blessings were exalted, so secret darts from thee have pierced me; and when I have ascended before men, I have descended in humiliation before thee. And now, when I thought most of peace and honour, thy hand is heavy upon me, and hath humbled me according to thy former loving-kindness, keeping me still in thy fatherly school, not as a bastard, but as a child. Just are thy judgments upon me for my sins, which are more in number than the sands of the sea, but have no proportion to thy mercies : for what are the sands of the sea ? Earth, heavens, and all these, are nothing to thy mercies. Besides my innumerable sins, I confess before thee, that I am debtor to thee for the gracious talent of thy gifts and graces, which I have neither put into a napkin, nor put it, as I ought, to exchangers, where it might have made best profit, but mispent it in things for which I was least fit: so I may truly say my soul hath been a stranger in the course of my pilgrimage. Be merciful unto me, O Lord, for my Saviour's sake, and receive me unto thy bosom, or guide me in thy ways."

ON SUITABLE ATTIRE.

No. 270.   SATURDAY, December 30, 1710.   [Steele.]

Cum pulchris tunicis sumet nova consilia et spes.
HOR. 1 Ep. xviii. 33.

In gay attire when the vain coxcomb's drest,
Strange hopes and projects fill his labouring breast.

ACCORDING to my late resolution, I take the holidays to be no improper season to entertain the town with the addresses of my correspondents. In my walks every day, there appear all round me very great offenders in the point of dress. An *armed* taylor had the impudence yesterday in the Park to smile in my face, and pull off a laced hat to me, as it were in contempt of my authority and censure. However, it is a very great satisfaction that other people, as well as myself, are offended with these improprieties. The following notices, from persons of different sexes and qualities, are a sufficient instance how useful my Lucubrations are to the public.

" Jack's Coffee-house, near Guildhall, Dec. 27.

" Cousin BICKERSTAFF,

"It has been the peculiar blessing of our family to be always above the smiles or frowns of fortune, and, by a certain greatness of mind, to restrain all irregular fondness or passions. From hence it is, that though a long decay, and a numerous descent, have obliged many of our house to fall into the arts of trade and business, no one person of us has ever made an appearance that betrayed our being unsatisfied with our own station in life, or has ever affected a mien or gesture unsuitable to us.

"You have up and down in your writings very justly remarked, that it is not this or the other profession or quality among men that gives us honour or esteem, but the well or ill

I I

behaving ourselves in those characters. It is, therefore, with no small concern, that I behold in coffee-houses and public places my brethren, the tradesmen of this city, put off the smooth, even, and ancient decorum of thriving citizens, for a fantastical dress and figure, improper for their persons and characters, to the utter destruction of that order and distinction, which of right ought to be between St. James's and Milk Street, The Camp and Cheapside.

"I have given myself some time to find out how distinguishing the frays in a lot of muslins, or drawing up a regiment of thread laces, or making a panegyric on pieces of fagathy or Scotch plaid, should entitle a man to a laced hat or sword, a wig tied up with ribbands, or an embroidered coat. The college say, this enormity proceeds from a sort of delirium in the brain, which makes it break out first about the head, and, for want of timely remedies, fall upon the left thigh, and from thence, in little mazes and windings, run over the whole body, as appears by pretty ornaments on the buttons, button-holes, garterings, sides of the breeches, and the like. I beg the favour of you to give us a discourse wholly upon the subject of habits, which will contribute to the better government of conversation among us, and in particular oblige, sir, your affectionate *cousin,*

"FELIX TRANQUILLUS."

"To ISAAC BICKERSTAFF, Esquire, Censor of Great-Britain.

"The humble petition of Ralph Nab, Haberdasher of Hats, and many other poor sufferers of the same trade,

"Sheweth,

"That for some years last past the use of gold and silver galloon upon hats has been almost universal; being undistinguishably worn by soldiers, esquires, lords, footmen, beaux, sportsmen, traders, clerks, prigs, smarts, cullies, pretty fellows, and sharpers.

"That the said use and custom has been two ways very prejudicial to your petitioners. First, in that it has induced men, to the great damage of your petitioners, to wear their hats upon their heads ; by which means the said hats last much longer whole, than they would do if worn under their arms. Secondly, in that very often a new dressing and a new lace supply the place of a new hat, which grievance we are chiefly sensible of in the spring-time, when the company is leaving the town ; it so happening commonly, that a hat shall frequent, all winter, the finest and best assemblies without any ornament at all, and in May shall be tricked up with gold or silver, to keep company with rustics, and ride in the rain. All which premisses your petitioners humbly pray you to take into your consideration, and either to appoint a day in your Court of Honour, when all pretenders to the galloon may enter their claims, and have them approved or rejected, or to give us such other relief as to your great wisdom shall seem meet.

" And your petitioners, &c."

Order my friend near Temple-bar, the author of the hunting-cock, to assist the court when this petition is read, of which Mr. Lillie to give him notice.

" To ISAAC BICKERSTAFF, Esquire, Censor of Great-Britain.

" The humble petition of Elizabeth Slender, Spinster,
    " Sheweth,

That on the twentieth of this instant December, her friend, Rebecca Hive, and your petitioner, walking in the Strand, saw a gentleman before us in a gown, whose periwig was so long, and so much powdered, that your petitioner took notice of, and said, "she wondered that a lawyer would so spoil a new gown with powder." To which it was answered, " that he was no lawyer but a clergyman." Upon a wager of a pot of coffee we overtook him, and your petitioner was soon convinced she had lost.

" Your petitioner, therefore, desires your worship to cite the clergyman before you, and to settle and adjust the length of

canonical periwigs, and the quantity of powder to be made
use of in them, and to give such other directions as you shall
think fit.

"And your petitioner, &c."

Query,   Whether this gentleman be not chaplain to a regiment, and, in such case, allow powder accordingly?

After all that can be thought on these subjects, I must
confess, that the men who dress with a certain ambition to
appear more than they are, are much more excusable than
those who betray, in the adorning their persons, a secret
vanity and inclination to shine in things, wherein, if they did
succeed, it would rather lessen than advance their character.
For this reason I am more provoked at the allegations relating
to the clergyman, than any other hinted at in these complaints.
I have indeed· a long time, with much concern, observed
pretty fellows in sacred orders, and shall in due time let them
know, that I pretend to give ecclesiastical as well as civil
censures. A man well-bred and well dressed in that habit,
adds to the sacredness of his function an agreeableness not
to be met with among the laity. I own I have spent some
evenings among the men of wit of that profession with an
inexpressible delight. Their habitual care of their character
gives such a chastisement to their fancy, that all which they
utter in company is as much above what you meet with in
other conversation, as the charms of a modest, are superior
to those of a light, woman. I therefore earnestly desire our
young missionaries from the universities to consider where
they are, and not dress, and look, and move like young officers.
It is no disadvantage to have a very handsome white hand :
but, were I to preach repentance to a gallery of ladies, I would,
methinks, keep my gloves on. I have an unfeigned affection
to the class of mankind appointed to serve at the altar, therefore am in danger of running out of my way, and growing too
serious on this occasion ; for which reason I shall end with
the following epistle, which, by my interest in Tom Trot, the
penny-post, I procured a copy of :

"To the Rev. Mr. Ralph Incense, Chaplain to the Countess Dowager of Brumpton.

Sir,

"I heard and saw you preach last Sunday. I am an ignorant young woman, and understood not half you said : but ah! your manner, when you held up both your hands towards our pew! Did you design to win me to Heaven or yourself? Your humble servant,

"Penitence Gentle."

END OF THE TATLER.

No. 271. TUESDAY, January 2, 1710. [Steele.]*

The printer having informed me, that there are as many of these papers printed as will make four volumes, I am now come to the end of my ambition in this matter, and have nothing farther to say to the world under the character of Isaac Bickerstaff. This work has indeed for some time been disagreeable to me, and the purpose of it wholly lost by my being so long understood as the author. I never designed in it to give any man any secret wound by my concealment, but spoke in the character of an old man, a philosopher, an humourist, an astrologer, and a Censor, to allure my reader with the variety of my subjects, and insinuate, if I could, the weight of reason with the agreeableness of wit. The general purpose of the whole has been to recommend truth, innocence,

---

* "Steele's last 'Tatler' came out to-day. You will see it before this comes to you, and how he takes leave of the world. He never told so much as Addison of it, who was surprized as much as I ; but, to say the truth, it was time, for he grew cruel dull and dry. To my knowledge he had several good hints to go upon ; but he was so lazy and weary of the work, that he would not improve them."—Swift to Mrs. Johnson.

honour, and virtue, as the chief ornaments of life ; but I considered, that severity of manners was absolutely necessary to him who would censure others, and *for that reason, and that only*, chose to talk in a mask. I shall not carry my humility so far as to call myself a vicious man, but at the same time must confess, my life is at best but pardonable. And, with no greater character than this, a man would make but an indifferent progress in attacking prevailing and fashionable vices, which Mr. Bickerstaff has done with a freedom of spirit, that would have lost both its beauty and efficacy, had it been pretended to by Mr. Steele.

As to the work itself, the acceptance it has met with is the best proof of its value ; but I should err against that candour, which an honest man should always carry about him, if I did not own, that the most approved pieces in it were written by others, and those which have been most excepted against, by myself. The hand that has assisted me in those noble discourses upon the immortality of the soul, the glorious prospects of another life, and the most sublime ideas of religion and virtue, is a person who is too fondly my friend ever to own them ; but I should little deserve to be his, if I usurped the glory of them.* I must acknowledge at the same time, that I think the finest strokes of wit and humour in all Mr. Bickerstaff's Lucubrations, are those for which he also is beholden to him.

As for the satirical part of these writings, those against the gentlemen who profess gaming are the most licentious ; but the main of them I take to come from losing gamesters, as invectives against the fortunate ; for in very many of them I was very little else but *the transcriber*. If any have been more particularly marked at, such persons may impute it to their own behaviour, before they were touched upon, in publicly speaking their resentment against the author, and professing they would support any man who should insult him.

---

* Addison was the assistant here alluded to.

When I mention this subject, I hope major general Daven-
port, brigadier Bisset, and my Lord Forbes, will accept of
my thanks for their frequent good offices, in professing
their readiness to partake any danger that should befall me in
so just an undertaking, as the endeavour to banish fraud
and cozenage from the presence and conversation of gentlemen.

But what I find is the least excusable part of all this work
is, that I have, in some places in it, touched upon matters
which concern both Church and State. All I shall say for this
is, that the points I alluded to, are such as concerned every
Christian and freeholder in England; and I could not be cold
enough to conceal my opinion on subjects which related to
either of those characters. But politicks apart.

I must confess it has been a most exquisite pleasure to me
to frame characters of domestic life, and put those parts of it
which are least observed into an agreeable view ; to enquire
into the seeds of vanity and affectation, to lay before the
readers the emptiness of ambition : in a word, to trace human
life through all its mazes and recesses, and shew much shorter
methods than men ordinarily practise, to be happy, agreeable,
and great.

But to enquire into men's faults and weaknesses has something in it so unwelcome, that I have *often* seen people in pain
to act before me, whose modesty only makes them think themselves liable to censure. This, and a thousand other nameless
things, have made it an irksome task to me to personate Mr.
Bickerstaff any longer ; and I believe it does not often
happen, that the reader is delighted where the author is
displeased.

All I can now do for the farther gratification of the town, is
to give them a faithful explication of passages and allusions,
and sometimes of persons intended in the several scattered
parts of the work. At the same time, I shall discover which
of the whole have been written by me, and which by others,
and by whom, as far as I am *able*, or permitted.

Thus I have voluntarily done, what I think all authors should do when called upon. I have published my name to my writings, and given myself up to the mercy of the town, as Shakspéare expresses it, "with all my imperfections on my head." The indulgent reader's most obliged, most obedient, humble servant,

RICHARD STEELE.